Praise for *What I Left for You*

In this beautiful tapestry of a novel, Li~~~~~~~~~~~~~~~~~eys of a grieving social worker on a quest ~~~~~~~~~~~~~~~~~ly's past and a university lecturer thrust in~~~~~~~~~~~~~~~he Nazi occupation of Poland. By honor~~~~~~~~~~~~~~~~~~~~~~ of the Lemko Rusyn people, *What I Left for You* poignantly reveals a lost narrative of the Second World War. Readers will not soon forget this powerful tale of love and sorrow, fortitude and faith.

–Amanda Barratt, Christy Award-winning author of
The Warsaw Sisters and *Within These Walls of Sorrow*

Devastating, yet inspiring. Through two intriguing heroines, *What I Left for You* illuminates the story of an oft-oppressed minority group in Poland in World War II. Liz Tolsma uses her personal search into her family history, her usual faithful attention to history, and her very human touch to pen a novel that draws you in and holds you as you hope for Helena and McKenna to find what they've lost. A novel you won't forget.

–Sarah Sundin, bestselling and Christy Award-
winning author of *Embers in the London Sky*

Impeccably researched and beautifully written, *What I Left for You* is an unforgettable tale of human resilience, loyalty, and the power of family. Spanning several generations and alternating between two timelines, Liz Tolsma expertly transports the reader from a young woman's journey through modern-day Poland to the frightening reality of German occupation. When an unexpected twist merges the two women's lives, the resulting shockwaves had me holding my breath to the final page. Liz Tolsma is a masterful storyteller. Her personal connection to the story makes this tale even more unforgettable. A must read!

–Renee Ryan, award-winning author of
The Last Fashion House in Paris

With her exquisite writing style and expressive voice, Liz Tolsma has once again crafted a memorable World War II story that will burrow into your heart. This dual timeline story features two compelling protagonists bound together by their shared lineage to a people group whose heritage was almost destroyed. Liz's personal connection as a Lemko-Rusyn descendent adds poignant depth to her captivating novel.

–Johnnie Alexander, bestselling, award-winning author of
Where Treasure Hides and *The Cryptographer's Dilemma*

WHAT
I LEFT
FOR YOU

ECHOES
of the PAST

WHAT
I LEFT
FOR YOU

LIZ TOLSMA

BARBOUR
PUBLISHING

Cover model: © Richard Tuschman / Trevillion Images

Published by Barbour Publishing, Inc., 1810 Barbour Drive, Uhrichsville, Ohio 44683, www.barbourbooks.com

Our mission is to inspire the world with the life-changing message of the Bible.

 Member of the
Evangelical Christian
Publishers Association

Printed in the United States of America

In honor of the Lemko Rusyn diaspora around the world. May we always remember the land that birthed our ancestors and cradled our people for hundreds of years. *Slava Isusu Khrystu.* Glory to Jesus Christ.

EPIGRAPHS

Whose peacocks are these, that graze by
themselves in that green oak tree grove?
Oh mine, mine, I raised them, oh while you were at war.
You raised them, but why did you not sell them, these peacocks of yours?
I did not sell them, because I was waiting
for you, to return from the war!

~Traditional Lemko song sung by tinkers, men who traveled to repair pots and told stories and sang songs while they did so

By the waters of Babylon,
    there we sat down and wept,
    when we remembered Zion.
On the willows there
    we hung up our lyres.
For there our captors
    required of us songs,
    and our tormentors, mirth, saying,
    "Sing us one of the songs of Zion!"
How shall we sing the LORD's song
    in a foreign land?
If I forget you, O Jerusalem,
    let my right hand forget its skill!
Let my tongue stick to the roof of my mouth,
    if I do not remember you,
    if I do not set Jerusalem
    above my highest joy!

PSALM 137:1–6 ESV

WHO ARE THE LEMKOS?

When I first had the idea for *What I Left for You*, it was going to be a story about Ukrainian Jews fleeing to Lemkovyna during WWII and finding refuge there. As I researched further, I discovered that the Lemkos had a fascinating story of their own experiences during and after WWII, a story that very few people knew. I'm Lemko on my maternal grandmother's side, and so I could do no less than write about my people.

The history of Lemkovyna and the Lemko Rusyn people is complicated, but scholars agree that the Lemkos came about through the combining of several Slavic tribes isolated by the Carpathian Mountains. Their traditional homeland encompasses what is today southern Poland, northern Slovakia, and western Ukraine.

The Lemkos have their own language, though it shares characteristics with several Slavic languages. They have their own customs, their own traditional dress, and before the diaspora, most of them practiced the Greek Catholic faith.

Christianity was brought to the Lemko Rusyns in the ninth century by Saints Cyril and Methodius from Greece. When the schism occurred in 1054, the church retained its Orthodox ties until 1646 when sixty-three Transcarpathian Orthodox priests joined the Catholic Church. And so was born the Greek Catholic Church, which uses Eastern rites while maintaining ties with the Roman pope.

This people group is referred to by several names, including Lemko, Lemko Rusyn, Rusyn, Ruthenian, Carpatho-Rusyn, and trans-Carpathian Rusyn. Some call them Ukrainians, but most Lemkos would balk at that designation.

GLOSSARY

Lemko Rusyn words

Please note that Lemko is written in Cyrillic. When changed into the Latin alphabet, spellings vary greatly. What I'm providing here are either transliterations of Lemko words or Latin spellings that come from the very closely associated Rusyn language with the pronunciation then transliterated from the Cyrillic. There is some overlap between Lemko Rusyn and Polish, as well as Ukrainian.

baba – grandmother

ďakujem (ja-KOO-you) – thank you

dushko moja (DOOSH-co MOY-uh) – sweetheart

Ljublju tja (loob-LOO-cha) – I love you

mojou sestrou (MOI-oh SESS-trō) – my sister

nie (yeah with an *n* in front) – no

nyaňo (NYAN-nyo) – Dad

Pan (PAHN) – mister

Pani (PAHN-ee) – married woman

proshu (PRO-shoe) – please

Slava Isusu Kyrustu (SLAH-vuh ZHESS-oo CREEST-oo) – Glory to Jesus Christ, often used as a greeting

tak (pronounced like it looks with a soft *k*) – yes

Polish words

ciasto z śliwkami – plum cake

dziękuję (jen-KOO-ya) – thank you

dzień dobry (jen-DOUGH-bree) – hello (good day)

grosz (GRAHS) – 1/100 of a złoty

nie (yeah with an *n* in front) – no

obwarzanek (ob-var-ZHAHN-ek) – a Polish-style bagel with a larger center hole and twisted dough. They are sold from carts around Kraków for just a few złoty each, less than one US dollar.

pączki (POONCH-key) – a rich, sweet fried Polish donut made with eggs, sugar, and milk, and filled with prunes, rose cream, cherries, strawberries, chocolate hazelnut, chocolate cherry, or any number of other fillings.

Pan (PAHN) – mister

Pani (PAHN-ee) – married woman

Panna (PAHN-uh) – unmarried woman

proszę (PRO-shay) – please

tak (pronounced like it looks with a soft *k*) – yes

złoty (ZWAH-tay) – Polish currency

German words

Bahnschutz – railway police

halt – stop

ja – yes

nein – no

schnell – fast

CHAPTER ONE

My beloved Lemkovyna,
You are my earthly paradise.
My heart is yearning for you,
I dream of you.

You are most dear to me
Because you are my mother,
Oh, how it tears at my heart
To write about you.

~From "Song of Lemkovyna"

Tuesday, March 24, 1942
Kraków, Generalgouvernement, Poland

There are days that change the course of our lives, that inexorably shift the sands beneath our feet. I've had many of those over the years. Some of those, when I woke up, I knew the coming hours would alter my life. Others came as a shock. A surprise that woke me from a complacent slumber.

How was I ever naive enough to believe that life would never change, that the river of my days would always follow the same path? I should have known that with each turn of the sun, something altered, whether it be a small shift or a cataclysmic shake-up.

When the dirty Nazi boots trod across the fields and hills of my beloved

Poland, the ring of hobnails echoing off the cobblestones of the narrow, medieval streets of Kraków, I had expected that. Everyone living in the country had.

For months, years, that madman across the western border had been railing and screaming and whipping his people into a frenzy. It was only a matter of time until he and his troops crossed the invisible line separating the two countries. Until Poland came under his control. And that bloody September morning came, along with the myriad of changes that accompanied it.

For many nights afterward, my sleep was restless. Then complacency set in once more, and I grew used to the soldiers patrolling the streets, used to white armbands with blue stars encircling my Jewish friends' arms.

And then came the insistent, persistent pounding on my door in the middle of the night. It roused me, but several moments passed before I shook the sleep from my brain enough for me to register what was happening. Once I did, the pounding in my head matched the knocking at the door. These days, such an occurrence could mean only one thing.

Though I moved after the roundup of intellectuals just two months after our land was sullied by the Germans, and though I kept my head low, the Nazis must have finally caught up to me. The knocking continued as I pulled on my bathrobe, my hands shaking, the satin belt slipping from my fingers as I worked to tie it around my waist. I took the time to slide my feet into my embroidered bedroom slippers.

After a deep breath, I finger-combed the tangles from my hair and opened the door. "Jerzy!" I sagged against the doorframe. "You gave me the fright of my life."

My old friend pushed his way inside and locked the door behind him. His usual easy smile didn't grace his thin face, and new lines spread from the corners of his eyes.

Only once before had I seen him in such a state, when our occupiers arrested him and the other professors at Jagiellonian University. The day that he spared me and my friend and fellow university lecturer, Risa Birkha, from long months in prison and possibly death. I grabbed his skinny upper arm and squeezed. "What is it? What's wrong?" My pulse pounded in my neck.

"Oh, Helena, it's awful." He scrubbed his stubble-covered cheeks. "It's Risa."

Just something about the way he said it—soft, defeated—sent a chill through me. "Is she. . .?"

"Not yet. At least I don't think so."

"How do you know?"

"My neighbor, Józef Adamowicz, told me. He is a friend of the doctor in the Jewish ghetto and has been going to the gate every day to bring clothes, food, and medicine. I've been asking him for any word on Risa and the baby. He came just now and told me she is very ill. Likely not to live through the night."

"*Nie*, nie, nie." I turned in small circles as I struggled to make sense of something that made no sense. That never could. This couldn't be happening. Already Risa, my dearest friend, my Jewish friend, had endured so much, including the loss of her husband at the hands of those German monsters. And now she was dying. "I want to see her."

Jerzy held me by the shoulders and gave me a small shake. "How do you propose we get into the ghetto?"

That was the question.

Jerzy squeezed me even tighter. "Józef hasn't gained access, and he's bringing clothing."

"There has to be a way." I spun around a few more times, my mind whirling as well. Then I snapped my fingers. "Bread. We'll bring bread. And if we can get some vodka, we can bribe the guards."

"What bread? There is little enough for us. How can we pretend we're making a delivery of bread?"

"We don't have to fill our baskets. All we need is enough to cover the top. Do you have your ration book?"

"*Tak.*"

"So do I. We will use all the coupons we can. I don't mind going the rest of the month without if I can feed a few mouths along the way. But I need to see Risa, and I have to find out what has happened to her child."

"But vodka?" He released his grip on me.

"You had to be resourceful to survive the camp. We'll be resourceful now."

"I don't know if this is the best plan."

I touched his sunken face, so care-worn even though he was in his early thirties. "You have been through so much. No one blames you for not wanting to risk another imprisonment. If you don't want to come, I understand. But with or without you, I will go. You wouldn't have come here and awakened me at this hour if you didn't mean for me to help Risa."

Jerzy sighed, his thin shoulders rising and falling. "I thought you would want to know. I should have realized you wouldn't stand by and do nothing. That is against your nature." He gazed at me, his eyes soft, a tenderness there I had never seen before. "You're right, of course. Risa would want to see you. You must go, but not alone. I will come."

I opened my mouth and drew in a breath.

He waved away my forthcoming objection. "Nie. You will not do this alone. No negotiating on this point. Take it or leave it."

Despite the seriousness of the situation, I lifted one corner of my mouth. "You leave me no choice, do you? If it won't be too much for you, then fine."

He hesitated, just a fraction of a second, then straightened his shoulders, much the way he had that fateful day the Nazis marched the professors out of the Collegium Novum more than two years ago, even after the soldiers had struck him, the sound reverberating in the high-ceilinged hallway.

The day he saved my life by lying to them that I wasn't intelligentsia.

Within a matter of moments, I pulled on a warm dark green dress, my coat, and my black head scarf with colorful embroidery that I brought from my childhood home. "Our first stop is the bakery." I grabbed a basket, and we headed down the stairs and out the door.

By the time we reached the street, Jerzy was panting for breath.

What those beasts had done to a strong man in his prime was despicable. "Let's rest here."

He shook his head. "There isn't time to waste."

"What good will you be if you faint on the street?" This time I waved away his objections, so we stopped for a few minutes in front of the building while he caught his breath, and then we wound our way down the dark streets.

Always before, these streets had teemed with life, both day and night. University students, housewives, and businessmen mingled here, scurrying to and fro, shopping, relaxing, celebrating.

Now they were quiet. Not even ghosts haunted them. Our footsteps, which before would have gone unnoticed, reverberated off the buildings like gunshots. I glanced up to a window where a young child sat between the parted lace curtains with his nose pressed against the glass. A slender woman pulled him away.

With our ears as tuned as foxes' and our eyes as sharp as cats', we slunk toward the bakery. I held my breath in anticipation of running into an olive-clad soldier, ready to spring around corners or into doorways if we spotted any patrols.

Thank the Holy Father that we didn't run across anyone. The tubby baker, whom I had known my entire time in Kraków, was kind enough to allow us to purchase a good quantity of bread and even gave us a bottle of vodka, no questions asked. *Pan* Laska had always been kind to me, and I hadn't misplaced my trust.

The walk was long from Old Town to the ghetto. My skin crawled, as if a thousand cockroaches raced over my arms and legs. We came to the bridge across the Vistula River to make our way into the area of the city where the ghetto walled in the Jews, and exposed as we were, it was a miracle we weren't caught breaking curfew. My temples throbbed.

After we made it across the silvery snake-like water, we stood at the ghetto's entrance, well before the end of curfew. A stucco gate straddled the road, two large, arched entrances topped with other arches, the shapes reminiscent of Jewish headstones. A not-so-subtle hint at the fate that awaited many of those imprisoned here.

Several guards mingled to the side, the tram tracks that ran inside mocking those who were forbidden to leave.

We approached the entrance, my tightening throat threatening to close and cut off my breathing. I struggled to keep my hands from shaking, but I turned to Jerzy. "Let me do the talking. The guards might be more easily persuaded by a woman's charms."

He raised one eyebrow then sighed. "I suppose you're right. No one can resist your smile. It is bound to get you whatever you want."

I didn't have time to mull over his strange pronouncement, because we came to the gate that shut the Jewish race away from the rest of the world. Lifting my chin despite the churning in my stomach, I marched right up to the guard and gave him that smile that Jerzy talked about. "*Dzień dobry.* Good morning to you. We have come with the bread."

The soldier pursed his lips, his little Hitler-like mustache dancing with the movement. "That isn't much. And where are your passes? It's illegal for you to be out this early."

And it wasn't. The basket was small, but Pan Laska had insisted on filling it. Fast, fast. I had to think of an explanation fast. "The truck broke down. Once the repairs are made, the rest will be delivered. This is for those in the hospital only."

Time hung suspended while the guard pondered whether to allow us through. I flashed him another one of my apparently persuasive smiles and even batted my eyelashes, though I would rather have vomited on his polished boots. But whatever it took to see Risa.

The guard moved closer, a frown turning his mouth into an upside-down crescent. "Papers. Both of you." His Polish was poor.

I dug in my coat pocket then handed them over, and he looked both Jerzy and me over. I resisted the urge to cross my arms over my chest. After a short eternity, he handed them back. One hurdle down.

"Still no passes. Basket."

We gave it to him. He rummaged through it, digging all the way to the bottom, several of the rolls dropping to the muddy ground, ruined. Then he drew out the bottle of vodka and smiled.

I swallowed and nodded. "For you and your friends to enjoy. A thank-you gift for allowing us in."

"Very good." He took one roll for himself and tossed a few to his comrades. By the time he finished, the basket was less than half full, but he finally passed it back, and I grasped it with all my might.

At long last, having forgotten about passes, the guard swung open the huge arched door with a creak. Not until we were inside and around the corner did I lean against one of the neglected buildings and allow myself to breathe. I turned to Jerzy and chuckled. "You shouldn't have doubted me."

"Helena Kostyszak, you are one formidable woman. I vow to never doubt you again."

"Where is she?"

"Actually, it wasn't a bad idea to tell the guard that the bread was for the hospital, because Risa is there."

"Do you know where that is?" An awful stench reached my nostrils and churned my stomach even more. The putrid odor of garbage, excrement, and decaying bodies permeated the air. Even when I returned home—if I returned home—it was bound to take several baths and a number of good scrubbings to wash the odor from my hair and clothes.

But it was nothing compared to the suffering of the residents. That was the worst. Even in the stillest part of the night, the moans and groans of the sick, the suffering, and the dying filled the air. No crickets. No tram bells. No songs from those drunk on vodka.

Just weeping and wailing.

"We need to go this way." Inside the walls, Jerzy had regained some strength, some of the confidence the Nazis had stolen from him in the labor camp. There was a glimpse of the man he had been before. The Germans had released him only a few months ago, so it would take time for him to be rid of the haunting behind his eyes.

We wound our way down the cobblestone streets, the buildings here not as well kept as those in Old Town. Everywhere I glanced in the dim almost-dawn light, everything was gray. Gray buildings. Gray streets. Gray bodies in piles on the corners.

As the ghetto was compact, the Jews stuffed in a small area, our walk was short. Soon we came to an orange-beige three-story building with a row of narrow, rectangular windows above all else. Compared to the rest of the buildings in the area, this one was in good condition. But that was saying little.

Jerzy led the way to the wrought iron gate in front of the door.

"This is it? They use this building for the hospital? No wonder so many people are dying."

"The doctors can do nothing about the poor circumstances. The Jews are dying because there isn't enough medicine, because the conditions are unsanitary, because food is sorely lacking. That is what killed Risa's husband. What brought her here."

I swallowed the lump in my throat but made my steps purposeful as we entered the hospital. For Risa, I would be strong. I would keep my fear from showing.

As we entered, the door protested the movement. This time Jerzy took the lead, stepping to the desk just inside the entrance. "Dzień dobry. I would like to see Risa Birkha."

The odors of festering wounds and death permeated the hospital walls. It was all I could do to keep from losing the part of a roll Jerzy and I had shared.

The man behind the desk nodded and stood. "I am Dr. Julian Aleksandrowicz. You are friends of hers?"

"Tak. We were colleagues from the university and are good friends. Józef Adamowicz told me she was gravely ill."

Though the doctor was a youngish man, the large bags underneath his eyes gave him a much older appearance. "I am so sorry about her. If I had the proper medication to treat her, we could do something. Then again, if the Nazis didn't shut us in like animals, worse than animals, she wouldn't be this ill. Enough about that. Come with me."

He led the way up the stairs then down the center of a crowded room, the patients moaning on thin pallets on the floor. Many were littered with sores or were nothing more than flesh-covered skeletons.

My throat burned, but I schooled my face to keep my overwhelming emotions from showing.

Dr. Aleksandrowicz stopped in front of one of the pallets. "*Pani* Birkha, you have some visitors."

If he hadn't called Risa by name, I would never have recognized the woman in front of me as my years-long best friend. She had lost a considerable amount of weight since I last saw her, just two years ago. Her dark eyes were sunken in her gaunt face, and her once lustrous hair lay tangled and matted around her shoulders.

She moaned, and I scooted around the doctor until I knelt at her side and clasped her by her very hot hand. "My dear, dear friend."

Risa's eyes fluttered open. "Helena?"

"Tak, it's me. And Jerzy is here too. We brought you some bread."

"Not much time."

"You have plenty of time. Time to watch your daughter grow into a fine woman, time to meet your grandchildren. So no more talk of that."

"Listen to me."

I leaned forward so I didn't miss any of Risa's faint words.

"My husband is gone."

"I know, and I am heartbroken." I shook my head. Poor Risa, facing all this without her husband. What insanity ruled the world?

"Take care of her."

"Of Teena?"

"Tak."

"You know I will do anything for you. Of course I will take care of her, at least until you can do so yourself, until you regain your strength. She needs her mama. She needs you, so don't you go leaving her alone."

"Wish I could stay." Risa gasped for breath. "Love her."

"Of course I will. And she will know and love you too."

"*Dziękuję.* Thank you."

Moments later Risa's chest ceased its rising and falling, and her hand went limp.

CHAPTER TWO

As soon as the guard checked the identification papers in my shaking hands on my way out of the dingy ghetto, I broke into a run. Jerzy called after me, his voice stronger and not as thin, but I didn't slow my stride. I sprinted through the streets now bathed in daylight, across the bridge, and back toward Old Town. When I finally ran out of breath at the south end of Planty Park, I slumped on a bench, hunched over, and released my pent-up sobs.

Risa was gone. Dead. Her daughter now an orphan.

How did we, the people of Poland and the other denizens of the world, allow such a horrific fate to encompass Europe? For years we turned a blind eye to the screeching lunatic with an iron grip on Germany and placed our trust, our security, in the hands of the French and English, who only placated him. Who, in the name of peace, allowed him to follow whatever whim entered his mind.

What a sick, twisted, evil mind it was.

Now we, those who had been forced to bend the knee to him, reaped the harvest of the seeds of apathy we had sown for so many years.

Since Risa and I met at university almost ten years ago, she had been such a bright light in my life. When I arrived in Kraków, I knew nothing about living in a city, getting around, or being on my own. For the first several months, life outside of Dubne and Lemkovyna was overwhelming. I missed Mama more than I ever believed possible. Ever since *Nyan'o* died, I planned to leave home, get an education, and take care of her the way she deserved, but when it came to pass, the separation was almost too much to bear.

There was no one more special to me than Mama. It was she who stroked my hair from my fevered brow many nights. Mama who slaved to provide the potatoes and cabbage on the table. Mama who counted out the precious coins and bought a string of paper flowers to decorate our tiny cottage.

In order to take care of Mama as she deserved, I had no choice but to leave her behind. And there was a hole in my heart.

Then Risa came into my life. Since we were among the few women at the university, it was inevitable that we would find each other and discover all we shared. She was more than my friend. She was my ally.

We studied together, rented a flat together, and laughed together. The sharp edge of homesickness dulled, and soon I found myself enjoying Kraków.

Even when her husband entered the picture, he and Risa never made me feel like I was in the way or interfering with their time together. The only change came when they married and I had to find my own flat. By then the city had become my friend and the clanging of the tram at night was like music. Kraków's trees were its magnificent old buildings, and its hills were the shop-lined cobblestone streets. My eyes no longer widened at the numerous food options right outside my door. My stomach no longer rumbled from sunup to sundown.

And now both Risa and her husband were dead. Gone. Their lights snuffed out long before the evenings of their lives. I banged my fists on the wooden bench, ignoring the pain. Above me, flying over Wawel Castle, the Nazi flag with its hated swastika flapped in the breeze. If I had encountered a soldier in that moment, I would have spit in his face.

It wasn't fair. True, as a Lemko, a much-derided minority, I had experienced enough persecution in my life, but nothing like this. The Nazis didn't treat Jews as second-class citizens. Nie, they treated them worse than swine.

It was the Nazis who were the swine.

A breeze blew off the Vistula, cooling my heated cheeks.

Several minutes passed before someone slipped onto the bench beside me. I didn't have to turn to know it was Jerzy. His scent, a mixture of onions and old books, gave him away.

I scooted closer to him, and he held his arms open to me. What a welcome embrace, a solace, a refuge. I soaked his wool coat with my tears. In turn, he wet my hair with his own weeping.

When we were both spent, he released his hold on me, and I shivered. "I can't believe it." My voice caught, and I swallowed hard.

"I can't either. She was so vibrant, so full of life."

"They have stolen everything from her, even the breath from her body."

"Not quite everything."

I leaned against him. "What do you mean?"

"Teena. Her daughter is still alive."

"For now. I promised Risa I would care for her, but how am I supposed to do that? I don't even know where she is. Likely in the ghetto, but where? How am I supposed to find her? And when I do, if she is there, how do I get her out?"

"Okay. Take a deep breath. One thing at a time."

I obeyed his instructions.

"First, we have to find Teena. It will do us no good to get into the ghetto again only to discover that she is elsewhere. Once we locate her, then we can formulate a plan to free her."

I drew air into my lungs and released it little by little. "How do we find her?"

"I'll ask Józef. If he can get word to Dr. Aleksandrowicz, he probably knows about Risa's daughter."

It took everything inside me not to stand from the bench and shake my fists at heaven. None of this was fair. None of it. Too many people suffered. Those who had already faced too much hardship in their lives were mired in terrible trials.

As I bent over my knees, Jerzy rubbed my back. He was my rock. "I know. I know."

"Do you?"

"All too well."

I glanced at him from the corner of my eye, his thinning hair now gray at his temples. Many might believe him to be older than the young man he was. "I suppose you do. The labor camp must have been awful."

"Someday, maybe, I will tell you. Now is not the time." He gave a slight nod in the direction of a German soldier just down the park's path from us. "Nor the place."

Of course. The air around us crackled with danger. Even when the sun shone, a black cloud hung over the city. Citizens dragged their feet when they walked, and smiles graced faces only on rare occasions.

Instead, the streets teemed with fear and anxiety. At times the Nazis arrested people just for stepping foot outside their homes. Many of those disappeared. Vanished.

Jerzy and I sat still and silent until the soldier passed by without paying any attention to us. At last my breathing eased and my muscles relaxed. But I remained on alert.

"Getting Teena will be dangerous." Jerzy rubbed his now-calloused hands on his well-worn but neatly pressed pants.

"Tak." Even the thought of it was fraught with danger. One wrong move, and the Nazis wouldn't hesitate to do to us what they had done to hundreds, thousands, maybe even hundreds of thousands.

"Are you sure you want to move forward?"

I snapped my gaze to Jerzy. "Of course. I intend to keep Teena and take care of her as my own." The words came to my lips without thought, but no thought was necessary. "Risa would have done no less for me. When I was alone, she befriended me. I owe her a great deal."

"So you are doing it to repay a debt?"

"Nie. Much more than that. It would be wrong to leave a helpless child to possibly die when I could rescue her. Where I grew up, far too many children passed away. My own parents lost two girls before me.

"We see every life as precious, bestowed on us by our Creator. No matter that Teena is Jewish, she matters to God. So I will do whatever I can to make sure she survives this madness."

"Then I will walk every step of the way with you. You are a courageous woman."

"Or crazy. Time will tell."

Jerzy laughed then, and the tension of the moment broke. But the awareness of what it could cost to save Teena's life cloaked me. If I pondered it too long and hard, I might lose my nerve. Better just to put a plan together and execute it without examining it too much.

Jerzy stood and helped me to my feet. A true gentleman. "Let's go to my flat. We can speak to Józef and see what information he can give us."

We strolled along the tree-lined path of Planty Park as if we didn't have a care in the world. Every now and then, a tram clanged by, a flash of color beyond the still-bare branches. Normal life trying to go on as it always had.

Even when it would never be the same.

We came to Jerzy's building. No longer did he live in a comfortable flat like he had prior to his arrest. The stairwell leading to his floor was dark and dank and unheated. His apartment was small and crowded, the stained, peeling wallpaper dulled by cigarette smoke.

When the Nazis had taken him and the other intelligentsia to the camps, he had lost everything. Even now the only work he'd managed to secure was as a street sweeper. The pay was barely enough to keep body and soul together.

There was no mistaking the hunger in his eyes or the jutting of his bones. I was far too familiar with it.

Other than a couple of wooden kitchen chairs, a pile of blankets on the floor, and a few pots and pans, Jerzy had nothing. I shook my head. "I should bring you some dishes and some silverware. And if I can come up with enough fabric, I might be able to sew some curtains to keep the chill from the room."

"It's not fancy."

My chest burned. "How could they come and take away everything you worked so hard for? Why do some people oppress others?"

"Ah, we would both be far richer if we had the answer to those questions. I do have some tea on the shelf if you would like to light the stove and make yourself a cup while I run downstairs to talk to Józef."

"No need, unless you want some." I refused to take what little he had, though pity would strip away the bit of pride and humanity he clung to.

He raised an eyebrow.

"Let me put the kettle on, and we can both have some when you return."

He nodded. Dignity was one commodity we still possessed. Maybe less than before, but we had some.

He left the flat a moment later, and I lit the stove and pulled the kettle forward. If nothing else, the tea would warm us. Spring had yet to put in much of an appearance.

My position as a tutor to a German family kept me warm and fed, though I was forced to lie and say I had received my education because I was half German. Otherwise, I would have joined Jerzy and the other intelligentsia in the labor camp. I managed to send some money to Mama, though not as much as before the invasion.

By the time Jerzy returned, I had two cups of tea steeped, and I handed him one of the chipped brown mugs. He took it and sipped.

"What did you find out?"

"Teena is at one of the orphanages in the ghetto."

"There are orphanages there? As in more than one?"

"There are, unfortunately, many orphans."

The tea turned bitter on my tongue. "How does Józef recommend that we get Teena out?"

"He didn't say, and I didn't ask. My suggestion would be to go about it much the same way as we got in this morning."

"Will the guards be suspicious? They will figure out we aren't delivering bread."

"We will pray there will be different men there tomorrow."

"Tomorrow already?" So fast. No chance to prepare for a small child. No pram, toys, or even clothes. "Tak, I suppose there is little time to waste. We have no idea how Teena's health is or what is happening to her or when the Nazis might decide to do something to those innocent little ones."

"Exactly."

"Getting in is one obstacle. Getting out will be the bigger one. I suppose you have a plan for that as well?"

He nodded. "Of course I do." He went on to share how we would go about secreting Teena from the walled ghetto.

When he finished, I pursed my lips. "It is risky, but there is no easy way to go about it. We will have to pray and leave what happens in the Holy Father's hands."

"Do you believe He will hear us?"

"If I didn't believe that, I would have no hope." Though it was becoming more and more difficult for me to keep that flickering flame alive.

CHAPTER THREE

For our struggles and our tortures
God will reward us,
Our bitter difficult life
Will become sweeter for us.
Receive with love this letter,
Written in blood,
From our aching hearts
Watered with tears.

~From "Song of Lemkovyna"

Thursday, August 3, 2023
Suburban Pittsburgh, Pennsylvania

All that was left was a diamond ring. Hopes and dreams a lifetime in the making shattered in mere seconds and the million shards scattered to the wind.

A life turned upside down by a few words that cut like broken glass and left scars that might never heal. The cruelty of it all hit McKenna Muir in the middle of her chest. A sucker punch.

The ring sat on the cool marble bathroom vanity, glittering under the strong lights, almost taunting her. A reminder of a happy time not so long ago when life was bright and full of promise.

When all of her childhood dreams were about to come true. A wonderful husband, a beautiful home, and children to fill their days with laughter. A sun-drenched tomorrow that came to an end in one single stroke of lightning.

Now all that was left was a diamond ring.

Though she swiped away the tears that cascaded down her cheeks, she couldn't keep up with the flow. Her throat burned. She grabbed the ring, took it into her bedroom, and stuffed it in the deepest recesses of her underwear drawer.

If only it were that easy to put away and forget the events of the past several days. To erase her memory or turn back the clock.

She returned to the bathroom and swallowed two ibuprofen to ease the headache banging inside her skull. Even though she finger-combed her hair and splashed cold water on her face, she was still a wreck, eyes bloodshot, light brown hair tousled.

This week wasn't supposed to go like this. Life wasn't supposed to turn out this way. A mere seven days ago, everything had been perfect. Well, almost perfect. To her, it had been idyllic.

She'd been blind to everything happening right under her nose.

"McKenna? Are you here?"

Taylor's return to their town house broke the peace and quiet that allowed McKenna to wallow in her sorrow. To pity herself for all her trouble and heartache. To pretend for a moment the world hadn't ended.

"Yes, I'm here." She said it in a go-away-and-leave-me-alone tone of voice.

Taylor, however, was not one to be deterred. "You're not fine, I can tell." Her voice now came from the other side of the bathroom door. "I'm coming in. Are you decent?"

"No."

"Now you're lying." The door protested being opened and the floors squeaked as Taylor entered McKenna's sanctuary.

She turned and forced herself to lift the corners of her mouth. "See. Nothing wrong."

"Haha. I've known you for every one of my twenty-seven years, so you can't pull anything over on me."

It was true. Taylor did have this uncanny sense of knowing just what was going on with her. They were almost like twins—born on the same day, moms were friends, and they went to the same church.

"This has to do with Chris, doesn't it?"

"It doesn't take a rocket scientist to figure that out."

"Sarcasm doesn't become you, Ken." Tay spouted one of their moms' favorite sayings.

"Sorry."

"No need. I get that you're hurting. Care to talk about it?"

"Not really. It's embarrassing. Like, how could I have been so blind? The signs have been there for a while."

"Did he cheat?"

Cheat? What a funny word. Like sneaking a peek at a classmate's paper in junior high. There should be a different term for it when a guy built up a girl's expectations and aspirations and then dashed them cold.

Could he have cheated when he and McKenna weren't sleeping together, when they'd agreed to keep that for marriage? But the snake did go behind her back and was well and truly in love with his new girlfriend before McKenna ever put two and two together. "I guess in a way. He's with Courtney now."

"Guess he has the alliteration thing going for him."

McKenna left the bathroom and plopped face-first onto her unmade bed, startling her black cat and sending him scrambling. "Usually I appreciate your humor. Today I could do without it."

"Sorry." Taylor sat beside her. "I'm here to listen if you're ready to share."

At some point, people were going to have to find out why the engagement was off. McKenna sat up. "Pinkie swear that you'll keep this just between you and me for now. If anyone asks, tell them you promised not to say a word. I'll let people know in my own good time."

Tay held up her pinkie. "I promise." They locked fingers.

"Okay. Here goes. You probably noticed that we haven't been going out as much, and he hasn't been here a ton. I chalked it up to him having to study for his bar exam. That's intense. But no, he wasn't studying. At least not all the time. When his nose wasn't in a book, apparently his lips were locked on Courtney's."

"Who is this Courtney?"

"I don't know. Some friend of his sister or something. She swears she didn't know about her brother's, um, unfaithfulness, but I have to wonder. Can I trust anything that comes out of the mouth of anyone related to him?"

Tay shrugged while McKenna picked a few black cat hairs from her light pink duvet. She glanced at Noir, now curled on her pillow at the end of the bed. Cats had it made.

"How did you find out?"

"He took Courtney to some fancy dinner to schmooze with local politicians, and she posted about it on Instagram and tagged him." Chris had always had a pile of political aspirations.

"Maybe he knew you wouldn't be able to go."

"It was last Saturday night. You know, the night I sat here by myself in my pajama pants and a hoodie consuming way too much popcorn while watching *Pride and Prejudice*?"

"Oh. And how could you watch that without me?"

McKenna gave Tay a side-eyed glance.

"Maybe it was platonic."

"Definitely not. She was dressed in this sparkling, skin-tight red gown and was draped all over him. He definitely had no objection. In fact, he hasn't smiled at me like that in months."

"Did you confront him?" Tay just about jumped up and down on the bed. She loved any and all drama.

"Of course." McKenna pinched the bridge of her nose to keep from bawling like a baby. "He didn't even try to deny or justify it. He just told me it was true and then erased me from all his social media."

"You didn't scrub him from yours?"

"Of course I did. After I finished crying. By then I wasn't even a memory to him. But I did keep the ring. It's the least he owes me."

Tay rubbed McKenna's back. "I'm so sorry. It's awful that you have to go through this. But can I be honest?"

"Always." Oh, would she live to regret that word?

"Chris drove a wedge between you and your family and pulled you away from the church. I can't say I'm going to miss him. I just hurt for you."

For two years now, Mom and Dad had been preaching the same thing to her. How he had managed to find things for them to do on Sunday mornings that meant her missing any kind of service.

And they were right. He had controlled and gaslit her, convincing her that leaving the church was all her idea. That any problems between them were because of her distrust of him.

He had changed her into a person she didn't know anymore. A person she didn't care for one bit.

She swiped away a few more tears, even though Chris wasn't worth crying over. Somewhere along the line, she had fallen more in love with him than with God.

And that wasn't a good thing. Right now the heavenly Father she'd loved all her life seemed more distant than the farthest star in the farthest galaxy. "I hate that you were all right all along."

"Trust me, none of us are happy we were. None of us are going to tell you we told you so. We all hate to see you so miserable. If I ever run into Chris, I'm going to kick him good and hard in the shins."

McKenna couldn't help a small chuckle. "Please don't do that. If you do, you'll have to kick me in the shins because I've been as much a fool as him. Maybe more. So many people warned me about him, but I refused to listen. Blinded by love is a real thing." How could she have been so stupid?

"At least you found this out now and not after you married him."

All McKenna could do was nod. Chris may not have even gone through with the wedding. Then again, he might have. She covered her eyes and worked to breathe evenly to keep from crying. Again. "And you know what else is getting me down?"

"Hmm?"

She had never admitted this to anyone. She was only admitting it to herself as she said the words. "My job is burning me out."

Taylor sucked in a breath. "What? I thought you loved being a social worker."

"I do. I did. I don't know. I don't know anything these days. It's hard though, meeting these families, these kids, that are just a mess."

"It's got to be tough to have to deal with that."

Tay had no idea.

"Wait a minute." Taylor was bouncing on the bed again. "I have an idea. Something that could be good for both of us. And it would be so much fun."

"No, I'm not going to an amusement park with you. Roller coasters and I don't get along."

"And don't I know it. Just hold on. Wait a second, and I'll be right back. Don't go anywhere."

"Where would I go?"

As she exited the room, Tay waved her hand. "It's just an expression. You're so literal."

It couldn't have been more than a minute before she was back with her laptop. Once more, she hopped onto the bed. With McKenna's weak stomach, it was a miracle she wasn't seasick by now.

Tay opened the top, woke up her computer, and went to the internet.

"You could have done this on your phone, you know."

"Call me a little old-fashioned. Sometimes things are easier to see on a big screen." She typed in a few words that McKenna couldn't make out. "Do you remember when we took our DNA tests?"

"Yeah, and it turned out just like I thought it would. I'm from southern Poland. But what does this have to do with my awful job and, you know, Chris?"

"You could work on your genealogy and put your family tree together. I'll do mine too. We'll get a membership to the site where we took our DNA tests and see what we each come up with. If nothing happens with it, at least it'll take our minds off our troubles for a while. We should have done this eons ago. Let's make the time for it now."

"What troubles do you have that you need the distraction?"

"Oh, plenty. Plenty. See this broken fingernail?" Tay stuck out her pointer finger that had a small chip in the hot-pink nail polish. "The worst kind of tragedy you could imagine." She lay back in a dramatic half swoon.

McKenna whacked her over the head with one of the many decorative pillows scattered on her bed. "You are crazy."

"For some reason, that's what everyone says about me." She sat up.

"I'm glad you're my bestie." McKenna hugged her. "You get it, you sympathize with me, and then you don't allow me to eat an entire chocolate cake."

"All in a day's work."

"I wish I could be more like you."

"Hey, no." The laughter fled Tay's eyes. "You're you, and you're pretty special the way you are. Chris is an idiot not to see that, but I do. Don't go changing, not in the least. One of these days, a guy is going to notice how great you are. In the meantime, you'll have to put up with me."

Now McKenna swooned backward on the bed. "Oh, the horror. The inhumanity."

They both laughed until they cried. But the tears that rolled down McKenna's cheeks soon changed to weeping that came from deep inside her soul.

Because Chris had ripped so much from her and left her a different person. One she wouldn't have recognized two years ago.

No matter what she did to try to mask the pain in her gut, nothing would. Her life was a jigsaw puzzle. Nothing but pieces lying in disarray.

CHAPTER FOUR

Friday, August 4, 2023
Suburban Pittsburgh, Pennsylvania

The overhead lights buzzed, echoing in McKenna's head as she sat at her desk in her cubicle and reread the email from Cindy, her supervisor.

I've cleared your schedule for the morning. Please come see me in my office at 9:30.

No fluff to it. No *how are you doing* or *what's up*. Cindy hadn't even given her a choice of times. And had cleared her schedule. On a Friday. That meant she wouldn't be able to meet with the family she was working with until Monday at the earliest.

That was what set those little butterflies in her stomach tumbling around. She'd had a meeting set up with a mom of five who was out of rehab and working toward getting her kids back. At least some of them. It was an important meeting, an appointment she had to keep.

Since Cindy knew this, it made no sense for her to clear McKenna's schedule. None at all.

She glanced at her watch. 9:27. With her heart hammering in her chest, she got up from her desk and made her way to Cindy's office, taking the tiniest steps imaginable to put off the inevitable as long as possible.

But nothing could have prepared her for the sight of two police officers with Cindy in the crowded room. "What's going on?" She glanced from a rather petite female cop to a male one who towered over his partner.

The tall, dark-haired officer nodded in McKenna's direction. "Please, Miss Muir, have a seat." His gaze was steely, his jaw hard.

She moved a pile of papers and sank into the chair on the other side of the room.

"We'd just like to ask you some questions." The thin female officer smiled. "I'm Hailey Donaldson, and this is Wes Grange."

Were they going to play good cop/bad cop? She glanced at Cindy. McKenna's hands were sweating so much that they left marks on the chair's wood armrests.

"You don't have anything to be nervous about, Miss Muir." Officer Donaldson gave McKenna another smile then turned to Cindy and nodded.

Cindy leaned forward, her facial features soft, a balled-up tissue in her hand. "Do you remember a case you closed about six months ago regarding a toddler named Yasmine Brown?"

"Yes. We worked with the mother when Yasmine was born and did welfare checks on them regularly. Mom was doing great and so was baby." Yasmine had the biggest brown eyes that McKenna had ever seen, and they instantly won her over. "She even kicked out her boyfriend and got a restraining order against him."

Cindy dabbed at her eyes, and all the breath left McKenna's lungs. "The boyfriend, Hank, came back in the picture a few weeks ago. Last night he beat Yasmine to death because she was crying too much."

McKenna's entire body shook, and she hugged herself to still her limbs. "No. No, that's not possible. I ran into them in the grocery store a couple of weeks ago. They both looked so good, so happy. Belinda didn't mention anything about her boyfriend."

Officer Donaldson took the seat beside McKenna. "Was that the last time you saw Yasmine?"

She nodded.

"Did you, at that time, notice any bruising, cuts, or other injuries on her?"

This time she shook her head.

"When was the last time you visited them in a professional capacity?" Officer Grange crossed his well-muscled arms in front of himself.

Just that action alone was enough to send McKenna's heart rate through the stratosphere. She took a couple of deep breaths. "Um, I'd have to look on my calendar for the exact date, but I believe it was in the neighborhood of seven or eight months or so ago."

"Yasmine's mom said she reached out to you last week, but you never returned her calls."

What? If she'd seen Belinda's number, she would have known it. "No. I never heard from her. I don't know what happened there, but she didn't call me. I would have gotten in touch with her right away, just like I always did."

Officer Grange jotted something in his notebook. "We're going to have to ask you to come to the station, Miss Muir, and answer further questions. This is a homicide investigation."

She shuddered but stood. "Of course. I want to do everything I can to help bring Yasmine's killer to justice." This had to be some kind of nightmare. One she would hopefully wake up from very, very soon.

But nothing of the sort happened. Officer Grange held the door open and motioned for McKenna to leave Cindy's office.

"Do you want me to come right away?"

Officer Donaldson nodded. "If you could. The girl's mother, as I'm sure you can imagine, isn't in any shape to talk much right now. Any light you can shed on what might have happened would be greatly appreciated."

"Okay. My supervisor cleared my schedule, so I don't have any meetings this morning. I'm happy to do all I can. Your investigation will show that I didn't receive any calls from Yasmine's mother."

"I don't know if that will be necessary." But Officer Grange's deep voice was cool.

Even though she wasn't the one in trouble with the law, her knees were about as mushy as a pile of mashed potatoes. McKenna exited the office, her footfalls almost silent as she crossed the deep carpeting to her cubicle.

It wasn't until she got to her car that the tears came, hot as they tracked down her face. How could someone commit such a horrible, despicable act on a defenseless child? Maybe Yasmine was upset, or perhaps she wasn't feeling well. A little loving and cuddling might have been all it would have taken to soothe her.

The sun shone through the windshield, so bright it was almost blinding. At the edge of the parking lot, a plot of black-eyed Susans danced in the light breeze. A car came and another left. Behind her, where there was an elementary school, a bell rang, and the music of children's laughter filled the air.

Life was going on.

But how? Deep inside McKenna, this was a black, cold, rainy day. Even worse than losing Chris. That didn't compare to Belinda's loss. How she must have had her heart ripped from her chest when she knew what that man did to her baby.

Officer Donaldson knocked at her window, and McKenna lowered it. "Are you going to be okay? Do you need some tissues? We'd be happy to drive you to the station and back here when we're done. We don't want you to be on the road in such a state."

McKenna swallowed and shook her head. "I'll be okay. Thank you for your concern."

"We don't want you to get into an accident."

"I won't." She dabbed her eyes with the tissue she'd gotten from the box she kept between the front seats. "If something changes, I'll pull over and give you a call."

"That's a great idea." Officer Donaldson returned to her vehicle where her partner waited behind the wheel.

How she managed to drive herself to the station with the officers right on her tail was beyond her. Somehow, though, she didn't pass out and didn't have to pull over because of her tears.

Before she knew what was happening, she found herself sitting in a sterile, windowless interrogation room with nothing but a small table, a few hard chairs, and a camera in it. She pulled her hair away from her face.

Several minutes passed before the two officers entered the room. Officer Donaldson set a cup of coffee in front of McKenna. "You look like you could use it."

"It's that bad?" McKenna gave a hollow laugh.

"No, just women's intuition."

Officer Grange harrumphed.

"And I'm sorry we have to use this room. There's a meeting in the conference room, so this is all we have available."

"It is a little intimidating."

"Don't worry. We just want to get more of a feel for the relationship Belinda had with her boyfriend and with her daughter, what first caused social services to get involved, that kind of thing."

McKenna nodded. Thank goodness for Officer Donaldson; otherwise, she'd be an absolute wreck. The guy cop was none too friendly.

Hours ticked by as they threw question after question at her, many of them repetitive. She hadn't taken the time to eat breakfast, and lunch passed without a break. Her head buzzed.

It must have been the middle of the afternoon when Officer Grange finally snapped his notebook shut. "Would you mind if we searched your phones and other records at your home and office?"

"I would have to consult my supervisor on that. And I hope you believe me that I take my job to keep children and families safe very seriously. If it had been in my power to prevent this, I would have."

"About the phone and other records, ma'am?" Officer Grange wasn't about to let that topic go.

"Am I in trouble?"

Thankfully, Officer Donaldson stepped in. "We just want confirmation of everything you've told us, and we need to weigh it against what Belinda and her boyfriend are telling us."

They had talked about this in school, and they had training for such cases at work too. It wasn't outside the realm of possibility for a social worker to be held somewhat liable, especially financially, if they neglected to report any abuse.

But that hadn't been the case with Yasmine. McKenna honestly hadn't seen any marks on the girl in her most recent visits. Or even a few weeks ago. "May I call my supervisor?"

"Go ahead. Take all the time you need. Would you like a sandwich or something?"

At least the female officer was a little more understanding. "That would be wonderful."

"And a diet pop?"

"Yes, please."

Officer Donaldson grinned again. She really was quite pretty, with blond hair and smooth skin. "You'll feel better once you get something in your stomach. We'll step out while you place the call."

"Thanks."

They left the room, and McKenna dialed the number. Cindy confirmed what she already suspected. Because this was a homicide case, they needed to allow the authorities to see the records and go through her work phone. "I'm awfully sorry this happened."

"Thanks, Cindy. I know I did right by Yasmine. Honestly, I can't believe she's gone. She was a little bubble of light. Now snuffed."

"Some go their entire careers without having this happen. It's a shame this came while you're young, but I know how much you do for each of your clients."

"Thanks. Your support means everything."

Neither officer had appeared by the time she hung up with Cindy, so she called Taylor. Confidentiality had prevented her from sharing much information with her best friend, but while she was on the case, she had told her that she was working with the cutest little kid. Now that this story would be splashed across the news, she gave Tay a brief rundown on what happened.

"Oh, sweetie, that's awful. If only there was something I could do to help."

"There's nothing, but thanks. I have a feeling I'm really going to need your listening ear and your shoulder in the coming weeks. This is way worse than Chris."

When Officer Donaldson returned with a turkey sandwich and a Diet Coke, McKenna handed over her work phone. "I'll have to go back to the office and go through the files."

"We spoke to your supervisor, and she's going to make sure all that gets done."

Not a moment later McKenna's personal phone dinged with a text from Cindy telling her she had everything under control at the office and that McKenna should go home and try to get some rest.

God bless that woman. No wonder they had become something of friends.

As soon as the police allowed her to leave, she made her way down the hallway, the concrete blocks painted a putrid green unsettling her stomach. She checked out at the front desk and stepped into the fresh air.

The sun was still shining. How dare it do that? How dare it bring light and warmth on such an awful day?

McKenna glanced up, and there was Taylor, waiting at the bottom of the steps. Once McKenna traversed them, Taylor wrapped her in a gigantic hug. "How are you doing?"

"I've been better, honestly. This is all so surreal. Yasmine's death, my questioning by the police about every one of the case's details."

"Then it will get straightened out in a jiffy, and life can go back to normal."

But even normal, even what life was like at 9:27 this morning, was nothing fantastic. "I don't think it ever will be again."

"Well, I just happen to have a gift card to our favorite restaurant, and I have the online order ready to go. Just have to hit Send. So you go home and take a hot shower, and I'll be there in a little bit with good food."

"Thanks. What would I do without you?"

"Let's never find that out. How about some chocolate too?"

"Of course. Chocolate makes everything better."

But as McKenna slid behind her car's steering wheel and scrolled through her phone, reality slammed her between the eyes.

Nothing would be better for a long, long time.

Because there were a couple of calls from an unknown number. The ones she'd ignored as possible spam.

Could those have been from Yasmine's mom?

The police, who had downloaded the information from her phone, would find out.

CHAPTER FIVE

Terrible things happened,
We were chased from our mountains,
From you, our loving mother,
Separated from us forever.

Oh, how heavy is my heart
That we are separated,
And throughout this strange land
We are scattered.

~FROM "SONG OF LEMKOVYNA"

Wednesday, March 25, 1942
Kraków, Generalgouvernement, Poland

The early spring day was drawing to a close, and the shadows that crossed the wood floors in my flat lengthened. The fragrance of frying onions and cabbage mingled in the warming air. Children shouted as they raced down the street, returning home from the German-run schools.

Only the youngest could attend and then only long enough for their teachers to indoctrinate them into Nazi ideology. The Polish language was forbidden. Being smart was forbidden. Some days it was almost as if breathing was forbidden.

I examined myself in the mirror, the silver peeling off it, fluffed the brown hair I had always wished was blond, and smoothed out my simple brown dress with faded red buttons down the front. Tonight I had to blend in with the Jewish workers returning to the ghetto after their shifts at outside factories.

It wouldn't be difficult. Never in my life had I had money for fine dresses or frippery, and now what little I did own was wearing out. New dresses were out of the question, a luxury very few had the money or the ration coupons for.

From my scarred and warped wardrobe, I drew out the large black overcoat with big inside pockets that Jerzy had given me. Why he had it, I hadn't questioned. But it was this coat that would be the key to our success or failure in secreting Teena from the ghetto.

I fingered the armband in the pocket, again not questioning where Jerzy had come into possession of such a thing. A thing that sent the hairs on the back of my neck and my arms standing as straight as soldiers.

It was fine that he refused to tell me. He had his secrets, and I would never push him to reveal them. In such days, being stupid and not knowing much could play in your favor.

So much pretending, so much acting went on just to survive underneath the Nazi thumb. Life was nothing more than a charade, a game. One with winners and losers.

The stakes were high though. The winners controlled the citizens like puppets. The losers were shot in the streets.

Would Uncle Michal be disappointed in me if he ever discovered I pretended to be uneducated? Or would he understand why I was forced to? In America, though they were now in the war, life was so much different. Perhaps when the conflict ended, I would finally be able to persuade Mama to leave our home for a better place.

It would break my heart to turn my back on my beloved green hills, but a land flowing with milk and honey beckoned to me. Now more than ever.

Never mind. There was no time to think about that. I slid my feet into my most scuffed and practical oxfords and slipped from the flat. After a short walk down Długa Street, Jerzy met me at the tram stop. Soon we were aboard and headed toward the ghetto.

He stared straight ahead at some unseen sight for the entire trip, even though I studied his strong profile most of the way. Perhaps the danger of what we were about to do weighed on his shoulders too. After all he'd already endured at the hands of the Nazis, it must.

The bell on the tram chimed as we traveled down Kraków's ancient streets, the happy, normal sound of it in stark contrast to the world around us. Our stop was next, and I nudged Jerzy in the ribs to rouse him from his thoughts.

For our safety, we had agreed to disembark a couple of stops before we needed to get off. As we strolled toward one of the outside textile factories where Jews were forced to work, Jerzy took me by the hand and squeezed my fingers, his clammy against mine. "Are you ready? It won't be a pleasant night."

"I know. But if we manage to get Teena out of that horrible place and somewhere safe, it will be worth it." Despite my confident words, my stomach muscles clenched and relaxed and clenched again.

He drew me into a side hug. "For Risa. Remember that. This is for Risa."

All I could do was nod. If I spoke, I would lose my composure. And since I was playing a part on a stage, I could not break character.

After about thirty minutes, a group of thin, worn, bedraggled women exited the factory. I reached into my outside coat pocket and pulled out the rough, off-white armband marked with a blue Star of David and slipped it over my wrist to the middle of my upper arm.

Jerzy did the same and gave me a wide smile and a peck on my cheek. "I'll see you inside." He would come later when the men returned from their work detail. There was no way he would blend in with the hunched-over women.

Once fortified with a deep breath, I entered the stream of ladies exiting the factory and bent my head like most of them did. There was almost a rhythm to the way they shuffled their feet, and I shuffled in time with them. Even though the weather was far from summerlike, sweat covered my body and brought a chill.

How could these women do this every day? Long hours bowed over machines, their rations not enough to sustain them. Even Lemkos didn't have life this hard. At least we worked in the fresh air and ate the fruit of our labors.

Most of the women had bandaged fingers from their work. I stuck mine into my coat pockets. Without the same wounds, I would break character.

Up and down the line, marching with the women, were soldiers with large brown and black German shepherds and guns. Imagine that. Dogs and guns to guard a group of hungry, overworked women. If it weren't so serious, it would be laughable.

In front of me loomed the gate, the same one I had passed through last night. The same pressure built in my chest, and I held my breath as I marched through it and into the walled, overcrowded section of the city. I was near the end of the line, and once the last woman was through, the gate clattered shut behind us and the ladies scattered to their respective residences.

I made my way to the hospital to wait for Jerzy, but I didn't have long before he appeared around the corner. As he went by, I fell into step with him.

We continued toward the orphanage, dodging bloated bodies piled on the street, some covered with damp newspapers or threadbare gray blankets and others without any covering at all. Before my roiling stomach rebelled, I turned my head. There was no dignity here, even after life. Though I breathed through my mouth, the foul odor of death lingered in my nostrils.

After a short walk, we arrived at the nondescript gray two-story building, some of the bricks chipping away in the face of the elements. We climbed the two crumbling steps that led to the bare wood door, the paint peeled away long ago by the wind and the rain.

With a creak, Jerzy opened the door and stepped aside so I could enter first. From upstairs and both sides of me came the wails of infants and the cries of little children. Everyone else in this miserable place went about in silence, heads down, tongues muted, ears shut.

Not so the littlest of them. They protested with the lusty cries that the rest of the prisoners bottled up. That they couldn't allow to escape their lips.

Only these tiny ones expressed their true emotions.

No one met us in the front, so I made my way down the hall with its sagging wood floors and peeked into one of the rooms. A nurse dressed in blue with a not-quite white apron covering her held a child in one arm, his bottle propped against her sagging bosom while she leaned over a crib and fed another infant.

I rushed forward. "Here, let me help you, *proszę*." I grabbed the bottle the woman held and scooped the infant into my arms.

The woman sighed, her chest heaving. "Dziękuję. There are too many of them and too few of us."

All around the room lay small babies, most of them with heads of dark hair. A few slept, but others cried and cried, their faces red and wet with tears. "I'm happy to help."

The woman studied me up and down then shifted her gaze to Jerzy, who had since entered. "Who are you, and what do you want here?"

Even with meager rations and worn-out clothes, Jerzy and I were in much better condition than anyone else in the ghetto. "I am—was—a friend of Risa Birkha. She passed away last night."

The nurse stepped backward, closer to the wall, and pulled the infant in her arms tighter to her. "Many die each night."

"We are not here to harm you or any of the children. I loved Risa like the sister I never had." I swallowed against the ever-rising tide of tears. No ocean would be large enough to hold all of them shed throughout Poland.

"Ever since I came here from the countryside, she was with me and helped me. Now it is my turn to help her daughter. I'm looking for Teena Birkha. I plan to take her out of the ghetto and give her the best life possible."

The woman jiggled the child she was feeding, and I did the same with the squirming infant in my arms. "Where did you meet Pani Birkha?"

Other than to those who knew me before the invasion, I didn't speak to anyone about my education or my work at the university. But here with this woman, in this place of the most cruel and intense persecution, I could be honest. Had to be honest. "Risa and I were both lecturers at Jagiellonian University, she in the department of psychology, and I in the department of anthropology."

"I knew Pani Birkha."

I released a pent-up breath. "Then you'll allow me to take Teena? One less orphan with an uncertain fate." Though all of us walked an uncertain fate every day.

"Tak."

With the single word, the heaviness that had weighed on me since Risa's death lifted off my shoulders, at least a little bit. Plenty of danger still loomed in front of us before Teena would truly be safe.

The nurse called for another attendant to come and be with the babies; then she led us to an equally crowded nursery on the second floor. She made her way to a crib underneath the streaky two-over-two window and lifted a sweet little dark-red-haired baby from the crib.

I couldn't help but cover my mouth. Until this point, I had never seen six-month-old Teena. She was so beautiful, perhaps even more beautiful than her mother. The nurse brought her to me and placed her in my arms.

I snuggled her close to my chest and kissed the top of her head.

"You will take good care of her?"

"The best. I would give my life for this little one. She is absolutely precious to me."

"We are so grateful. Teena is a delight, and she is blessed to have a woman like you who loves her and would risk her life for her."

I stroked Teena's hair. "I would do anything for her. How long has she been here?"

"Her mother took ill almost a month ago. Some of the babies here survive only a few days. Pani Birkha did all she could to make sure her daughter was well cared for. And to know that she won't have to live in this miserable hole gives me that much more hope for her survival."

"You have my word. And I will pray for the Holy Father's blessings on you and on all the children here, that He will keep you in safety and good health."

All the nurse did was nod. Tak, it was difficult for any of them to believe that the Holy Father continued to bless them. After all, they believed He had stolen Risa from her daughter.

Jerzy touched my shoulder, infusing me with warmth. "We should go."

The nurse stepped forward and kissed Teena on both cheeks then uttered something in Yiddish. Perhaps words of wisdom or of blessing. "How will you get her out of here? You are taking her away, aren't you?" For the first time, she pointed to our armbands.

"Don't worry, we are Gentiles. These were to get us into the ghetto and to get us out. We don't want to draw attention to ourselves. And it's better if you don't know how we are going to manage to spirit Teena to freedom."

"I understand." Once more, the nurse kissed the child.

Jerzy rubbed Teena's head. "We should get out of here. Curfew is coming."

With the cries of perhaps a hundred babies ringing in my ears, I exited the orphanage, Jerzy right behind me. As I stood in the street that overflowed with rubbish, I peered at the window on the second floor at the building's left end. "Perhaps one day, Teena, when this madness has run its course, you or your children or grandchildren will return here and see where you lived the first days of your life."

I tucked the small child into the large inside pocket of the oversized coat to test how well she would do in there and how conspicuous it made us.

Jerzy walked backward facing me. "Just keep your hands over the front of yourself and no one will notice the difference."

From inside the coat, Teena let out a wail. One that could get us killed.

Already those few who roamed the streets flashed us sideways glances. I released Teena and cradled her close. For over a month, she hadn't had a mother's love. She would have it now and have it in abundance. "We will have to drug her."

"Dr. Aleksandrowicz will help with that."

We continued toward the hospital.

But this was only the first step in a journey fraught with danger.

CHAPTER SIX

There was too much suffering. Too much pain. Too much dying.

As I made a vain attempt to sleep on the ghetto's hospital floor, the only place we found room to shelter, all around me came the weeping, wails, moaning, and groaning. Throughout the night, as we waited for the morning work details to leave so we could slip out, it never ceased. Every now and again, one voice went silent, never to be heard again. But then three others joined the ongoing lament.

Little by little, the Nazis sucked the life out of everyone around us. The Jews the fastest, but the rest of us eventually. If only the Allies would arrive and end our misery.

Without medicine or proper supplies, there was little the overworked doctors and nurses could do for their patients. Risa and many, many others would never have fallen ill if conditions were better. And when they had, with the right drugs, they could have been cured.

It wasn't enough that the Nazis worked their prisoners like serfs. It wasn't enough that they didn't give them food to keep their bones from jutting out underneath their skin. Nie, they had to go one step further and take away even the most basic health care.

And beside me, on the cold tile floor that was not a good bed, little Teena wept for the mother taken from her far too soon. The mother she should never have lost. I gathered her close to keep her warm and to comfort her. Her little shoulders shook, and she pushed on my chest.

I was not who she wanted, and I could not blame her for rejecting me. In time perhaps she would come to love me. And in time I would tell her about the beautiful woman who gave birth to her.

Now that I had charge of her, though, how would I care for her? I was a single woman who had to work. Taking Teena with me to my German employer's home was out of the question. Perhaps my downstairs neighbors would watch her. They had a little girl of their own.

Neighbors. What would they think when I came home with an infant? Suspicions and rumors were sure to fly fast and furious. How could I explain Teena's presence? Maybe I would have to say that she was my sister's child from Dubne. Something like that.

And rations? She would need proof of identity to get a ration card for milk. There was too much to think about, too much to consider. Too much that could go wrong.

As shafts of daylight peeked into the windows, the handful of people on the floor around me roused, and I rubbed my gritty eyes. My legs ached from standing and jiggling Teena a good part of the night.

The child was mourning. Somehow or another, she must sense all she had lost.

It was all I could do not to cry with her.

Jerzy sat up and pulled me down beside him. "Have you been awake all night?"

"Do I look that bad?"

His nod was almost imperceptible, just enough to let me know that I did. "You should have woken me."

"One of us had to get some sleep."

"We need to be sharp this morning. When we return to your place, you can rest, and I'll watch Teena for you."

"You? Have you ever been responsible for a small child?"

"I do have three younger sisters, and from time to time Mama had to go to the market and left them with me. How much experience do you have?"

I shrugged. Beaten at my own game. "My two older sisters passed away a few years before I was born." In Lemkovyna, losing a child was not an uncommon occurrence. Many women carried that heavy burden on their shoulders.

He smoothed a lock of hair away from my face, his touch so gentle. An unnamable emotion flashed through his eyes. "We will do this together. I will not leave you to take care of Teena alone. No matter what, I will always be here for you."

"Dziękuję. That means so much to me." I touched his once-smooth cheek. He had lost as much as anyone because of the war.

Little by little, all around us, the ghetto came to life. Dr. Aleksandrowicz, who had arranged these accommodations for us, arrived at the hospital early to make sure we had all we needed and were ready to go. He also brought some drops he had gotten at the pharmacy to make Teena sleep so she would be quiet when we left the walled area of the city.

Jerzy clapped him on the back. "We owe you so much and are so grateful for your help."

"If only other children could be saved. But I can't say more. Just take care of this little one and of yourselves. May you be blessed."

"And you." I kissed the doctor on both bearded cheeks then tucked Teena inside the large coat. With her dark eyelashes brushing her fair skin, she had an angelic appearance. My heart twisted, a physical pain in my chest. Risa would never get to see her daughter grow up. Teena would never know the mother who loved her more than her own life.

What a poor mite to have lost so much at such a tender age.

"Are you ready?" Jerzy slipped on his armband and then passed mine to me.

The weight of Teena inside the coat made putting it on more difficult, but I managed it. "Tak."

"Good. The women going to the factory should be heading out in just a little bit. I will meet you at your flat as soon as possible."

"Be safe." I also kissed his cheeks.

Again, there was that emotion in his eyes, one I couldn't put my finger on. "And you."

With that, I stepped from the hospital and onto the street. No smells of breakfast cooking, just odors of death. No shouts of happy children on their way to school, just the cries of the sick and dying. No chattering conversation as people headed to work, just the guttural shouts of the guards moving along the weak and tired.

I fell into one long column of women who shuffled their feet. Careful to hold my arms over the baby, I walked as the others did. Head down. Shoulders slumped.

The closer I came to the ghetto's boundary, the drier my mouth went and the more my legs turned to jelly. All I had to do was get through the gate and away from the line without anyone noticing me. That was it. Nothing more.

So simple.

So difficult.

"Hey, I don't remember seeing you before." The middle-aged woman next to me flashed me a narrow-eyed look.

"I-I'm, I just arrived here. I've been in hiding. Tak, in hiding all this time, and they found me."

The woman shook her head. "I think you might be trying to get out of the work detail in the quarry at Plaszów." She elbowed the woman beside her. "What do you think? Have you seen her before?"

"Never. Your first day, you say?"

"Tak."

The first woman shook her head, her thin, graying hair swinging with the motion. "I don't believe you. You're looking for a way out of the work assigned to you. And you should be ashamed of yourself. Young and strong and well-fed that you are. How do you manage that?"

I sucked in a lungful of air. "I—"

"My bet is she lets the guards have their way with her, and that is how she manages to keep from starving to death." The second woman spat on the ground.

"Never. I would never do such a thing. It's like I told you."

The first woman waved away my words. "No more. We know the kind of woman you are. You would do anything to help yourself. Anything at all. Pitiful."

If they only knew. Then again, what difference did it make?

The second woman nodded in the direction of the guards. "We should let them know she is trying to get out of the real work, taking a job someone older or weaker might need."

"That's exactly what I'm going to do."

"Nie!" Cold shot through my body. "I will go back to my job. I promise I will. Just whatever you do, don't tell the guards. Proszę. Look. I'm getting out of the line now." And I did.

The column, one long snake of thin, empty-eyed women, marched by. I hid in the shadows of one of the buildings until the women were almost past.

Then I spotted another opening, one away from the guards, and I slipped into the line.

This time I didn't dare look up until, far behind me, the gate shut with a thud. A divide between those who walked in relative freedom and those whose moves the Nazis controlled. I shivered and hugged Teena tighter.

Without lifting my head, I snuck peeks from the corners of my eyes to ascertain where the guards were. Not seeing any, and with buildings all around, I slipped from the line and scurried to the safety provided in the gap between two of the buildings.

I patted Teena's bony back. The baby continued to doze. Between the medicine and not sleeping all night, she should be out for a good long while.

In the darkness of the alley, I pulled off the armband and, since I would never go back to the ghetto, ground it into the dirt then strode as fast as possible in the opposite direction.

Running would only call attention to myself, but that's what every part of me screamed to do. Instead, I maintained a brisk pace, every sense, every muscle on high alert, until I was on the other side of the bridge from the ghetto.

I plopped onto a bench along the water and pulled the sleeping baby from inside the coat. As the wind blew cold across the water, I cradled Teena to my chest and rocked back and forth. "Praise the Holy Father, we made it. Praise the Holy Father."

Teena didn't so much as stir. This was an opportunity for me to gather and fortify myself with several deep breaths. With my nerves steadied, I headed for the nearest tram stop. Though I avoided taking them to save money, today I splurged. Getting home that much faster, behind closed doors where there was a measure of safety, would make spending the *złoty* worth it.

Within half an hour or so, I had climbed the stairs to my flat, emptied out the drawer at the bottom of the wardrobe, filled it with blankets, and settled Teena in it, praying all the while that she wouldn't wake and alert the neighbors to her presence. Then I sank onto my lumpy dark green davenport.

Though a cup of tea would warm and relax me, I had no energy to go to the stove and put on the kettle. Sleep overtook me until someone shook me by the shoulder. I rubbed my eyes until I came around fully. Jerzy stood over me. What a wonderful sight he was. I jumped up and gave him a quick hug. "You made it."

"Tak. How did you fare?"

"I had a bit of a problem."

"What happened?"

I explained what the women said about me. "I can't imagine what they go through every day. Some of those jobs must be terrible for them to get so upset when they believed I was getting out of hard labor."

"That's just it. It is hard labor. Very hard labor. Many who are assigned to that detail don't live. That's what Dr. Aleksandrowicz told me. You saw for yourself what life is like inside the walls. It must be ten times worse at one of the camps."

"I'm thankful I was able to get out with Teena." A tremor passed over me, shaking me from head to toe.

Jerzy pulled me close. "That had to be awful."

"It—it. . ."

"What is important is that we both made it and that Teena is with us."

"The only question that remains is what we do from here. My mind was so occupied with rescuing her and everything that has happened in the past day and a half that I never thought about how I would go to my job with Teena here. Who is going to take care of her? I have to bring in an income."

"I have to work as well, with what pittance I get from the job the Nazis allow me to have."

The tea would taste even better now, so I went to the tiny kitchen to brew some for both of us, the leaves in my jar almost gone. A few more cups, and there would be no more until maybe the end of the war. Who knew?

At that point, we both needed it, so I set the water to boiling. "I also worry about the others in this building. They know I'm not married, and when they last saw me, I wasn't expecting. What am I to say if they question where this baby came from?"

Jerzy rubbed the top of his head. "All excellent questions. Life is getting more difficult by the day. The Nazis would love nothing more than to get their hands on all three of us."

"Do you think we need to hide?" Though my hand shook, I managed to pour the water over the leaves in the strainers.

"I don't know. At the very least, we have to remain inconspicuous. Stay out of trouble."

"That's easy for me, but for you to stay out of trouble. . ."

Jerzy gave a hearty chuckle, and it was a balm to my heart. For a long time after he returned from the camp, he didn't even break a smile. Perhaps some of the trauma he endured there was fading. If I could take him to my beloved hills, the peace and quiet and fresh air would be sure to heal him.

Wait. Could that be the answer? A place to earn a small income, have someone watch Teena, and remain out of sight.

When I left Dubne more than fifteen years ago, I never dreamed I would yearn as I did now to return to the place that had brought such misery to us and an early death to my dear nyan'o, my father. Kraków was my escape, my way out of the crushing poverty that came with being Lemko, though my love for the land of my birth, my people, never waned.

But now. Now the world was topsy-turvy, and Lemkovyna appeared like a paradise on earth. "We could go home." I threw out the suggestion without meeting Jerzy's gaze.

"Kraków is my home."

"I don't mean your home. I mean mine. Dubne. It's so tiny and tucked away in the Carpathian foothills. No one would ever think to search for us there. It would be safe for Teena and for both of us."

"You couldn't show up there unmarried and with a child."

I glanced at Teena, her tiny hands fisted, her mouth working in her sleep. "I could say I was widowed."

"I have a better idea. If you're up to it, that is."

CHAPTER SEVEN

For justice, truth and liberty,
Heavenly God, I pray to you,
Give us strength to survive our sorrow
And to hope for a better plight.

~From "Song of Lemkovyna"

Friday, August 4, 2023
Suburban Pittsburgh, Pennsylvania

Still sitting in the police department's parking lot, McKenna scrolled through her personal phone to find three calls from the same number last week. She hadn't answered any of them. Whoever had been trying to reach her hadn't left a voicemail or a text.

How was she supposed to know who it was? All the caller ID said was that it was from an unknown number. Did she have to listen to everyone looking for money and every political candidate so that she didn't miss any client calls? Most of her clients didn't have her home number.

Part of her wanted to dial it and find out if that was truly Yasmine's mom. She thought about it for a moment, her finger hovering over the screen. Then again, it might look bad, might look like she was trying to influence Belinda. If the cops searched it again, she couldn't have them seeing her reaching out now.

She threw her phone on the passenger seat and headed home, blaring her favorite music to drown out the thoughts swimming in her head. She didn't have far to go until she arrived. Good thing, since she was barely holding it together.

She picked up the phone to take it inside, and it unlocked, revealing an email from Cindy. The subject line was *One more thing*. More bad news? Now what?

She waited until she was inside and dropped her purse onto the kitchen counter. She'd forgotten to get the mail, but that was the least of her worries. With a few taps, she opened Cindy's email.

Please don't reach out to Belinda or to her family. They are furious and blame the social system for failing Yasmine. I'm sorry about all of this.

None of the niceties they usually exchanged. But she was right; it wouldn't look good if Cindy favored McKenna. That was probably why she had to keep it professional.

The shower Taylor had suggested was calling her name. That was the best thing about this town house they rented. Good, steaming-hot water to wash away her cares.

But her cares weren't that easily scrubbed away. They remained like a weight around her neck. She dressed in her comfy shorts and an oversized T-shirt and combed her wet hair into a ponytail. A little better, but not much.

Taylor arrived soon after McKenna finished in the bathroom, the odors of cumin and chilis filling the house as she unpacked burritos and chimichangas. Then Tay laid a couple of good European chocolate bars on the table.

What should have had McKenna's stomach rumbling sent it tripping over itself instead. To please Tay, she stuck a smile to her lips. "Thanks, bestie. This is so nice of you."

"Hate to be the one to say it, but you don't look much better than at the police station. Just more comfortable."

"Oh, Tay, what am I going to do?" McKenna slid into a chair and covered her head. "I could—"

"Nope, I'm not about to let you think like that. Have faith. I know you almost better than you know yourself. You would never intentionally put a child in harm's way."

"That's it. It wasn't intentional, but if I didn't take those calls and it turns out they were from Belinda, then I was negligent."

Taylor sat and moved all the Mexican food to the opposite side of the table, only keeping the candy bar, which she offered to McKenna and which McKenna brushed away. "Listen to me, sweetie. Did you get some calls?"

"Yes. But from an unknown number. I haven't called it because I don't want the cops to think I'm trying to do something underhanded."

"Good move. Did the person leave any voicemails or texts?"

"Nothing. And as far as I know, Belinda didn't try to contact anyone else in the office. If nothing else, she also had Cindy's number."

"There you go." Taylor took a paper plate, set a burrito on it, and placed it in front of McKenna. "You have nothing to worry about because you did nothing wrong. Nothing. It may take some time for all this to sort out, but there is no way anything bad is going to happen to you."

"You don't have a crystal ball or a direct line to God."

"Ah." Taylor sat back, broke the chocolate bar in half, and took a bite. "That's where you're wrong. I do have a direct line to God. It's called prayer."

"But you can't see into the future."

"I do know who controls what's going to happen."

McKenna got up and moved to the kitchen island, where she leaned against the cool granite countertop. "I don't know. If nothing good is going to come of all this, then why would He put me through this torture? Why did this have to happen at all, especially to a sweet, innocent baby?"

"One thing I don't have is all the answers."

With her hand fisted, McKenna worked to scrub away the terrific headache the ibuprofen hadn't touched. "I need answers. That baby didn't deserve to die, and I may well have been able to prevent her death."

"I know. But we can't stop evil. That's a force far greater than us."

Just then her phone chose to ring. She went to answer it, but her eyes widened when she picked up the phone and glanced at the screen. "It's Chris." Could this day get any worse? "Go away and leave me alone!" she yelled at the phone even though she hadn't answered the call. For some reason, it felt really good.

"Let me handle this. You shouldn't have to deal with him." Taylor touched the green button.

"What are you—"

"Why, hello, Chris. Imagine you calling."

McKenna paced back and forth behind the island.

"I know you didn't call to talk to me, but it's nice to hear your voice anyway. How have you been?"

What on earth was Taylor thinking by talking to him? To the guy who broke her heart.

"Oh, that's great. I'm so glad you're happy with the woman you left my best friend for. That kind of makes it all better, doesn't it?" Tay flashed McKenna a smile.

"No, I'm not going to hand the phone to her. I'm enjoying our conversation. Aren't you? I mean, it's been a while since we caught up."

"Taylor." McKenna whisper-yelled her friend's name.

"I'm doing great. Thanks for asking. At least now I don't have to worry about how McKenna's fiancé is treating her. So that's one thing off my plate."

"Hang up."

Taylor shook her head. "The ring? I don't know what she did with it, and it's not really my business to ask her. Touchy subject and all. Though if she were to ask my advice, I would tell her to sell it and make a bunch of money. That would be the least she deserves."

Now Chris' voice came through the line loud and clear. "I want my ring back."

"Do you need it to propose to the other girl?"

"Taylor." This time McKenna didn't even attempt to keep her voice quiet.

"I never said she wasn't here." Tay shot McKenna quite the narrow-eyed look. "I did say that I wasn't going to hand the phone to her. And I meant that. That's a hard no from me."

"It doesn't belong to her." Chris' face must have been turning the color of tomato soup. He was easy to anger. That should have been a red flag to her from the start.

"You know, you caught us at a bad time. We're just about to have dinner, but it's been great talking to you. Let's say we never do this again though. Toodles."

McKenna stood with her feet apart. "What on earth did you do that for?"

"Just having a little fun."

Against her will, one corner of McKenna's mouth turned upward. She quickly turned it down again, but not before Taylor noticed.

"See, it was fun." Tay nodded as she spoke.

"I'll bet he has smoke coming out of his ears."

"Wouldn't doubt it."

"And I don't plan on giving him his ring back. You don't think he'll sue me for it, do you? A court case is the last thing I need."

"Naw, he's too much of a chicken. He always was a whole lot of hot air and not much else. Use that ring to buy something nice on our Cancun trip."

All the joy leaked out of McKenna. "I don't know about going now. It seems wrong to leave the country, sit in the sun, and have a good time right after a little girl was murdered."

"You aren't under arrest or anything."

"Yet."

"And you never will be. You told me once that social workers can't be held criminally liable for a death unless they were grossly negligent. Which you weren't. Now let's dig into this dinner. I, for one, am starving. And I know you hate cold food."

Between the meal that McKenna suddenly found herself famished for and the movie *Pride and Prejudice* that they watched and the copious amounts of chocolate they consumed, the two of them managed to pass the evening.

But Taylor couldn't entertain McKenna forever. Nor should she have to. At some point, she was going to have to face what happened to Yasmine and her possible role in it.

She sat on her bed and found the news article about Yasmine on her phone.

TWO-YEAR-OLD KILLED BY MOTHER'S BOYFRIEND

Police have taken twenty-two-year-old Hank Turnbull into custody for beating his girlfriend's two-year-old daughter to death when she wouldn't go to sleep.

First responders got the call about a child not breathing around 11 p.m. on Thursday night from the 1300 block of West Maple Avenue. When they arrived at the home, they discovered Yasmine Hull unresponsive. She was declared dead on the scene.

A preliminary autopsy report found that she suffered multiple skull fractures, three broken ribs, and a broken leg. There were also numerous bruises and lacerations. The cause of death was determined to be homicide by blunt force trauma to the head.

Yasmine's mother, Belinda Little, had a restraining order against Turnbull, but neighbors report that she had recently taken him back.

"She just let him come near that baby, and I can't believe she did

that. Now that sweet baby is gone," said a neighbor who asked not to be identified. "Where are the social workers who were supposed to be looking out for this family? Where is justice in this system?"

Police say Turnbull is in custody and is expected to appear in court on Monday. They refused to answer questions about anyone else liable in the case, stating, "We are investigating how such a heinous crime was committed."

A fund has been set up to help with funeral costs for Yasmine. Final arrangements have yet to be made.

McKenna ran to the bathroom and lost her dinner. How could Hank have done something so despicable to such an innocent child? And because she wouldn't go to sleep? Kids were like that sometimes.

Back in her too-pretty-pink bedroom, she pounded her pillow. This wasn't right. Yasmine never should have been treated this way.

Waves of grief washed over the sands of her anger, cooling it.

All this because she didn't want to be bothered by potential spam.

If that was Belinda calling, she should have picked up the phone.

If only.

CHAPTER EIGHT

After a restless night's sleep, a long run, and another shower, McKenna sat at the kitchen table with an insulated tumbler filled with highly caffeinated, highly creamed and sugared coffee. Maybe it wasn't the best choice, seeing how buzzed she was. Her hands shook enough without the coffee.

She was only about halfway through her cup and already bored with silly cat videos when Taylor came in with several bags of groceries. McKenna eyed her. "You're bright eyed and bushy tailed, especially for a Saturday. What has you so chipper this morning?"

"I'm in a baking mood. Thought I might try some cinnamon buns, though after reading the recipe, we might have them in time for dinner instead of breakfast."

"I don't think I can eat much anyway."

"You need a distraction."

"My run was great and so was the shower, but Yasmine's death is never far from my mind."

"No, I'm talking about a real distraction. Something that uses brainpower."

"Okay." McKenna drew out the word. Tay could come up with the craziest schemes. Her conversation last night with Chris was just one example.

"Trust me on this. I got you a subscription to the site where you got your DNA tested, and now you can look at records and build a family tree like we talked about. You're always telling me you want to know more about your mom's mom's side of the family. This is your chance."

McKenna bit the inside of her cheek. "I was thinking about taking a sabbatical, just to catch my breath and process everything. I have plenty of time saved up."

"That's a great idea. Because you have one of the toughest jobs on the planet, you deserve it."

"Okay. I'll give the family tree thing a go and see where I end up."

"That's the spirit. Go grab your computer while I make myself a cup of coffee. Fifteen sugars and ten creams, right? That's how you like it?"

McKenna shot her a *whatever* glance. "I can't believe you've been going without some caffeine running through your veins."

A few minutes later she was seated at the table once more with her laptop in front of her. She logged on to the site and scrolled around. "Hey, this is kind of cool. I found my *baba* already to build a family tree. See, here she is in the 1950 census. Two years old. Maria Dudik."

She clicked on the thumbnail of the census document, and it brought up a larger version. "Johnstown, Pennsylvania. That's where my baba grew up." She touched Baba's name on the screen.

She squinted to get a better look at the entry. The handwriting was in a very fancy, loopy script that wasn't easy to make out. It would be simpler if she had the big screen from her work computer.

Some distraction this was turning out to be. She leaned forward a little. "It says her parents are Paul and Helen Dudik. Okay. That's something. Baba never told me their names. Then again, I never asked."

She worked for a while longer, searching Paul and Helen. The census record stated they were born in Poland, but she was coming up empty on that front.

All kinds of websites had genealogical information, and there was so much to sift through that before she knew it, three hours had passed. Wow. It was great for getting her mind off her troubles and wasting the day. And she thought Pinterest had been the black hole of time.

While McKenna worked, Taylor kept herself busy in the kitchen preparing the cinnamon rolls. It was that heavenly scent of spice that drew McKenna from her somewhat frustrating search for her great-grandparents.

"Are you hungry?" Taylor stood with a large teal oven mitt on her hand, holding a piping-hot pan of deliciousness.

"I wasn't before, but I am now. What have you created?"

"I like to call it heaven on earth."

"Let's dig in."

"We need the cream cheese frosting first. That doesn't come until they're cool."

"There is no way I'm going to wait. And remember, hot food."

"It'll slide off."

"I don't care. I'll scoop the frosting into my mouth after each bite. How's that?"

Taylor shrugged. "Suit yourself."

McKenna bit into the cloud-soft dough, the sweetness of the cinnamon-sugar filling dissolving on her tongue. The frosting's tang was the perfect finishing touch. "You're right." Her mouth was still half full. "Heaven on earth."

For another minute, she forgot her troubles. Then her phone rang, pulling her from the delicious world of sweet rolls.

Another unknown number, but there was no way she was going to let the call go, no matter what kind of sales pitch she had to listen to. She swallowed and touched the green button. "Hello."

"Why did you allow him to do that to my baby?"

"Belinda? Is that you?" She probably shouldn't be having a conversation with her, but at least she hadn't initiated the call.

"My baby is gone because of you."

"Did you try to call me the other day? The number came up as unknown. If I had realized it was you, I would have answered. Even if you had left a voicemail, I would have gotten back to you."

"So now you're blaming my daughter's death on me? 'Cause I did call."

The throbbing in McKenna's head started again. "No, I'm not blaming you at all. What I'm saying is that the person who should be blamed is Hank. He's the one who did this to Yasmine. He's the one who beat her. And I'm so, so very sorry about that."

The line went silent for a moment, and then came a soft sniffling. A complete one-eighty from the anger a moment ago. "My baby. How could I have allowed him back in my life? He told me he was a different man. But he wasn't. No, he was the same old Hank who wanted nothing to do with my sweet baby."

"Men like him can be very persuasive. They make a good case for themselves, and you wanted to believe him. You always want to believe the best about people. And that's not a bad thing."

"Well no more, I tell you that. Never again am I going to trust any man. They're snakes in the grass, every last one of them."

Though McKenna was inclined to agree with her, she didn't say so. "How are you holding up?"

"My baby is gone. How do you think I'm holding up? Awful. Terrible. I can't sleep. I can't eat. I can't do anything but think about how Yasmine will never get to grow up, how she'll never get to go to prom or get married or have a baby of her own. I was gonna teach her that you should get married and not fall for the first guy that makes you feel special."

"You were a great mom to her. Whatever you did, you did it out of love. I saw how much you wanted the best and how you were working on making a good life for her."

"But then I let that piece of dirt back into my home. He's not even Yasmine's dad. And right away, I was scared. That's why I tried to call."

"I would give anything if I could go back in time and answer the phone. Why didn't you call Cindy? Or the cops?"

"I was scared. I had to use a different phone, a friend's phone, and then he figured out what I was doing."

"Belinda, did he hurt you?"

The pause was so long that McKenna checked to make sure she hadn't lost her signal. "Belinda?"

"No."

"Okay. If you say so. But the police can introduce additional charges if he did. Keep that in mind."

"Okay."

"Again, I'm truly heartbroken over Yasmine."

"Why? Why do babies have to die? Why are families torn apart by hatred?" Belinda's voice was thin, and it warbled.

"I don't know."

"Thank you for being honest. Everyone has been giving me one answer or another, but none of them make sense to me."

"None of this makes sense. Just know that I'm going to be praying for you." They weren't allowed to say this at work, but at this point, she didn't care. There was nothing else to say.

"I miss my baby."

"I do too."

"Thank you, McKenna. I just wish you would have answered."

For a long while after Belinda hung up, McKenna stared at her phone. It took Taylor touching her shoulder to bring her back to the present. "I couldn't help but overhear."

"Did I do the right thing by talking to her?"

"I don't know."

"Too many of life's questions don't have answers." McKenna pushed her now-cold cinnamon roll away and poured another cup of lukewarm coffee.

"You were right to tell her not to blame you or herself but to blame Hank. I suggest you take your own advice."

"I think I'm going to go to my mom's house. Ask her some questions about her family."

"Do you want me to go with you?"

Right now she wasn't good company. "No, thanks. I would ask Mom for some of her famous pumpkin muffins for you, but I think you're good on the sugar right now."

"Yeah, I suppose I am." Taylor's tinkling laugh filled the open room.

Mom and Dad lived only about thirty minutes away. Far enough that McKenna was able to live her own life without interference. Close enough that when she needed a parent or two, she could get to them without much trouble.

She turned on Christmas music and blared it through the car and turned off her thoughts. It might be the end of August, but carols could sweep away a bad mood like nothing else.

She pulled up to the gray two-story colonial where she'd grown up and entered the mudroom. "Mom?" She made her way into the kitchen.

Mom came from upstairs, still trim from the long walks she loved to take. "Kenna. What a nice surprise. What brings you by?"

Within half an hour, she'd poured out the entire sordid story to Mom. Somehow a box of tissues appeared in front of her, but she got through it with dry eyes. She must have cried out all her tears. Or maybe it was Mom's steadying presence.

"Aw, hon, I'm so sorry you're having to go through this. Are you okay for money if you take a leave of absence?"

Leave it to Mom to have that foremost in her mind. She wasn't emotional like McKenna was. Practical. No nonsense. That was Mom. "I'm fine. I just need someone in my corner."

"You have lots of someones standing beside you."

"Thanks. So what can you tell me about your family? How much do you know about your grandparents?"

"Not much. They didn't talk about the past. They were always very focused on the present and the future."

"But they were born in Poland."

"That's my understanding. From what I know, life wasn't easy for them before they came to the States. But you know, when I lost my first baby, she came to me. Time was taking a toll on her by then. It was only a year or two before she died. I remember her holding my hand and telling me that she understood."

"So she lost a baby?"

"By then I'd learned not to ask questions about the past. She wouldn't have answered anyway. But yes, that's the impression I got."

"What do you know about them?"

"They lived here in Pennsylvania. When they came, there were lots of people like them in the area, so they felt at home. They spoke in their native language. Polish, I guess it was. I never learned it. My mom had an uncle or a great-uncle that lived near us, but he died when I was very young."

"Well, that's more than what I had to go on before."

"And I do have her prayer book. When she died, she left it for me."

"Yes, I know. You keep it on the nightstand next to your bed. Are there any clues in there?"

"Just her name, Helen Dudik. That's all."

"This information should give me a good start. Thanks."

"I'm glad you found a hobby. Good for you. The Dudik women have always been strong. I like that you're taking after them."

But was she truly strong? Because inside, she was crumbling.

CHAPTER NINE

Lemkovyna, beloved mother
Hold me close to you.
Is there a better place to rest
Than being near you?

~From "Song of Lemkovyna"

Thursday, March 26, 1942
Kraków, Generalgouvernement, Poland

There were small moments, like the subtle shift of a river, that moved my life in a direction different than what I planned. Though the change didn't appear great at first, over time it moved farther away from the course I originally set.

As soon as Jerzy said he had a better idea for our safety, as soon as those words passed his lips, there was a small movement. Or maybe not so small, because this changed everything. How I looked at him, how I thought of him.

What I did.

I stared at him openmouthed, not quite believing I heard him correctly. "You want to do what?"

"I'm serious. Getting married is the most sensible solution to our problems." He raked his hair.

"Getting married is the craziest suggestion I have ever heard. There is no need to involve yourself in this business. It was my idea to rescue Teena, so I am the one who will take care of her." I kept my words soft as I glanced at the infant, now my child, my daughter, still asleep in the makeshift bed.

When I placed the cup of tea in front of Jerzy, he touched my hand, his so warm. A strange tingle shot through me. So strange. "You don't have to raise her on your own. Risa was my friend too."

"You have already done a great deal. You don't need to burden yourself with a wife and a young child. With the war, who knows what is going to happen tomorrow." It was the unpredictability of life that was the hardest. Not knowing what the day would bring. Any one of them might be the last.

"Being married to you would not be a burden." His pale cheeks pinked.

This tender demeanor from him, almost as if he truly wanted to marry me, flustered me, had my heart flapping like a bird. My teacup rattled against the saucer as I carried it to the table. Before my legs gave way, I sat on the hard wood chair.

"Think about it."

The trouble was that I was giving this idea consideration. Just as marriage would be no burden for him, being married to him would be no burden for me. He had always held a special place in my heart. For a while, I believed it to be a good friendship.

He had saved me, me and Risa, when the Nazis arrested the intelligentsia at the university. Was that where this funny tickling in my stomach came from? Did we share something more than friendship?

Maybe that was what it was. Maybe it was more. Many marriages were built on less than the friendship we shared. "Mama will be upset that we did not marry in our local church." The church was central to Lemko life and culture. All important events took place there.

"If she would like, if you would like, we could have a civil ceremony here and have our religious marriage conducted at your church."

My heart grew butterfly wings and fluttered inside my ribs. "You would do that for me?"

"I did not plan on running anywhere, but when I make a commitment, I make it with my entire heart. This might not be the conventional way of starting life together, but I want to do right by you."

Tak, our story might not have the most usual start, but this was war. How many had the wedding of their dreams these days? Absolutely no one. I licked my lips. "If you're proposing to me, Jerzy Bielski, then I happily accept."

The grin on his face stretched from Russia to France. I found myself turning up the corners of my mouth, then laughing.

"I don't have much to offer you."

"And I have nothing to give you."

From her little bed, Teena cried. "I hope that's a cry of approval from our daughter." Jerzy's shoulders straightened. Teena would be his daughter too.

I chuckled and picked her up. Our daughter, as Jerzy had said. That was what she was. "Do you know a priest you can trust? We will need her baptized so we can get papers for her. I would wait until we get to Dubne, but she should have them before we travel."

"I can find a priest who will do that. There are few left who haven't been deported, but the ones who are here will be more than happy to thumb their noses at the Nazis. Let me go find one, and I will put together what little I have. Then we can get married and be on our way."

Before I could string together a coherent sentence, even a coherent thought, he was out the door. I paced the room, jiggling Teena to keep her quiet. "What on earth have I done? I must be out of my mind to marry someone I only ever considered a friend. Jerzy is kind and thoughtful. He saved my life. But marriage? I must be out of my mind. What do you think?"

Teena cooed a sweet baby sound.

"You are right. I will be giving you a mama and a nyan'o. That is what I have to keep in mind. This isn't about me anymore, but about you too. About what is right and best for you. I can hear your mama in my head. She would be happy, I think. She would laugh and call us crazy, but she would also be very pleased that we are going to give you a complete family."

Teena entwined her fingers in my hair.

"Tak, you are the reason for this and where my focus needs to stay. So when I promise to love and cherish Jerzy for the rest of my life, a vow that I take seriously, remember that I am taking that vow for you too."

Teena gave a contented sigh.

"That must be your signal of approval." My heart settled into a steady rhythm as I laid the baby on top of the blankets and went to pack my belongings.

My frugality meant I hadn't accumulated much in the way of goods and trinkets over the years. Between watching every *grosz* and sending home as much as possible, I had kept to the bare necessities. Just enough to provide for myself, so that Mama would have plenty.

I did pack my few serviceable dresses and my bedding, my teapot, and my pot and pan. Keeping in mind that I would have to get them all in a suitcase and also juggle Teena, that was enough to take with me. I would have to dip into my savings to purchase some clothes for her, at least enough until we got home and Mama could sew a few things for her grandchild.

The smile on Mama's face at having a grandchild would be worth everything. If I had a camera, I could capture it forever, but since I didn't, I would have to imprint it in my memory, a precious image I could take out and examine anytime.

All in all, it didn't take long for me to put everything together. There was no time to sell the bed and the table and chairs. They would stay for whoever occupied the flat next. Among other matters, I had to write to my employer and my landlord and tell them I was leaving. I would, however, give no forwarding address. With Risa gone, there was no one here I trusted with my secret.

Soon to become our secret.

Once packed, I picked up Teena again and walked the creaky wood floor with her, jiggling her as I went. What would Jerzy expect of me as his wife? I pressed my stomach to stop it from jumping around. From what he had said, he wanted to be married to me in more than name only.

For most of my life, my focus had been on getting an education and taking care of Mama. I had never given much thought to marriage. My life had a different purpose after Nyan'o died. I turned from daughter to provider.

But now I was about to become a wife.

I warmed from the tips of my ears to the tips of my toes. Not an unpleasant thought. If Jerzy decided he wanted a full marriage, I would be prepared. And I would give myself willingly.

I had always thought a great deal of him. In fact, it would be wonderful to have a man look after me for a change. It had been far too many years since Nyan'o had died. Far too long that I had been on my own and had to be self-sufficient.

After another hour or so of waiting, of snuggling with Teena, of pacing the floors, Jerzy returned. His green eyes glimmered in the dusky light. "Everything is set. Are you ready to go? Ready to become Pani Bielski?"

I stole a quick peek in the mirror hanging on the wall. The colors in my navy-blue dress with red polka-dots were faded from far too many washings. Even though I had cinched the red belt as tight as it would go, it was still loose. And my blue pumps were scuffed.

He came behind me and squeezed my shoulders. "I will only be gazing into your face. No need to worry about anything else, though you do look lovely. You always do."

I fiddled with the belt once more. These compliments coming from Jerzy's mouth were strange and sent little sparks through me. It would take some time to get used to them, so I turned to him. His coat was threadbare and in need of a good brushing. But he had slicked back his light brown hair and had shaved. A sprinkle of freckles was strewn about his nose. "And you are very handsome. Any girl would be fortunate to marry you."

He picked up his suitcase as well as mine while I brought Teena, wrapped in blankets. I left the flat's key and a note underneath my landlord's door on the main level. I would drop the letter to my employer into a post box along the way.

A short time later we stood in front of the priest Jerzy had found. He smiled at us, as well as Teena. "May God Almighty bless both of you for what you are doing and for how you are caring for the least of these, one of His."

When I had awakened this morning on the floor of the hospital in the ghetto, I had never dreamed I would end the day as a married woman. Yet here I was, vowing to be faithful to Jerzy until death alone parted us.

And I meant every word. Every single one.

Jerzy made the same promise to me. And the way he gazed at me, steady, unwavering, told me that he intended to keep his vow.

After we partook of the Eucharist, the priest pronounced us man and wife and blessed us. Along with our marriage certificate, which he dated two years earlier than this day, he also baptized Teena and handed us a certificate for her.

"And now I have a small gift I would like to offer to you to celebrate your marriage and to thank you for taking in this child. The bed in the rectory is small, but you are welcome to use my room."

"Oh, we can't." Out of habit, I had spoken, the words coming out before I consulted my husband, but when I did turn to him, he nodded. "Where would you sleep?"

"This will be a good opportunity for me to spend the night in meditation and prayer. Always a proper activity for the spirit and the soul."

"Dziękuję. We will take you up on your offer." Jerzy shook the priest's hand. "You have been very kind to us, and we will never be able to repay you."

"You can repay me by staying safe and protecting this precious new life. I will leave you now. May God the Father watch over you in all your journeys." He strode down the aisle and out of the sanctuary, leaving us surrounded by a sacred peace.

For a while, I reveled in it, the candles flickering off the gold-covered statues and altars throughout the church. The stained-glass windows tinted the late-afternoon light and splashed it over the stone floors. Incense sweetened the air.

Jerzy sat in the front pew, which was well-worn by centuries of worshipers, and closed his eyes in prayer. I joined him, Teena on my lap.

Holy Father, You who see all and know all, watch over us, Thy servants, all the steps of our days. Whether our travail in this world be long or short, may Your blessing rest on us, Thy servants.

Jerzy continued to bow his head, but I couldn't remember the rest of the words from the prayer book. Oh, I had left it in my flat. What would I do without it? How could I lift my petitions to heaven without it?

Jerzy's lips moved, though no sound came out. I pulled Teena close and closed my eyes, unable to say anything to the Holy Father. For a moment, I drank in the silence of the church. Then I crossed myself. *I ask this all in the name of the Father and of the Son and of the Holy Ghost. Amen.*

I opened my eyes to find Jerzy staring at me. "You resemble a Madonna."

Though I didn't usually blush, I might have at that compliment. "Don't put me on such a level, or I will surely disappoint you every day. You know me well enough to know that I am not perfect. I have my faults and my failings, as do you."

He widened his eyes and opened his mouth, and I almost burst out laughing in church.

"Let's be honest and open with each other and never go to bed angry." I touched his face. "That's what Mama said made her marriage to Nyan'o work."

"She sounds like a very wise woman. I look forward to meeting her."

"She is going to love you."

"Well, my wife, are you ready to go?"

I picked up Teena. "We are ready to follow wherever you lead."

"But you will have to do the leading to Dubne. I have no idea how to get there." He took me by the hand and ushered me out. The rectory stood beside the church, and when we opened the door, the sweet odor of pork knuckle and the almost tangible tang of sauerkraut filled the air.

"The housekeeper must have prepared this for us. How lovely and thoughtful of the priest." I unwrapped the blankets that cocooned Teena, pulled a bottle I had gotten from the orphanage from my suitcase, and prepared it for her.

While I ate, I fed the baby. Soon the little one fell asleep. Jerzy cleared the plates, and together we washed them and put them away. As I rinsed out the sink, Jerzy came up behind me.

"Helena?" His breath tickled the back of my neck, though he didn't touch me.

My hands stilled. "Yes?"

"You are so dear to me."

"And you to me as well."

"Thoughts of you helped me survive the labor camp. When I didn't know if I would be able to go on another day, I prayed for the strength to live through the next hours so I could come home to you."

I spun to face him, almost nose to nose. "I never knew that."

"It's the truth."

Warmth spread through me. Thoughts of me had sustained Jerzy in the worst of conditions, and my heart swelled. What might be the kernels of love stirred.

And then, with my body trembling, he led us to our marriage bed.

I lay awake long into the night, long after my new husband snored beside me on the narrow bed. Life might hold joy or sorrow for us, love or indifference, plenty or want.

For not the first time in my life, I longed for a peek into my future. What joys or sorrows waited on the path before us?

CHAPTER TEN

Saturday, March 28, 1942
Near Dubne, Generalgouvernement Poland

The undulating tree-blanketed hills of my beloved Lemkovyna increased in height with each kilometer that the train clacked over the rails. Jerzy managed to occupy Teena through most of the four-hour trip, so I stared out the window at the changing landscape.

For the first time in years, I was coming home, and my entire body tingled. Though the classical buildings of the beautiful city of Kraków were stunning and left me breathless the first time I saw them, they couldn't compare with the hills rising in front of me.

I was almost home.

My breathing slowed, and my shoulders relaxed. That was the effect of the hills on a Lemko. That was what it meant to trod the land of our ancestors.

Though I hated having to part with some of the precious złoty I had been saving in a jar in my kitchen for so long, there was no way Jerzy and I could walk with the baby and our items from the rail station to the little village of Dubne.

We hired a kind farmer with tanned skin and a slump-backed horse to take us home in his rickety cart. He and I chatted in Lemko for a bit, him asking about Kraków and what it was like to live in such a large, cosmopolitan city, something he had never experienced and likely never would. I kept most of the details to myself.

Jerzy tapped my shoulder. "What is he saying?"

I sucked in a breath as I clung to the edge of the seat. Why hadn't I thought of it until now? My new, well-educated husband spoke several languages, but Lemko wasn't one of them. It might resemble Polish in some ways, but he wouldn't understand everything. And he certainly wouldn't be able to hold a conversation in the language. The only language of most of the Lemko people.

"I never thought... I'm so sorry. Here we are, traveling to our new home, at least for a while, and you can't communicate with the people here. What are we going to do? I got so caught up in Teena and making sure she was safe that I forgot about you." How could I have not had a thought for him? What kind of wife was I?

He rubbed my hand between his to warm it. "Don't fret. I am sure that I will pick it up soon enough."

"But almost no one in Dubne speaks Polish."

"Then I can learn from you."

How like him to maintain such an upbeat attitude. Likely what saved him in the labor camp, why he lived until the Nazis decided to send home the professors they had arrested from Jagiellonian University.

"I am plucky. You might have to be my teacher and interpreter for a while, that's all."

"Ďakujem."

"I can guess at that one. Does it mean thank you?"

"You are right. I truly did marry a very smart man."

Teena woke and cried, and Jerzy took her from me. "Look, little one. This is where we are going to live, all three of us together. Have you ever seen such a beautiful place? Nie, you haven't, have you? Grass is a novelty to you, I suspect."

While he entertained her, I turned my attention to the countryside around me, more and more familiar with each turn of the cart's wheels. I also constructed possible scenarios, how Mama would react when I walked through the door into my family home.

She might well be rather upset that I married someone who was not a Lemko. For hundreds of years, we kept to ourselves, marrying within our own enclaves. Or she might be angry that I risked my life to save Teena.

Then again, one look at Teena, and Mama would be in love. I kissed the baby's red, downy head, and she reached out and patted my face. Already she was becoming used to us. But how I ached for Risa to be here too.

As the farmer urged his horse and cart on, the yet-to-green hills grew taller, the terrain, steeper. But where the fields once would have been covered with sheep, there now were none. According to what Mama wrote, the Nazis had confiscated most of them. How did they expect the people to make a living from this poor, rocky soil without their animals? Their prized possessions.

Despite the grim circumstances awaiting us, life here had to be better than in the crowded city. A measure of peace and security must remain in this place.

My heart ticked up a few beats per minute the closer I got to Dubne. Quaint villages with a mixture of thatched-roofed, tin-roofed, and tile-roofed homes lay tucked in the valleys between each hill.

Here my ancestors had lived for hundreds of years. Not easy years by any means, but years in which we were left alone to live and speak and worship the way we pleased.

Fifty years ago, when Uncle Michal moved to America as a very young man, it was the Hungarians who had persecuted us, and many of us had left. Now it was the Germans who oppressed us, but this time there was nowhere to go.

Jerzy leaned over to whisper in my ear. "What has you smiling so much?"

"Am I?"

"Oh, tak. Are you ever."

"We don't have much. You might be surprised at how poor we are."

"If you are wondering if I will think less of you because of your background, don't. I never could. After the labor camp, nothing would surprise me about the way some people treat others."

How well he knew me already. Perhaps it would help our marriage that we had been friends first. "I don't know what we are going to do for a living."

"The Lord will provide."

My faith, always wobbly, was a mustard seed compared to his. I had much to learn from him. "Look, over there." My exclamation startled Teena, who wailed at this pronouncement.

Jerzy jiggled her, and she quieted. "What is it?"

"I used to play with my friends on these hills. On that tree there, we had a long rope with a large knot tied at the bottom, and we would swing from it. More than one of us broke our arms jumping from it."

"Were you among them?" His eyes sparkled.

"Nie. As Mama's only living child, she would have had my head on a platter if she found out I so much as swung from it. I never told her what I did."

"What else do you recognize?"

"There's the windmill. See it? Not as grand as the ones in the Netherlands, but we don't have as much water to pump. This way, we can get it up the hills to make it easier to carry to our homes."

Jerzy nodded and bounced Teena on his knee. "What else?"

"Around the bend here, in just a moment, you will see the church's three spires."

"Three?"

I held my breath as the farmer navigated the curve. In front of us rose a church, wood shingles covering the sides, wood dome spires rising from it, the tallest at the entrance and the shortest where the altar was inside. A Greek Catholic cross topped each spire. Unlike the Roman Catholic one with a single crosspiece, these crosses boasted three, the bottom one on an angle. "Isn't it beautiful?"

Set among the flowing hills, the sky cerulean blue behind it, the sight of the church never failed to steal my breath.

Beside me, Jerzy let out a sigh. "It is magnificent. You only ever talk about how poor this region is. You never speak of its great beauty."

"Really?"

"Not that I recall. Then again, even poets would fail to do it justice."

A short time later the horses clopped past the church and down a few homes until we reached house number twenty-three. The house my family had lived in for generations. At times as many as eleven people had dwelled here. Today it was just Mama.

Well, we would grow it by three.

Jerzy handed me Teena, hopped down, then took her back and gave me a hand. He was a gentleman, that was for sure. After paying the driver, we turned to the log house with a wooden roof sloped on all four sides. After standing for many years without a chimney, it now had one.

If my schooling had been for nothing else, it had been to give Mama a stove with a proper chimney so she wouldn't get ill and die from inhaling smoke over the years. Not like Nyan'o. On the day he died, I swore to myself that Mama would never suffer the same fate. I was heartbroken at having lost my father. I couldn't have Mama torn from me too. I took Teena, and, clutching her, no longer able to hold myself back, I hurried to the door and stooped as I entered. "Mama!"

The short, slight woman with gray hair pulled into a bun turned from the stove. The lines around her eyes deepened as a smile creased her face. "Helena! *Dushko moja*, what are you doing here? I thought you were in Kraków. And who is this with you?"

I turned just as Jerzy straightened from entering. The low doorway was to remind us about moving from outside to inside. A reminder that the home might be small and smoky, but it was a roof overhead.

"Mama, this is my husband, Jerzy Bielski, and our daughter, Teena." The baby gummed Jerzy's finger.

Mama raised both of her eyebrows and stood frozen for a few seconds. "Husband? Daughter? I don't understand." She flicked her gaze between Jerzy and me.

"Sit down." I nodded toward the chair beside the rough wood table with chunky round legs.

"I should at least get you a cup of tea. The Nazis have taken so much, but they can't take the dandelions." That is what we did, no matter the news a guest brought to our house. We always offered them refreshment and a place at our table. And Mama was renowned for her hospitality. She bustled toward the stove, stoked the fire, and filled the kettle with water from a pail. "Oh, Helena, this chimney is wonderful. I feel like a rich, spoiled woman to have such a thing in my house."

I couldn't stop the warmth in my chest as I helped Mama get the teacups.

"If you had let me know you were coming, I would have baked something. I am almost out of bread as it is."

"We don't need anything. You should sit and rest and talk while I feed Teena."

Again, Mama glanced at the baby and then at me. With her mouth wide open, she watched as I prepared the bottle and sat to give it to the baby.

"She doesn't look anything like you. Or your husband. Jerzy is your name?"

Jerzy scrunched his forehead. Of course, we had been speaking Lemko. "He doesn't understand, Mama."

"So he is not Lemko?"

"He is not. If you would sit, I could tell you everything."

At last she settled in the chair, a steaming cup of dandelion tea in her hands. "What is it that you have to say to me?"

"Jerzy is a friend from the university. That is where we first met. He was a professor of economics there, so we were colleagues."

"You have been traveling with a man not your husband? Your nyan'o would have had a heart attack hearing that." Mama's face flushed as red as the fall leaves on the hillsides.

"He is my husband. Let me finish the story." I managed to tell her about Risa and all that had happened in the past few days. "So you see, there is nothing we are doing wrong."

"You are telling people that Teena is your child when she is not."

"The conditions in the ghetto were appalling. If I could describe it to you, though I cannot bear to. Sooner or later Teena would have died. Or been killed by those monsters."

Mama nodded. "They have come and taken so many young men from the village to work camps. Or so they say." She rattled off a few names, all people I knew. In a town of only fifty houses, there were no strangers.

How would Jerzy assimilate to life here? Not just the language, but he wasn't used to our way of life or our way of worship. All of our superstitions and our traditions.

When I had first gone to school in Nowy Sącz to study beyond what I could learn in our little village, it had been so scary. Everything was different, and I ached for home. In time I had adjusted, but these hills would always be where my heart belonged.

He must miss his home and find this place as strange as I found Nowy Sącz. But he smiled at me, and I did my best to interpret. In this way, we carried on a conversation with Mama. When we finished, she clapped her hands once. "You will have a wedding here, of course, with all our friends. And I will prepare the feast."

"No need to go to that expense. Besides, we are not supposed to be newly-weds. Remember, we have been married two years. Two years ago yesterday. These days there isn't money for a party for our friends and neighbors."

"Times have always been hard. The war hasn't changed that much."

"You don't have the sheep anymore." I stared at the empty dirt stall right there in the living and cooking space.

A wood rail partitioned it from the rest of the house, a wood manger nailed to the wall on one end. Whether a sheep or a pig, it was the family's most treasured possession, and we couldn't take the chance of someone stealing it or a wild animal killing it. So it lived inside.

"We will have a proper celebration of your marriage, even if it is two years late. Everyone will expect that, so that is what we will do."

And when Mama spoke, her word was her decree.

After darkness fell and we had eaten a simple meal with Mama and had gotten Teena settled for the night, Jerzy and I lay in bed together.

He stroked my cheek. "I feel badly about your mother sleeping in the kitchen."

"She wanted to give us our privacy. We may pretend differently, but we are truly newlyweds. She doesn't mind."

"What did she say about me being Polish and not Lemko?"

"Not too much. She would have preferred that I marry a local man, but in time she will come to love you and welcome you as part of our family. As long as you treat us both right, that is."

Jerzy's warm laugh filled the small room. Waves meant to represent the hills had been painted on the whitewashed wall in bright red, yellow, and orange. Loops had been brushed above them with brightly colored leaves around the edges to remind us of the local trees. Icons of saints hung on the wall, festooned with paper flowers in the same colors.

The circumstances that brought us here might not have been ideal, but home cradled me and comforted me.

Jerzy pulled me close, and warmth filled me, something akin to feathers tickling my stomach.

His voice rumbled in my ear. "I have to admit to being worried. What if the Nazis come again for any young men they might have missed? I don't want to be separated from you."

After what I suspected he endured at the hands of our occupiers, it was no surprise that concern followed him even here. "Don't fret. Everything will work out. They have the men they need. Dubne is the safest place on the planet right now."

But I feared those words might not be the truth.

CHAPTER ELEVEN

Many others also died,
They are no longer with us,
But since they were righteous from birth,
They went to their reward.

Lord, have mercy on them
Do not remember their sins,
Take innocent souls from here
Give them heaven for their troubles.

~From "Song of Lemkovyna"

Monday, August 7, 2023
Suburban Pittsburgh, Pennsylvania

Oppressive. That just about summed up the day. The heat was oppressive. The pouring rain in the middle of the thunderstorm was oppressive.

And what McKenna was about to do was oppressive.

The weight of it sat on her shoulders and pressed on her chest. She parked her car far from the funeral home door. Many had shown up to pay their respects to a little girl whose life was stolen from her.

This wasn't going to be easy. Nothing was right about a wake for a two-year-old. The needless death of an innocent child caught in the crosshairs of two people who didn't like each other.

McKenna took in a long, deep breath, opened her umbrella, and made a dash for the door, water splashing onto her bare shins as she sloshed through the puddles on the way inside. The funeral home lobby was full of people milling about. Across the room were two large pieces of poster board covered with pictures of Yasmine.

Other than Belinda, McKenna knew no one else there, so she wound her way through the gathering, the chatter quiet among them, entered the chapel, and took a seat in the last row of chairs. She bowed her head in an attempt to still her racing thoughts.

Even with prayer, she was unable to block out the mental image of Yasmine's final moments. So little, yet she must have been so afraid. And in so much pain. She didn't have love and peace surrounding her. Quite the opposite.

McKenna dug in her purse for a tissue to dab away her tears.

As she stared at the small white casket at the front of the chapel, sprays and bouquets of pink roses surrounding it, someone touched her shoulder.

"Are you the social worker?"

Here came the blame. She steeled her spine and turned to the gray-haired woman. "Yes."

A small smile played on the older woman's lips. "I'm Yasmine's grand-mother. I thought I recognized you. You were at Belinda's once when I stopped by."

Ah, now McKenna recognized her. Her hair had been long and piled on top of her head at the time. Now it was shorter and straight. "It's good to see you again. I'm so sorry for your loss."

"Thank you, dear. It's tough, but I take comfort in the fact that she's in Jesus' arms right now and has a much better home in heaven than she ever did here."

"That's so true."

"It's not Belinda's fault. Hank could be very persuasive when he wanted to be. He knew how to get his way with her, but I wish she never would have let him back into her life. Then we'd have Yasmine running around and laughing and growing up."

"Yes, he had a silver tongue."

"But God knew what He was doing. He just wanted her in heaven and decided it was time for her to go home to Him."

"That's a lovely way to put it. You're a remarkable woman."

"Naw, it's not me. It's Jesus inside of me. And if you'll excuse me, there's someone else I'd like to greet."

"Of course. It was good to see you again. My prayers will continue to be with you and your family."

"You're so sweet. Thank you." The woman moved away, her shoulders a little more stooped than the last time McKenna had seen her.

The service passed in a blur. Too many tears to count fell in that room. Touching tributes to the sweet toddler McKenna had known and who would always hold a special place in her heart.

Afterward, spent from the emotion of the day, she gathered her purse and headed for the exit.

"McKenna. Wait."

She turned to find Belinda hurrying after her. They embraced and held each other for a long time, both of them silently weeping. At last McKenna stepped back and pulled out two tissues from her purse—one for herself and one for Belinda.

"I'm so sorry for your loss."

"I should have listened to you. You were right about Hank, and I knew it, but I wanted to have my own way. It was so selfish of me. And I'm sorry I was mean to you the other day." Belinda sobbed harder.

"It's not your fault."

"But it is. If I hadn't let him come back around. . ."

"You don't know. He could have returned without your permission. He's the one who was selfish, who put his wants and desires over that precious baby's."

"But if I had listened to you."

"We can't go back, much as we would like. Right now all we can do is lean on the Lord and trust in His goodness and sovereignty."

Sitting in her car a few moments later, McKenna reflected on the words she'd spoken to Belinda. None of this was good. Yasmine's grandmother had said this is what God wanted, but how could that be? That was an idea she didn't even want to entertain.

Jesus loved little children. He welcomed them. He warned against those who harmed one of them to the point of saying it would be better that they drown. Yes, one day, both on this earth and in the next life, Hank would get his just deserts. But Yasmine? She was an innocent little girl who did nothing to deserve the horrific way she died. McKenna's words to Belinda had flowed from her tongue with little thought. Did she believe them?

None of it made sense. How could a sovereign, loving God have allowed something like this to happen? And to a child, no less.

Was that even a God she wanted anything to do with?

Her heart was as muddled as ever when she got home. Taylor sat cross-legged on the couch, a bowl in her hand and beauty tutorials from YouTube on the television. "Hey, I saved you some soup. How did it go?"

"It was very sad, as you can imagine. And I'm not hungry. I might need another one of your prescribed showers."

"Come and sit for a little bit. You can have my crackers. You have to eat something."

McKenna slipped off her shoes and parked herself next to Tay. She nibbled on one of the saltines.

"I've had a brilliant idea."

McKenna stared at the ceiling. Tay had far too many brilliant ideas.

"No, I mean it this time. This one is really good. Have I ever steered you wrong?"

"Two words. Punta. Cana."

"Fine, there was that, but this is different. You need a break. Even your supervisor said so. You took a few months of sabbatical, right?"

"Yeah." McKenna drew out the word.

"And I have a few weeks of vacation saved plus some PTO. Instead of Cancun, this is the perfect opportunity for us to go to Poland and find out more about your family. I don't know about you, but I'm really enjoying this genealogy stuff. My family has been in the US for a long time, but yours hasn't."

"I don't know anything about them yet, not even the town or city where they're from."

"Well, duh, we wouldn't be able to get away for a while. That will give you some time to do your research and compile everything we need."

"Won't it be boring for you?"

"My life is boring. My family's boring. Both sides came here from England before the Revolutionary War. Period. End of story. If I want to find out more, I can do that from right here in the US. And if it would make you feel better, we can stop in England."

"I don't know. It might be better if I went back to work next week and kept busy that way." Then again, going into the office, being involved in other families' lives, might be difficult.

"You're exhausted and grieving. If you don't take time for yourself, you're going to end up burned out, and that's the last thing your supervisor is going to want. She'll understand that you need the time and will know that you'll come back rested and ready to take on what is a very demanding job."

"A rest does sound delicious." Just the idea of not having to set an alarm for the next few months was something she could get behind. "All right. I'll do it. I won't go back to work yet."

"That's the spirit. Now how about binging on a few episodes of our favorite baking show?"

"No can do. I have genealogical research to conduct."

Taylor threw a pillow in McKenna's direction. "What have I done? I've created a monster."

McKenna threw the pillow back then settled herself on her bed with her laptop. There was so much to sift through. First of all, she ordered DNA tests from different sites to see if she might come up with additional matches. Then she tried again to make some headway in finding her elusive relatives.

She read a number of articles on genealogical research and ordered a couple of books then settled in for a few videos. All of it was helpful but not specific to what she needed to know.

Following a knock, Tay peeked into the room. "I'm going to bed."

"Bed?" McKenna glanced at her watch. Sure enough, it was that late. "Oh, I didn't realize what time it was. It feels like I just sat down. One thing leads to another to another, and suddenly you're off to bed."

"Well, some of us have to go to work tomorrow."

"If I'm going to have to listen to this for the next couple of months..."

Tay entered and sat on the bed beside McKenna. "What have you discovered? That you're related to a movie star or someone else famous?"

"Not anything. This Polish research is intense. The spellings of the last names are all over the place. As you can imagine, the immigrants didn't speak English when they came to the States, so everything got messed up. Polish is pronounced nothing like it looks."

"I'll bet."

"I wish I could play Scrabble in Polish. With all the *J*s and *Z*s and everything, I'd win for sure."

Tay laughed, hugged McKenna good night, and left the room. She worked for a couple more hours before forcing herself to close her laptop and crawl underneath the covers.

But with the lights off and her mind not occupied, the images that had earlier filled her brain returned with a vengeance. A little child's broken and bloodied body. Her screams and cries for help as she died.

How was Belinda able to stand the pain? And that question about God allowing the deaths of innocent children in such a violent manner haunted McKenna. Was what she told Belinda true? Did what Yasmine's grandmother had said hold any merit?

It was difficult to fit that into her belief in a loving heavenly Father who cared so much for little ones. The mental pictures flashed back and forth between Yasmine's body and Jesus with the children on His lap.

Her tears came, hot and fast. She missed Mom and Dad. She missed Chris. He'd been a jerk, but at least he'd been a shoulder to cry on.

The ache in her chest grew until it almost consumed her. With only the glow from the streetlights slanting through the windows and illuminating the way, she grabbed a box of tissues, wiped away the tears that still fell, and padded into Taylor's room.

Like they'd done in middle school and high school when they had sleepovers, McKenna crawled into bed with her best friend.

Tay stirred. "What's wrong?"

"Just about everything." McKenna spoke the words on a fresh sob.

Taylor wrapped McKenna in an embrace and smoothed back her hair like Mom would if she were there. "It's going to be okay, Ken. Just give it time, and it will get better."

"Will it?"

"He will never leave you nor forsake you. That's what we were taught from the time we were small."

"I—I failed her. I failed her."

"No, you didn't, sweetie. You can't think that way. You just can't. Beating yourself up isn't going to bring her back. If justice is served, Hank will spend the rest of his life in jail. And God will judge him for his crimes. But you did nothing wrong."

"Why, Tay, why?"

"None of us has that answer."

CHAPTER TWELVE

Friday, August 11, 2023

McKenna took one last gaze around the town house to make sure everything was in order. She'd spent all morning—all week, really—cleaning and scrubbing and tidying in preparation for Baba's visit. She even made Baba's favorite salmon dinner with boiled potatoes and green beans. The fishy odor already permeated the house. Taylor had decided to spend the night at a friend's place until the smell was gone.

McKenna fluffed the pillow that said A HOUSE ISN'T A HOME WITHOUT LOVE and sprayed another round of air and fabric freshener over the couch and the love seat. Noir was hiding under the bed, but he had left his cat odor all over the place. Just as she was straightening the silverware on the table, which was precisely at five, Mom and Dad pulled up with Baba.

She'd told them they could come anytime, but Mom was a stickler for punctuality. Perhaps McKenna wasn't because it drove her so crazy. At any rate, she couldn't wait to give Baba a hug. She ran to the car and enveloped her in an embrace.

The familiar and comforting scent of jasmine floated from Baba, like coming home. Though she was still as thin and as straight as ever, there were more wrinkles around her eyes. Maybe it was just from the big grin she gave McKenna.

"Oh my dear, how good to see you. You're skinny."

No one had told Baba about the broken engagement. At least that was what McKenna believed. She'd commanded Mom not to share the information until she was ready to talk about it. The subject would have to be addressed tonight.

But not now. "Funny coming from you and how little you are."

"I've always been that way. Genetics. Mama was the same as me. So that's how it is."

"Well, I have a meal inside that's sure to put a little weight on your bones."

"I hope it's salmon. Somehow you cook it better than anyone else." They made their way up the walk to the front door. "I never had it before I was married, but we ate it on our honeymoon, and it was the best thing I ever tried."

"Of course I made it for you. With everything else you like."

"Chocolate cake?"

"The best chocolate cake ever." McKenna opened the door, and Baba stepped in and inhaled.

"Ah, yes. I already know it's going to be delicious."

Mom kissed McKenna's cheek as she passed on her way to the kitchen. "What can I do to help?"

"Everything's ready. I just have to put out the ice water." That was one benefit of punctuality. McKenna could have dinner ready at the right time, and it would never get cold.

"Okay, I'll pour that."

Dad kissed McKenna as well. "How's my pumpkin?"

"Okay." She sighed.

"What's this?" Baba pulled out a chair at the head of the table and seated herself. "That didn't sound like a very cheerful and upbeat response."

"We'll talk about it more over dessert. There are so many other things I want to hear about from you."

Dad said grace, and McKenna passed the dishes around the table. Baba took her time, savoring each bite. "I don't know how you do it, dear, but it gets better and better every time I have it. Maybe you're in the wrong profession."

Mom and Dad shot McKenna narrow-eyed looks. She shrugged. Mom pointed at Baba. The time had come. McKenna drew in a long, ragged breath. "There's something I have to tell you. I'm on a sabbatical from my job, and I broke my engagement with Chris." There. She'd ripped the bandage off.

Baba dropped her fork onto her plate with a clatter, and her dark blue eyes filled with tears. "Oh, I'm so sorry to hear about Chris. He always seemed very attentive to me, but sometimes it didn't feel genuine. His manners were forced, maybe?"

"He put on a good front." McKenna took a long drink of water. "But he's in the past. Next time I'll be warier."

"Don't shut the door on your heart and lock it tight. Grandpa and I shared a wonderful love until the cancer took him, but I wouldn't have traded those years for anything, even knowing how few they would be."

"But you never married again."

"Ah, I was old enough by then. And I'd had my one great love. Who was I to ask God for more than that? All I'm saying is not to give up on love. You never know what your heavenly Father has in store for you."

"Okay. I promise." It would take an act from the Almighty for her to open her heart again.

"And tell me why you're taking a break from your job. Did something happen?"

While Baba and the rest of the family finished their dinners, McKenna shared with her about Yasmine's death and how difficult it had been. "But I do have some good news."

"Good news is like water in a dry desert." Baba nodded, her hair as white as fair-weather clouds. "I always like good news better than anything."

"Who doesn't?" McKenna laughed at Baba's mantra, one she had repeated for as long as McKenna could remember.

"Well, out with it. I could keel over at any moment and never know what you have to tell me."

"You aren't going anywhere, and we all know it." McKenna stood and gathered two plates.

"Oh no you don't. Sit down and tell me."

"Over cake and coffee. Then we can really enjoy it."

"You're the worst tease of all." Baba laughed, a hearty, rich laugh.

Much to Baba's chagrin, McKenna made a show of moving at a snail's pace, but at last she had the coffee and cake served and she rejoined the others at the table. "So I've been doing some research on our family's history while I've been off."

"You have? That sounds interesting." With little emotion behind Baba's words, it was hard to tell if she was excited or not.

"So far I haven't found too much. I requested your parents' death certificates to see if that would shed any light on the situation, but I was hoping you could tell me more. Do you know what their birthdates were or where they were born or anything like that?"

Baba shook her head. "They never really did anything for their birthdays. I only knew their years. Their death certificates won't tell you anything that I don't know because I was the one who gave the information for those."

"Do you have your birth certificate? That might list your mother's maiden name."

"Oh, that I know."

Mom tilted her head. "You never told me what it was."

"I guess you never asked. You must not have had to make one of those family trees in school."

"I guess not."

"Anyway, it was Kostisak."

McKenna grabbed a pad of paper, one where she had scribbled a bunch of notes, and a pen. "How do you spell that?"

"I think it was k-o-s-t-i-s-a-k. But that's only a guess. You know, my parents had it very hard during the war, so they didn't talk about their lives in Poland very much."

"Poland is where they were born?"

"I believe so. The borders have changed so much in the years since then, but I'm pretty sure they said Poland."

"What did they have to say about their life during the war?" McKenna pushed away her cake. This was much more interesting.

"Just what I said, that it was hard. My dad would sometimes talk more about it, but Mama never did. Whenever I tried to get her to say anything, she cried. Anything about that time, anything about her life before coming to America, Mama never wanted to discuss."

"I wonder why that was?"

"My dad would say things about how hard it was, how hungry they were, and how they were in constant danger. When I pressed him for details, he would say nothing more."

"So you don't know where they came from?"

"The southern part of Poland, in the foothills of the Carpathian Mountains."

McKenna scribbled down this information. "This is more than anything I've been able to come up with so far."

"Why didn't you ask me?" Baba patted her hand.

"I. . ." McKenna dabbed at a cake crumb, dark against the light blue tablecloth. "I didn't want to tell you about Chris."

"You were going to have to tell me at some point, or I would have looked pretty silly showing up to your wedding with no one else there." Baba winked.

"I just didn't want to disappoint you."

"How could realizing that Chris wasn't the man you were meant to marry disappoint me? I would have been more let down if you had married him and then realized you were with the wrong man."

"I guess so. But everyone warned me for so long, and I was stubborn about listening to any of you. I thought I knew best, and when I found out I didn't, it was hard to admit that you were right all along. That stung."

"Oh, sweetie." Mom rubbed the back of McKenna's hands. "He was a very good actor, especially around you, not allowing you to see through his costume and stage makeup."

"But I should have listened. How could I have been so blind?"

Mom patted her hand. "What's important, like Baba said, is that you came to see the light before marrying Chris. Our hearts ache for you, they do, but better now than later. I know that doesn't bring much comfort at this point. I just pray that it will down the road."

"Okay." McKenna pushed back her chair and stood. "That's enough of that for now. Let's move on to happier subjects, shall we?"

"Did your mother tell you I got a new cat?"

"No, Mom didn't mention it to me." McKenna stared at Mom as she strode by with an armload of plates.

"It must have slipped my mind. But it is an awful lot of cats to be taking care of at your age."

"I'm not that old, thank you. You'd better be careful, because you'll be here sooner rather than later. And they keep me company."

"Well, I think it's wonderful for you to have a new friend." McKenna picked up a few plates.

"Oh, it is. His name is Smoky because he's the most beautiful gray color. Oscar doesn't think much of him, but they'll be great friends before long, I just know it. And the girls already love him."

"I bet they do." That would be Baba's two female cats. If Taylor was more of a fan of the creatures, she and McKenna would have a houseful themselves.

With three women cleaning up the kitchen, they managed to get the dishes done in no time, even with Dad underfoot trying to sneak another piece of cake. Mom had to keep him away because of his prediabetes.

They finally went to sit in the living room. Soon the cards would come out for pinochle, but a few minutes like this were welcome. McKenna snuggled against Baba, who stroked her hair. "Are you really doing okay?"

"I am. Some days are better than others, but this genealogy project is helping to keep my mind occupied."

"What do you plan to do from here?"

"Now that I know your mother's maiden name, I'll do a little more research, but I'm planning on going to Poland to do some in-person digging."

"By yourself?"

"Tay is going to come too. And Poland is one of the safest countries in all of Europe for Americans. Kraków is especially friendly to tourists, and I heard that it's even safe at night, as long as you keep your wits about you."

"Wow, imagine going there. What a wonderful opportunity you have."

"You should join me."

"I don't know. That jet lag might be more than this old body can handle. But when you go, will you do a favor for me?"

"Sure. What is it?"

"Will you find my sister?"

CHAPTER THIRTEEN

Gallows, gallows,
They hang them there unconcerned
The best sons of Lemkovyna,
Without a case or proof.

Though innocent, they are guilty
That their homeland is Lemkovyna
That it is a Slavic land and
On it reside Rusyn tribes.

Lemkovyna is wailing
The whole country is covered with blood.
There is pain everywhere, crying and sorrow,
Tears and blood to fill an ocean.

~From "Song of Lemkovyna"

Monday, June 28, 1943
Dubne, Generalgouvernement, Poland

After fifteen months in Dubne, I had grown accustomed to being back here spending the nights in my husband's arms, our daughter slumbering beside us in the bed against the wall.

I had grown accustomed to the peace and quiet of my homeland. What a welcome relief from the frantic pace of Kraków, especially after the invasion. At night all that was discernible were the stars hanging in the sky over our heads and the crickets singing their lullabies in the grazing fields.

I had grown accustomed. And complacent.

And so I snuggled closer to Jerzy, his arms now muscled by farm labor encompassing me. There was no need to hurry out of bed. In five more minutes, the daily chores would still be waiting for me.

Here life remained little changed except for the missing men and missing animals. And it was as good as it could be in those turbulent times.

Just as I was about to throw aside the covers and begin my day, the roar of motor engines filled the air, stirring Jerzy and Teena from their slumber. The toddler cried, and Jerzy lifted her from beside him, nestling her close to himself, whispering to her words that I couldn't make out.

Across the room, in the only other bed in the house, Mama sat up and rubbed her eyes. "What is it? What is happening?"

"Autos. Trucks." Jerzy flicked his gaze toward the window, headlights flashing across its still-dark background like scenes on a film at the cinema.

"Germans." My stomach dropped like a broken elevator. Now what did they want? They never arrived this early.

"Has to be." Mama stood and slipped on her housecoat. "Lemkos only drive carts pulled by donkeys."

"I was afraid of this." Jerzy handed Teena to me and got dressed himself. None of us bothered to light the lamp but used the shine of the moon to move about the small room. There wasn't much to bump into or trip over.

"Why?" I bounced a now-screaming Teena on my hip.

"I didn't want to worry you. . ."

"But. . ." I touched his muscled forearm.

Jerzy had proven to be a good provider and protector of our little family. He never shared much of what was going on in the outside world with me.

Perhaps to shield me from worry. Perhaps to shield me from trouble. But I was made of sterner stuff. Before I ever came to Kraków, before the Germans paraded on our streets, I had endured much.

Poverty. Injustice. Loss.

"This has to do with your visits to the partisans, doesn't it?" I kept my voice low so Mama wouldn't hear, but that was almost impossible in the cramped living quarters.

He pursed his lips.

"Why do you refuse to tell me, no matter how much I beg? I see. I know. Sometimes you are gone from the farm all day. You return home quiet and withdrawn. It can be nothing else."

"You don't need to know."

"But I do." I worked hard to control the pitch of my voice. "Look at those trucks out there. This affects me."

"It's better that you are in the dark."

"Not any longer. *Proshu*, tell me. Treat me as your equal, as you once did."

"How can I love you and have you drive me crazy at the same time?" The muscles under my fingers tightened. "A group of partisans attacked a German transport near Gładyszów a few days ago in an attempt to arm themselves for a revolt. My guess is this is in reprisal for that."

"Gładyszów is so far away and has nothing to do with Dubne. Why would they come here?"

"Who knows why the Nazis do what they do? For one man we kill, they kill a hundred."

Did he realize he implicated himself in that statement? "So what do we do?"

Mama took Teena from my arms. "We sit here and wait for whatever fate they have planned for us." She sighed a heavy sigh, the weight of years of trouble wrapped into it.

I shivered and pulled some clothes from the chest at the end of the bed so Teena and I could get dressed. "We won't wait like sheep on the hillsides to be taken away."

A shot rang out, and a woman's scream rent the night, chilling my blood. I dressed faster and wound a light blanket around Teena. "That sounded like it came from the Dubnianskii home."

"Hurry." Jerzy tied his boots. "Mama, come on. Get your shoes on, and let's be off."

"Where?" Mama raised her hands as if she was surrendering. "Where shall we go? To the forests? They will find us there. To the mountains? They will hunt us down there as well."

"Any moment, the Nazis will come knocking at the door." Much in the same way my knees knocked together. "We can't allow them to find us. Think of yourself and Teena. We need each other. Hurry, proshu. We at least have to try to get away."

Mama rose, but much too slow for Jerzy's liking. "Come now, let's go." He tied Mama's shoes and picked up Teena. The four of us slipped out the door.

Up and down the dirt road shone the lights from the cars and trucks. Many of the villagers, roused from their beds, stood in the grass at the road's edge, watching as the uniformed soldiers led men, women, and even a few children out of their humble dwellings and into the idling trucks.

Jerzy crooned to Teena, into her ear so that I had to be right next to them to hear it. On feet as silent as a fox's, we slipped around the small house, smaller than my flat in Kraków, up the hill, and into the night.

By the time we got to the top, Mama was out of breath and I was panting.

Jerzy motioned us forward. "We have to keep going. We have no idea if they brought dogs or not."

"I heard none." Mama slowed even more.

"We can't take any chances. Helena, help Mama. In a little while, we'll be able to rest."

Down one hill we trudged and up another, deeper into the forest.

After an hour or so, he stopped, a light ahead of us in a small clearing.

"Is this where you go?" I came alongside him.

"Tak. We'll be safe here."

"With the partisans?" Mama's shrill voice would alert the Germans all the way in Gładyszów.

"Hush. We have to be quiet." It was enough that Jerzy had to keep Teena from waking and crying.

"Hello? It's Jerzy with my family." His Lemko language skills were improving by the day.

A short, thin man with a long beard and long, curly hair stepped away from the fire and into the thicket where we stood. "What are you doing here?"

"Reprisals, Ivan, reprisals for Gładyszów." Jerzy shook his head. "Why they would pick Dubne? I don't understand, but they have."

"It's not just Dubne. Listen."

The fire popped and crackled, and then a noise rose from the valleys that sent goose pimples up and down my arms. Weeping. Wailing. From every direction, every Lemko village in the area. "Do they mean to slaughter us all?" My legs shook, and I barely held myself upright.

Ivan stroked his beard, the stench of weeks without a bath clinging to him. "They would like nothing more than to wipe all Slavs from the face of the earth, and that includes the Lemkos. But tonight it's about getting even. No, more than getting even. It's about at last having some sort of provocation they can point to for their murdering and arresting innocent men, women, and children."

I bowed my head and beseeched heaven to make it stop. Make it all stop. All the loss. All the pain. All the bloodshed that left Lemkovyna's soil red.

"This is my wife, my mother-in-law, and my small daughter. We need a haven."

Already once, Jerzy and I had fled the Nazis and their crazy Aryan ideal. It would rip my soul from my body to have to leave Lemkovyna for places unknown. Life now was filled with too much running and too much hiding. Tonight had shattered the illusion I had built that Lemkovyna was safe.

Ivan motioned us into the clearing. "For tonight you may stay, but this is no place for women and children. It's not safe. We're involved in the fighting, in protecting our homeland and our way of life. You don't want anything to happen to them."

"For the night then." Jerzy clapped Ivan on the back.

"And what happens after that?" I followed the men into the circle of light where a dozen other equally ragged men sat, many puffing on cigarettes.

Jerzy handed Teena to me. "I'll return home in the morning to get a better idea of what is happening there. The Germans prefer Blitzkrieg, so it's likely they'll be gone by then."

"And it is just as likely they will set a trap for us and will be waiting to take us away." Mama puckered her entire face.

Close to the fire, a log lay on its side, and I took Teena and sat there, the warmth of the flames heating the already warm summer night, the smoke keeping the mosquitoes at bay. "Do you have to go, Jerzy? What if something happens to you?" In Kraków I was an intelligent, independent woman. Here, in this place and time, I had come to lean on him.

And found it wasn't all that bad.

"Ivan is right. We can't stay here more than tonight. From here the Lord will lead us in the way we should go. If we can't trust Him, there is no one to trust."

He was right, as he usually was. I had married a very wise man, and that was more than just his book learning. So for tonight, and only for tonight, I would trust the Lord to watch over us. Tomorrow I would have to make the choice whether or not to put my faith in Him once again.

Within a short amount of time, we had Teena bedded down and Mama snoozing beside her, the crickets serenading us. Jerzy stood at the edge of the clearing, speaking to several of the partisans. From the way they got on, their heads bent together, they knew each other.

I picked my way toward them.

"Do you think it's wise for us to stay in this position, or should we find another place to gather and formulate our plans?" When I stepped on a twig and it cracked, Ivan broke off his thoughts. "Go to sleep with your mother and daughter."

"Nie. I am not your average village woman, and I have been kept in the dark far too long. The time has come for me to know what is going on. Exactly. I need to understand what difficulties might lie in front of my family."

Jerzy nodded but didn't smile. "My wife is a highly intelligent, educated woman. We met at Jagiellonian University where I—"

"That's enough. When you first found us and we discovered you weren't Lemko, I told you then I didn't want or need to know anything about you but that you would not betray us. You have proven yourself a friend to our people. I need to know nothing more." Ivan directed his attention toward me. "You are better off with your mother and daughter."

"But I understand things beyond this part of the world, and I want to stay informed."

"Helena." Jerzy reached for me, but I backed away. In Dubne I was content as a housewife. Here, not anymore. I thirsted for knowledge. I hungered for work. "It is not in me to stay in my tiny house with my daughter, much as I love her. If nothing else, I need to know."

Jerzy sighed, much as Mama had before. This war was aging everyone before their time. "Go ahead."

Ivan picked up the conversation. "I say that we must move. The Nazis will comb every square centimeter of these woods and search behind every tree until they root out the last of us. They won't rest until we are all dead."

Perhaps it had been better to remain in the dark. I shook my throbbing head. No. Knowledge was the most powerful weapon anyone could possess.

Another man, this one taller than Ivan but no less bedraggled or smelly, cleared his throat. "We can't keep running. Eventually they will catch us. What we have to do is prepare to fight."

"I disagree." This man—or boy, really, as he had no facial hair—stood with arms akimbo. "At some point, tak, we have to fight. We are not ready to do that now. We need more time. More arms. More men."

I cast a glance at Jerzy, who shook his head. How long would he stay with us before his convictions compelled him to join these partisans? I stepped away from the group, and he followed.

"I know what you're thinking, and I am committed to protecting our family. That vow I made before man and God, I take seriously."

"You won't hold out forever."

"For now, then. I promise to stay with you for now. Until there will be no choice but for me to leave and do my part. I have come to love Lemkovyna, and I don't want to see anything happen to it or to its people." He traced my jawbone, eliciting a shiver, and I leaned into him. "Especially not to you or Teena. You are precious to me."

"I understand. I truly do. But I don't want to lose you. There has been too much of that already."

"Do you want to see them drive us from this place?"

"This has been our homeland for six hundred years. Even though I chose to leave, it was to make a better life for those who remained. Lemkovyna is imprinted on my heart and will always be a part of me."

"Then you understand."

"Just keep me informed. Don't treat me as if I don't have a brain in my head."

"I would never do that. In many ways, you are far smarter than I am."

"Ďakujem. Ďakujem for treating me as your partner in life. We are in this together, for better or worse."

For many minutes, as the men argued and the stars shone in the heavens above us, Jerzy and I stood together, wrapped in each other's embrace, one with each other. One soul, one life in front of us.

A streak of pink tinged the eastern sky. Morning was coming. Soon it would be time for Jerzy to leave and find out what had happened in Dubne. If it was safe for us to return.

But last night had shattered all hope that Lemkovyna was a haven.

There was no such place anymore.

All too soon, Jerzy kissed the top of my head and shrank away into the woods.

CHAPTER FOURTEEN

The day without Jerzy stretched into eternity. The sun moved through the sky at the pace of a lame donkey. Teena was hungry and fussy, even though I did everything possible to keep her occupied. The men shared with us what they had, but it was not enough to keep a child's stomach full.

With a stick, I drew a picture of the sun in the dirt, but Teena stomped her tiny feet and erased my etching with her hand, covering herself in dust. I was at my wit's end.

Mama came and joined me on the log where I sat then picked up Teena and held her close. Of course, my daughter snuggled close to Mama and sucked her thumb, content for the moment.

"How do you do it?"

"What?" Mama shrugged.

"Manage to keep her calm when no matter what I try, she fights me."

"You are anxious about Jerzy. Even though she's small, she picks up on your moods, especially when you are tense."

"Aren't you concerned about him? What might have happened to him?"

"Who, by worrying, can add an hour to their life?"

From the Bible. So easy to say. So difficult to live. "I can't help it. Too many scenarios are playing in my head. What if the Nazis weren't gone? What if they set a trap for him? What if he never comes back?"

Mama shifted Teena's weight. "Listen to all those what-ifs. You don't know that any of that has happened or will happen. There is no use in concerning yourself and upsetting your child over a mere possibility."

I leaned against Mama's shoulder. The one I had cried on when I was little. The one that had carried the weight of caring for us after Nyan'o died. Like Teena, I found it a safe place to rest. "Have I told you how much I love you?"

"Many times. And I love you too. What a comfort you were to me after your nyan'o passed away. And so hardworking, giving me that wonderful chimney and the money that kept my belly full. I could not have asked for a more wonderful daughter. I am so proud of you."

My heart swelled with the praise, and I kissed Mama on her cheek. "No woman should have to suffer the way you have."

"It is how life is for our people."

"But it doesn't have to be. It can be better."

"And people like you will make it so."

We sat in the silence for many long moments, just a mother and daughter with a bond like no other. Before I became a mother myself, I didn't understand that connection. That deep, abiding love a mother has for her child.

I understood it now, even though I hadn't carried or given birth to Teena.

Time, distance, circumstances, would never break it. Never, ever, could anyone, despite their best attempts, sever it.

Forever, she would be my mother. The woman who had raised me and cared for me, loved me and cried with me. And forever I would be her little girl. The child in pigtails who skinned her knee and sat in her lap and wanted more for her.

"I'm scared, Mama."

"I know, dushko moja. We all are. What times we live in. But no matter what, we can cry out to God."

The words meant little to me when she said them to me as a child and even now didn't register much, but the way she spoke them, full of confidence and acceptance, soothed my soul.

Still, it ached because Jerzy had yet to return. Thoughts chased themselves in crazy circles in my brain. Something must have happened. Perhaps the Nazis were still there and had arrested him. Maybe he had fallen down one of the steeper slopes and hurt himself. He might be lying there unable to move. Or worse.

As the shadows lengthened and the light faded through the canopy of the trees, Ivan came to me as I walked with Teena. "How is she doing?"

"Fine, as long as I keep her distracted. I know you want us gone, but I cannot go anywhere until Jerzy returns. If he does."

"You are good people, I can tell. And any family that belongs to Jerzy, we will take care of. But I am thinking of your safety."

"Is there anywhere safe these days?"

Ivan shrugged. "In the arms of our Holy Father."

"I don't know what could have happened to him. He left at dawn, so he should have returned hours ago."

"He will be back. Whenever he comes to us, when we aren't busy with our plans for fighting the Germans, he talks on and on about his family. He loves you all a great deal."

That managed to tease a smile from my lips. Our casual friendship had always been comfortable, and that hadn't changed after our marriage, but we spoke little about love. And I loved him. If I didn't, I wouldn't be fretting about him so.

"Your husband, though he's not Lemko and he comes and goes, has become valuable to us. He is very intelligent and good at strategizing."

"That makes me happy. And thank you for not shunning him because he isn't Lemko."

"He's a good man. In these days, we cannot judge based on someone's ethnic group. A fellow Lemko could turn us in to the Nazis as fast as any Pole. And a German could turn out to be a friend more than the Rusyns."

"I've broken many stereotypes and many traditions in my day. Some don't like that I have married outside our community. Then again, they didn't like that I left Dubne for school and then the university."

"You are a unique woman, that much I can say. But the world is widening and changing. I don't know how much longer we can remain an isolated, insular people."

"You are right."

Ivan left me, and soon he invited us to the crackling fire for the evening meal of potatoes and cabbage. Just as he finished saying the blessing over the food, Jerzy appeared in the clearing.

Oh, what a wonderful sight he was. Leaving Teena sitting on the log, I rushed to him and drew him close. "Where have you been? We have been so worried."

"Ah, you can't get rid of me that easily. There were some matters I needed to take care of there."

"Like what?"

He took me by the hand and led me toward the fire ringed by the haggard men and Mama. "Let me share it with everyone at the same time so I don't have to repeat it."

We settled on the log beside each other, shoulder brushing shoulder. Ivan offered tin plates of food to us, the aroma familiar. My soul sighed.

"So what did you discover?" Ivan held his plate in his hand but didn't eat.

As Jerzy chewed a bite of potato, he shook his head. "Nothing good. The cries of weeping we heard last night were from villages all around. Dubne, Obručné, Leluchów, every village and every family in Lemkovyna has been visited by the Nazis. So many men have been taken away to the Jasło prison."

"Nie. Nie." More lost from our small village. "Who?"

He gave the names of three young men, boys I had grown up with, now married with children. All were innocent men who farmed the land and herded sheep to eke out a living. Without their husbands, the women would be hard pressed to survive. I fisted my hands. "You have to help them."

Mama fed Teena a bite of potato and scowled. "Do you wish to lose your husband too?"

"Of course not, but we can't allow the Nazis to take these men away. They did nothing wrong, nothing at all, yet they are punished because someone dared fight back against them."

Jerzy rubbed my tense shoulder muscles, relaxing them in the way only he could. "Ivan and the others and I will discuss this, and we will see what we can do. Perhaps there is a way to free the men. I don't know."

"So what do we do now?"

"We go home. The Nazis have taken their revenge, so no one is in danger anymore."

"And you?"

"I will continue my work."

That meant he would still be involved with the partisans, putting his life at risk. The only difference now was that I knew. And would worry more than I already did.

He scooped more cabbage from his plate. "One more night here, Ivan, if you don't mind. In the morning, I will take my family home."

He nodded. "Whatever you need."

Just as we had the previous night, Jerzy and I spent some time together after Teena and Mama were asleep. I leaned against my husband. "Did the soldiers destroy anything?"

"Just the hearts of many of Dubne's residents."

"I cannot figure out why they target innocent people. It would be one thing if they had been involved in the act of sabotage, but they weren't. When the attack took place, they were on their farms, so why would the Nazis come after them?"

"Who knows why they do what they do. Lemkos, Jews, Poles, anyone they don't like or don't deem worthy, they want to get rid of them. Annihilate them. And if no one stops them, that is just what they will do."

"I want to help." The words slipped unchecked from my mouth, or I would have stopped them. Then again, nie, I would have allowed them. I had helped Risa and Teena, but it wasn't enough. There were too many others who needed our assistance.

"Nie."

"Tak. With the planning, at the very least."

"If you get caught. . ."

"Teena and Mama need me, that is true. But they need you too." What would I do without my friend, my companion, my lover? "We all do. My brain is slowly shriveling and dying. I need to put my knowledge to work. Saving Risa was not enough."

"But think of her daughter. You have to keep thinking of her. Without you, what will happen to Teena and your mama?"

"Just let me talk to you about matters and help in any plans you might make. Let me contribute some way or another."

Jerzy studied his dirt-crusted, sole-flapping shoes for a moment. Three and a half years of war had changed us. "There's no discouraging you, is there?"

"You know me too well."

"I do. Once you set your mind to something, it's as good as done. Just like your mama. I suppose I have no choice. But if I tell you to step back because it's getting too dangerous, you must listen."

"As long as you don't coddle me."

"Would I ever do such a thing? I know better."

"Good. I appreciate you treating me like an intelligent human being."

He held my hand and rubbed circles on my thumb. "Because you are.

Things are different now though, than when we first met. Now you are my wife and the mother of my daughter."

I reached up and stroked his cheek. If he didn't shave soon, his beard would come in as scraggly as Ivan's. "Do you want to know something?"

"What?"

My heart could no longer contain my feelings. *"Ljublju tja."* I stood on my tiptoes and kissed the tip of his nose.

He leaned over and drew me to himself, so close that his heart pounded against my chest. "Oh, Helena. We might not have the most conventional of marriages, but I wouldn't trade it for the usual courtship for anything. In the long run, God brought us together, and I am glad He did."

"Me too. And I pray that He never separates us."

"Ljublju tja."

All too soon, we broke contact and bedded down for the night, once again in each other's arms. Thankfully, even though we were at a higher elevation, the weather was warm.

Come morning, we made our way out of the forest and down the hills to Dubne. The sight in front of me sent a burst of warmth through my limbs. Jerzy was right. The Germans hadn't touched anything. The church stood in its place, undisturbed. So did the houses, many of them that had sat in the same spot for generations.

Nothing was better than stooping and stepping over the threshold into our small dwelling. After I settled Teena, I leaned against the wall and closed my eyes.

I was a woman torn in two. I loved the place of my birth, this simple village with its hardworking, loving people. My family. After all, I was related to most everyone here in some way or another.

At the same time, I loved learning and the world beyond these walls. Soaking in all that knowledge and living in the city had spoiled me forever. There was more beyond these hills to explore and savor.

Or there had been before the war. By the time it was over, there might be nothing left.

Jerzy came and kissed my temple, ending my musings.

"Where is Mama?"

"Out getting water. You asked me to keep you informed, so I will. I spoke with Ivan before we left this morning. We plan to mount a rescue of the men from Jasło prison. There are no details yet, as we need to conduct surveillance and organize with the Polish Home Army, who has prisoners there too. It goes without saying that this comes with plenty of risks."

"In order to get weapons to facilitate the raid, there will have to be more attacks on the Nazis."

"Likely."

"But it can't end like before. Otherwise, it will only make the problem worse."

"Maybe there is another way to get the weapons without ambushing the Nazis."

I nodded. "That would be best. This is where reconnaissance comes in. Before any plans can be made, we need to know exactly what we are dealing with."

"Right. We shouldn't plunder the Germans before we know what we're up against. This isn't the Thalerhof concentration camp where your people were taken in the Great War. Jasło, from what Ivan was telling me, is a building in the center of town, which makes everything different."

"Easier in some ways, more difficult in others. I know you and those men, and I have faith in all of you, that you'll be able to do this."

"With your help, of course." Jerzy chuckled, a sound that warmed me from head to toe.

"Of course. We are partners, after all."

"You know, your mother is out of the house, and Teena is sleeping." He eyed the bed we shared.

"I have work to do."

"The floors are dirt. They don't need to be swept."

"You are very tempting, you know." I wiped my hands on my skirt and stared at the floor he had mentioned. "Before I lost my position at the university, that was the next thing I was going to do for Mama. Get her wood floors so she wouldn't have to try to keep a dirt floor not so dirty. So she would be comfortable." Now that was an impossible dream.

"She appreciates everything you did for her and doesn't begrudge you what you weren't able to accomplish."

"Wood floors. Such a small thing, and yet now who knows if or when I will ever be able to turn them into reality. Even if you could make them yourself, the Nazis won't allow us to cut the trees that grow in our own village."

"Compared to the animals and food they demand of us, it is a small thing."

"These small things end up being big things."

"You worry too much." Jerzy kissed my temple. "Let's make use of this time alone."

On our way to the bedroom, through the window, from the corner of my eye, I spied the neighbor woman, Pani Chomiak, running up the path to the house, her face flushed.

I clutched my chest and rushed to the door to meet her. "What is it? What's wrong?"

"Your mother. You have to hurry. Come quickly."

CHAPTER FIFTEEN

Oh, you are a beauty, Lemkovyna,
Our country, you are priceless to us.
Even if one were to go over the whole world
From pole to pole
One would never find such a place,
Lemkovyna is a foretaste of paradise.

~From "Song of Lemkovyna"

Friday, August 11, 2023
Suburban Pittsburgh, Pennsylvania

Baba, what are you talking about? You don't have a sister." McKenna leaned back in her chair and fastened a stare on her grandmother, whose white hair was perfectly coiffed.

"You never told me about a sister, Mom."

Baba brushed some imaginary crumbs from the baby-blue tablecloth. "That's because I don't know much about her. Growing up and even into my adult life, Mama never said a word about her. It wasn't until she was dying that she told me she had another daughter. All those years, I thought I was an only child."

"Wow." McKenna gripped the edge of her chair. This made the search for her family all the more important. And time sensitive. Baba, though she might be mistaken for seventy, was aging.

"I'd always brushed off Mama's words as the confused mumblings of a dying woman. Sometimes at the end, she didn't make sense. But I wonder. Since that day, I've wondered. If you could answer that question, that would mean the world to me."

"That's insane, thinking you were the only one for all that time. I wonder why she never told you."

"I'm a mother." Baba glanced at Mom, light shining in her gray eyes. "There's no love like it. For whatever reason, if this is true, Mama was separated from her daughter. That had to be incredibly painful. I can't imagine what it must have been like for her. Probably too painful to talk about."

"That could well be the reason." Mom fiddled with her napkin.

"Something awful must have happened to separate them."

Baba nodded. "Must have. If it's true, it's awful how much my parents suffered all those years."

"I promise to do my best to find her, Baba. I'll turn over every stone I have to in order to do it."

"I'd love to meet her." Baba's voice cracked. "Before I die, I'd love to meet my sister."

"If she even exists." Mom was always the practical, levelheaded one.

"I don't know." Baba twisted a ring on her finger. "Something deep in my heart says she does."

"Okay. Let's go over some of what you do know." McKenna spent the next hour picking Baba's brain for anything she might recall, anything her parents or some other relatives said that might be helpful.

As Baba spoke, McKenna entered the information into her computer and looked up some of the details. "This is frustrating. I can find their immigration records, which list no child, and their records here in the States, but there is nothing about them from Poland. No church records, no marriage record, nothing."

Baba suggested multiple spellings of her parents' last names, but McKenna still came up empty.

"You know, my mother always said they spoke low Russian, or a peasant's version of the language, but when I asked her if she could understand what Khrushchev was saying on television, she couldn't."

"That's an interesting tidbit. Something I'll have to look into. You don't happen to have their death certificates, do you?"

"Like I said, the death certificates won't be of much help to you. And I think I got rid of those a long time ago. Too much junk cluttering up the house."

"Okay. I think I'll pull them anyway, just for reference."

"Don't pressure yourself too much in having to discover this information for my sake."

"If nothing else, I want to help you figure out if she exists, okay?"

"Okay. That would be nice." Baba stood. "And now I need to excuse myself." She left the table and headed in the direction of the bathroom.

McKenna turned to Mom. "What do you think? Does Baba have a sister?"

"She never mentioned it to me, and I don't remember her mother saying anything. Nothing is impossible though. But like Baba said, don't kill yourself over this. I know how you get. You're like a pit bull. Once you latch on to something, you don't let go."

McKenna shook her head. "Don't worry. I'll take good care of myself. This is supposed to be a time for me to heal, so that's what I'm going to do. Change my scenery and think about something else, anything other than what happened to Yasmine."

"I hope you can do that. I really do."

So did McKenna.

It took the ringing of the doorbell to break McKenna out of her semicomatose state as she sat at the dining table and stared at her computer. Most days she was happy enough to spend her time cleaning, running, and baking, in addition to digging for any information she could come up with on her ancestors.

Not today. No, today was different. It should have been special.

Yasmine's first dance recital. McKenna had helped Belinda find a studio that gave lessons to underprivileged girls, and Yasmine ate it up. The invitation to the show that Belinda had given her at the grocery store still hung on the fridge with a magnet.

Senseless.

God, why? It was a prayer she'd prayed a thousand times over the past few weeks.

One for which she still didn't have an answer.

Beside her laptop sat her Bible. She'd promised herself she would read it today and see if God had anything in there that might give her comfort.

It remained unopened. She had no will to do anything. Maybe a nap would help. The nightmares that plagued her left her drained. Then again, if she dared close her eyes, they might return.

The doorbell rang again. It must not be the delivery guy bringing a package. And her car sat in the driveway, so she couldn't ignore it. Whoever it was knew she was home.

Another *ding dong*. "Okay, okay, I'm coming." She fluffed her hair that she had yet to comb today and wiped her lips in case she had dried yogurt on the corners of her mouth.

The moment she opened the door, she almost slammed it shut.

Chris stood on the stoop.

"What are you doing here?" She had to shut the door. Not let him into her home. Or her life.

"Can I come in?"

No. "Yes." Her mouth, apparently, wasn't about to obey instructions from her brain.

He blew out a breath. "Thanks." He stooped to take off his shoes, a rule of hers.

"Don't bother. You won't be staying long." That was better.

"I just want to talk. Clear the air between us. I had to come in person because you blocked me everywhere else."

"And I should have locked the door."

"Please, just hear me out."

She fiddled with her smartwatch until she came to the stopwatch. "I'm going to be generous and give you five minutes. Starting now." She punched the green button.

"The rumors you heard about me going out with Courtney are true."

"I thought you were trying to make amends."

"What I mean is that I did go to that gala with her. And not telling you about it to begin with was a huge mistake. I see that now."

McKenna bit her tongue to keep another snarky response from bursting out.

"But it wasn't what you think."

"Oh, really. You two looked awfully cozy. Like lip-locked cozy."

"We were not kissing. I have no idea where you got that impression."

"From the picture your sister took of you and what's-her-face at that benefit and tagged you in. You were on full display for the world to see. A little sloppy of you, actually."

"She's my sister's friend and wanted to come. She has political aspirations of her own."

She pursed her lips. "Why did you have to keep it a secret if it was innocent?"

"Come on."

McKenna shook her head. "You know what. Leave. Just leave. I'm not going to do this with you. Not today. Not ever."

"Baby, there's only one thing I want."

She crossed her arms and nodded. "Here it comes. You want the ring back. Fine. If that's what it takes to get rid of you for good like some pesky fly, then you can have it." She stomped upstairs to her bedroom, thundered back down, and threw the ring at him. "Now get out." She pointed to the door and held her breath, her entire arm shaking.

He stooped down, stood up, and left. When he did, McKenna released her breath and went to turn the lock. When she did, she stepped on something with her bare foot.

The ring.

Why on earth hadn't he taken it?

CHAPTER SIXTEEN

Friday, September 8, 2023

Though it was first thing in the morning in the Pittsburgh area, it was well into the afternoon in Poland, so McKenna picked up her phone and placed a video call. The online reviews of this in-country genealogical researcher were great, and for the first time since Yasmine's would-have-been dance recital, a little twinge that might be anticipation plucked at her.

The call rang a few times before a thirtyish man with blond hair and the perfect five o'clock shadow answered. "Hello, McKenna. It's nice to meet you."

Filip Jankowski's English was flawless. "You too. I've been looking forward to getting some help with tracing my grandmother's family in Poland."

"Excellent." He spent a few minutes going over some of the services they offered, including research, in-country guides, and locating missing family members.

Those were the things that had piqued her interest in this particular company. "I don't know anything about my family except my great-grandparents' names. And there's a rumor that my grandmother has a sister, though it could be nothing more than a rumor."

"But sometimes rumors have a little bit of truth to them, no?"

"Yes, I suppose that's right."

"Let's start with your great-grandparents' names."

"Paul Dudik and Helen Kostisak. I'm not sure on the spelling of either of them."

"Hmm." He stroked his chin and stared at the ceiling for a moment. "Both of those names are interesting. They aren't usual Polish names. I believe they're Lemko."

"What? I've never heard of that."

"Many people haven't. The Lemkos, sometimes considered Carpatho-Rusyns, settled in the southern region of Poland, northern Slovakia, and western Ukraine hundreds of years ago. They have their own culture, their own form of Orthodox Christianity, and their own language."

"Rusyn. Like Russian."

"Though the words are similar, they are two very different things."

"My grandmother says that her mother spoke low Russian."

"It is possible that she meant Rusyn. It's worth checking out."

"Okay. I'll look more into that."

"The Lemkos were very insular people, usually marrying other Lemkos."

"So it makes sense both my great-grandmother and great-grandfather would be Lemko. Do I have that right?"

"You do."

"My great-grandmother was a very intelligent, highly educated woman."

"That's not what you expect to find with a Lemko. They were extremely poor and didn't have many opportunities to go to school beyond the absolute basics."

"From what I understand, my great-grandfather was a simpler man. More down to earth."

McKenna jotted a few pages of notes over the course of their conversation. Her great-grandparents' death certificates had arrived in the mail, and unlike what Baba told her, they did have their birthdates on them, so she passed those on to Filip.

The phone call, of course, triggered the need for more research, so McKenna was back on her computer as soon as she and Filip hung up. She absorbed every word she read about the Lemkos. The poor people had been persecuted for hundreds of years, first as serfs, then as peasants.

She'd had about ten minutes of work time when Taylor entered the town house. McKenna pushed her laptop back. "Guess what?"

"You don't give a person much time to get inside, do you?"

"This is too good. Filip, the genealogical researcher in Poland that I talked to, told me my great-grandparents were Lemko."

Once Taylor came up the stairs from the entry, emptied the containers from her lunch bag, and settled on the sofa with a cup of tea, McKenna filled her in on everything she'd learned that day.

"Wow, that's kind of cool."

"Isn't it? And kind of sad too. I hate all that those people had to suffer throughout their history just because they were different from those around them."

"Not much has changed, has it?"

"I suppose not." McKenna got up, made herself a cup of tea too, then sat beside Taylor. "Well, do you think you're ready to take a few weeks off work?"

"Oh, are you saying that it's time to go to Poland?"

"I think so. Filip is going to do some research before I get there, but he's actually familiar with the Lemko people, so he knows what he's doing. And I want to be there to see everything and help if I can."

"Does he think he'll be able to find your grandma's sister?"

"We talked a little bit about that. The first thing is to find where my great-grandparents were from and where they lived. Then we go from there."

"Let's do this." Taylor bounced a little bit on the couch, and McKenna bounced right beside her.

Tuesday, October 3, 2023

As the regional jet broke through the clouds on its approach to Kraków, McKenna got her first glimpse at the land of her great-grandmother's birth. Green fields spread out before them like a quilt, dotted with the occasional house. Rivers and lakes interspersed the green with a bit of blue. The closer they got to the ground, the thicker the homes became.

More and more houses and businesses. Roads with cars darting about. In many ways, not so different from the States. They crossed a highway, and a minute or so later, they touched down, the reverse thrusters pushing her against her seat. And then they slowed and turned off the runway.

Green surrounded the airport, and in the distance, low emerald hills rose like an old city wall.

She squeezed Tay's hand. "Can you believe it? We're here. Actually in Poland."

Taylor returned the squeeze. "I haven't seen you this excited since...Well, it's been a long while. Already the trip is doing you good."

"I feel like it is."

The pilot parked at the remote stand, and while everyone emptied their carry-ons from the overhead compartments, she texted Filip that they had arrived. A couple of minutes later, he let her know he was at the airport and gave her instructions on how to find him. As she and Tay emerged from the passport control area, there he stood, holding up a sign with McKenna Muir written in large letters.

"Hello, Filip. It's nice to meet you in person. This is Taylor Ashby, my friend."

"Good to meet you too. Did you have a good flight?"

"Yes." McKenna managed her large suitcase and her carry-on as they made their way to the exit. "But it was long, and I'm tired."

"You will wake up when we get outside in the sunshine. For now we will stay in Kraków and do some research in my office. When we have a little more information about your family, then we will take a trip. Does that sound okay with you?"

"That's what I had planned on."

"Perfect. Let's get to work."

They dodged the traffic of the suburban section of Kraków and then rode on old city streets, charming buildings from bygone centuries lining the way. Filip proved to be quite good at navigating his small car around the automobiles and trams that traveled the same roads.

He wiggled into a tight parking spot. "Here we are." The building was pale yellow with tall windows crowned with raised triangles. A dark wood door with a chevron design, patinated round metal pulls, and a sunburst window above it welcomed them into a bright, open, modern workspace with long tables instead of cubicles.

What a world of difference from her cramped office. And whether it was from the jet lag or just being in an office again, a wave of grief washed over her.

Filip led them to a large table at the end of the row where a laptop and several books occupied the space, as well as a pen holder and a pad of lined paper.

McKenna glanced at the front window and the car beyond it. "Will our bags be safe?"

"They will be fine. No worries. Let's start the easiest way. We will go to a records search site and see what we find." He woke up his laptop, and she pulled hers from her bag. Even Tay got in on the action.

The other genealogists in the room tapped away on their computers or talked on their phones in a mixture of English and what was probably Polish. As time passed, McKenna's eyes grew sandier. She would need sleep soon. She'd gotten some on the plane, but it wasn't like curling up in bed.

Just as she was about to call it a day, she stumbled on an immigration record for an Anna Kostisak who had come to the United States in 1923 and was heading to her uncle Michael's house in Johnstown, Pennsylvania. On the scanned-in copy of the record, in very light pencil, was written Michael's address on the same street Baba still lived on.

McKenna sat up straighter and scrolled across to the next column. Under "Closest relative in country of origin," it listed Anna's father as Lucas, and he lived in Dubne. "I have something."

All the clacking of computer keys in the entire office stopped, and the weight of ten stares sat on her shoulders. She studied the track pad on her computer, her face warm. Yep, she'd gone and been the loud American most Europeans didn't care for. "Sorry." This time she whispered.

Filip touched her arm. "Don't worry about it. We all get excited when we make a big discovery."

"I didn't mean to shout."

"It must be big."

She couldn't contain the smile that popped out on her face. "Listen to this." She shared with Filip and Tay what she'd found. Before she even finished telling them, Filip stood behind her and peered over her shoulder at her computer screen.

"Before I came, Baba told me everything she knew about her family. It wasn't much, but she did mention that her mother's uncle Michal lived right down the street from where she now lives."

"That is a very good lead. Take a screenshot of that and record it in the spreadsheet I sent you an example of."

It had proven to be a valuable tool in saving all the information she gleaned, so she did what Filip asked. "What do you think of it?"

"You said your great-grandmother had an uncle named Michael in the United States."

"Yes. He's the one who paid for her schooling."

"So your great-grandmother may have had two uncles, perhaps. Michael in the States and Lucas in Dubne, who was Anna's father. Michael could have both paid for your great-grandmother's schooling and helped his niece Anna emigrate. This gives us additional branches to explore and might help us in following them back to find out more about your family."

Taylor came and stood beside Filip, also peering over McKenna's shoulder. "Wow. Look at how much you accomplished, and we just got here."

"I know. I can't wait to dig in further." McKenna yawned. "My spirit is willing, but my flesh is weak."

Tay chuckled. "I know. At this point, I can barely keep my eyes open."

"Then let me take you to your hotel." Filip shut his laptop and straightened a few papers on his desk. "Tomorrow, after you have rested, we can work again. I have a few ideas of where we can do more research."

"You had me at hotel."

Filip cocked his head.

"Sorry. An American idiom. Some sleep sounds very good right now."

"Then we will go. Do you need anything to eat?"

McKenna and Taylor glanced at each other then shook their heads. "I'm too tired to think about food." McKenna yawned again.

"Okay. I will tell you that by your hotel, parking is very hard, so I will just drop you off. It is not far from here, but with your suitcases, you don't want to walk."

Within five minutes, Filip had dropped them and their luggage on the sidewalk. He was right about not being able to park. It was a busy street with a tram line, and he wasn't allowed to block traffic.

Within half an hour, they had checked into a boutique hotel, their room small but charming with a brick wall behind the beds. Soon they had showered and snuggled under the thick duvets.

McKenna was almost asleep when her phone rang. Mom. She couldn't ignore it. "Hello."

"I'm sorry. Were you sleeping? I must have gotten the time difference wrong."

"Just about asleep, but it's early here. Jet lag is taking its toll."

"Maybe you should call me back later then. I want you to get some rest."

"Well, now that you've called, you might as well tell me why, because I won't be able to sleep if you don't."

"I was listening to the news on the radio this morning and heard something really awful."

If McKenna hadn't been awake before, she was now. "What?"

"Belinda took her life last night."

CHAPTER SEVENTEEN

Benevolent and Almighty God,
You too at one time suffered,
Help us live through this calamity,
We will faithfully serve You.

The Way of the Cross is ahead of us
But look to God.
God will help us, God is our strength!
Truth always wins over wrongdoing.

Boldly with Christ all the way to Golgotha,
Let's have hope, faith, and will.
In a sea of suffering, full of crying and pain,
God grant us a better plight.

~From "Song of Lemkovyna"

Wednesday, June 30, 1943
Dubne, Generalgouvernement, Poland

That cry from Pani Chomiak scraped against the nerves in my chest. Mama. Something was wrong with my dear, precious mama. I couldn't breathe.

As soon as the cry came, Jerzy rushed from the house, and after a moment working to get my legs moving, I followed, leaving Teena sleeping on the bed.

I drew in a much-needed breath, and despite my husband's longer legs, I soon overtook him. I had to be with Mama, the woman who had given me so much.

Mama was old. Maybe not in the world's years, but in Lemko years, she was well advanced in age. This was what all my hard work was designed to prevent. Soon I was running in time to the beat of my heart. I slid down the steep incline.

And then, even though I had been panting a few moments ago, now my breath caught in my throat. There lay Mama on the ground, as pale as any ghost who might haunt the surrounding forests.

I rushed to her side and knelt in the grass, pulling her onto my lap. "Mama, it's Helena. I'm here. Don't worry. Everything is going to be fine. Holy Father, protect her." I wiped away either sweat or tears from the side of my face.

Jerzy arrived and sank down beside me. I leaned against him, my rock.

"Mama, can you hear me?" I watched for her chest to rise and fall. It did, though only a little bit and slowly. When I touched her hand, it was chilly. "Nie, nie. Mama, you can't leave me. Proshu, don't leave me. You have to stay here and watch your granddaughter grow up."

Mama remained unresponsive. There was no doctor to call. The one who had lived in Leluchów had been taken away a while ago.

Then Pani Chomiak huffed onto the scene. "Has anyone called for Pani Bosak? She knows how to care for the sick and what herbs to use."

Herbs? They were going to be no good if Mama had suffered a heart attack or a stroke. My time in Kraków taught me that we needed a hospital and medical equipment. Even then, that often wasn't enough.

The next minutes blurred by in a haze. Two men—very possibly Jerzy and another neighbor, Pawel Dudiak—picked up Mama, brought her to the house, and laid her on her bed. Her complexion matched that of her snowy pillowcase.

Pani Bosak came and administered some herbs. During the next few hours, villagers stopped by to check on the patient. Some brought a few potatoes or a loaf of bread, any kind of offering as a testament to their love and concern. Pawel came twice to check on her.

All the while, I held Mama's hand, feeling for a pulse every now and again. Thin and thready, it was there. "You can wake up, Mama, anytime you want. Just open your eyes and let me know you can hear me. Or squeeze my hand."

Mama's fingers tightened around my hand. I sucked in a breath. "Oh,

Jerzy, did you see that? She can hear me. Do it again, Mama, do it again."

And she did.

"Thank You, Holy Father." The tight band around my middle loosened. "Someone get her a glass of water." When Jerzy handed it to me, I brought the cool liquid to Mama's lips.

She opened her mouth, and I tipped the glass so a little would run into it. "That's so good. Keep it up. Just a little more for me."

She drank again.

No sooner had I set the glass on the hard-packed floor beside the bed than Mama's eyelids fluttered, her lashes dark against her pale skin.

I stroked her wrinkled cheek. "I'm here, Mama. We all are. Wake up so that we can see you're going to be okay."

As if following my command, she did, at first squinting, even though the room's interior was dim. "What is all this fuss?" Though her voice was weak, her words were strong and clear.

I couldn't help but laugh. "You gave us quite the scare. Do you remember what happened? How were you feeling before you lost consciousness?"

"Dizzy. Hot." She furrowed her brow.

Jerzy stroked Mama's thinning gray hair. "Perhaps all you need is some rest. Maybe it was the heat that got to you."

"Do you have any pain?" I continued to rub Mama's hand, bringing a little warmth to it.

"Nie. Thirsty. Still hot."

"Then drink a bit more, and we'll get a cool cloth for your face."

Mama closed her eyes again, and when her chest rose and fell in a steady rhythm, I followed Jerzy to the home's main room. "I am not a physician, but it doesn't appear to me that she's suffered a heart attack or a stroke. What do you think?"

"If I had to bet, I would say that she got overheated and maybe dehydrated. Let's see how she responds to some rest and something to eat and drink." He kissed the top of my head and gave me a brief hug, just enough to reassure me.

It was one of the benefits of marriage that I enjoyed the most. He was always with me in the midst of crisis. With him by my side, I was never alone.

Jerzy refilled the glass of water while I found a rag and dipped it into the bucket. "I'll stay here today, but if your mother is doing better tomorrow, I have to go."

"I understand."

"We need to implement our plan to rescue as many as we can from Jasło. The Nazis are sure to be mistreating them. If we don't act fast, many of them could be dead before we can get there."

"You're right. I can't begin to think about the torture they might be suffering at their captors' hands."

"Unfortunately, I can."

"In these years, even as we became one and a family, you have never shared with me what happened when the Germans held you."

"I would rather not relive it. And it's best that you not know. What is important is the future, not the past." He kissed me again, this time on the lips, and then went into the bedroom with the now-full glass of water.

When I entered, Mama was pushing herself up by her elbows in an attempt to sit. I shook my head. "Nie. You will spend the day in bed, taking a much-deserved rest. Take it easy. Pani Chomiak came and took Teena a while ago, so I can give you my full attention."

"I heard you talking."

By this time in my life, I should have learned that nothing was secret within the intimate confines of a Lemko home. Or within the small Lemko communities. "That's nothing to worry about. There are people who will bring our men home from those who stole them from us."

"Is it dangerous?"

Jerzy handed me the glass of water. "It will be hard, but the plan Ivan and I are putting in place is going to be good. One that will ensure the survival of as many as possible. To raise our chances of success, only he and I know the plan. And Helena, because she insisted. That way, no one can betray us."

"I don't want my daughter to end up a widow the way I did, so young, no one to support us."

"I am going to do my best to make sure that doesn't happen. I have a beautiful wife and a daughter that I love more than anything in the world. When I have so much to live for, I have so much to fight for."

After Mama fell asleep, Jerzy and I stepped outside for a breath of fresh but hot air. "I hope you meant what you said, that you have much to live for."

"Of course I do."

"Then you will return to us." I had come to depend on him more than I would have thought possible. Love must have had that effect on me.

"I will do everything in my power to make it so. Ultimately, it's up to God."

"I know. Just don't do anything foolish or rash."

"I won't, but those men need our help."

"Before Mama took sick, I was going to ask to come to the forest with you to assist in the planning."

"I will tell you everything I know when I know it."

"I had thought I could go to Jasło with you to be the lookout."

"You would have been a very pretty distraction for the guards, but I will not allow you to put yourself in danger. Not with Teena and your mama depending on you. There is no guarantee this will go well, no matter how carefully we plan."

"I understand. And I know why you're doing what you're doing."

"I have come to not only love you and your mama, but I have come to love your people and your way of life. Whatever I need to do to protect them, I will. All of human life is precious."

Before we returned inside, Pawel Dudiak came down the drive, waving something in his hand. "You have mail." He was one of the few in the village that could read well.

Because of Dubne's remote location, mail didn't arrive often, and very few received correspondence from the outside world. When it did, it filled everyone in the village with much excitement and caused a great stir.

"It's addressed to Helena Kostyszak. It didn't come through the regular post but by special courier." Pawel stopped in front of me and handed me the envelope. He gave me a wide grin and brushed a strand of light brown hair from his forehead. A long time ago, we'd had a crush on each other, one the distance between Dubne and Kraków had extinguished.

Once I had studied the handwriting on the outside, I turned to Jerzy. "It's from Jadwiga, one of the secretaries at the university. What could she want?"

"You will never know unless you open it."

"I will leave you to your mail." Pawel turned to leave.

"Ďakujem. I appreciate you bringing this to me."

"Things may have changed, Helena, but I would still do anything for you." He waved at me and then ambled down the lane.

"I am glad I married you first." Jerzy hugged my shoulders. "If not, Pawel might have snatched you up."

"It was nothing more than a childhood infatuation. You aren't jealous, are you?"

"Why would I be when you're my wife?"

I returned my attention to the letter, turning the envelope over and over in my hand. "How could Jadwiga have found us here? We didn't tell anyone where we were going." The paper shook as I held it.

Jerzy took it from me and sliced open the envelope. "Would you like me to read it to you?"

"Tak, proshu."

"My dearest Helena,

"I am taking a guess and assuming that you have returned to your home village for safety. I went to your flat, but the superintendent said you disappeared a while ago. Jerzy seems to have also disappeared again. Perhaps he is with you?

"Things in Kraków have been quiet. Too many residents have been taken away. I am sure you heard of the liquidation of the ghetto. What a sorry business that was. I wonder what has happened to Risa. As for me, I remain here and try to keep my head down and myself out of trouble.

"There is a group of us who would like to start the university again. Tak, I know it is forbidden by the Germans, but we want to do something underground. Clandestine. It is not right that our bright young men and women are denied an education just because of the occupation.

"So that is why I'm writing to you, and to Jerzy too, if you know where he is. We would like for both of you to return to Kraków to resume your duties at the university. Of course, we cannot meet on the university grounds, but we would meet in flats and homes and even churches throughout the city.

"Please consider returning. The pay won't be as good as it was before, but it will be something, and in these days, that is all we can ask. Think about it and let me know as soon as possible. We would like to start classes in September, maybe even earlier.

"If you are unsure, then come and see me, and we can discuss this face-to-face. I hope I can convince you to make this move. Perhaps this time you can persuade your mother to come with you.

I anxiously await your reply.

"Your dear friend, Jadwiga."

I bit the inside of my cheek, chewing it raw. No wonder it came by courier with no chance of the Nazis opening it. "What do you think? Is this a good opportunity?"

"It certainly is intriguing. Of course, it would mean me giving up my work with the Lemko partisans."

"We don't have to go until after the raid on Jasło. Perhaps, like she said, we can just travel there and talk to her about the possibility. In the meantime, I can see if Mama would be open to the idea of the move. What can it hurt?"

"This is something you really want, isn't it?"

"Tak. I need to use my mind again. Proshu, Jerzy, I want to discuss this with Jadwiga. I love my land, my people, and my family. But I need intellectual stimulation as much as I need air."

"Fine, then. Just to make you happy."

Now all I had to do was convince Mama to go to Kraków. Because I would never leave her behind.

CHAPTER EIGHTEEN

Tuesday, August 3, 1943
Dubne, Generalgouvernement, Poland

I stood hugging myself, staring at the night sky speckled with stars. My little town had succumbed to slumber, and peace settled over the area. Even the few remaining sheep had quieted their bleating. Only the occasional bark of a dog broke the stillness.

My arms were stiff, either from today's hard work or from missing holding Jerzy. Without him, I was empty.

Inside our home, Mama and Teena slept together. Ever since Mama's episode a little over a month ago, Teena was attached to her. Wouldn't leave her. Even insisted on sleeping in bed with her, which I hadn't had the heart to discourage. In the end, it was good medicine for Mama.

Their bond continued to strengthen, and I loved her all the more for accepting Teena as one of her own instead of rejecting her because she was Jewish. It made no difference to her. A child was a child, no matter who the parents were, and every child deserved the right to be nurtured, to grow and blossom.

But what about Jerzy? I turned to the hills surrounding me, though the slice of moon that shone did little to light them. For a few days, he had been gone to the forest to finalize the plans for the rescue of the prisoners in Jasło.

I couldn't go with him, wouldn't go with him this time. Mama was better, but I wasn't comfortable leaving her alone, especially with Teena to care for.

If something happened while I was gone, my grief might break me.

A twig behind me cracked, snapping me from my thoughts. Before I had a chance to focus on the dark shadow, I was caught in an embrace, the fresh-air odor clinging to my husband. I would know his scent, the feeling of his arms around me, anywhere.

I kissed him, long and hard, until he pushed on my shoulders to break our connection. "Woman, you will start something we won't be able to finish." His voice was like a low growl.

"I missed you."

This time he kissed the top of my head, likely not wanting to stir the passions that had risen with the last one. "And I missed you. But we have hit a snag with the plan."

"What is it?" If they couldn't rescue the prisoners, those men were as good as dead.

"Ivan has fallen and broken his leg. Rather badly, I'm afraid. Our plan depends on someone taking his place as lookout. Someone already familiar with what we're about to do."

I held my breath, but I could have predicted his next words.

"I need you."

He had been good to his word, reporting on how he and Ivan were going to secure the men's release. On some points, I had added my advice. "Nie, you know I can't leave Mama and Teena. They need me. What if something happened to Mama while I was gone? Or Teena? You are asking the impossible."

He rubbed my goose-bumps-covered arms, even though I was plenty warm. "What other choice do we have? Most of the men are in the forests or in labor camps. You know each detail. We will be gone only three days. Four at the very most. Have Pani Chomiak come and stay with them. She will pamper them as if they were at the spa taking the waters."

Despite the gravity of the situation, I could not imagine Mama's reaction to the water from the nearby mineral springs. Once, a colleague at the university had gone and brought back a bottle. At the fish-tank taste, I almost gagged.

"They will be in good hands. We are scheduled to leave tonight. In fact, we should have already been gone, but Ivan's injury has slowed us. I would not ask this of you if it weren't of the utmost importance."

"How can I go?" Nyan'o had passed away while I was staying with my cousins in Leluchów, and I hadn't had the chance to say goodbye. If Mama fell ill again while I was gone, and the worst happened. . .

"In times of war, we put our own needs aside and give our best to the greatest good."

We had done that for Teena, and it had proven to be the biggest blessing in our lives. Though it tore me apart inside, Jerzy was right. I could do no less for my own people. "Make the arrangements with Pani Chomiak. I will pack."

After a peck on the cheek, he disappeared into the night.

"Holy Father, proshu, don't let this be a mistake."

Thursday, August 5, 1943
Jasło, Generalgouvernement, Poland

Darkness fell on the sleepy little town. With a curfew in place, the only creatures roaming the streets were a few cats and the mice they were chasing. Through an open window down the street came an infant's cry.

Getting here had been grueling. Because of our lack of travel papers, a must when moving about the country, we were forced to stick to the back roads and mountain trails. After a couple of exhausting days, Jerzy and I had arrived not long ago and had met up with those from the Polish Home Army.

Though I was hot and filthy, I had no time to clean up. In a short time, our detailed plan would be implemented. The rain was doing a good enough job of washing away some of the grime.

Hand in hand, Jerzy and I headed toward the prison. The whole time, my heart pounded in my ears, drowning out all other sounds, even the rain pelting the pavement. He squeezed my fingers, a small measure of reassurance.

Really, this was a crazy mission. Several men, one paid-off guard, and a woman, and we believed we were going to get into the large prison complex and free Polish political prisoners as well as the Lemkos held inside.

The others in the group, who had scattered as we entered the city, met us. I only knew them as Paw, Korczak, Boruta, and Dąbrowa, and of course, Jerzy. And that was for the best. Together we slunk through the rain-soaked yards of private homes, the grass slick underneath our feet.

All was dark. Even the moon was snuffed out, covered by the thick, heavy clouds that unleashed their payload. Mud sucked at my one remaining pair of shoes, tightly laced oxfords.

A wire fence loomed in front of us, separating one neighbor from the other. Jerzy lifted the bottom, and I crawled through the muck to the other side. I wiped my mud-caked hands on the wet grass. After moving across three streets this way, we left the cluster of homes behind and came to a cornfield.

My entire body shook. This could go very right or horribly wrong. Those were the two outcomes. Korczak had commanded absolute silence, so the questions and objections that raced across my tongue died.

A moment later he motioned for all of us to get down. Crawling through the stalks that pulled at my hair was not something I would have chosen to do.

By now mud caked every part of me, including my pants, my hands, and my hair. The rain only made it thicker and heavier and now did nothing to wash it off. I would never get the stains out of my clothes.

The men were all young and strong. Most of them had trained for this type of physical activity. They knew just what to do and didn't tire despite the conditions.

For me, the trek was much more difficult. We hadn't crawled far before my forearms burned and sweat mingled with the deluge. Compared to this, the small home I shared with my family was a palace.

I kept my focus on Mama and Teena, asleep in their beds a two-day trek from here. If Jerzy and I and the others didn't succeed, they would be alone with no one to support them.

They would struggle to survive.

So I couldn't fail. While in school, fighting against my gender and my ethnicity, I had dug deep inside and discovered a tenacity I hadn't known I possessed.

I tapped into that again, staying close to Jerzy's heels, Paw right behind me.

At last the cornfield gave way to a row of hedges lining a road, and across the road sat a large, rectangular compound. Other than the front building, a high wall surrounded the remainder of the prison.

Here we had to remain until our contact inside signaled us with a light. I shivered, now soaked and chilled, my hair falling in wet, muddy strands around my face. Jerzy pulled me close, his body heat warming me through.

Any minute now Three, our inside man, would let us know the time had come for the raid. Then again, it would be a miracle for anyone to see the light from his torch through this downpour.

The ground beneath me rumbled, and the crank of engines filled the air, drowning out even the patter of the rain. I turned to Jerzy.

From what I could make out, his eyes were wide. So these were German trucks then, much as I suspected. Sure enough, a few minutes later the cars and trucks, almost hidden by the sheets of rain, pulled up to the prison gate.

Jerzy and I and the rest of the group slunk behind the hedges, and I lost sight of what was happening. All the while, I hardly dared to breathe. Only small intakes of air when my body screamed for oxygen.

And then the cars and trucks turned around, their headlights sweeping the row of hedges where our group hid. Jerzy pushed my head down. I lay there in the mud, my arms and legs stiff and sore. *Proshu, Holy Father, keep us safe.*

A moment later the engines roared, and then the sound faded little by little until only the ringing of the rain on the pavement was left. The Lord heard my prayer, and I managed to breathe freely once more.

But not for long. Again, Germans broke the silence, this time with the clack of their hobnail boots against the road. Soldiers were right at our fingertips.

How many more close calls were we to have tonight? I licked my dry lips and allowed some of the rainwater to run into my mouth to soothe my parched throat.

At last the men moved away, and then voices came from the area of the gate. The long-awaited light flashed, breaking the darkness like the dawn. Three approached the gate. With the signal given, the men left me, sprinted across the road, and then were adjacent to the wall with the gate.

The key grated as Three turned the lock, and all the men, including my husband, disappeared inside the compound.

I remained alone in the mud, the rain pelting me. Every second that passed was a lifetime. Carefree childhood days spent frolicking barefoot in the mountain meadows, all of that cut short by my father's death.

School days in Nowy Sącz, struggling with the Polish language, behind in all my classes but still managing to graduate with the best grades of all the pupils.

Happy times in Kraków as a student and then a lecturer. Jadwiga. Risa. Jerzy.

I pawed the ground beside me until my hand bumped one of the rucksacks that the men had left behind. Precious provisions for prisoners who were likely starving. When they came out—not if but when—it would be my job to hand out food to the men.

The rain slackened, but I remained cold and tired and caked in mud. Even at our poorest, we had always been able to wash in the stream or tote water to heat on the stove to bathe.

I wiped the dirt from my eyes so I wouldn't miss the men coming out of that gate. Time ticked away, though I had no inkling of how much. The precious watch I had bought myself in Kraków with one of my first paychecks lay at home in Dubne, safe from harm.

Lights flicked on in various rooms in the prison, a good sign that the men had managed to subdue the guards and get inside. A few moments later Paw stepped outside of the gate, a machine gun now in his hand. That meant they had gotten to the armory. With a weapon depot on the grounds, the partisans had no need to raid German military transports. No chance of being caught doing so. No chance of further reprisals.

Still, time passed on the back of a tortoise. I bit my lip until I tasted blood.

A gunshot from inside startled me and started my heart pumping like it had never pumped before. Who was shot? Not Jerzy. *Holy Father, not Jerzy.*

I kept my gaze trained on the prison gate. Paw didn't move. No one went in, praise be, but no one came out. How long until they had all the cells opened?

And then Paw flicked on his flashlight and motioned for me to come. I rose, and it took a moment for me to gain my footing on the wet ground, but then I bounded across the road and past Paw into the prison.

Though I had never been inside such a place before, I didn't take time to examine my surroundings. Instead, I followed the directions of someone dressed in Gestapo garb who had a gun trained on another man dressed in the same uniform. This must be our insider.

My legs burning, I hurried until I came to the prison kitchen. Loaves of leftover bread lined the counters. On the counter behind me, I found several burlap bags that had likely once been filled with potatoes, and I stuffed a couple with all the bread they would hold.

Next I ran down a long corridor, my shoes tapping against the slimy stone floors, until I came to a door. I opened it, but it was nothing more than an office. I tried several more doors until I arrived at a supply room. From there I grabbed blankets and rushed back to the gate, where I deposited my treasures.

"The office is over there." Paw nodded in the opposite direction without ever taking his attention off his prisoner. He held out a piece of paper, which I grabbed.

As soon as I had it, I hurried to the office, one large reception room opening into several other rooms. Korczak had instructed me which offices I needed to visit and which safes had to be opened. Somehow he had obtained the combinations. There was no point in asking how. One of our Nazi prisoners must have been tortured enough or promised enough to give it up.

I stepped inside the first room, a rug softening my footfalls, though my shoes would leave it covered in mud. With the aid of my flashlight, I bypassed a large metal desk covered in neat piles of paper and came to a huge gray floor safe on the other side of the room.

Though my hands shook, the knob cool under my fingers, I managed to correctly dial the combination on the second try. The heavy door swung open. Inside were stacks of złoty. I swept all the paper money into one of the burlap bags. This would assist the freed prisoners to flee to safety and restart their lives.

Once I had that, I moved to the next office. Again, it was carpeted, and the beam from my torch illuminated a room that was laid out much the same as the previous one.

This time the safe's lock released on my first try. Maybe I was getting to be a little too good at criminal activity. However, unlike the previous safe, this one contained travel documents and blank identification papers. Once we were away from the prison, Korczak and the others would pass them out so the men could secure what they needed to start over. They would leave some for Jerzy and me when we released the Lemkos.

I also put these in the burlap bag but kept a few out for myself and my family. Traveling here without permission had been difficult and dangerous, as would be making the trip to Kraków. These would ensure our safety.

When I had gathered everything I needed, I hightailed it back to the yard just as Jerzy led out a contingent of about sixty men and even a few women. One man was carried out because he had been badly beaten.

To keep from weeping at the sight of the emaciated prisoners, I busied myself by passing out the provisions. As soon as I had given everyone food, a blanket, and blank identity papers, Korczak and Boruta led the column of parolees through the gate with Dąbrowa bringing up the rear.

But now the hardest part of the mission remained. While the others had freed the captives from the Polish Home Army, it was up to Jerzy and me to get out the Lemkos still behind the prison's bars.

CHAPTER NINETEEN

We carry a great wound in our heart,
Daily we ask God to help us
Survive our bitter life,
So all will end well.

~From "Song of Lemkovyna"

Tuesday, October 3, 2023
Kraków, Poland

McKenna gripped the phone in her hand. The tram rumbled by, vibrating the bed. She couldn't have heard Mom right. "What did you say?"

"I'm so sorry, sweetie. They interviewed her mother on the news, and she said that Belinda just couldn't handle life without Yasmine and that the guilt of bringing Hank back into their lives was eating her up."

Her head throbbed. "This is senseless."

"It is a real tragedy. Belinda is as much a victim of Hank as Yasmine was."

"If only I had known. If I had seen, been more attentive when I ran into them that day in the store. But Belinda assured me everything was going well. And then I saw her at the funeral. She was so, so sad, but she had just lost her daughter."

"Honey, please don't blame yourself. You couldn't have known what was going on behind closed doors. Belinda was very good at hiding what was happening from the world."

McKenna wiped away tears. Her muddled, jet-lagged mind couldn't comprehend everything. "I really need to get some sleep. Thanks for letting me know."

"I wish I didn't have to call you about this. Rest well, sweetie. I'm glad to know you're there safely, and I can't wait to hear about everything in a few days when you aren't so bushed. I love you."

"Love you right back."

They hung up, and McKenna sat with her phone in her lap, just staring at it. Taylor crawled out of bed and came and sat beside her. "I kind of heard."

"Belinda is dead now too."

"That's so awful."

"Hank ruined so many lives. So many. And it just keeps getting worse. If only I could have gotten through to Belinda about him. I wish I could have convinced her not to ever have contact with him."

"You got her to get a restraining order. She chose to allow him to come back."

As the tears came fast and furious, McKenna held her aching head. Tay rubbed her back, and she relaxed.

"Why don't you just lie down and close your eyes? I'll get you some melatonin to help you sleep. We both need it. Since we have plenty of time here, we can stay in bed as long as we want tomorrow."

"I won't even be able to go to the funeral. What will her mother think of me?"

"She knows you care about her and about her daughter and granddaughter. You were there for Yasmine's. If it makes you feel better, you can send flowers."

"That would be nice."

Taylor went to the bathroom and returned with the melatonin and a wad of tissues.

"Thanks. You always know just what I need."

"How about I plug in my white noise machine? Would that help?"

"It would."

But nothing really helped. Not the jet lag, the melatonin, or the white noise machine. McKenna dozed off and on and maybe got a couple of hours of deep sleep, but she woke up about as groggy as when she went to bed.

Taylor, on the other hand, must have slept like a log, because she woke up as bright and chipper as. . . Well, it was just kind of annoying how awake she could be so early in the morning.

McKenna managed to drag herself out of bed and pull on a pair of jeans and a flowy top.

"Do you know what you need?"

"About ten more hours of sleep?"

Tay threw a pillow at McKenna's head. "A brisk walk outside. We've been sitting or lying for a couple of days now." She pulled the curtains open. "It's a beautiful day to explore this amazing city."

"Fine. I could use something to eat." Though it would probably taste like sawdust.

"Pączki! It's pączki day."

"That's only the day before Lent. And I've never had one."

"How can you call yourself a true Pole?"

"I'm Lemko, not Polish, remember?"

"We are going to remedy your ignorance of pączki right now."

"But I'm not having a prune one, I'm telling you that right off the bat."

"I'm sure they have other flavors. Come on."

"And I need my coffee."

"I'm sure we can find some of that too."

They left the hotel, and Taylor, with the map pulled up on her phone, led the way toward the pączki. Funny how the sun could shine, the birds could sing, and people could go about their everyday lives even when others around the world were in so much pain.

Though her heart ached, she strolled alongside Taylor, past buildings that had stood for hundreds of years, down Długa Street, across a busy road, and to a park. "This is beautiful."

"I knew a walk would do you good."

They continued past a round brick building with multiple spires, though it certainly wasn't a church.

"That's the Barbican, part of the old gateway into the city."

"My own private tour guide."

Taylor tossed her a crooked grin.

Beyond the Barbican was a bricked plaza with a white stone and redbrick wall, a tower constructed of the same materials rising from it, and an arch cutting through it for pedestrians. Above the arch was a stone carving of a fierce, crowned eagle with long talons.

They passed through the arch. When McKenna turned around, on the other side was a carving of an armored man with a flag.

"That's St. Florian himself."

"Next thing I know, Tay, you're going to charge me for this tour."

"That will be three złoty, please."

"At least you aren't expensive."

They moved with the flow of tourists down the street a little way before Tay halted. "And here we are."

The pączki bakery didn't have any inside seating. In fact, there was no inside for the customers at all. The public stood on the street and placed their orders at the counter after having perused all the flavors in the glass case.

A mere ten mouthwatering minutes later, they were seated inside a coffee shop with their pączki and McKenna's requisite shot of caffeine. She bit into the sugar-covered doughnut, just nicking the chocolate hazelnut filling. "Oh my goodness. These are fabulous. I'm never missing pączki day again."

Tay licked some sugar from the corner of her mouth. "I told you so."

McKenna managed to down all of the treat and her coffee. But she couldn't keep Yasmine and Belinda from her mind. This was such a beautiful world but one so filled with pain. What a dichotomy. How was she supposed to make sense of it all? How could she enjoy such an interesting place, a place where she could enjoy the simple pleasures of coffee and pączki, while two lives had been lost because of the hatred and violence of one man?

"Okay, Ken, I can see that faraway look in your eyes, like you're thinking about home."

"I can't get Belinda or Yasmine from my thoughts."

"Well, I'm not going to allow you to go to a dark place. I mean, look at where we are. This city is amazing, and we've only scratched the surface."

"Maybe we should go see what, if anything, Filip has turned up."

"We will. Later. I'm sure he has other clients to work with. Right now it's time to explore. All around Old Town is a park. Planty Park, though I'm sure I'm pronouncing it wrong."

"After this breakfast, a walk does sound good. Let's do it."

They left the touristy street lined with restaurants and gift and souvenir shops, ambled back through the gate, and wandered to a greenbelt that surrounded Old Town. Couples strolled together, and McKenna's heart broke a little more. Chris would have loved Kraków. He'd always been drawn to architecture. He was kind of a nerd that way.

That was another thought she worked to banish.

As they meandered along the paths, they passed a large oak tree with unique leaves that were both dark and light green. McKenna stopped to snap a picture.

"According to my phone, this is Jagiellonian University."

"That makes me wonder. Baba said that her mother was highly educated, even had a college degree. Maybe she went to this school. It looks like it's been around for quite a while."

"Well, it wouldn't hurt to check." Taylor charged ahead.

That was one good thing about traveling with her—she wasn't shy about anything and would always ask. A long time ago, when they still very young, she'd told McKenna that all people could do was say no.

So there they were, after a couple of false starts, in front of the main university building where the administrative offices were housed. The imposing, grand, redbrick building offered five soaring arches, and above that, five two-story windows. Even higher, above the windows, were the crests of the university benefactors. Standing tall above it all was, per Taylor's phone, St. Stanislaw bearing a shield with the same Polish eagle that was on the gate.

They climbed the steps, passed through the arches, and entered the building, beautiful mosaic floors under their feet. In the first office they came to, Taylor stepped up to the thin, blond woman behind the desk. "Dzień dobry."

"Dzień dobry." The woman then took off speaking in rapid Polish.

"Do you speak English?"

The woman smiled and tucked a curl behind her ear with a manicured hand. "Of course. How may I help you?"

"I don't know if you have any information on who studied here in the 1930s, but my friend is wondering if there is any way you could tell if her great-grandmother was a student here." Taylor blurted everything out before McKenna even had a chance to open her mouth.

"I am very busy, but you came a long way for this information, did you not?"

"Yes. All the way from America. And my friend is searching for her great-grandmother and trying to put together a picture of her life. We know she was an educated woman, so we thought we'd stop in and see if she was a pupil here."

The woman hemmed and hawed a bit. "It would be very unusual for a woman to be educated in university in those days. You don't speak Polish?"

They both shook their heads.

"Okay. I will look. Write her name here." She pushed a piece of paper and a pen toward McKenna. "Include when you think she would have been here. Then I don't have to search so much."

McKenna jotted down the information and handed the paper to the secretary. "Dziękuję. I really appreciate you taking the time to do this."

"I will look when I have lunch. Come back at two, and we will see what I have found. My name is Karolina, by the way."

"Dziękuję, Karolina. We'll be back later."

They stepped outside. "See." Tay gave McKenna a playful poke. "I told you that all she could do was say no, but she said she would look for the information."

"You were right. I'll admit it. Part of me can't believe she's actually going to search. Things are different here than at home."

"And someone who studied at the university at that time probably isn't alive anymore, so she can't get into trouble giving out that information."

"That's also true." They strolled the grounds for a while, winding their way through a beautiful garden filled with colorful flowers. Taylor once again pulled out her phone and informed her that this was part of the university.

After a while, they made their way back to the Collegium Novum. "I know it's before two," McKenna said as they climbed the steps, "but let's wander the building and take a look. From what we saw before, it seems very beautiful."

"It is. Look at this." As they stood under the arches, Tay handed McKenna her phone. "Copernicus and Pope John Paul II went here. We can't claim to have gone to school at the same place as anyone that important."

"That's cool. To think that my great-grandmother might have studied where they did is amazing. She really must have been smart."

"Don't get your hopes too high. Karolina hasn't told us anything yet."

"You're right. I'm so glad you always keep my feet on the ground."

"That's what I'm here for."

"Come on. Admit that you're here for the pączki."

"Okay. That might have something to do with why I jumped on a plane and flew all those hours and all those miles."

"I knew it." They laughed together as they entered the building. They meandered farther in this time. McKenna couldn't take in everything at once. "Look how high the ceilings are."

"Wow, everything is marble. Even this staircase. They must have had some very generous donors. Let's go upstairs."

The same beauty and splendor awaited them there, with marble balconies overlooking the first floor and more floors tiled with terra-cotta, black, white, and ivory mosaics. McKenna whipped out her phone to take a picture. "This is amazing."

"Hey, look over here." Tay stood in front of a bronze plaque with a group of three lights above it. Nearby was a set of wooden double doors, all carved. "You have to read this."

For the freedom of spirit and service to science and nation of Jagiellonian University professors deceitfully and forcefully taken away from this hall and imprisoned by the Nazi occupant on November 6, 1939.

"Whoa." McKenna glanced around, attempting to conjure in her mind a picture of Nazi soldiers in this very hall, weapons in their hands, the footfalls of their boots echoing off the vaulted ceilings. "What happened to them?"

"I'm trying to look it up." Taylor was busy on her phone. "Ah, it's two. We have to go back and see if Karolina has found anything. I'm sure she can tell us more."

They descended the stairs and returned to the administrative office, which was humming with activity.

When they entered, Karolina came from behind her desk. "I have quite the story to tell you."

CHAPTER TWENTY

McKenna stood in the middle of the busy university office and clasped her hands. What kind of news might Karolina have for her and Tay? From how she'd said it, it must be big. Perhaps the first clue on her trail to trace her great-grandmother.

"I went into the student records and did find that Helena Kostyszak was a student here in the early and mid-1930s. She not only completed her baccalaureate degree, but she earned her doctorate."

"Doctorate?" McKenna shook her head as if to clear away the cobwebs. "She had a doctorate? I mean, I know she taught at our local university, but I believed she had received her advanced degree in the States."

"Yes. What is pretty amazing is that your great-grandmother managed to earn one. It was unusual for women to even be allowed to study here in those days. The campus had just opened for women. Only a few earned doctorates."

McKenna gazed at Taylor. "I never realized she was so incredible."

"Now we know where you get your brains from."

"Judging from her records, she was a very bright student. She would have to be in order to accomplish all she did with the obstacles she faced. But there's even more."

"More?" McKenna stared at Karolina, openmouthed. "What could be better than this?"

"Your great-grandmother taught here. While not allowed to be a full-tenured professor, she was a lecturer. She was one of two female professors.

One was Jewish. Your great-grandmother was here until 1939."

McKenna's heart skipped a beat. "Wait a minute. 1939. That's when the Nazis invaded. We were just upstairs and saw the plaque in front of that lecture hall."

"Room fifty-six. Yes. That is where the Nazis brought the professors, telling them there was to be a lecture on changing the curriculum to fit the German ideology. Instead, they took away 183 people."

"Is there a way to find out if my great-grandmother was among them?"

Karolina pulled a sheet of paper from a manila folder on her very organized desk. "I already did. This is the list of those taken to the prison here in Kraków. From there, they went to Sauchhausen, and then to Dachau."

McKenna scanned the page. All men. She moved farther down the list but didn't see Helena's name. "So my great-grandmother wasn't arrested."

"No women were. Only men. Somehow she managed to escape or something. There is a story about a man who helped save the two female lecturers by concealing the fact that they taught here. His name was Jerzy Bielski."

"Do you know the name of the women he saved?"

Karolina's blue eyes sparkled as she pulled out another sheet of paper. "Do you see the names here?" She pointed at a spot on the page.

"Jerzy Bielski, Risa Birkha, and..." McKenna gasped. "Helena Kostyszak. Wow. He saved my great-grandmother."

"He did. It is an interesting story, especially since, as I said, Risa was Jewish. The two women would have been pretty close, because it was them against all the men."

McKenna nodded. "Very true. So did Jerzy Bielski go to Dachau?"

"Yes. About thirty of the men died either at one of the camps or soon after their release."

"They were released?"

"Apparently there was some sort of deal worked out with neutral parties that freed the prisoners. By 1941 all of those arrested who were still alive had returned home."

Tay whistled, but not too loudly. "You have an amazing family, Ken. Mine could never compare to this."

"I have one more thing for you."

"This is almost like that television show where celebrities find out about their ancestors. They always dig up something really interesting." McKenna stood on her tiptoes.

Karolina handed two sheets of paper to her. "These are the employment records I have for your great-grandmother, Jerzy, and Risa. You'll find their birthdates and where they were living in Kraków at the time."

"Oh. Oh." She took the papers and worked to catch her breath. "You don't know what a gift you've given me."

"And you have given the university a gift as well."

"I have?"

"We are working to put together what happened to some of these people who were taken away during the war. In fact, we had no idea about any of them after the raid. So now we can fill in that missing piece. We would like to have a picture of you."

McKenna grimaced. "I'm still pretty jet-lagged, and so I haven't done much with myself. My makeup didn't cover the black circles under my eyes this morning. If everything goes to plan, I'll be here for several weeks, maybe even a couple of months, so if it's okay with you, I'd like to come back another day for that."

"Of course. Let's exchange information, and we can set a time when you can speak with the university president and have your photograph taken."

"The president?"

Karolina nodded. "Give me your number so I can text you, if that's not a problem for you."

"It's not." McKenna provided her information. "Thank you so much for everything. I appreciate it."

"We both do." Taylor wasn't about to be forgotten.

"I hope you have a pleasant stay. Let me know if there is anything I can do for you."

Once they exited the building, McKenna stopped short of the first step. "Can you believe that?"

"It's wild. Here we thought your great-grandmother was from a small town, but we manage to find her at a university in the big city."

"If Helena was from Dubne, where her uncle Lucas lived, this must have been such a change for her. But what a strong woman she was. And that's what Baba and Mom keep telling me. That she was one of the most resilient people they ever knew. I guess she had to be to deal with everything she did."

Taylor made her way down the steps, and McKenna followed. "Even if you find out nothing else about them, that's a pretty big chunk of information on who she was as a person."

"Oh, wait. We have their addresses on their employment records." Any residual heaviness lifted from McKenna's shoulders. "We can go see where they lived."

"That will be interesting, but I'm getting hungry. How about we grab a bite to eat first?"

"Sounds good to me." They searched for something close by and found a milk bar. McKenna had read about those before coming. They were started during the Communist era and were good, cheap, and traditional.

After they each had a fortifying bowl of very delicious borscht with something akin to tortellini in it, they set out to find Jerzy's apartment. "I imagine it must be pretty nice if he was a full professor at the university. He must have been making a good wage."

Taylor pointed out the turn they needed to make. With McKenna's lack of directional skills, the job fell to Tay. "I suppose, especially compared to the many poor people around."

They made several more turns, the city easy enough to get around, especially with the map open on Tay's phone. On her own, even with how straightforward the city was laid out, with her poor navigating skills, McKenna would be hopelessly lost. "This is it."

The building in front of them wasn't very spectacular. In fact, with its brown-gray stucco exterior and pretty standard windows, it didn't stand out. Only the three arches on the bottom floor set it apart. Then again, it was a far sight better than where Belinda and Yasmine had lived. "Maybe he had the penthouse."

Taylor laughed. "Apparently professors didn't make as much money as we thought. And maybe it was nicer years ago."

"True. I bet it would have been more than Helena would have earned had she stayed in Dubne, if that's where she's from. Her uncle certainly was. I'm disappointed that Helena's records don't show that information."

"We aren't going to solve the mystery all in one day. Practice some patience. And we still have to go see your great-grandmother's flat. Doesn't *flat* sound so European?"

McKenna shook her head. "You sound like an American trying to be posh. Now don't I sound British?"

The laughter that followed was a balm to McKenna's soul. For a little while, it washed away the lingering sadness.

Tay consulted her phone once more. "Look at this. Her apartment was on Długa Street, the same street we're staying on."

"That's crazy. Are you sure?"

Tay handed her the folder with the information. They blocked part of the sidewalk, but the pedestrians just moved around them, rather unfazed. Sure enough, the address said Długa Street.

"What are we waiting for? We can see her place and then go back to the hotel for some rest."

"That sounds great." They traversed the few streets over and the couple of blocks up until they were almost across from where they were staying. "How is it that we picked a hotel so close to where Helena lived?"

"It's wonderful." Taylor's huge grin was infectious.

"And the building is amazing. Look at that architecture." McKenna pointed to the second-story windows framed by intricately carved stone and the third-story ones with less-detailed carvings. "In my art history class, we studied some of this, but it's so different than looking at it in pictures."

"Way better."

An older woman, bent and leaning on a cane, exited the building.

McKenna sighed. "I wish we could go in and see where Helena lived so long ago."

The woman stopped. "Excuse me." Her English wasn't as good as that of the younger generations, but it was far better than their Polish.

"Yes?"

"Were you talking about Helena?" Her sharp blue eyes sparkled.

"I was."

"Who lived here a long time ago?"

"In the 1930s until at least 1939."

"Oh my." The woman swayed on her feet, and McKenna grabbed her by the elbow to steady her. "You mean Helena Kostyszak, don't you?"

"How did you know?"

"I was a young child then, and I've lived in the same flat all my life."

"That's incredible."

"Ninety years old and going strong."

"So you knew my great-grandmother?"

"I remember her. Would you like to come in and I can tell you about her?"

Overcome, McKenna covered her mouth and nodded.

"But you were on your way out." Taylor was keeping her wits about her.

"Never mind. Just for a tin of food for my cat. She has enough until tomorrow. My name is Pani Piotrowska. Come, come."

McKenna and Taylor followed the elderly woman inside to her apartment on the second floor. Though they had to climb a flight of stairs, Pani Piotrowska managed them quite well.

She unlocked the door and ushered them into a tiny but neat apartment. So far, McKenna had yet to spy a speck of dirt, either inside or out. This city was the cleanest ever. Though the space hadn't been updated in a while, Pani Piotrowska had a bright couch, a utilitarian kitchen, and two doors. One must be to the bedroom and the other to the bath.

"Now you ladies sit down and tell me where you're from while I get some tea."

They introduced themselves, and McKenna explained what had brought them to Poland. "So you knew my great-grandmother?"

"I did. Of course, I was still very young, hard as that is to believe, but I thought she was the most beautiful woman I had ever seen. Not very tall, but she held herself, I don't know how you say it in English, but like she was grand. Never like this." Pani Piotrowska slouched.

McKenna laughed. "I've only seen one or two pictures of her."

"Oh, I wish I had one. I am sorry for that. But I can tell you what she was like."

"Yes, please."

"As soon as we have tea." They chatted for a few more minutes until the kettle sang and Pani Piotrowska poured the hot water over the leaves. McKenna got up and took the cups from her.

The old woman settled herself in a chair just opposite them in the small space. "One reason I remember her was because she was always so kind. Whenever she spoke to me, she looked me in the eye and made me feel important, not like a fly about her head."

"Oh, that makes me happy." McKenna rubbed her chest, just above her heart. "What else?"

"Mama said she was saving money, but every once in a while, Helena would bring me a sweet. Mieszanka Wedlowska chocolates. Until the war came, that is. And she had a beautiful laugh. When I heard yours, it reminded me so much of hers."

A happy tear gathered in the corner of McKenna's eye, and she brushed it away.

"And then one day she left everything behind and disappeared."

CHAPTER TWENTY-ONE

The prison gates were opened
The imprisoned were saved from death
They're returning to their families
But wonder for how long
They'll find themselves in their homes
After such a heavy-hearted time.

~From "Song of Lemkovyna"

Thursday, August 5, 1943
Jasło, Generalgouvernement, Poland

Freedom. Judging from the men's wide smiles, they relished even the rain on their faces. Still, their gazes darted around. Freedom was fleeting, something to be cherished for however long it lasted.

Because freedom could be yanked away without notice. Captivity was what was long-lasting.

Now with the Polish Home Army marching their released captives away, Jerzy and I turned our attention to freeing the Lemkos still held here. Thankfully, all of the guards were locked in solitary confinement, a place where they had tortured their prisoners just hours before.

This time I entered the prison following in Jerzy's wake. Dampness and humidity seeped through the stone walls. The wet floors were slippery and

WHAT I LEFT FOR YOU

treacherous underfoot, and I steadied myself against the wall.

My hand came away sticky, but I didn't dare dwell on what might be the cause.

The smells were even worse. Human excrement. Blood. Decay. They all mingled into an odor so putrid that even the most seasoned stomach wouldn't be able to stand it.

I turned and retched.

Jerzy hurried to my side, rubbing my back while I finished emptying my stomach of its contents. "Why don't you wait outside? This is too much for you. For anyone."

"Nie, I am fine. Or I will be." I covered my nose and mouth, the fragrance of yeast from the bread I distributed still clinging to my hand, providing a little bit of relief. "If you can do this, so can I."

He continued leading the way down the darkened, arched corridor, only the thin stream of light from his torch piercing the cloying darkness as he opened cell doors. Finally, he came to one occupied by a man I recognized from a neighboring village. "Atanas Petronchak. At last we find a Lemko."

The thin, frail man held out his filthy hand, and I clutched it. Likely the first human touch he'd felt in months. At least the first friendly human touch.

"Where are all the others?" Jerzy steadied the man, who swayed on his feet.

"Your accent gives you away. You are no Lemko."

Though Jerzy had worked hard on learning our language, he could not get rid of the Polish sound of his words. "This is my husband." I stood beside Jerzy. "The Polish Home Army freed its prisoners. We're taking care of the rest, and we'll assist you in getting home safely."

Atanas harrumphed.

We couldn't allow the wound of distrust to fester. For the escape plan to be successful, the freed prisoners had to follow Jerzy without question. "He has been working with the partisans in the mountains. Doing good work. All along, he's been in on the plan. If you can tell me where Vasyl Horniak is, he will vouch for my husband."

"You are very naive. Did you believe the Germans would go easy on us? Of all those taken in the raid, there are only four left. And Vasyl isn't among them."

The world around me spun. Jerzy's strong arm steadied me, but I still collapsed into his arms. "Four?" The word squeaked past my throat.

151

"Four. I would tell you what they did to us, but you would faint if I did. They are brutes who treat the rats who infest this place better than they treat us."

I choked back the sob that rose in my throat.

"Monsters." Jerzy voiced my exact thoughts. "Show me where the rest of the Lemkos are. We will make sure you all get home without incident."

At last Atanas nodded, pointing out the cells that held his fellow Lemkos. While Jerzy opened the remaining doors, I gathered my people and provided them with bread and some clothing I found. Two had oozing wounds. Once outside, once morning came, I might be able to treat them.

If I could stomach it.

In the meantime, I ushered them into the fresh air. Jerzy needed to hurry before any more Germans came, before the morning shift of guards arrived.

Dawn was not far off before he joined us. "We had better go. This took more time than I anticipated."

We scurried along as fast as the prisoners could manage until we came to a fence. There was no way but to scale it, and the men were weak. Both Jerzy and I had to boost them over. Not long afterward, another fence blocked our progress. Then another.

Precious seconds and minutes ticked by. Finally, we reached the railroad tracks. Though the thought of riding a train was heavenly, it wasn't possible. We had no papers and no permission to be out and about.

We halted at the tracks, and Jerzy did a quick search for any railway police. If we ran into the *Bahnschutz*, all of this would be for naught.

I held my breath while he scanned the area. He flicked his torch back on and motioned for us to follow. Though I worked to tread lightly, the gravel crunched underneath my feet as we crossed the tracks in the railyard.

In front of us rose a large white church that glowed despite the unrelenting rain. A redbrick wall surrounded it, and several dormitory-style arms radiated from it. Jerzy had told me about this convent during our planning.

Oh to be able to take refuge inside its walls and underneath its red tile roof. Just for the night, for a little sleep and shelter from the storm. A slice of heaven on earth.

But to avoid putting anyone else in danger, we slogged on.

And *slogging* was the right word. The relentless rain was good in that it erased all traces of our footprints in the mud. On the other hand, it made the muck thicker and heavier, soon coating everyone's boots. Not far into the trek, my legs burned with the effort, and my sweat mingled with the rain.

Because I brought up the rear, I kept an eye on the men we were leading into the forest. They were frail from malnutrition and often stumbled over rocks and exposed tree roots.

Then Atanas' knees buckled, and he fell to the wet earth.

"Jerzy!"

Everyone turned and came to help. From my rucksack, I withdrew a bit more of our precious bread and a canteen of water. I lifted his head. "Come on. Take just a little."

His eyelids fluttered open. "The Holy Father has sent you to us."

"Eat a bit, and you will feel better. We need to get farther away from the prison before morning, before they send out soldiers searching for us."

"Tak, tak." Atanas ate a few bites of bread that I fed him and drank a bit of water. Just that small amount of sustenance was enough to revive him. A few minutes later he sat without assistance.

"Are you hurt, or are you going to be able to continue walking?" I screwed the cap onto the canteen.

"I can go on, but if this happens again and I hold you up, then leave me. What is one life worth compared to five others?"

"Every life is precious, created by God for a special purpose, so we aren't going to leave you. You can lean on me."

"You're a wisp of a woman."

"But stronger than I look."

Jerzy nodded. "That she is. Until we manage to find a walking stick that will work for you, lean on her. Helena, if it gets to be too much, let me know."

"I will. We need you leading."

Before we resumed our trek, I passed out more bread to the prisoners. Jerzy and I refrained from taking food from them. We had started this journey strong and healthy.

As soon as Atanas was able to stand and walk, we were on our way again. As we moved in the forest, the canopy above provided some shelter from the rain. Here it was only damp, not soaking.

At least Teena was safe at home with Mama, dry underneath our roof. Jerzy had needed my help, and I willingly gave it, but my heart ached with missing my daughter. So far, God had not seen fit to bless us with a child, but Teena was a solace. A joy.

Risa would be proud of her little girl, at how bright she was, how cheerful and loving. Though she was growing and getting heavier, she still loved for anyone to pick her up, sit her on their lap, and tell her a story.

Already I had been gone for much longer than I had ever left her. It would take us double the time to return home, if not more, with these feeble men.

For a while during our trek, I played movies in my head about the first thing I would do when I got home. I would scoop up Teena and kiss her all over her little face. Tell her how beautiful she was and how her mama loved her so much.

Teena wouldn't know that I spoke both of myself and Risa.

At last the sun pinked the sky, and Jerzy called a halt to our march. I passed out breakfast, but even though we had planned on rescuing more prisoners, our store was already running low. At least it was summer, and we might be able to find food by foraging.

The men gathered piles of leaves, curled up in them even though they were damp and the mosquitoes swarmed them, and soon they were snoring. Jerzy made up the same makeshift bed for me. "Sleep for a while. I'll keep watch."

But I wasn't ready to rest. Instead, I drew him close. Lines radiated from his green eyes, and his beard was thickening. I smoothed his hair away from his forehead. "You are exhausted. Can't we all sleep? We must be safe here."

He sighed, confirming my worst fears. "I don't know how the Germans do it. Maybe it is not as bad in the other occupied countries as it is here, but somehow they have men crawling everywhere, like ants over a picnic. We thought we would be safe in Dubne, but Nazi boots didn't spare even that isolated hamlet."

"I know. And yet I can't wait to return there. At least we will be together again."

"This separation from Teena has been difficult on you. I shouldn't have taken you from her."

"What is done is done. It's too late to rehash that. I'm glad I came. I understand you and what you endured better. And it makes me want to fight harder to rid these monsters from our land."

"Have you changed your mind about going to Kraków?"

Had she? Once she had left Dubne in search of a better life. But it had been lonely, and nothing there matched her beloved hills. "Maybe. I don't know. We have the means to forge travel papers, but... I only wish there was a place for me to teach closer to home."

"I know."

"And Mama. How could I take Teena from her? They are so close and love each other so much. If Mama refuses to move, then I can't leave."

"You're a wonderful mama to Teena. I've watched your love for her grow."

"And I've watched yours. You're a terrific father."

He bent down and kissed me. "We'll stay home then, with our daughter and your mother if she won't leave. Our little family."

"If so, will you continue your work with the partisans?"

"Would you have me do any less?"

I had no answer. All I wanted was for him to stay beside me, but he wouldn't be the man I had come to love if he did that. I kissed him then stepped from our embrace. "I'm going to get some sleep. Make sure not to tire yourself too much."

Our entire group slept until almost dark then set off once more. Two days passed, and we drove deeper into Lemkovyna. One by one, the men broke off to travel to their villages, until only Jerzy and I were left.

Up ahead was the much larger town of Tylicz, spread across a couple of rolling hills. Even though the walk was only a few hours more from here to Dubne, we needed to stop and get something to eat. Our supplies had run out long ago, and my stomach wouldn't stop rumbling. My body trembled from fatigue and hunger. Without sustenance, I would never make it home.

Another day was breaking over Lemkovyna. As soon as we filled our bellies, we would return to the relative safety of the woods. By this time tomorrow, we would be in Dubne. Reunited with our beautiful daughter.

"Over there are a few houses." Jerzy pointed to the slope-roofed dwellings not so different from those in Dubne. "Perhaps one of the women will sell us some bread."

"That would be wonderful." Once again, my stomach growled in agreement, and we both chuckled. "I'm glad we saved those few złoty."

"This will be just enough to get us home. If I know your mama, she'll pull up all the potatoes and cabbages she can and fix us a feast."

"Stop. You're making me even hungrier."

Then, out of nowhere, a German dressed in a gray-green uniform, a metal helmet on his head and round glasses perched on his nose, appeared in front of us.

My knees went soft, but I managed to stay upright. The one time we let our guard down, and we came face-to-face with the enemy.

"Identification and travel papers. Now."

CHAPTER TWENTY-TWO

A steely-eyed Nazi soldier stood in front of me. I couldn't move. Couldn't breathe. Beside me, Jerzy stiffened.

"I said I need to see your papers now. Right now."

Jerzy didn't reach for them. He too must have been in a state of shock.

The soldier struck him on the side of his head with his rifle butt. Blood flowed from the wound and stained Jerzy's beard red.

How dare they do such a thing to my husband? To treat him in such a manner. Heat flared in my chest, my legs thawed, and I positioned myself between the Nazi and Jerzy. "We will get our papers." I spun and faced my husband, speaking in Rusyn to ensure that the soldier couldn't understand. "Are you hurt? Look at what those brutes did to you. Come on, you have to at least give him our identity papers."

"German. Polish is forbidden." The Nazi shoved me out of the way, and I stumbled backward, scraping my palms on the ground as I caught myself. "Speak German."

Only because of my schooling did I understand what he said. Any other Lemko wouldn't know the language. But I refused to reveal that information to the soldier. Instead, I pretended like I understood only the basics. "Identity papers. *Ja.*"

As I stood and wiped my bloody hands on my very dirty pants, I spoke again to Jerzy. "We have to give him something."

My soft words resulted in another shove to the ground, this time with the soldier pinning me to the cobbled road with his boot.

"Jerzy." I filled my voice with as much pleading as I could. He had to take action or this Nazi would hurt us. Maybe even kill us.

At last he broke out of his daze and knelt beside me. "They've hurt you."

"I'm fine." My hands stung and pain radiated from my tailbone, but I would save that information for later. There was no need to upset him.

"Look what you did to my wife." Jerzy came to his feet and stood nose to nose with the soldier. Actually, a little more like nose to forehead, since Jerzy was taller and broader than the skinny but muscle-bound man.

"You will hand over your papers."

Jerzy complied by retrieving our identity papers from the rucksack he carried.

I rose and scanned the area for an escape path. But in the few minutes we had been here, our situation had attracted a crowd, and there was nowhere for us to go. If we ran, the people, if they didn't stop us, would at least slow our getaway.

From the corner of my eye, I spied Jerzy glancing around. His shoulders slumped as he must have come to the same conclusion as me. Our situation was grim.

Hopeless.

The soldier studied the papers, nodding his head a time or two. My mouth was dry. Maybe he would allow us to go after all. Perhaps he didn't know that Dubne wasn't near here. I prayed that he didn't.

"Travel documents."

Nie, nie. The two words I begged God he wouldn't say. But he did.

Jerzy shrugged his shoulders as if he didn't know what the soldier was talking about. That earned him another blow to his head.

"*Halt!* Halt!" I screamed at the Nazi.

"Then give me your travel papers. You are not from around here. I know you understand me. Now show them to me. If you don't have them, then I have no choice but to take you in."

"*Nein!*"

The soldier nodded and grinned. "I knew you were playing dumb. Intelligentsia, are you? I should have known."

Both of us remained as mute as rocks. I trembled from head to toe and bit the inside of my cheek to hold my tears at bay. What was going to happen to us? Why had I ever left Teena? That was the most irresponsible, foolish thing—

"All right. Come with me. Let's go." He shoved us in the direction of a truck with several young people already sitting in the canvas-covered bed. Such was our fate.

Jerzy climbed aboard first then lifted me inside. This had to be a bad dream. Any moment I would wake up in my bed in Dubne beside my husband, Mama and my daughter across the room.

"Where are we going?" Jerzy spoke in German. There was no longer any reason to hide that we were intelligentsia. "Where are you taking us?"

"The Fuhrer requires your presence in Germany to work in his factories and to build the Third Reich to further glory."

Germany. "Nein! Nein! You cannot take us there. I have a baby at home who needs me. Please, don't do such a thing. Think of your own family."

"Think of yours before you wander around the countryside without proper permission. And if your child is Aryan enough, perhaps that child will be of some use to us."

I clamped my mouth shut. What had I said? I should never have mentioned Teena. The soldier had seen our papers and knew our names and where we lived. It would take very little work to discover Mama and Teena.

Jerzy wrapped me in a side hug, drawing me to himself. Oh, how I relied on him and needed him now more than ever. Without him I would collapse and never rise.

"I just told them about Teena."

"I doubt they want a toddler and an old woman. What they need are able bodies to perform the hard labor that their soldiers would otherwise be doing. With the invasion of the Soviet Union, they are stretched thin. Besides, she is not Aryan enough for them."

That was true. "They can't take me away from her. Not from her or Mama. They depend on us. Without us, they won't survive."

Jerzy tucked a stray strand of my hair behind my ear, one that had come loose from the scarf on my head. "Don't fret about them. We will pray to the Holy Father and ask for protection for all of us. Don't worry. This won't last for long."

What did he mean? The war or this separation or both? But instead of asking for clarification, I peered through the opening at the end of the truck bed, into the soft morning light brightening the mountains that I so loved.

The sun's rays bathed the trees and colored them pink and pale orange. Lemkovyna, my beloved homeland. How long would I be away from it and from those I loved? I would never be able to bear this.

To me, this was worse than death.

I had lived away from Lemkovyna while in Kraków, but my homeland was close. Whenever I wished, I could return.

That was not the case now.

The truck's engine rumbled to life, its gears ground, and the mountains outside the truck grew smaller as the kilometers slipped away.

I turned to Jerzy. "You worked for the Germans and were their prisoner once before. What was it like?" I had to prepare myself for what lay ahead. For whatever fate awaited me.

Everyone in the truck—the strapping young man with a scar down his cheek, the three adolescent sisters with matching black scarves on their heads who clung to each other, the man who sat with his hands clenched and the muscle in his jaw jumping—all turned their attention to Jerzy.

His eyes glazed over, and a shutter came halfway over them. Tak, he often cried out during the night and woke drenched in sweat but never told me about the nightmares. "To survive, you will have to be strong. While I'm not Lemko, my wife is, and I've lived among you for several years now.

"In your blood is the will to survive. Draw on that, and it will see you through many hardships. Trust in almighty God to watch over you."

"Bah." The angry young man spat out the word. "Is this His idea of watching over us? He does no better than us. It's His fault I walked into their snare."

The truck bumped over some rocks or something, jostling all of us. Jerzy held on to me. "Like those bumps, there will be times when life will be rocky and difficult. But don't allow them to break you. Never allow them to break you."

Talk resumed among the other occupants, but as the vehicle sped farther and farther from Teena and Mama, Jerzy stared straight ahead.

"Will they allow us to remain together?"

He stroked my cheek, a gesture of his that always relaxed me. This time a shiver ran down my arms. "I don't know, my love."

"Tell me the truth. I need to know what lies ahead."

We must have traveled half a kilometer before he answered. "Nie. They will separate us. And when they take you from me, I need you to be strong. Never allow them to see how this is tearing you apart. That will give them control, which is what they want the most."

"I promise to be strong. At least I will try." But it wouldn't be easy.

All too soon, the truck braked to a screeching stop in front of a nondescript building, the top two floors beige stucco, the bottom level covered in stone.

The soldier was there, and several others exited the building, all with weapons in their hands, coming against unarmed young people. "Out, out, let's go."

I clung to Jerzy as we slid to the ground, crushing his fingers in my grip, as if that might glue us together in a bond our captors wouldn't break.

"Move, move." One of the tallest ones jabbed Jerzy with his rifle butt.

With all of my strength, I held my husband upright, and together we entered the building.

The soldier stood in front of us and rocked back and forth. "You have been chosen to go to the Fatherland to work. Don't worry, because life there will be good. We will pay you and give you good housing and plenty of food. Life will be better."

Jerzy squeezed my hand tighter. He knew the truth, and now so did we all.

The Germans, always so meticulous with their paperwork, documented each of the dozen of us then handed our papers back.

After that began the long nightmare. Already my head swam from lack of sleep and food and from fear and worry. But the Nazis marched us the short distance to the station, and as soon as the freight train pulled in, one of the guards jumped off, flung open a door, and, at gunpoint, ordered us inside the already crowded car.

The stink inside was a thousand times worse than at the Jasło prison. My stomach churned, and I fought back the bile rising in my throat.

"Cover your nose with your scarf. Perhaps that will help." Jerzy, always there. Always dependable. I breathed through the fabric and pushed away the horrible thoughts of our inevitable separation.

For days we traveled westward, more and more kilometers between us and Mama and Teena. Between where we should have been. How divided was my heart, between being there with Jerzy and longing to be home.

At times he comforted me, and at times I comforted him. That was what marriage was supposed to be.

One night he whispered to me in the darkness as the others around us slept. "I am so frightened. I told the others to be strong and to rely on their faith, but mine is as small as a mustard seed."

"I am scared too. We know conditions won't be like they are telling us. This train is testament to that. How will we survive? Yet we must. When I want to give up, which is almost every minute of every day, I think of Teena and of Mama and how they need us. Somehow we must find a way back to them."

"My main concern is you. You were already weak then they arrested us."

Every day or so, when the train stopped, the guards allowed us out to stretch our legs and passed us some dry brown bread. Most of it crumbled before I even got it to my lips. Jerzy and I were both dizzy and weak. Each stretch period, we stumbled more often before gaining our footing.

"The next time the train stops and they let us out, several of us are going to try to get some more food. Even a bit of grain from the field. Anything at all."

What was he thinking? Being treated like a dog must be affecting his reasoning. Driving him mad. "You are talking crazy." I shook my head, just a little at first then with more vigor. "That is forbidden. If the Nazis catch you, they will beat you or kill you. I need you. Stay inside. Don't risk your life for a bit of grain. I'm begging you. Proshu, proshu, stay with me."

"Everything will be fine. You can't go any longer on the rations they feed us. Or don't feed us. You have to remain strong for Teena."

"Proshu, Jerzy, nie. We will trust the Holy Father. Isn't that what you always say?"

"His provision is right outside the doors." Jerzy's voice was firm and strong. Never had I heard him so determined. For hours I pleaded with him, but like a mountain, he would not be moved.

And just a short time later, the train halted and the guards slid the doors open. As before, they allowed us to disembark and stretch our legs, but always under heavy surveillance.

Though I clung with all my might to Jerzy's hand, he tugged from my grasp. When the guard turned his back for a moment, he sprinted away. Several others did as well.

Then gunshots rang out.

CHAPTER TWENTY-THREE

A whole century will pass,
We will grow,
Our enemies will perish,
We will remain here.

Because this is our Rusyn land
It is our fatherland,
It is our inheritance,
It is the cradle of Holy Rus'.

~From "Song of Lemkovyna"

Wednesday, October 4, 2023
Kraków, Poland

McKenna fiddled with the handle of her teacup as she stared at the older woman sitting across from her. "My great-grandmother disappeared?"

"*Tak.* Just like that, at the beginning of the war. She worked hard and maybe late, so sometimes it would be a while before we saw her, but this had been a long time. Too long. Mama didn't say anything about it, but when I asked where *Panna* Kostyszak was because I missed my sweets, she changed the subject."

"Did you ever find out where she went?" McKenna leaned across the wobbly table, willing the woman to give her an answer. A clue, at the very least.

"We never did."

McKenna sat back, deflated.

"One day the owner of the building came and said that your great-grandmother hadn't paid her rent for the month. That's when we realized she'd had to disappear. Or had been taken. You never knew in those days. I knew she taught school, and many teachers vanished at that time."

"Taken?"

"Oh, it was awful. People like my uncle, young and strong, were snatched by the Nazis every day and sent to labor camps. You were afraid to be on the street because you never knew when a soldier might grab you and put you in a truck. That I do remember because I was a little older then."

"That's terrible. I never knew."

"Americans and many others think it was only the Jews who were forced away. And it was horrible what happened to them. But we Poles suffered as well. Papa used to smile so much, but the war changed him into a grim man.

"Anyway, the owner said your great-grandmother had taken some of her things with her. Not much, but the necessities. We did notice, when he let us in the flat, that pictures were missing from her dresser and so were her clothes, her bedding, some of her pots and pans."

"That makes sense."

"I'm ashamed to say, but we took some things from her place. Pots and pans that she left, a few dishes, a blanket."

"Don't feel guilty. I think she would have been happy to know that her things were being put to good use. Her daughter, my grandmother, is not a wasteful woman. She uses every bit of everything."

"Poverty and war will make you like that. And I guess it gets passed through the generations. I am sorry I can't tell you more." The older woman patted McKenna's hand in a motherly gesture.

McKenna shook her head. "There is nothing to be sorry about. You gave me more information than I ever had about her and her life." She drained the last of her tea and went to the kitchen sink to wash it.

"Oh no, dear. Just leave it." The older woman's chair scraped the battered wood floors. "I have all day with nothing much to do except wash a few teacups."

"It's not a problem at all." But it was, because she had no idea where the soap was.

"Before you go, though, I have something for you. Wait here, and I will be right back." The woman shuffled away.

McKenna glanced at Taylor, who stood beside her, both of their backs to the sink. "Wonder what it could be."

"Maybe something your great-grandmother wasn't able to take with her."

"Wouldn't that be something." McKenna's heart rate kicked up a notch.

She surveyed the small kitchen with its three-person table tucked against the wall across from them. Above the table hung a picture of the Virgin Mary with the infant Jesus. Though the room showed signs of age in the golden-yellow wallpaper and the matching counter, it was as clean as a hospital.

Everywhere in this country was that clean. Perhaps that was where Mom got her neatness obsession from. McKenna had inherited that gene as well.

The small electric clock beside the picture ticked away the minutes until Pani Piotrowska returned with a package wrapped in tissue paper. "It first sat in my mother's drawer. When she passed away, I got it and have had it in my drawer ever since." She handed it to McKenna.

"What is it?"

"Open it, and you will find out."

She unwound the paper, careful not to tear it. Inside was a book with a black cardboard cover. On it was some kind of impression, but it had been so well used, it was impossible to make out anymore.

The cover was no longer attached to the book, so she set that aside and came to the front page. The letters were Cyrillic in style. Written across the top was АНГЕЛЪ ГОСПОДЕНЬ. There were plenty of other words, all in what she assumed to be Cyrillic, none of which she could read. There was a date. 1909.

The illuminations around the edge of the page were of two angels standing on what appeared to be mums. She squinted a little to make out the faint pictures. Above the angels were several other cherubs, and above them all was what must have been a dove. In the upper left-hand corner was maybe a chalice, and in the upper right were the stone tablets of the Ten Commandments.

All in all, it was beautiful. McKenna looked up at Pani Piotrowska. "Do you know what it says?"

"I have no idea. I can't read that kind of writing. It must be Russian, that's all I can figure."

McKenna would have to ask Filip. Perhaps he would know.

"What I do want you to see is on the inside of the cover."

McKenna picked that up again and turned it over. There was handwriting. Faint, but handwriting. *Helena Kostyszak. Dubne, 1930.* Whatever this book was, it had definitely belonged to her great-grandmother. With a feather touch, she wisped her fingers over the words.

Helena had held this. Had written inside of it. Had used it so much it was falling apart. A lump settled in McKenna's throat. "Dziękuję. I can never thank you enough for taking such good care of it all these years."

A tear trickled down the woman's wrinkled face. "I never would have thought that her great-granddaughter would show up on my doorstep all these years later to claim it, though every time I see it in my drawer, I say a prayer for that person. For you."

Now McKenna's own tears flowed. "Thank you a thousand times over." She swiped away the moisture and swallowed hard to regain her composure. "Would you mind if we took a picture together?"

"Of course, we must. And I will give you my phone too, and you can take a picture for me as well."

So they stood together in that little time-warped kitchen, McKenna towering over the slight old woman and holding the book. Taylor snapped a few pictures with McKenna's phone and then a few with Pani Piotrowska's.

"We should go and let you be. But we're staying just down the street, and so I will come visit you again."

"That would be wonderful. You are welcome anytime. If you need anything, let me know. You are special to me because your great-grandmother was so kind to us. She was a very good woman." Pani Piotrowska pulled McKenna to her level and kissed her three times on the cheeks. "Until we meet again."

"Yes. Until then."

A few moments later, after they'd exchanged contact information with Pani Piotrowska, McKenna and Taylor were outside of the building, standing on the sidewalk as the tram rumbled past.

"Wow." Tay's eyes were huge.

"I know, right? Just wow. Whoever thought when we went in there that I would come away with a piece of my great-grandmother. Even if I never find out anything else, today was amazing. This book will stay in our family from now on."

"What a wonderful keepsake. I don't have anything like that from my family."

"Somehow I have to figure out what it says."

"And we have to get Pani Piotrowska some of that chocolate."

"For sure. But I'm never going to remember what kind it was because I have no idea what she said."

"Then it'll be a great challenge to try to find the right thing. Maybe it'll take us a couple of tries."

Since neither of them were very hungry, they grabbed some snacks from the corner store. While there, they checked out the supply of chocolate. There was Ptasie Mleczko, Krowka, Michaszki, and Mieszanka Wedlowska.

McKenna studied all the options. "I know it was two words long."

"Well, that's something. It brings us down to two."

McKenna tapped her chin and went back and forth between them, one in black and blue wrapping and the other in colorful packaging with bright birds on it. "I just don't think I'm going to be able to know for sure."

"Then let's get both." Tay's voice was bright, as she was a true chocolate connoisseur. "And some for ourselves to try."

They returned to the hotel, chocolates in hand. With a great deal of internet searching, McKenna managed to get a Cyrillic keyboard to use on her computer then worked to type the words from the book into the translation program.

The first part, according to the program, said "Angel of the Lord" in Bulgarian.

"Bulgarian?" McKenna raised her eyebrows. "What in the world?"

"But it does make sense because of all the angels drawn on the side."

"Okay. I guess you're right."

The next part read "Prayer Book" in Russian.

"Now it's Russian? What's going on?"

Taylor shrugged. "No idea." She handed McKenna a piece of chocolate, the one from the bird package.

It was a small piece but thick and rectangular. And marshmallowy good. McKenna savored every bit before getting back to work.

Next up was "For children. Blessing Kurt Tulia." This was supposedly Ukrainian. Then in Russian was "Yell. Mook."

"That makes zero sense."

By this point, Taylor was laughing. "The program just can't make up its mind what language this is supposed to be. Keep going. I can't wait to see what's next."

There was only one word left, and it translated to "Hungary" in Mongolian.

They both lay back on McKenna's bed and giggled. "Mongolian. That's not even anywhere near here."

In between laughs, Taylor drew in several deep breaths. "It has to be some other language. One that's kind of a mixture of all of those."

"But Mongolian?"

"I have no idea. I didn't think they even used Cyrillic. Guess I was wrong. But if it is a prayer book, that's really neat." She handed McKenna one of the small packages of Mieszanka Wedlowska.

McKenna unwrapped it and popped it into her mouth. Absolutely delicious. She never would have pegged the Polish for making good chocolate, but they sure did.

"Even if it's a book on how to wash clothes, I still think it's cool to have. Dad would say that God works in mysterious ways. Imagine Him bringing us to the right house, and imagine that the woman who came out of the building at just the right time was there in the 1930s and remembered my great-grandmother."

"That's wild. We've only been here a short time, and already you have a great story to tell."

McKenna sat up and picked up the book again. She opened to the signature inside the cover. *Helena Kostyszak. Dubne, 1930.* "Look at this, Tay. It's proof of what we suspected. Helena was born in Dubne. Or at least lived there in 1930. You know, I never searched for that town."

In no time, Taylor was on the internet and sucked in a breath. "Ken, you have to see this." She passed McKenna her phone.

There was a shot of the most beautiful wooden church she'd ever seen, set against a backdrop of green hills. "It's gorgeous."

"That's in Dubne, which is a very small town. See, look at this drone view of the village." Tay took the phone back, found the page, and handed it to McKenna.

Only a few homes sat huddled together in a valley, surrounded by trees and large hills. Maybe even small mountains. Beautiful but remote.

A thought struck her. "If we go there, perhaps we'll be able to locate Baba's missing sister."

CHAPTER TWENTY-FOUR

Filip gave a wide grin as both Taylor and McKenna entered his office the following morning. "It is good to see you."

"Do we look better than when we got off the plane?" Two solid nights of sleep had pretty much erased McKenna's jet lag.

"That is not a fair question to ask a man. No matter which way I answer, it will be wrong." He chuckled.

"You're right. My apologies. We feel better, at least."

"That is good. Now you say you found some information yesterday. You are a very good detective. Maybe I should hire you to work with me."

The thought of not having to go home and face Yasmine and Belinda's family and not having to jump back onto the hamster wheel that was her job was tempting. "I do have my life and my career."

"I understand. Now tell me what you discovered. I am very interested."

McKenna went over the events of the previous day. So much happened in a short stretch of hours, it was hard to believe. Then she pulled out the prayer book. At least that was what she believed it to be. "Pani Piotrowska gave me this. I'm not sure about my translation, but I think it's a prayer book. And it has my great-grandmother's name in it."

She took a deep breath and handed it to Filip. He was gentle with it and lifted off the cover. "She's been keeping it all this time?"

"In her dresser drawer, praying that one of Helena's descendants or family members would come. I can't believe she did that."

"Pretty amazing, I would agree." He studied the book for several minutes, handling it with a great deal of care.

"So what do you think?"

"The illustrations do make me think it could be a prayer book, though I don't know Cyrillic, so it is difficult to say. But what is interesting me the most is this name. Dubne. Though it is a very small village, I have heard of it. And if that is where she was born, she is definitely Lemko."

"And do you think she was born there?"

"Those records would be on file with the local church. Let me do some searching and see what I can come up with using the information you gave me. Knowing where she was born will help."

"That's great. Is there anything I can do in the meantime?"

"Hang on. Let me make a phone call." He pulled out his cell, dialed a number, and spoke to whoever was on the other end in Polish. After a conversation of several minutes, he hung up. "That was a friend of mine. He is more familiar with the Lemko language. I will give you the address, and you can take the book to him."

"That's wonderful. Thank you so much, Filip. You're a man with many connections."

"That is my job. I would be no good without them." He gave McKenna the address and showed her how to purchase tram tickets on her phone and how to validate them once on board.

She and Taylor left the building and headed in the direction of the tram stop. "Another adventure for us." Tay kept up such a brisk pace that McKenna was huffing and puffing to stay in step with her.

"Slow down."

"We're going to miss the tram."

"There's another one a few minutes later if we do. We're in no rush."

Tay slowed a little. "Sorry. I guess I'm excited."

"It is thrilling to be making headway on my family's history. I can't wait to see what Filip locates in the records."

"Next trip is going to be to England to research my family. Hopefully I can dig up something half as interesting as yours."

"You have no idea if mine is the least bit interesting. We could be as boring as plain milk."

"Somehow I don't think that's going to be the case."

They crossed the road, the traffic stopping for them as the new law there required, but just missed the tram. Good thing, because it gave McKenna a chance to catch her breath. They stood beside the shelter, waiting for the next one, when her phone rang.

Chris. What on earth could he want? "It's Chris."

"Don't answer it."

But Taylor's warning came too late. McKenna had already pressed the green button. "Chris?" She had to shout as another tram—not the one they were waiting for—rumbled by.

"Thanks for answering."

"How in the world did you know how to contact me?"

"I saw from Instagram you were in Poland, so I figured I had to use WhatsApp. I took a chance."

"What's going on? And it had better be an emergency."

"Do you have a few minutes to talk?"

She stared into the clear blue sky. Everything in her screamed for her to end the call immediately. "Fine." She motioned to Taylor that she was going to step toward Planty Park just behind them.

She got away from the noise of the main street and sat on a bench shaded by tall trees. "Okay, I'm in a quieter spot, so I can hear you better. What is it?"

"I need my ring back."

McKenna gave a sarcastic half laugh. "I don't get you at all. You came to my house, demanded the ring, so I gave it to you. Funny thing, though. You never took it. What was that all about?"

"I never asked for it. I told you there was only one thing I wanted. You assumed what that was."

"Then what could it be?"

"It doesn't matter. Those circumstances have changed. Right now I need my ring."

"You had your chance."

"You don't want me to sue you."

McKenna's heart seized for a second. "You wouldn't."

"Let's settle this before it comes to that." Chris' voice was as cool as an ice rink.

"You had your chance to take it. I don't understand why you left it on the floor like you did."

"That was then. This is now."

"I can't get it for you at the moment."

"Is there a way for your mom to let me in your town house?"

"There is no way you're going to step foot in my house. Or contact my family. I will let you know when I get home—it may be a while—and then we can meet at a neutral site for me to give it to you." A couple walking past stared at her. Right, almost everyone in this country spoke quite good English, she was finding out.

"Thanks, baby. You were always a peach. Never change." Chris ended the call.

A peach? Really? That's what he thought of her? Heat rose in her chest and was probably steaming out of her ears. Why, then, did her throat burn? Nuts. She was going to cry in the middle of a public park in the middle of a foreign country.

She channeled her anger again. If only he would have taken the ring that day, she could be done with him. She should have run after him and forced him to leave with it.

A minute later she returned to the tram stop. Taylor narrowed her eyes and frowned at her.

"What?"

"Why on earth would you take a call from him? Do you know how many trams we've missed?"

"We'll catch the next one. I can't run away from the past forever. At some point, I'm going to have to confront it head on. Because my great-grandmother never spoke about hers, it seems to me that she never faced it. But I will."

"So what did Prince Not-So-Charming have to say?"

"He wants his ring back."

"The one he didn't take from you the other week?"

"That exact one."

"I hope you shut him down cold."

Thankfully, their tram pulled up at that precise moment and left them busy trying to figure out how to validate their tickets on their phones. They finally settled in their seats and headed toward Filip's friend's place.

"Don't think you can get away without answering that question."

"Which one?"

The glare that Taylor shot her could have leveled an entire army.

"I told him I would give it back once I'm home."

Tay gasped. "If we weren't in public, I'd whack you upside the head. He doesn't deserve it."

"I just want to be done with him. To never have to think about him again. What if he took me to court over it? I don't really want it anyway."

"I get that. But as long as I'm with you, you're not to take another call or text from him. Even when I'm not beside you, you aren't. Am I clear?"

"Yes, Mother."

Taylor crossed her arms and leaned back in her seat. Guess it was a good thing there were witnesses.

Only a few minutes later, they arrived at their stop. With Tay's phone to help them navigate, they soon arrived at Andrzej's place. Filip said he worked from home and didn't mind being disturbed, especially since it was the lunch hour.

He answered the door, his dark-brown hair reaching to his shoulders and his beard rather scraggly. But he shook their hands, and there was a slight sparkle in his blue eyes. "Welcome. Come in. Filip told me to expect you."

McKenna gave him a smile. "Thank you for seeing us. We appreciate it, especially on short notice."

"That is no problem. I need a break from work. Let me pour the tea, and then you can show me what you have brought."

Five minutes later they were seated on a white couch in a rather stylish apartment with white walls, beautiful old molding painted black, and a white tin ceiling painted black in the middle.

"So tell me about your family. My great-great-grandfather was Lemko, so I know the history. I have always been fascinated by it. So hard their lives were."

"My great-grandmother, from what we can tell, was born in Dubne. Before the war, she worked at Jagiellonian University, where she was a lecturer."

"That's unusual for your great-grandmother to teach there. First of all, it was almost unheard of for Lemkos to be educated past their third year. Second of all, she was a woman. When was she there?"

"In the late 1930s."

"Oh my. Really? That is extraordinary. Let me look up something." He went to his computer that was set up on a very neat, contemporary glass desk and did some searching. "What was her name?"

She told him.

"Did you know that she married Jerzy Bielski? He spent time in a concentration camp at the beginning of the war, and they were both taken to a work camp in 1943."

"What?" Helena had been married before her great-grandfather? What happened to her first husband? And a labor camp. Wow.

Whatever she had survived, it must have been horrific. No wonder she never spoke about the past.

CHAPTER TWENTY-FIVE

Cursed be the moment
When the strong enemy came from hell
And brutally deported us,
Our happiness came to an end.

It was difficult to depart,
To bid farewell to you,
For you are our loving mother.
Pain, sorrow, crying out.
To seek our fate out in the world,
Crying out bitterly often.

~FROM "SONG OF LEMKOVYNA"

Tuesday, August 10, 1943
Somewhere between Poland and Germany

After the gunshots, the world fell silent. Everyone from the train hushed, even the wailing infant. The German shepherds that had been barking and snarling shut their mouths.

The world held its breath. I bit the side of my hand to prevent the cry that was strangled in my throat.

Whatever lay ahead, I wouldn't be able to face this ordeal without Jerzy. I wouldn't be able to face life without him. He'd become my heartbeat. My soul.

Exhaling and inhaling another deep breath, I allowed my gaze to wander the field. Four bodies lay on the ground.

One of them was Jerzy's.

Now the scream burst from my lips. "Nie! Nie! Jerzy, nie!"

Someone pulled me toward the train. Though I wriggled and fought to break free, they held me firm. "My husband! They've shot my husband! I have to go to him."

"If you do, they will shoot you too." The voice was deep but firm.

"I don't care. Let them. They've taken my life with his."

"Nie, they haven't. Don't let those pigs win. Don't give them the satisfaction of shooting you too."

I slumped against the man who held me tight, and then the hot, bitter tears came. Like a ceaseless river, they flowed. There weren't enough to express my sorrow. In the space of days, I lost my husband, my daughter, my home.

Everything I held dear, the Germans ripped from me.

They had left me destitute and alone. Utterly alone.

The black-clad soldiers herded us back into the car and slammed the door shut, metal grating on metal. The lock clicked into place. Though fresh air had filtered in during the stop, as soon as the doors shut, the fierce odor rose again.

With a shudder, the train pulled out of the station. What about Jerzy? "My husband. We can't leave his body."

"What are you going to do? There is nothing. Pray for his soul. That is all that is left."

A hollowness, like none I had known before, filled me. Left me an empty shell of the woman I had been mere days before.

My irresponsible choices tore me from my daughter and even killed my husband. Though he begged me to go to the prison with him, I should have thought of a different solution, one that wouldn't have taken both of us from Teena. If I hadn't been along, he wouldn't have been worried about me. Wouldn't have left the train car to take care of me.

What a foolish, selfish woman I had been, only thinking about myself and how dissatisfied I was at home. I never should have asked to be included in the plans he and Ivan were making. If I hadn't known anything, he wouldn't have asked me to go. Maybe he would have even made it home without being arrested.

I was reaping the consequences of my choices. God had forsaken me and left me alone in the world. Because of my sin, He had stripped me of all in my life that was good.

The train chugged westward, toward Germany, away from Mama, Teena, and Jerzy. I couldn't allow myself to dwell on what would happen to his body. No proper burial for sure. No community coming to mourn together with me. No procession to lay him to rest in the cemetery.

If I thought too much about it, I might go insane.

Maybe I was already crazy. Perhaps this was nothing more than a delusion. That had to be it. "Tell me this isn't real. Proszę, tell me this isn't real."

But the man who held me upright didn't say the words.

"Then this is not my imagination."

"Nie. More than anything, I want to tell you this is a nightmare. In a way, I suppose it is. But it's a living nightmare."

A living nightmare. A living pit of blackness. No light. No peace. No joy. The Nazis had done it. They had left me broken.

For a couple more days, the train snaked through the countryside—or so I assumed—stopping every now and again to pick up more passengers bound for Hades. Otherwise, when we stopped now, they didn't open the doors, not even for a moment. Not to give us food or water or to empty the bucket that served as a toilet.

Not that I had any desire for food. If I wasted away, what difference would it make?

I gave myself a mental shake, banishing those thoughts to the furthest recesses of my mind. Teena and Mama were my priorities now. They had to be. For them, I had to stay alive. Some way or another, when this madness ended, I would return to them. Though I would be forever broken, unfixable, I wouldn't give in and die.

I had a daughter. Risa's precious gift. Whatever I had to do to get back to Teena, that was what I would do.

For Teena. Only for Teena.

The train chugged onward. With such little room to move, my legs cramped. I ran out of tears to weep. Inside and out, I was dry.

The train halted again, but this time was different. From down the line came the squeak of metal doors opening, the chatter of voices.

Then our door slid open, and sunshine filled the inside. I blinked against the sudden brightness.

"Out. Out. *Schnell.* Let's move."

I jumped from the train car to the gravel below, falling over and catching myself with my hands. Pain shot through them and up my arms, but I had no time to assess my injuries. The guards pushed us along the platform and lined us up, men on one side and women on the other.

If Jerzy had lived, this was where they would have separated us.

"Line up! Five deep! Arm's width either side and in front and behind. Move it! Move it!"

My head buzzing, I stumbled as I fell into position. For hours, as the hot sun beat on my head, I stood with the other women on the train platform. Guards with guns and growling dogs patrolled the group, up and down, up and down. Often civilians accompanied them. From what I caught of their conversations, they were checking out the women, determining our suitability to work in whatever industry they ran.

I pushed my black shawl from my head, welcoming that small relief from the heat. Sweat slithered down my back and the sides of my face. Oh, how lovely a bath would be. A place where I could have a good, long cry.

But it was not to be. Here and there, guards took groups of women to the side. I refused to ponder where they might be going. Instead, I stood, swaying from time to time, staring straight ahead.

At last my turn came. Two guards with similar large, brawny builds, one with a cleft chin, pulled about two dozen of us away from the larger group. Now the guards stood to the side, and the prospective so-called employers examined each woman.

These farmers and factory owners were determining if we were fit for the type of work required. Once they did, they bargained with the soldiers.

In other words, we were being sold as slaves.

A few women were pared from our group. The rest of us were taken to a waiting truck and once again piled in the back then whisked away from the train station and through the good-sized town.

After a short time, we came to the opposite side of this smaller city, then to a complex of buildings. They escorted us to a dormitory, very sterile except for the bars on the windows and the armed guards patrolling the grounds.

In a haze, I went about claiming a bunk toward the middle of the room and then reported for showering, delousing, and the sewing of a yellow diamond with a purple *P* in the middle onto my dress. All my clothes. Much as the white-and-blue armband had marked Risa as a Jew, this marked me as a Pole.

It took all my willpower not to shout that I was Lemko, not Polish. Little good that would do. I was Slavic, and that was all that mattered.

Then it was on to duty in what turned out to be a textile mill. Tiny bits of fibers floated on the air, lodged in my throat, and sent me into a coughing spasm. I wasn't the only one given to a fit of hacking. From the emaciated appearance of some of the women and their hollow coughs, it was clear they had been held prisoners for quite some time.

Is that what fate awaited me? A slow, sure demise? Perhaps Jerzy had been right to run from that train. His death was quick and, I prayed, painless.

Nie, for Teena's sake, I had no choice but to remain strong. I couldn't allow myself to get sick. No matter what, I had to survive so I could return to my mama and daughter.

More than ever, Teena needed me. The poor tyke had already lost one mother. She didn't need to lose another.

So as the foreman hustled us from one part of the factory to another, giving each job a brief overview then hurrying us to the next station, I paid as much attention to him as possible.

A beautiful young girl, still nothing but a child, her blond hair falling in curls around her shoulders, leaned over to me as we made our way to the next piece of machinery. "I am going to forget this."

What was a child doing in a place like this? "I'll listen for both of us."

"I'm scared I'm going to make a mistake."

"Quiet!" the round, red-faced overseer roared.

"Don't worry." I spoke in a whisper. "I will help you as much as I can."

"Dziękuję."

After the foreman introduced us to the carding machines, the spinning machines, and the weaving machines, among others, our overseer assigned us our tasks. Mine was to watch the winding machines to ensure the spindles didn't become stuck. If they did, I had to get them moving once more.

It was dangerous work to be sure. To avoid losing precious time that would slow the war effort, we couldn't shut down the machine. If I wasn't careful, I might lose a finger. Or a hand. Or worse, God forbid, if my clothing got caught in the spindles.

I drew on every ounce of memory to conjure up the foreman's instructions. One of the women at the spindles did her best to guide me. "Silence!" The dour-faced foreman cracked a whip across the woman's slender back.

How could he have even heard her above the clatter of the machines? I had a difficult time hearing myself think. I mouthed "sorry" to the woman who had been whipped then moved to the next stuck spindle.

Between the hours on the train, my overwhelming grief, and now hours upon hours on my feet, by the time the whistle blew to mark the end of the day, I was more than exhausted.

A frail, adolescent prisoner ladled thin soup into my tin cup, a single potato floating like an island in the middle of it. In addition, I received a slice of very dry brown bread that soaked up the soup like a sponge. To wash it down, I drank a cup of the bitterest coffee substitute known to man.

I choked it down, silently reciting my mantra. *For Teena. For Mama. For Teena. For Mama.*

While I ate, I examined the other women. Like me, they all wore yellow diamond patches with purple *P*s. The woman I now sat beside hadn't come with us, so I turned to her. "Are there only Poles here?"

The woman, thin lines ringing her mouth, gave a sardonic laugh. "Nie, but you won't see anyone else. They are afraid of our diseases."

"What diseases?" What infirmity was there that only affected Polish women?

"The disease of being Slavic. We are kept separate. In our own rooms, the Russians in theirs, the Ukrainians in theirs. Those here from Germany and Western Europe are treated much better. But we will never see them. I'm Gośka."

"Helena."

Gośka continued to talk as I finished my meal, if it could be called that, but I tuned out most of what she said.

When I returned to the dormitory room—really, barracks—I found my spot, curled up on the bunk, and sobbed.

I would never see Jerzy again or have him by my side. He wasn't here to comfort me or to give me strength. What would he be saying now? Likely reminding me of the promises of Scripture and telling me I needed to pray and stay strong.

I whispered into the darkness. "I'm trying, my love, I'm trying. But it is so hard without you. Surviving here may be impossible."

CHAPTER TWENTY-SIX

Sunday, February 13, 1944
Germany

I lay in my bed and stared at the bunk above me in the dormitory. Three levels from floor to ceiling. For almost six months now, I had stared at the same bunk.

Six months. Six months since Jerzy had died. Six months since I had last held Teena or kissed Mama's cheek. Long, exhausting, depressing months. Yet the hands on the clock moved and the pages on the calendar turned.

"Save, O Lord, and have mercy on my mama, my daughter, and my people according to Your blood; and from Thy mighty and merciful hand, grant them all Thy good things, both in this life and in the life to come."

Though I prayed this very inadequate supplication from the prayer book, the heavens remained silent. Perhaps there was no longer any point in lifting petitions to a God who had turned His back on His creation.

I studied my fingers, now red and raw in places and scarred and calloused in others. All from yarn. At least today was the Sabbath, a day off from making German military uniforms. A few hours of peace. The factory owner required that we participate in services. Though it wasn't the Greek Catholic faith my people had practiced for centuries, the Lutheran services were interesting. Similar in some ways, very different in others.

Lonia, the young blond girl from the day of our arrival, appeared at the edge of my vision. "Can I lay with you?" As she made the request, her voice was soft and timid, and she studied her shoes.

I scooted over. "Of course." It turned out that Lonia was only thirteen. No one could blame the girl for missing home. If the ache in my chest was as wide as the Baltic, the ache in Lonia's must be as wide as the Pacific.

"Do you know what today is?"

I stroked the girl's silky hair, widening the wound in my own heart. "What?"

"Today is my fourteenth birthday."

I raised myself on one elbow. "Fourteen? Why didn't you tell me earlier?"

"What difference would it have made? Could you have baked me a cake or bought me a gift?"

"You never know. You just never know."

"That's okay. I only want one thing. To go home. To see Mama and Papa and my sister again. I wonder if they miss me as much as I miss them."

"There is no doubt they do. Do you mind me asking again why you are here when you are so young?" To this point, she had resisted sharing her story.

A cloud misted her eyes. "Agata got her summons to appear for work in Germany. Mama and Papa were afraid to let her go. Thinking the Nazis would never take someone as young as me, they sent me instead.

"But the Germans didn't care. They just wanted someone to work here. When Mama figured out they were going to send me anyway, she stood at the school window where we were being kept and screamed and screamed. It did no good."

"Oh, how awful." That mother must be berating herself every day for sending this young child to work in Germany. I understood her pain. "Your mama feels terrible about all this and misses you every day. I miss my daughter, Teena, and I know where she is."

"Someday, after this awful war is over, I would like to meet your daughter."

"And I would very much like to meet your family as well." The war hadn't been going to plan for the Germans. Their push into the Soviet Union was halted and was now a full-out retreat. My German language skills came in handy, as I was able to glean quite a bit from listening to the foremen's conversations.

"Maybe I will be home for my next birthday."

"Maybe. Your family would be so happy." I held back the suspicion that her parents and sister might no longer be there when she returned.

"I am so thankful God sent you to me. It would have been awful to be alone this entire time."

"One of the other women would have looked after you. Maybe Gośka."

"Not the way you have."

"You take away some of my loneliness, so I'm thankful for you too."

We lay together for a while. Even though the factory wasn't running, we were still required to sweep the factory floor and clean our dormitory on Sunday afternoons. It was this brief two-hour break that was the only true rest we had all week.

After a while, Lonia stirred. "I have to go to the toilet. I'll be right back."

She had been gone for a while when a heart-freezing scream came from the direction of the water closet.

Lonia's scream. I recognized its high pitch from the nightmares she suffered on a regular basis. I jumped from the bunk, bumping my head on the bed above but ignoring the pain. In a flash, I raced down the hall to the restroom. All the time, Lonia's screams continued.

I tried the door, my hands sweaty, but it was locked. "Lonia? Lonia? What is happening?"

More screams were my only answer.

"Can you open the door?"

"Help me!" The end of the plea was cut off, muffled as if someone held their hand over Lonia's mouth.

I glanced up and down the hall. The gray-haired matron peeked out of her office but made no move to come to our assistance. "Help us! Proszę!"

A few of our fellow prisoners, all with purple *P*s sewn to their work overalls, congregated. "We have to help Lonia," I pleaded. But no one moved.

From inside the toilet came a deep male voice. The overseer. "Go away, or I'll strangle her to death. And whoever I find out there."

More muffled cries came from Lonia.

"Back up, everyone." I motioned them to stop pressing so close to the door.

They all did my bidding. With every bit of my might, I kicked the door. Again and again. When my foot throbbed and I was out of breath, another woman kicked. Then I took another turn. The overseer must have been using his considerable girth to block it.

The matron finally left her office and made her way down the hall, keys jingling at her side. "Go back to your rooms. If this is the behavior you display on Sundays, you'll soon have no more days off."

A few wandered away, but I was not about to go anywhere. I had promised to take care of Lonia. With one last great kick, I broke the door in and gained access to the restroom. Though I was small and weak compared to the overseer, adrenaline must have given me superhuman strength, and I pulled him away from her.

"Get this brute out of here." I swallowed the names I longed to call him.

Another prisoner, a much bigger and more vigorous new arrival, managed to hold on to our warden long enough for me to scoop Lonia up and hurry with her from the water closet to the bunk. With the gentleness of a bubble floating to the grass, I placed her in the bed and covered the shivering girl with the thin, gray wool blanket.

By this time, the dormitory was abuzz with what had happened. The women crowded around Lonia.

"Get back and give her some air. Leave the poor girl in peace after the ordeal she's been through."

"He did that to me too."

"And me."

"And me."

It was too much. "Leave. Proszę. I'm sorry for all of you, I truly am. But Lonia is an innocent child. You must remember how it felt when this happened to you. Don't make it worse for her."

One by one, the women dispersed. I crawled onto the bunk and touched Lonia's shoulder. She flinched, and so I backed away. I sang to her, a Lemko lullaby, slow and sad.

> *Oj, wersze, mij wersze,*
> *Mij zełenyj wersze,*
> *Już mi tak ne bude,*
> *Już mi tak ne bude,*
> *Jak mi było peruse.*
> *Już mi tak ne bude,*
> *Już mi tak ne bude,*
> *Jak mi było peruse.*
>
> *Oh, my mountains, my mountains*
> *My dear green mountains*

Life has changed for me,
Life has changed for me.

The somber, almost chant-like haunting tune was perfect for the mood that permeated the barracks. How life had changed for us, never to be the same. We would all bear scars, horrible, deep scars that would never be erased.

Especially not for a fragile fourteen-year-old girl. Just barely fourteen. I was older and tougher, seasoned by the hardships of life. Lonia was not. She was but a tender green sprout. Or she had been until that monster trampled her with his boot.

Young shoots treated such didn't often rise from the dirt.

Over and over again, I crooned the tune until Lonia's shaking eased and she fell into a fitful slumber. Then I stroked her hair, as fine as spun gold, easing the tight bands in my own chest. Never again would I allow Lonia to go anywhere on her own, not even the toilet.

Especially the toilet.

The matron entered the room, her jangling keys announcing her presence before she lumbered through the door. They swung back and forth on her ample hips.

I rose to cut her off before she got anywhere near Lonia. "You should take better care of your workers."

Frau Albrecht shrugged. "You should mind your own business."

"Lonia is my business. She is a child who shouldn't be here in the first place. Then for you to sit by and allow that man to do what he did to a child—a child—is disgraceful."

Frau Albrecht slapped me across the mouth with the back her hand, sending me stumbling, bumping my hip on the bunk. The metallic flavor of blood filled my mouth. "No more talking. If you favor having a tongue, I would hold it."

"I will not when it comes to the treatment of children. She shouldn't be in this place, alone and vulnerable."

This earned me another slap, this time across the other cheek. My eyes watered.

"I said that is enough. You will not be able to protect her if you are sent away. Or worse."

Frau Albrecht knew how and where to hit a nerve. I clamped my lips shut to avoid saying anything that might earn me a harsher punishment or exile to a concentration camp. That would do Lonia no good. Then she would have no one to watch over her, and it would only mean harsher treatment for her.

"I knew you were a smart woman." The matron moved in Lonia's direction, and I kept pace with her.

When she came to the sleeping child, she spat on her then spun on her heel, as much as a heavyset woman could, and marched from the room.

Humiliation upon humiliation. Would this ever end?

When it came time for the Sunday afternoon chores, I worked double time so Lonia didn't have to get up. Every swish of the broom across the floor became a silent prayer. One swish for Lonia. Another for Teena. Another for Mama.

What were they doing? Was Mama well enough to take care of Teena? A swish turned into a prayer for myself. For peace. For patience. For reunification.

What good the prayers did, I had no idea. But even if God refused to listen, refused to answer, they gave me some peace.

When Lonia woke later on and got up, I went with her to the restroom. I gave her my portion of the evening's limited rations, though the child barely got it down before it came back up. All through the night, she either thrashed or wept. Little by little, I eased into holding her. When she finally gave in, she clung to me, and I clung to her.

Two lone figures, fighting an endless, losing battle. Two Davids against a multitude of Goliaths. Just as God had the ultimate victory in that skirmish, it would only be by His intervention that we would prevail over our enemies.

The bell rang to wake us for the next day's labor. I spoke softly into Lonia's ear. "It's time to get up."

"Just leave me here to die."

"Nie, I refuse to do that. You are young and strong. What that man did to you was meant to break you and give him power over you. Do not allow him the satisfaction. Show him that no matter what he tries, you will stand tall."

"I am so scared."

"Don't worry. As I promised yesterday, I am never going to leave your side. You will get sick and tired of me because I'm going to be like sticky glue to you."

That brought a hint of a smile to the girl's face, though no light reached her eyes. "Do you promise?"

"Of course I do. When I say something, I mean it. And I will do whatever

I must to keep you safe and try to get you an easy job for today."

After the bitter ersatz coffee and dry slice of dark brown bread, we headed to the factory floor. The whizz of machines filled the air, and the dust floated in the early morning sunlight streaming through the filthy windows.

I headed to the foreman, above the overseer, an older gentleman with white hair and a white beard. Too old to fight on the front, so he got this position. "I would like Lonia to work beside me today. And from now on. There are those who wish to take advantage of her."

He gave a slight, single nod. It was enough for me. We had graduated from the spinning room to the weaving room. I took up my station at the machine and positioned Lonia to my right. Praise the Lord for that small favor.

But then the overseer from yesterday strolled through the room, grasping a riding crop that he tapped against his thigh.

The sight of him sent a shiver through me.

Lonia fainted.

CHAPTER TWENTY-SEVEN

Oh, you are a beauty, Lemkovyna,
Our country, you are priceless to us.
Even if one were to go over the whole world
From pole to pole,
One would never find such a place.
Lemkovyna is a foretaste of paradise.

Cloud-draped peaks, steep mountains
Projecting upward, unsupported,
Stretching skyward up so high,
Your eye can barely see them.

~From "Song of Lemkovyna"

Monday, October 9, 2023
South of Kraków, Poland

The scenery outside McKenna's car window changed from crowded ancient city to busy modern city to traditional suburbs to green, rolling farmland. As Filip drove on, away from the hustle and bustle of Kraków until the crowded buildings gave way to scattered houses, something moved in McKenna's heart.

In the back seat, Taylor exclaimed over every little sheep in the field or red-roofed house they passed. McKenna, however, stared at the scenery. The bonds around her heart that the broken engagement had placed there and Yasmine's death had tightened—all were starting to loosen.

"You are very quiet, McKenna." Filip kept his concentration on the road in front of them.

"Does that mean I'm talking too much?" Taylor chuckled. "You can just tell me, and I'll shut up."

"Well, now that you mention it. . ." Filip's guffaw had both him and Tay cracking up.

But for McKenna, their chatter faded into the background. This sensation, this strange tingling inexplicably mixed with peace, fell over her. So much of it reminded her of home, of the hills of western Pennsylvania.

They were on their way to the town where they believed her great-grandmother had been born. A tiny village tucked into a valley. Yet it was almost as if she had already arrived. If anyone asked her, she wouldn't be able to explain it. Instead, she allowed all of it to seep into her soul. To burrow its way deep inside of her and expand until it filled her.

Perhaps that was why the Lemko people were close to God. There was something magical about this place. Out here there was no denying there was a Deity in control.

"What is it you are thinking about?" Filip's question drew her from her reflections.

"How amazing this place is. The farther we go, the more I am drawn to it."

"Yes, there is a magic here. The Lemkos, in addition to being very religious, were also very superstitious. It helped them, I suppose, to explain what they could not understand. They were and are a simple people for the most part. But they know and love beauty when they see it."

The journey continued. At one point, Filip stopped for gas at a very American-like gas station with a convenience store. She and Tay used the restroom and got a few bottles of pop, and they were on their way again.

Not long after their stop, the landscape changed even more. The undulations were greater, as if someone was gathering ribbon together in folds. Not scary heights, but heights nonetheless. The homes sat farther and farther apart.

Every now and again they passed through a small village, the houses just far enough apart for each to breathe.

And then Filip pulled the car to the side of the road and stopped. She turned to him and frowned. "What is it?"

"Look."

He pointed at a small, light blue road sign. Dubne. Underneath was a line drawing of a tire with snow chains.

"We are here."

McKenna stared at the sign, her heart a flying trapeze in her chest. "This is it?"

"It is."

"But there's nothing here. How can we be in the town?"

"That story, I will tell you later. For now, enjoy that we have arrived."

"I am. I can't—I can't quite believe it." Despite the remoteness of this village, her cell signal was strong enough to snap a picture of the sign and text it to Mom.

"Are you ready?"

When she nodded, Filip pulled the car back onto the road. They rounded a curve, and within minutes the church she had seen in so many pictures online came into view.

It stole what little air she had remaining in her lungs. "It's gorgeous."

Set partway up the knoll, the weathered wooden church stood magnificent against the brilliant blue sky. Wood shingles covered the outside much like a Cape Cod style home. Three spires reached heavenward, stair-stepped in height. Atop each was a cross with three crosspieces, the bottom one, the shortest, at an angle.

Filip parked in the gravel drive that led to the church. "Go ahead and take a look."

"This is where my great-grandmother and my other ancestors would have worshiped?"

"Yes."

She and Tay stood near the car, and she took pictures from every angle she could. The day couldn't have been any more perfect to get an amazing shot, even though she was definitely not a photographer. The spires reminded her somewhat of the onion-shaped domes on St. Basil's Cathedral in Moscow.

"Would you like to see inside?"

"Very much so."

They traipsed over the soft green grass, through a gate in a short stone wall, and up the concrete stairs that must have been later additions to the church. But when Filip tried the door, it was locked.

McKenna's heart sank. "To come all this way and not be able to get in." She sighed.

"Don't worry. I will see if someone has a key. You wait here, and I will be right back."

About fifty yards from the church was a two-story, white stucco house with a red-tile roof and red geraniums blooming in every window box. Filip knocked on the door but didn't get an answer. He moved away to the single-story house beside it, but when he did, the lace curtains at the second-floor window of the first home parted.

He returned a few minutes later. "No luck, I'm afraid."

"Someone is home next door." Taylor pointed in that direction. If Mom were here, she would swat Tay's hand. "We saw the curtains move."

He went next door again, and this time someone answered his knock. They chatted for a moment, and the woman disappeared inside for a couple of minutes before reappearing and stepping outside.

Taylor clasped McKenna's hands. "This is good. Someone must have the key."

McKenna hardly dared to breathe. To be inside of the church where her grandmother had once worshiped, to see where she had been baptized, was going to be incredible.

Filip motioned them over. "This is Pani Adamski. She is actually the mayor of Dubne, and she has the keys."

The stout, middle-aged woman with short, curly gray hair smiled at them and unlocked the door. The vestibule was nondescript, but the sanctuary beyond was spectacular. Bright paintings and carved, gilded woodwork surrounded McKenna. For poor people, the church was decked out. "Wow."

"Yes. It is very nice, you think?" Pani Adamski's English wasn't as good as most English they'd heard so far, but it was more than passable.

"It's incredible. We're Protestants, so we don't worship in places this elaborate."

"It helps us to focus on God." Pani Adamski moved to the front of the church and sat in the front left pew. "I come here most days to sit and think and pray. It is very quiet, very good for that."

"It must be." McKenna and Taylor slid onto the pew.

Filip joined them. "When your ancestors lived here, this was Greek Catholic, but now it's Roman Catholic, so some things have changed."

"We kept much the same. The icons are the same." Pani Adamski pointed to the cross at the top of the altar's back wall. "Jesus above all. Below Him, the twelve disciples. Then more saints."

The paintings were breathtaking as was the gold work around each of the icons.

Pani Adamski gestured around the room. "No benches a long time ago. Maybe for the old and ill, but that was after it was Roman Catholic."

McKenna nodded and absorbed all she could of this place. For people who couldn't read or write, the paintings and icons must have helped them learn about God. "Would it be okay to take some pictures?"

"Tak, tak." Pani Adamski stood as McKenna took two dozen or more photos. When she was done, the mayor led the way out of the church. "Long ago, this town much bigger. Fifty or seventy houses. Big families in each house. Now there are fifty people. I have many children and grandchildren. That is why I am the mayor."

Oh, how Baba would love to be here. She would exclaim over every little thing. Showing her the pictures was going to be so fun.

"Why are there so few people left?"

"After the war, many moved away."

"Do you know the name Kostyszak? That was my great-grandmother's name."

Pani Adamski shook her head. "That is a Lemko name, yes?"

"It is."

"Then you go see the man in the yellow house that way." She pointed toward where they had come. "He maybe tell you. That is the only Lemko family still here."

"Dziękuję. You have been very helpful. And thank you for opening the church."

"You are welcome."

If only McKenna had thought to bring a few items that she could give as presents. All she had to offer was her appreciation, which was so little compared to the gift of being able to see where her great-grandmother and those who came before her worshiped.

They returned to the car, and Filip backed out of the driveway. "What did you think?"

"It was amazing."

"We will see if this man knows anything about your family. It has been a long time since the Lemkos left, so I don't know."

Before McKenna could gather her thoughts and ask more questions, they pulled up to a yellow house on the edge of a farmyard. Chickens pecked outside of a red barn where sheep bleated. A rusty tractor sat to one side.

Filip cut the engine and opened his door.

"Can I come?" McKenna was dying to learn if this man had heard of her family.

"Of course. Both of you may."

McKenna and Taylor unbuckled and followed Filip to the home's door. Filip knocked, and soon a fiftysomething man opened the door and gave a single nod. He said something to Filip in Polish.

Filip answered him, and they conducted a back-and-forth conversation for a while, none of which McKenna understood. The man gestured quite a bit as he spoke.

Filip then turned to McKenna. "He says the name is familiar, but he doesn't know too much. His father would have, but he passed away several years ago."

McKenna slumped. They'd come all this way only to discover they were a few years too late.

"But his name is Pan Pyda, and he would like us to come in and have a cup of tea with him. He has something he thinks might help. He speaks no English, but I will translate."

"Tell him that is very kind and we would love to join him for tea." McKenna never bothered to turn around to get Tay's consent but knew she wouldn't mind.

In fact, Taylor entered the house ahead of McKenna.

The kitchen and living room area was covered in bright green wallpaper with pale yellow scroll designs. A picture of the Last Supper hung on the wall, along with several icons, strings of paper flowers draped over them.

A backless blue couch was built into the wall, and this was where the man motioned for them to sit. He went to the sink underneath the sunny window with several potted plants on the sill and filled the kettle then put it on the stove. Then he left the room.

Before the kettle whistled, he was back with a book, and he spoke to Filip, who interpreted. "This is a book his grandfather made. His father was only a little child at the time, but one day toward the end of the war, his grandfather wrote down who lived here and where."

"Really?"

"Yes. If your great-grandmother lived here, it will say."

McKenna took a deep breath and willed herself not to be disappointed.

CHAPTER TWENTY-EIGHT

McKenna sat on the hard blue couch made up of a thin cushion on a plank of wood and stared at the simple black book Pan Pyda held in his hands. He and Filip chatted for a while. She might die if they didn't get on with it.

The kettle whistled, and the man went to pour their tea after placing the book on a small round table in between two rickety wooden chairs. She was half tempted to pick it up and glance inside. The only thing holding her back was that she wouldn't be able to read it anyway.

So she took the cup from Pan Pyda with as big a smile as she could manage. "Dziękuję."

He smiled in return then continued his chat with Filip. Would they ever finish?

Taylor leaned over to whisper in McKenna's ear. "You're getting antsy."

"I wish they would stop chattering like old grandmas and tell me what's inside."

"You've waited this long. You can wait another few minutes."

"Easy for you to say."

They both sipped their tea, and after a long while, the men finished their conversation. Filip set his cup on the table and turned to McKenna. "You want to know what is in the book, yes?"

"Of course."

Pan Pyda opened it and handed it to Filip, who translated. "He says that in this book his grandfather wrote many notes about the village and the people who lived here up to WWII. He went house by house to document everyone."

"Why did he do that?"

"There was no census taken at that time, so this was the only way to preserve the record of who lived here other than the church records. He was one of the richer men in the area and the mayor, so he took it upon himself to write this down."

"What does it say?"

Filip handed the book back to Pan Pyda and said something. Again, they conversed for a while.

"I don't read Lemko, which is the language this is written in, so he will have to read it for me. Even for him, it is very difficult, but he reads a little and will try to figure it out."

McKenna nodded while Pan Pyda flipped through the pages.

"He's found an Anna Kostyszak, seventeen years old, living here with her father Lucas at house forty-five in 1920."

"That's not her. My great-grandmother's name was Helena, and she was born in 1909. She didn't come to the US until after the war."

Filip relayed the information. Pan Pyda turned a few more pages. He spoke, and Filip took the book from him. "Here's another record from 1930." He pointed at an entry. "This says Maria Kostyszak, a widow, living at house twenty-three. Daughter Helena was studying in Kraków."

"That's it. That's her." McKenna slid to the edge of the couch. "What else does it say?"

"That's all for that entry."

McKenna swallowed her disappointment along with her tea. But at least they had a house number, and now they knew the name of her great-great-grandmother. That was pretty exciting. Tay bounced beside her.

Filip nodded at the man. "There is another entry for that house number. It is from 1942. This says Maria Kostyszak was living in house twenty-three with her daughter, Helena Bielski, Helena's husband Jerzy Bielski, and their daughter Teena."

"Teena Bielski. That must be Baba's sister, the one she asked me to find." She held her hand to her chest, her heart thumping under her touch. "I wonder what happened to Helena's first husband and how come my great-grandmother was separated from her daughter?"

"That sounds like another mystery we have to solve." Taylor was entirely too giddy about more puzzles. McKenna was more of a get-to-the-point kind of gal.

"Does he have any information after that?"

"No, that is all he has."

Taylor squeezed McKenna's arm. "That's a bunch more than when we started this morning."

"You're right, but I feel further from the goal than ever before."

The man said something else to Filip then rose.

"He wants to take us to see where house twenty-three was."

McKenna folded her hands in front of her mouth. "Really?"

"The house is no longer there, but he knows where it sat thanks to his grandfather's notes."

They all piled into Filip's car and drove a short distance down the road that turned from asphalt to dirt. Houses were scattered about, and a few had fallen into ruin. No doubt that almost everyone left in the village was related to the mayor.

Pan Pyda pointed to one side, and Filip stopped the car then turned to speak over his shoulder. "This is it."

They all climbed out and hiked a short rise to a more level area in front of a steeper hill. A small pile of bricks lay in one area. There was no other sign that a house had ever stood there.

"He says that this is where house twenty-three was. It is unusual because it seems like there was a chimney, and most people didn't have that."

"Perhaps that's why my great-grandmother got an education and taught at the university. She wanted to give her family a better life."

"Aw, that's a sweet thought." Tay had her phone out and was taking pictures.

McKenna rubbed the goose bumps off her arm. "It's kind of crazy to be standing where my ancestors lived and ate and slept."

Pan Pyda gestured all the way across his body, taking in the entire landscape, and Filip translated. "Our life as Lemkos has never been easy, but in times past, at least we had each other. Look around you."

McKenna did just that.

"This used to be filled with homes. Women would hang the washing on the lines. Children would play in the lane. Men would laugh at their own silly jokes. Now it is silent."

McKenna frowned. "What happened to them all?"

Filip interpreted. "War. Hatred. Intolerance. That's what happened. Even today I cannot talk about it because it is too painful."

"Can you tell me what happened to my family?"

As Pan Pyda opened the book once more, Filip leaned over and studied what he was pointing out. "It's a single note. 'Taken.'"

"Taken? Where?"

Filip translated as the man spoke. "He doesn't know where. It could be any number of places, but he doesn't know for sure where they went. Just that they were taken. It is like the Lemkos in this village fell off the face of the earth. His grandfather would not talk about that part of his life."

McKenna rubbed her arms again. "I suppose there's nothing else here then. We've learned all we can in Dubne, unless you can think of anything else we should ask."

"No. We have a good start and a place to begin from."

"So you think you can find out more about my great-grandmother and maybe about Teena and what happened to her?"

"It will take more research, but that is why you are here, no? You did not think you would get all of the answers in a single day."

"I suppose not." McKenna sighed. "I should have expected this wouldn't be easy."

"Don't worry. We will find out what you want to know. Have patience."

Taylor laughed. "Patience is not McKenna's strong suit."

"Hey." But Tay was right. Life couldn't move fast enough sometimes. Mom told her to slow down and enjoy every minute because before she knew it, those times would be gone.

Filip relaxed against the car, arms crossed in front of him. "Take a little bit and enjoy this view. Enjoy being where your great-grandmother and possibly many generations before her lived. Once a house was in the family, it stayed in the family."

So McKenna inhaled the sweet, fresh air and drank in the sight of the green hills rising in front of her, of the large tree across the road that might have been there when Helena lived there.

What was life like for them? Hard, from everything she'd discovered. Yet Pan Pyda said they laughed and played just like people around the world.

They didn't have to be rich to be happy. In fact, they probably enjoyed the little things in life more than most.

Then again, there was Belinda. She was poor and miserable. But it was true, McKenna had witnessed pockets of pure joy when Belinda played with Yasmine and held her daughter close.

The part of the Bible where it talked about being content in all circumstances sprang to her mind. Somehow these people knew the secret to it. She had yet to find it.

After a while, Pan Pyda said something to Filip, who turned to McKenna and Taylor. "Are you ready to go? He needs to get back to work."

McKenna nodded. "Oh, of course. I'm so sorry for taking so long."

"This is not a problem. He has my information, so he will take some pictures of the pages in the book that talk about your family and send them to me."

"That would be wonderful. Dziękuję."

They climbed into the car and returned Pan Pyda to his home. The twenty-minute or so ride to another little village where they would spend the night passed in silence. It was over two hours to Kraków, and they had paid Filip for two days to show them around Lemkovyna. He used the map on his phone to find the way. It was weird to hear the directions in Polish instead of in English, but he found the narrow driveway that led up a hill without any problems.

As the sun descended behind the hills, he parked in front of a charming house that was almost Alpine in nature. The bottom floor was covered in white stucco, but the top was wood with several peeked dormers. There was even a balcony where bright red geraniums bloomed. McKenna couldn't get enough of it. "Wow, this is so charming."

"I have learned that Americans like charming. Anything old is charming to them." With a chuckle, Filip got out of the car and pocketed the keys.

A younger man greeted them in the foyer. He and Filip conversed for a while, and then the man led the way upstairs and showed them to their rooms before leaving.

"I will be right down the hall if you need anything."

It wouldn't be too difficult to find him. McKenna counted only four rooms.

"Feel free to explore. There is a gazebo in the garden or the balcony to sit on. You should relax for a little while."

She must really look stressed out. Maybe she had bags under her eyes yet from jet lag. "I'll try, and I'll work on finding out more about what happened to my relatives. Do you know why all the Lemkos were taken and where they might have gone?"

"I do have an idea, but that is something you should find out on your own."

"So you're giving me homework?"

"Pretty much." Filip grinned, and his entire face brightened. "I am going to take a nap. They will have dinner downstairs in a little while."

After they settled in their room with twin beds and a bunk bed as well as a private bathroom, Taylor and McKenna headed to the balcony to enjoy the sunshine and the balmy weather.

"Ah." Tay eased into a wicker chair with a bright yellow cushion. "Now this is the life. Peaceful, beautiful. I may never want to leave."

McKenna pulled out her laptop with a grunt and got to work on discovering what might have happened to her family. "I wonder if they were taken away by the Nazis. Pan Pyda did say that his grandfather wrote nothing more after WWII."

"But they weren't Jewish, so why would they be taken?" Tay sipped from her water bottle.

"I don't know. Maybe it has something to do with them being Lemko. It could be that the Nazis didn't like them either."

"That's possible."

"But why wouldn't Filip just come right out and tell me that?"

"He wants you to be the one to figure it out. Maybe he likes you and wants to hire you."

"If I had a pillow, I would throw it at you." McKenna narrowed her eyes. "But really. What happened to Teena and to Jerzy? Where did they go?"

CHAPTER TWENTY-NINE

People were starving
Because they did not feed them.
Mistreated them, like devils.
People were dying like flies.

~From "Song of Lemkovyna"

Friday, February 9, 1945
Germany

B ielski. What are you doing here? Report to work. Immediately. Or there will be consequences." The dour-faced matron frowned at me.

I smoothed Lonia's hair away from her pale face, her brow so hot beneath my touch. "I no longer care about your consequences. This is a child who is dying. A child. Despite the typhus outbreak, despite the fact that you refuse to get anywhere near us, you keep us working. Well, no more. This child isn't going to die alone."

"Have it your way. But trust me, you will suffer for what you are doing."

Like I hadn't suffered all along. Quite the opposite. For almost eighteen months, I had lived under the most horrendous circumstances, faced disease and starvation and cruel taskmasters, lost every bit of dignity. So what else did I have to lose?

Absolutely nothing.

Our treatment at the hands of the Nazis had brought Lonia to this place. She should be living the life of every almost-fifteen-year-old. Going to school and doing her homework. Chatting with her friends about the boys they liked. Spending time with her family.

Instead, she lay in this freezing, stinking hole, struggling to breathe.

I labored to form a prayer to the Holy Father. Almost a year had passed since I had prayed. Then one from the prayer book burst into my mind. Still, the words were difficult to say and believe.

Save, O Lord, and show Your mercy to the young and the old alike, those who starve, those without father or mother, those without husbands, those who are dying, those who mourn, those who suffer, those in prison, those who are persecuted for the faith. Comfort them. Be ever present with them. Comfort them, bless them, and deliver them. Show Thyself to be a God of mercy and of power.

Here I was supposed to bow three times, but I didn't have the strength to do so.

Save, O Lord, and show Your mercy to those who persecute me, for Thy name's sake. May I not yield to temptation, to curse them and die.

More bowing was required at this point, but I couldn't.

I had said the words, at least in my mind, that God should save and have mercy on my enemies. Did that include the Germans? Those who held us in this prison in unspeakable conditions? No one would even treat their pigs this way.

In Lemkovyna, if a family had a pig, they treated it as well as their children. It lived in the house with them. They made sure it was fed, even if the mother and father were hungry. When the winter winds blew and the snow covered the earth, they kept it warm.

There was none of that here.

Lonia moaned and writhed on the bed.

"Hush now, hush. You will be just fine."

"Water." The word was weak, barely a breath.

If only I could fulfill this girl's simple request. But I had no water to give. "You will get some soon." In heaven, there would be plenty of water.

"Mama."

"She loves you, that is for sure. She loves you, so don't worry about her. God will take care of her."

"Papa."

"The same for him. Even though they can't be with you in person, their prayers are going out for you. Do you feel them?"

Lonia nodded.

"Good. Very good. You rest and get stronger and stronger so you can see them soon again." Word whispered about the factory was that the Allies were closing in on Berlin in the west and that the Russians were fast approaching from the east. Not too much longer, and we would be free.

Lonia would be free before the rest of us. Soon her soul would fly away into the arms of the Great Shepherd.

What would we find when we stepped out of these gates at last? Sometimes planes rumbled overhead, shaking the entire building. In the village, air raid sirens sounded, but we were not allowed shelter here.

The Nazis didn't care if we lived or if we died.

And still, they kept up this charade of being in control.

Lonia's breathing was raspy. Her chest rose and fell only a few times every minute. I held her already-cold hand. As I had done after the overseer's attack, I sang.

Oj, wersze, mij wersze,
Mij zełenyj wersze,
Już mi tak ne bude,
Już mi tak ne bude,
Jak mi było peruse.
Już mi tak ne bude,
Już mi tak ne bude,
Jak mi było peruse.

Oh, my mountains, my mountains
My dear green mountains
Life has changed for me,
Life has changed for me.

Life was about to take a radical turn for Lonia.

Then, as death rattled her lungs, I prayed the Lord's Prayer. "For thine is the kingdom, and the power, and the glory, for ever. Amen."

No sooner had I concluded the prayer than Lonia took her final breath, and her eternal soul winged its way to glory.

WHAT I LEFT FOR YOU

I bowed my head over Lonia's body, and a mighty howl burst from my throat. "Nie! Nie! Holy Father, how could You allow this? She was a child. A child. Do You hear me? This happened to a child."

For the longest time, I wept and wept. Sorrowed for Lonia and for Jerzy. Sorrowed for myself and for Teena and Mama. Would we ever be reunited?

"How long, O Lord? How long do You expect me to bear this? I cannot go on. Take me too. I do not want to be in this world anymore."

I cried enough tears to fill all of Lemkovyna's streams, until I was spent. At some point, someone came in and removed Lonia's body. There would be no proper burial for her, especially not with the ground frozen. No prayers said over her.

One of the women—I didn't even bother to turn around to see who it was but guessed it was Gośka—rubbed my back until I fell into a fitful sleep, exhausted from keeping watch over Lonia.

By the time I woke, darkness shrouded the dormitory, and all was quiet. A few light snores came from the women, but in general, they all slept hard because of the grueling work.

Out of instinct, I rolled over and reached for Lonia, who had slept beside me since the attack, only to come up empty. No wonder I was cold. I got up and padded around the room. Weak, thin moonlight peeked into the room, illuminating the skeletal figures on their bunks made of boards.

I held out my own bony hands, so calloused they were unrecognizable. What did it matter? Lemko women worked hard all their lives and had red and rough hands. That was part of life.

But at least we had been free on our own mountains. As free as we could be without governing ourselves and having our own homeland. Lemkovyna was always part of some nation or kingdom or empire or another.

But never a prison like this. Not one where little girls were brutalized and where women died of starvation.

My tears came again, streaming down my face. If only I could go to the mountains and scream as loudly as I wanted. Because this wasn't fair. I yearned to understand.

But this was beyond understanding. Beyond bearing.

Over and over again, God had slashed my soul. Nothing remained of it but tatters and shreds.

In the distance came a dull roar, and a blast of light brightened the night.

Sirens screamed in town. All of a sudden, soldiers flooded the room. "Take your things. Everything. Head downstairs to the shelter. Schnell. Schnell."

The first time they had taken thought for us. Tonight, for some reason, was different. I gathered my few belongings and my battered brown rucksack. I had Lonia's with me as well. Perhaps I would get a chance to return it to her parents. Maybe by the end of the war, I would need to use some of what was inside of it. A ragged blanket. A couple of dresses. A once-sturdy pair of boots, now falling apart.

"Schnell! Schnell!" With their rifles, the guards nudged along those they thought weren't moving fast enough, including me, my feet as heavy as my heart. I picked up my pace and moved with the flow of women to the damp, dark basement. Unable to see much, I stumbled over something and landed in someone's lap.

That woman pushed me to my feet, and I moved toward the back, shuffling so I wouldn't trip, until I found an empty spot to sit. The bare earth was cold from the bitter winter.

Where was Lonia? I had to take care of her and make sure she got to the shelter. Just as I was about to call out for her, reality slammed against my chest.

Lonia was gone.

But at least she was safe.

An explosion rocked the earth beneath us, and a few loose stones fell from the wall. Would the entire building collapse on us?

Huddled there, my life hanging in the balance, with nothing else to do, I recited Psalm 51. They were the only words that came to mind, so ingrained they were. "'Have mercy upon me, O God, according to thy lovingkindness: according unto the multitude of thy tender mercies blot out my transgressions. Wash me thoroughly from mine iniquity, and cleanse me from my sin.'"

Even when I finished the entire psalm, the bombs continued to rain down. Women cried and screamed. Gośka, seated next to me, clung to my forearm.

I had been speaking in Lemko, but now I switched to Polish so that the others might say the Psalms with me. I started Psalm 130. "'Out of the depths have I cried unto thee, O Lord. Lord, hear my voice: let thine ears be attentive to the voice of my supplications.'"

As I recited the verses, more and more voices joined me until almost the entire shelter was filled with echoing words.

More rumblings. More bombs. The wail of sirens pierced even the thick stone basement walls. When we finished that psalm, we switched to 131.

" 'Lord, my heart is not haughty, nor mine eyes lofty: neither do I exercise myself in great matters, or in things too high for me. Surely I have behaved and quieted myself, as a child that is weaned of his mother: my soul is even as a weaned child. Let Israel hope in the Lord from henceforth and for ever.' "

We repeated these psalms over and over until the drone of planes quieted and the whistle of bombs stilled. I sat without moving, afraid to take a deep breath.

The sound of the siren changed. All clear. With a whoosh, I released the air from my burning lungs. We had survived. For tonight at least, we had survived.

Another twenty minutes must have passed before the guard allowed us to return to the barracks. My legs were stiff from sitting so long and from the cold.

"What an awful night." Gośka climbed the stairs beside me. "But thank you for the Bible verses."

"The bombing was terrifying."

"Do you think this means the war is coming to a close?"

"We can only hope that it does."

No sooner did we return to our bunks than the sirens screeched again. Once more we dressed, and our captors herded us downstairs and made us sit on the freezing floor.

This time another woman started the psalms, and I recited with her. All clear. Up the stairs. Another siren. Back down. Wait. Then up.

By now my body was demanding rest. A small bit of sleep, even with the bunk beside me empty.

But at five o'clock, like every other morning since I had arrived, the guards awakened us, told us to dress, and gave us a little bread.

Then we were sent to work.

I reached the end of my endurance.

CHAPTER THIRTY

Monday, April 2, 1945
Germany

Cold. So cold. The biting winds tore through my coat and stung my sagging flesh. With no fat on my body, I had nothing to insulate me. Though the bitter winter had lost the worst of its edge, I had yet to warm through.

Everything about me was icy. My fingers. My cheeks. My toes. My heart. My soul.

The numbness it brought to my mind was a welcome relief. No longer did I cry myself to sleep. No longer did I pine for Teena or Mama or Jerzy. My emotions were as frozen as the winter fields had been.

My burning desires had been extinguished.

I felt nothing.

That was only because the cold cauterized the gaping, bleeding wound in my heart.

Out here in the open field, there was nothing to protect me or the other women from the breeze. The Allies crept closer from the west, and the Nazis shut down the cloth factory. Now they forced us to dig ditches.

The ground beneath Lonia's thin-soled boots that I had taken to wearing was barely thawed. For what wasn't, we resorted to pickaxes to break through the frozen chunks of earth. With each swing of the axe, pain shot through my back and into my shoulder.

The callouses that my hands bore before were nothing compared to the blisters upon blisters that bloodied my palms. I wrapped them in dirty strips of cloth from one of Lonia's lightweight summer dresses, but that did little good.

The guards, large women who ate far more than we did, kept watch and ensured that each of us dug the prescribed size trench each day.

I would laugh at the irony of it all if my soul felt anything. We were fortifying ourselves against the victors we longed to welcome.

Perhaps I should work slower. Keep from building these obstacles to the inevitable arrival of the Allies. But no, the guards forced those who didn't work fast enough to stay out, even in the freezing nights, until the trench satisfied their requirements.

Perhaps I should run to the forest, the tall straight trees standing sentry not too far away. There I could find relief from the wind and make my way home to Mama and Teena. Teena wouldn't even recognize me anymore.

But then the picture of Jerzy's bullet-ridden body flashed through my mind. Nie, I couldn't take the chance. My daughter had already lost three parents. I had to make sure that I returned to care for Risa's child.

So I kept at the work, picking and shoveling and digging, my ears and fingers so cold. Some distance away came the retort of artillery fire. It didn't excite me. It didn't frighten me.

Night fell, and at least my trench was large enough for me to go to the dormitory, warm up a bit, and attempt to sleep before the bombing runs ramped up. We didn't bother to undress anymore because we were up so often during the night seeking shelter from our saviors.

Grośka came to me as I sat on her bunk and nibbled on a slice of dry bread. It stuck in my throat, but I swallowed to get it into my shrunken stomach. "Did you hear that a train was bombed on the tracks not far from here last night?"

"Tak."

"It was filled with potatoes, carrots, and bread."

I eyed Grośka, who had gone prematurely gray, her thin strands of hair hanging around her pallid face. "Why are you telling me?"

"Listen, the male guards are gone, off to fight on the front. The Germans need every one of them, no matter how young or old, to fight this losing battle. There are only a handful of female guards left."

A light broke over me. Grośka wanted to break out and steal whatever food might be salvageable from the train. "Women who have guns and won't hesitate to shoot us." But to eat an entire potato would be a luxury.

"Come with us. There are three others who are going with me to see what we can get. The more who dare this, the more we can bring back."

"But how will we cook the potatoes?" The carrots we could eat raw.

"We'll figure out a way. Our bunks are made of wood. We could break them apart and stuff them in the stove to get it hot enough." The little coal we were allowed wasn't enough to keep the barracks warm. "And if not, we will eat them raw. It's better than nothing."

If I keeled over from hunger and died in the field like several of the weak and old had already, what good would it do Mama and Teena? When the Allies arrived, I had to have enough strength to make the trek to Lemkovyna.

Back to those I loved. To a place where I could thaw from the outside in.

"Tell me what you want me to do."

It was a risk, but one I had to take. Women died here every day, their bodies left bloated on the ground. All the digging had to be for fortifications. The Germans demanded every ounce of our energy be focused on that task.

To eat was to live. And to eat, we had to steal.

Together with the others, we formulated the plot in record time. We had to go tonight. Tomorrow might be too late. For the first time in weeks, my stomach growled.

We slipped from our room, past the space that held the Russian women, then made our way down the stairs, holding our shoes the entire time so we didn't make noise.

There was only one guard just inside the door. If we could slip by her, we would be out. Every muscle in my body told me to bolt ahead and leave here as fast as possible. But I held back, taking no unnecessary chances.

At last the large guard nodded off, and Groska motioned us to follow her.

Surely my heart couldn't handle all these extra beats every minute. At some point, it was going to give out and stop pounding altogether. My hands sweated, even in the frosty night air.

We stole across the factory grounds to the gate. Groska hesitated, and I scooted in front of her. With a slight push, it swung open.

Why were we going for food and returning to these horrible conditions? To work that might kill us? A wicked wind kicked up.

That was why. My threadbare coat was hardly enough to protect me against the gust. A storm could arise at any time, and I would freeze to death.

Not to mention the patches with the purple *P*s stitched on every piece of my clothing. That would give away my identity in a second. Even if I tore it off, it would leave a dark spot where the clothing hadn't faded.

Once outside the gate, we pulled on our boots and sprinted from the factory yard, the muck sucking at our footwear. I scanned our small group, the moonlight illuminating wide eyes.

I tried to smile as way of encouragement that I needed as well. We couldn't fail. We couldn't. Each of the women smiled back at me. We were ready to go. It was a bit of a distance to the burg, but the need for food drove us ever onward.

As we trudged toward the town, no one spoke, but we all huffed and puffed. I used what little strength I had remaining left in my body. But I forged on, along with the others, until we came to the rail station.

On the tracks lay numerous broken, overturned boxcars, their contents spilling onto the ground. Wheels, chains, and twisted pieces of metal were strewn among potatoes, carrots, and boxes of canned peas. The bombs had ruined some of the food, but some remained unscathed.

Between the tracks, spots of red glowed from a wooden house, most likely what had been the station, judging by the smoldering platforms. At least the fires would keep us warm as we got on with the business of stocking up on food supplies.

Each of us carried a burlap bag snagged from the kitchen on our way out. After a careful look around to be sure that no Germans guarded the wreckage, we crossed to the cars. Thawed a bit by the smoldering fire, I gathered potatoes. A few were rotten. Those I cast aside, able to do so because there were more than enough for me to carry. I worked on loading the precious food.

Down the tracks, the others gathered carrots and tins of peas. There was no meat to be had, but living in Lemkovyna, I was used to surviving without it. Only in Kraków, in the days before this madness, had I allowed myself the indulgence of kielbasa or a pork chop once or twice a week.

But a potato was another matter. My stomach wouldn't know what to do with an entire one. Some were covered in filth, in debris from the bombing, but it didn't matter. I could wash those, and they would be fine. Groska wandered farther down the line, searching for whatever else might have been in the train that would be of use.

In the flashing light of a far-off bomb, a glint of metal caught my eye just beyond the pile of potatoes. I picked my way through the debris, careful not to step on anything sharp, and bent to pick up the tin.

Another burst of light, and I made out what the blue and white label said. Milk. Powdered milk. I blinked several times to ensure that what I held in my hand was real.

It was.

As I stood there, I shook from head to toe, and not from the chilly night air. This was almost too good to be true, like a gift that fell from the heavens.

I motioned to the two women near me. "Look what I found."

They hurried over and exclaimed in soft voices over my discovery. "We will have a feast. Let us help you carry it." The taller of the two women opened her burlap bag.

We finished, our sacks now bulging, probably too heavy for our weak arms to carry far, but Grośka wasn't anywhere to be found. I went down the tracks a bit, calling for her with a soft voice, one that she might not be able to hear. I was not about to take the chance of a Nazi discovering us.

We had to get back. Before I turned to where the others waited, I stared at the western horizon, star shells exploding in midair with a shower of lights like fireworks. They were almost beautiful.

A louder explosion rocked the ground, and I raced to the other women. "Let's go. Grośka will make her way back, but we don't want to get hit by shrapnel."

The other women agreed, so we picked our way through the debris-covered tracks, over the fields where we dug trenches, and through the building until we returned to our room.

Even though it was late and we would be up early for more back-breaking work, we tore apart a wooden bunk and shoved it into the stove, stoking the fire, then placed several potatoes on the top, turning them from time to time.

Just as they were ready, Grośka returned and slung her heavy pack on the floor.

I couldn't wait to share my discovery with her. "Guess what I came across?"

"Sausages? Cheese? Chocolate?"

"Now you are really making my mouth water." I reached behind me, pulled a tin from my bag, and crowed in triumph. "Powered milk. Cans and cans of it."

"Milk?" The lines that hardened Grośka's face softened.

"Tak. All we have to do is add water, and we will have a fine meal." I produced a small but sharp piece of metal, likely from the wreckage of the train, that I had brought back, and used that to open the lid.

Once we added water, the milk was creamy on my tongue and awakened my taste buds. Never had anything been so delicious. Though the potatoes were burned on the outside and raw on the inside, I devoured my share. What a feast. My stomach pained me, but I ignored it.

I was full. My hunger, now stimulated, grew. I hugged myself, desperate for Mama's touch. And from my less-icy heart came the tears.

Everywhere, I hurt. The numbness was better. Feeling was torture. Desiring what I could not have was going to send me over the edge into insanity.

I tossed and turned on my bunk all the short night. The shelling was the background music to my struggle to find a comfortable position and lose myself to sleep. Kraków and Lemkovyna belonged to another time, another person.

I was not the Helena Kostyszak who dreamed of changing her people's lives. What a lifetime ago that had been.

I was now the widow Helena Bielski who snuck out of my prison and stole food just to survive. Who wore the clothing and shoes of a girl who had died way too soon. I had seen too much.

I needed to shut off the memories and the dreams. Return to that numbed state that allowed me to live.

The call to duty came long before I managed any real sleep. Groska passed around a little more milk, and we split some of the leftover potatoes. We didn't dare down all our food in one sitting, because we might need to ration it.

At least today I had the strength to continue digging the trenches, pickaxe and shovel against barely thawed ground. A losing battle loomed on the western horizon as the blasts and artillery fire continued in the distance, though perhaps not as far away as last night.

Then came a louder boom, one much nearer than before. The ground shook. Some of the dirt fell from the piles where I had shoveled it outside the trench.

What were we even doing, building trenches when, at most, a handful of soldiers remained in the area? I dared to sling my shovel over my shoulder and gazed at the three guards standing watch over this ragtag group of women.

The guards huddled together, conversing about something or another. Every now and then, one of them glanced up, one right into my eyes. She saw me not working but didn't say a word. No threat. No retaliation. Nothing.

I nudged the women on either side of me. "Stop working. They are not worried about us anymore. They have seen I'm not doing anything and have yet to yell at me."

One by one, my fellow prisoners shouldered their tools. Another loud blast shook the ground, this time kicking up dirt at the edge of the field.

The Nazi women dropped their weapons and sprinted away from the factory. I stood there, my mouth wide open. What had just happened?

"They left us, didn't they?" Grośka pointed to where they had been.

"I think. . . I guess they must have, though I have no explanation for it."

"I do. They are cowards. But we are free."

"Free?" My mind couldn't comprehend the word.

"Tak. With no one overseeing us, we don't have to stay here if we don't want to."

Ah, freedom. That is what it meant. To come and go as you pleased. To work for oneself and no one else. The women with me whooped and hugged each other. Grośka swept me into an embrace, tears streaming down her cheeks.

We dropped our shovels and picks and left the weapons in the field for the Allies. As soon as the guards fled the school, we made our way inside.

This time we opened several cans of vegetables and milk and made a proper fire in the kitchen stove. Then we sat to a feast at the table in the dining room. Growing up, sometimes I didn't even have this much on my small table.

Just as I smacked my lips after consuming the last of my milk, the factory door creaked open and boots marched down the hallway. The rhythmic thumping, so reminiscent of the boots that day at the university at the beginning of the war, brought out goose bumps on my arms.

Before any of us helpless prisoners could react, five men entered. One dark-haired, dark-skinned soldier aimed his gun right at my heart.

CHAPTER THIRTY-ONE

Lemkovyna, miracle of nature,
Leaves, brooks and gardens,
Pine forests, streams and rivers
Hover magically.

~FROM "SONG OF LEMKOVYNA"

Monday, October 9, 2023
Muszyna, Poland

McKenna sat with her computer yawning on her lap, a new tab open on the internet browser. That was as far as she'd gotten. How could she concentrate on the screen in front of her when, if she looked up, the most beautiful view spread at her feet? The hill sloped downward to the red-roofed town below. Beyond that, another hill rose, and another one behind the first, a dark shadow against the brilliant sky.

Not since Yasmine's death—and maybe even a while before that—had she been able to sit and relax and not have other worries press on her chest. For a time, she allowed the peace of the place to invade her soul.

How was it that such beauty and such evil dwelt side by side on the earth?

She opened her eyes and caressed Helena's prayer book. Her one tangible link to the woman who had once called this area home.

Sitting here wasn't getting her any closer to finding out what had happened to her great-great-grandmother Maria during the war and the mysterious Teena, who must be the sister Baba spoke about. Well, it was time to put her sleuthing skills to good use.

She typed "Teena Kostyszak" into the search bar but came up without any good hits. Then she spelled Kostyszak all the different ways she could think of. Kostiszak. Kostisak. Kostishak. Still nothing.

It wouldn't make any sense to search for her using the Dudik last name. According to Baba, her parents didn't marry until after the war.

So McKenna switched gears and searched for Teena Bielski, Helena's first husband's last name. This time she came up with a few possibilities. By her calculations, the woman, if she was still alive, would be in her early eighties. Some of them McKenna could rule out because they wrote academic papers just a few years ago. Unless she was one bright lady who kept working.

Some of the results were in Polish, so it was difficult to read those. She'd come back to them if she couldn't find anything useful in English.

Facebook said there were some Teena Bielskis on its site. Since she had nothing to lose, McKenna logged in and searched for Teena there.

She got a few hits with that name, but the pictures didn't match with an older woman. Still, she clicked on each profile. Some lived in Poland, and a few were from Ukraine. Time ticked away as she made her meticulous search.

The results switched to Cyrillic letters, so then she had no idea what she was looking at. She'd have to get help from someone with those. Perhaps Filip's friend, the one who had helped with the prayer book, could write out the family name in Cyrillic for her so she could continue her search.

Just as she closed her laptop, a small headache sending her eye twitching, her phone rang. That eSIM card she bought was great. Even Filip didn't have much luck with his cell phone out here.

The caller ID read CHRIS. Apparently she shouldn't have gotten such a good SIM card, or she should have hidden away in the Tibetan mountains. Somewhere he couldn't reach her.

Tay leaned over. "Don't answer it."

"He'll just keep pestering me if I don't."

"After a while of not answering, he'll have to get the message that you don't want him to bother you."

Great advice, but McKenna didn't take it, pushing the green button instead. "Hello?" She strung out the word.

"Hi." Chris yawned. "Where are you?"

"In Poland, like I told you."

"Still?"

"Guess you aren't stalking me on social media, or you would know the answer to that question."

"Just tell me."

"Listen, I don't want to be mean or anything. I don't want to come off as spiteful, but it's really none of your business where I am. Since we aren't together anymore, you have no right to keep track of my comings and goings. You didn't have that right when we were together."

"When will you be home so I can get my ring?"

The guy couldn't get a single thing through his very thick skull. She stared into the gorgeous blue sky overhead, but no answer came from there. Tay was shaking her head.

What should she tell him? Her heart was tender from the breakup. And she was mourning Yasmine and Belinda. That was enough of a load on her shoulders for the moment. One of the purposes of this trip was to get away from her problems and focus on something else.

After all, this was her family's story. She already had Taylor along for moral support.

"Well?"

Oh yeah, he was still on the other end of the line. "I'll be home when I get home."

"Can we make a date for lunch when you get back?"

A little of her lost resolve returned. "Absolutely not. I'll mail you the ring by certified mail when I can."

"Can't we at least have lunch?"

"No. I'm sorry, Chris, but I have no desire to see you. Please, respect my wishes and leave me alone. When you broke things off, you shredded my heart." She swallowed the growing lump in her throat.

"But—"

"No. I'm working on putting my life back together. One that doesn't include you. You made that choice. Now you're going to have to live with the consequences. You have what's-her-name now." She ended the call.

Taylor stood from her wicker chair and cheered. "Congratulations. I consider that a small victory. Or maybe not such a small one. You stuck to it and didn't allow him to bully his way into your life. He closed the door. He has no right to open it again."

McKenna released her breath with a whoosh. "That was hard." Her understanding of what Belinda went through with Hank grew. Men could be persuasive. They could sweet-talk better than any woman and knew which buttons to push. If they said the right words, they could melt women's hearts.

And so Belinda, without the good support system that McKenna had, allowed that man with his sugary words back into her life.

"Bet it feels good, doesn't it?"

"Sure does."

"That's the biggest grin I've seen on your face in ages."

McKenna felt her mouth. Sure enough, she was smiling. After a phone call from Chris. "He's ridiculous."

"And you put him in his place. I'm so proud of you." Tay hugged McKenna.

The porch door opened, and Filip stepped out. "I heard a shout and wanted to make sure everything was okay."

"It's fantastic."

"She just put her ex in his place, so we were celebrating her finally letting him go."

"I'm sorry that you had to go through that, but it sounds like you are not?"

"For a long time, I was. Coming here on my own has shown me that I have plenty of backbone. If my ancestors could survive what they did, then so can I."

"You are right. You have Lemko blood, so that makes you strong. What is the word you use? Fierce."

McKenna out and out laughed. "I wouldn't call myself fierce, but thank you."

"Like a mountain lion, you are."

Now both girls giggled.

"What? That is not a compliment?"

McKenna shrugged. "I don't know. I've never been called a mountain lion before. I don't pounce, and I don't bite."

"Okay. That's a bad one. So are you ready for some dinner? The food here, it is very good."

"I didn't even get a chance to find out what happened to the Lemkos during WWII."

"Let's get something to eat, and maybe I will tell you then."

McKenna picked up her laptop. "Okay. We'll be down in ten minutes." The girls returned to the room to put away their things and to freshen up.

"You know, I think Filip has a crush on you." Tay applied some lip gloss.

McKenna pulled out her ponytail holder and brushed her hair. "Nah. He's just nice. It's part of his job. I'm paying him plenty of money to help me with my research and to show us around here." It had to be that. She was not ready in any way to be in another relationship. And then throw in the long-distance aspect? Forget it.

"Don't dismiss him so fast. He's a nice guy."

"You're single."

"And I plan to stay that way."

"Same here. Let's get something to eat. I'm starving."

When they came to the small dining room, they weren't disappointed in what the cook and innkeeper put in front of them. There was grilled kielbasa that had been charred so perfectly that it was sweet. The plate also boasted the typical pierogi that McKenna was used to—a Polish-style ravioli—as well as a different one where the outside was made of potato. Bacon glistened on top of both dishes.

No doubt about it. She would have to go on a serious diet when she got home.

Filip was already at the table, his hair freshly combed. He wore a blue button-down shirt and a pair of jeans. My, he was handsome.

McKenna all but shook herself. Tay was getting into her head far too much. "Hi. This looks delicious."

"Sit and try some."

McKenna said a silent prayer and dug in. Oh, goodness. The traditional pierogi were stuffed with potatoes and farmer cheese. The others had cheese on the inside. These didn't even come close to what Baba made, no offense to her. Just something about it was on a different level.

"I can see by your face you like this."

"They're delicious."

"I told you they have good food here. The best in the area."

Beside her, Tay moaned. "Oh, deliciousness. Sheer deliciousness."

They enjoyed their meal. With such a heavy dinner, no dessert was needed. Afterward Filip suggested a stroll, which McKenna accepted. "I need to walk off a bunch of these calories."

"The fresh air here will help to burn them away."

Tay headed for the stairs. "I'm going to call home."

McKenna reached for her, but she darted up the steps and out of her grasp.

"Enjoy." Taylor vanished around the corner.

When they got back, McKenna was going to give her friend a stern talking to.

"Shall we?" Filip held the door for McKenna, and she stepped onto the patio and then followed a path that continued up the hill.

Filip soon caught up to her, and no wonder. Even though she'd been going to the gym and was running on a regular basis before she left, she was not used to these steep hills.

As soon as she caught her breath, she turned to him. "I searched for Teena Bielski, and I have some possibilities, but I don't know if I've found her. Like I said, the time went so fast that I didn't have a chance to look up what happened to my people during the war."

"I think it will help to explain quite a bit if you understand the history of the Lemko people."

A notification on her phone distracted her. "It's another one of my DNA results. I took several of them, one before I even started this journey."

"Why don't you open it? Maybe that will help you find Teena."

With her hands shaking, she clicked the link.

CHAPTER THIRTY-TWO

No matter how fierce the war was
It did come to an end
Soldiers returned home
The remnants of Hitlerites were being finished off.

~From "Song of Lemkovyna"

Tuesday, April 3, 1945
Germany

When the soldiers aimed their weapons at me and the other women, I put up my hands but shouted at them in English. Without the field gray uniforms I was so used to making the cloth for, there was no doubt they were Brits or Americans. "Don't shoot! Don't shoot! We are Polish prisoners."

The group of uniformed men, all of them younger than me, lowered their weapons. I relaxed my stance but kept my hands clenched. I hadn't survived all I had to be gunned down by the Allies we had been longing for.

"You speak very good English."

"We have been working for the Germans for years. Look at what they have done to us."

One young man nodded, his metal helmet slipping with the motion. "You're nothing more than skin and bones."

"They beat us and kept us in deplorable conditions. What food do you have? Or fuel? We stole some potatoes and carrots last night, but we have little coal to cook them."

"There's a displaced person's camp in the village church. You aren't the only ones who have been held prisoner." The young soldier righted his helmet. His accent—whatever kind of English he was speaking—was very different from what I had learned.

"So we have to go there?"

A tall, slightly older soldier answered this time, and it was easier for me to understand. "Ma'am, you don't want to be traveling home right now, especially to Poland. The war isn't over, so you would have to cross enemy lines. And we've heard stories about the Soviets who occupy Poland." He shuddered.

"What kind of stories?"

"I can't talk about it, but it's enough to say that a woman doesn't want to be there on her own. Not even a group of women."

"But I have a mother and daughter who need me. My husband is dead, and they have no way to provide for themselves. I must return."

Grośka tapped me on the shoulder. "What are they saying?"

I relayed to the others what the soldiers had told me. Then I turned back to them.

"We can't force you to stay here. You aren't prisoners anymore, but we would advise you to stay put until at least the end of the war. One of these days real soon, Hitler's going to be defeated. Maybe then it'll be safe for you to leave."

"What about my family?"

The blond one shrugged. "Maybe at the camp they can help you. At least they have food and a way to cook and some medical help. You all don't look like you'd survive the trip to Poland."

I glanced at my hands, the bones prominent. What the soldier said was the truth. Before I could undertake the journey to Mama and Teena, I had to regain my strength. It would do no one any good if I died along the way.

They had been alone this long. For a few more months, hopefully they would be safe and cared for.

The soldiers escorted us through the field where only yesterday we dug trenches with German overlords watching our every move. How ludicrous it was now.

We arrived at the bombed-out train station where we had been last night.

WHAT I LEFT FOR YOU

In the light of day, the destruction was ten times worse than I had thought. Not only was the train destroyed, but the bloated bodies of German soldiers littered the tracks and the station. Only the wind and the cold kept the stench from being unbearable.

I turned from the horrific sight.

Too much. It was all too much.

The war had exacted too high of a price.

The shorter soldier with the strange accent had something about his eyes, something I couldn't define, that labeled him as kind, so I came alongside him. "I'm Helena Bielski. And you are?"

"John Gage."

"Thank you for all you and your fellow soldiers are doing, John."

"How long have you been here?"

"I was brought here in the summer of 1943."

"Do you have any relatives?"

"My husband was killed. My mother and daughter are at home, and I need to get back to them." I inhaled and pressed on my jittery stomach. "Can you help me get a message to them? They don't know whether I'm dead or alive. I don't know for sure if they survived or if they were also captured at some point."

"Gee, I don't know what I can do. That has to be awful. I'll sure give it a try. When we get to the church, let me know their names and where they're from."

"That is very kind of you. I thank you very much." The measure of comfort, though small, was a start. A start on my journey toward them. A glimmer of dawn at the end of a very dark night.

"You're welcome. It's the least I can do."

"Your accent. It is so different. Where are you from?"

"From near Nashville, Tennessee. It's in the South, so that's why you hear the accent. You speak very good English. Probably better than me."

I tipped my head. "I do not know about that. It has been many years since I have used it."

As we moved on from the station, we got to chatting, and he told me he had wanted to be a doctor when he was drafted early in the war. His plans were to return to school when the conflict was over.

Before we finished our conversation, we arrived at the church where the pews had been pushed to the side and cots set up. Cots with real blankets

223

and pillows. Tears pushed against the back of my eyes at the simple sight. While I had grown up very poor, I had always had a pillow.

A good number of thin, vacant-eyed former prisoners like me filled the sanctuary. How many other work camps had there been?

John stayed with me while a pleasant, red-haired young woman named Doris registered my information. "There's soup in the kitchen and some bread to go with it too."

I pointed to the burlap sack John carried all the way for me. "We brought some supplies. Potatoes, carrots, peas, and tinned milk. Perhaps that will help?"

"Oh, we're most grateful." Doris' green eyes lit with genuine pleasure, and warmth spread through me. At least we had been able to repay in a small way the wonderful people who were so generous.

At last I was able to return my attention to John, and we exchanged information. "Thank you so much for what you are doing to help me find my family."

"Don't thank me yet. I don't know what I can do."

Doris found me soon after John left. "Why don't you come with me, and I'll help you get some new clothes. There are some in the charity box that might fit you."

Grośka and the others were already there, sorting through the sweaters and skirts and socks. The bin even contained a few pairs of sensible oxfords. Grośka pulled out a bright red sweater and a blue dress dotted with red cherries. "This would look fabulous on you. All you need is red lipstick."

"I don't think it will be practical for getting home." Though it was pretty. I bent over to assess what the box contained and swallowed back a sob. Not since Kraków had I seen so many nice clothes in one place.

At last Doris persuaded me to take a pair of trousers, a blouse, a sweater, and a pair of shoes, plus one dress to wear when I got home and dresses for Mama and Teena. It was almost overwhelming.

Grośka now held three dresses. "I understand. This is so much to take in, isn't it?"

"It is. How did they put this together so fast?"

"I imagine they must travel with supplies. Doris told me that wherever they go, they are discovering Polish and other foreign workers, so they are setting up these camps. Soon we will be moved to a larger one."

I studied the church's vaulted ceilings above me and the stained-glass windows on either side. While it wasn't covered in iconography and it didn't boast gilt side chapels like the ones that always stirred holy reverence in me, it was pretty in its own way. Behind and above me rose the pipes for what must have been a grand organ. "I only want to go home."

"But John told you it's too dangerous. I plan on staying with the Allies for as long as possible, unless we somehow end up in Russian hands. I might not even return to Poland. What is there for us but devastation and destruction? Warsaw, from what we have been told, lies in ruins."

"Nothing can destroy the green hills of my homeland. No bombs, no bullets, nothing. No matter what may happen to the buildings or the people, the hills will stand forever. They will always be where my people belong. But maybe now I can persuade Mama to come with me to America where I can give her a better life." Oh, how I ached for Lemkovyna.

"For your sake, I will pray that you can find your family and get to wherever it is you want to go."

"Why will you not return? You never have told me anything about your family."

"Because they are dead. They have been for years, so that is why I have no desire to go back. The Germans may lose the war, but they defeated me. All I want is a fresh start to my life, if it can be rebuilt at all."

"Some say that God has a way of bringing beauty out of the ashes."

Grośka turned to me, her eyes dark, her brow furrowed. "Is that what you believe?"

"I used to. I don't know anymore."

"You lost your husband. Has anything beautiful come of that?"

The sharp pain that once inhabited my chest was now a dull, scarred-over wound, but it was still one that never went away. The longing for Teena was stronger now. The toddler I had left was a girl, a girl I didn't know and who wouldn't remember me. "I have no way of knowing. I can't see to the end of my life and what is going to happen."

"I can tell you one thing." Grośka fisted her hands. "Europe is a pile of smoldering ruins, if the rumors are to be believed. There is nothing beautiful here. Maybe I am starry-eyed over a place I have never been, but America is the land of opportunity. My cousin who lives there told me all about it. I plan to take advantage of that opportunity to forget and start new."

Who could blame her? Temptation to go there pulled at me almost as much as the siren call of the green hills of home. Nowhere on earth was as beautiful. Perhaps that was where God would reclaim the years the locusts had stolen.

I changed out of the filthy pants and shirt that I had worn almost every day for years. They were ripped at the seams, and the knees were almost worn through. The buttons on my blouse no longer matched. I had lost a couple along the way, and since I had no spares, some of the women shared a few extra they had.

Before I slipped on the new clothes, Doris filled a tub with water that she had heated on the stove. Several sheets provided privacy, a commodity I had not possessed in years.

The bath was sheer bliss. I even washed my now-long hair, and once I had scrubbed, rinsed, and dried off, Doris had a comb for me to run through my matted tresses. Tears sprang to my eyes. I was clean.

And it was heaven.

So that the other women had a chance to bathe as well, I resisted the urge to linger. I spread the provided sheets on the cot and fluffed the pillow, which soon cradled my head.

Just as I was nodding off, Doris entered the sanctuary and clapped her hands. "May I have your attention, everyone?"

The low din of voices trailed away, and the women who had been attempting to sleep sat up.

"I know many of you have just arrived, but I've been told that tomorrow you will move to a larger camp west of here near Osnabrück."

Nie, not west.

Not away from Mama and Teena.

CHAPTER THIRTY-THREE

My entire body went numb as I stared at the redheaded woman I had thought a saint earlier in the day. "No, no, I can't go to Osnabrück. Mama is old and Teena is just a child. They need me. I need them." My airway constricted.

Doris came and patted my shoulder while I clung to her other arm. "I understand that this is difficult, but believe me, you are far safer here than you would be on your own. There's no guarantee the Nazis won't arrest you again if they discovered you. You can't just buy a train ticket home. And once you got to Soviet occupied territory, things wouldn't improve."

"I know, but can you imagine how worried I am for them, how frantic they must be?"

"I'm sure you are concerned, but it isn't safe. As soon as the war comes to an end, which is only a matter of time, and things settle down, it will be much easier. Be patient just a little longer."

At Doris' wise words, I bowed my head and loosened my grip on her arm. But the weight on my shoulders pressed all the harder. I dreamed every night of holding Teena in my arms again, of living and working beside Mama, of taking them to Kraków, getting my job back, and providing well for both of them.

Such dreams were as far out of reach right now as the stars in the sky.

The next morning, along with the women I had been imprisoned with and many others from the area, I went to the bombed-out station, one track already repaired, and boarded a train belching smoke from the engine. This time we weren't packed into cattle cars. Instead, I sat on the comfortable seat and drank the coffee and sandwiches that Doris and the others offered. The coffee was black, but it was real, and I savored every last bitter drop.

Because of damage to the rails from Allied bombing raids, it was a full day's trip to Osnabrück. The walk from the train siding to an abandoned army barracks was short, but, weak and tired, I stumbled several times.

As we made our way to the now-empty, utilitarian buildings, I glanced toward the village. A spire rose above the roofs, and an ache almost consumed me for the three spires on the church in Dubne.

How long, O Lord, how long? For years, I had been without so much as a prayer book. My hands itched to hold one, and my eyes burned to read the supplications penned inside. Whether or not I believed they rose to heaven like incense, they were a comfort.

What destruction this conflict had caused, not only to Europe's infrastructure but also to people's lives. Families were torn apart. Many innocent civilians were dead. Others would bear forever the scars of what happened to them.

The huge complex, now empty of Nazi soldiers and their blood-red flags with black-as-sin swastikas, hummed with activity. Military personnel bustled about, as did nurses and others from relief agencies.

With Doris beside us, we entered the walled and gated compound. I fought to keep my breathing even and my memories of the ghetto and the prison factory at bay. This was different. Very, very different.

Doris stopped and spoke in a low voice with a man, and then she turned to us and nodded. "Before you can go into the barracks, you all must be deloused."

I leaned in just a little, unsure I had heard right. "Deloused."

"I'm so sorry." Her hair swung as she shook her head. "It's for health reasons and sanitary conditions. Believe me, I wish I could spare you, but it must be done. Don't worry. A woman takes care of it, and you don't need to undress."

Different from how we were treated when we arrived at the work camp, but frightening to us nonetheless.

I turned to the others. They and Grośka stared at me, eyes wide.

"We must do as they ask if we are to find shelter here and a way home. At least they care about our health. That is already a sight better than the Germans."

A couple of the women frowned.

"I will go first." I slung off my battered rucksack, and Doris directed me to a chair. A young woman approached me, a white kerchief on her head and a bright green apron with red flowers covering the front of her blouse and her skirt.

She held a smoking pot with a long spout. "Don't worry. This won't take long, and I promise that it won't hurt." She chuckled, and I joined her, if for no other reason than to ease the tension flowing from my former prison mates.

The dark-haired, dark-eyed woman puffed the smoke into each of my sleeves and down the front and back of my coat.

"Now lower your head."

I followed her instructions, and she directed the smoke over my hair.

And that was it. I stood and motioned to the others. "Nothing to it."

Within a few minutes, Doris led us toward the barracks.

Here I was registered as a resident of the camp, giving such information as my name, birthdate, and place of birth. A medical exam followed, and at long last, after I was found not to carry any contagious diseases, another woman handed me a blanket and a pillow of my own.

All I had in the world besides the few clothes from the charity box.

Still, it was more than I had as a prisoner. Grośka and I picked cots next to each other and made our beds, claiming our small spots in the world.

She stood with her hands on her nonexistent hips and surveyed the barracks we now called home, the hum of voices enveloping us. "I wonder if we are still prisoners or if we're free to come and go as we wish."

"A very good question. They can't hold us here, can they? They're our liberators, not our captors."

"Maybe we can go into town and get jobs. Or at least walk around and enjoy the fresh air."

"Did we not have enough of that digging trenches?" I elbowed Grośka. "It would be nice to get out of the stench in here, though it isn't as bad as the prison."

The stink of body odor testified to the inadequate number of bathing facilities. If we could get jobs, perhaps we could even secure a flat where we could live until it was safe to return home.

Oh, to have my own home again. It was a goal I had often doubted of achieving.

"What is the first thing you're going to do when you walk through your front door?"

"We only have one door." I gave a saucy tip of my head. "Other than hugging Mama and Teena until they can't breathe, I'm going to go to church and thank the Holy Father for bringing me home, because then I will know that He does answer prayers."

She shrugged. "I'm not sure I believe in God anymore. How can I? There is so much evil in the world. If He existed, He could have stopped it. He could have stopped my family from being murdered, and your husband. He could have prevented your separation from your family."

"I. . ." I had no words. What she said was true. God could have stopped this madness from ever happening. If He had, my family would be whole and happy. Then again, I likely wouldn't have married Jerzy and would have missed out on the joy he brought to my life.

But Risa and her husband would be alive. Teena would be with her parents. We would all be teaching at the university.

After God had taken so much away from me, would I ever be as happy as I had been before German tanks rolled across Poland?

I hadn't been brought up to question God. It wasn't done. Instead, we went to church every Sunday and performed our duties and kept the feast days and festivals and all the rituals.

"You have wrinkles between your eyes." Grośka stepped in front of me. "I didn't mean to make you think so hard. I forget sometimes that you taught at a university."

"Thinking isn't a bad thing. We do it to form our opinions of the world, and it is how we digest and make sense of what we see. So your words did bring up questions in my mind, things I have to mull over."

"Not right now. Let's ask Doris if we can leave, and then let's explore the town. It will be nice to feel normal again."

"Won't the German people resent us?"

"Maybe Doris can tell us that too. Mama always told me that you won't know unless you ask."

So we did, but Doris shook her head. "I can't stop you, but I would advise against it. First of all, you both look like you would blow away in a strong gust of wind. And there aren't jobs to be had or much food available. This is a country still at war. What is available is expensive and takes ration coupons that you don't have."

I fisted my hands. "So we are really still prisoners. Isn't that what you're telling me?" If only I could take one breath, one single breath, as a free woman.

"No, not prisoners. All I'm doing is advising caution. Stay here for a while, get your strength back, and then you can make decisions about your futures. Soon the war will end, perhaps in a matter of days or weeks. Then you can return home."

Much as my heart wanted to disagree, my head understood. "I long for home."

"Then put on some weight so you have strength for the journey. We're just getting these displaced persons camps up and running. From what I've been told, they are going to work on getting everyone home again as soon as possible."

As I unclenched my hands, the back of my throat burned. The question came again. *How long, O Lord, how long?*

"Would it be possible to post a letter to my family?"

Doris straightened the creased cap on her head. "That's an excellent idea. It may not be easy, and it may take some time for the note to arrive, but it would allow you to communicate with them."

"I don't know if John will be able to get the one I gave him through to them. If he can, at least I would be able to let them know I'm safe." At last, a way to connect with Mama and Teena.

Doris hunted a sheet of plain white paper, a pen, and some ink. With nothing else to write on, I lay on the cold, hard concrete floor beside my bed and penned the letter. Someone would have to read it to them, but there were those in Dubne who could, including my old friend Pawel.

Dear Mama,

Slava Isusu Khrystu. Tak, do not be surprised to finally hear from me. I am alive. Soon after we helped to release the Lemko prisoners at Jasło, we were apprehended for traveling without proper papers. We were so close to home. From there we were sent on a train to Germany to work.

Jerzy died on the way. I am heartbroken, but it has been years now, so the shock has worn off. I will tell you more when I get home.

I don't know when that reunion will be. Right now, I am still in Germany, now liberated, being looked after, regaining my strength, and waiting for the war to end so that I can travel safely. There is so much I long to tell you, but more than anything, I long to hug and kiss both you and Teena.

I pray that you both have stayed well. I cannot wait to get back to you and start our lives afresh. Not a day has gone by that I haven't thought about you. Is Teena well? She must be so big by now.

I'm running out of room on this page, so I will close and try to write again very soon. Much love to both of you. Give kisses to Teena and tell her that her mama loves her very much and will be home soon.

Your devoted daughter,
Helena

Though I folded the paper and slipped it into an envelope that Doris provided, I did so with a sigh. There was so much more to tell Mama, but it would have to wait until we were together. Whenever that would be.

Doris promised to send the letter the next day, and with nothing else to do, I returned to my cot beside Grośka.

"I thought you'd have a grin from here to the Polish border after being able to write home."

"Inside maybe I have one, but not that big. I don't want to seem ungrateful, because at least I have a family to send this to, but it's the not knowing that is the most difficult. If I didn't know if Jerzy was alive or dead, it would be torture."

"Never apologize for your feelings. Not to me anyway. I understand. I have been able to mourn and have had time to come to terms with what happened to my family. You don't know what has happened to yours, and that must be awful."

"How about happier subjects. Tell me where in the United States you want to go."

"Chicago. It sounds so exciting. Buildings taller than we can imagine, all kinds of people, bright lights. Most of all, life. I want to be surrounded by life."

"That makes sense."

"And there are plenty of Polish people in Chicago, so maybe I would be able to talk to some and find a community there. If you could go, where would you settle?"

"I would like to see the wide-open plains, though it would feel so different from home. I can't imagine land that is flat, where the sky is big overhead. It must be something. I have an uncle in Pennsylvania. Maybe he would take me there."

"From what I hear, there are many beautiful places to visit, and I plan to see them all."

"Remember that the United States is a very big country. You haven't even seen all of Europe."

"But in America, they have cars that can take you wherever you want to go. My cousin has one."

I couldn't help but hug Groska. "I hope, my dear friend, that you get to see everything you want to see and to experience all that life there has to offer."

"And even if you don't move there, you will come to visit me, won't you?"

"I will have to see."

I couldn't blame Groska for making plans, for looking to the future. But what did the future hold for me?

CHAPTER THIRTY-FOUR

Monday, June 4, 1945
Osnabrück, Germany

I held the whisper-thin paper in my trembling hands. Though I hungered for the words on the page, I couldn't control the shaking that blurred the Cyrillic letters I hadn't read in many years. I took a few deep breaths, sat on my cot, and put the paper beside me.

Words from home. Precious, precious words from home, written by Pawel Dudiak.

> *Dear Pani Bielski,*
>
> *We did receive your letter. Please accept my apologies for not writing to you sooner. Life in Dubne has been chaotic. Maybe you have heard, but the Polish Army and the Soviet NKVD have been conspiring to rid Poland of the Lemkos. Of all they call Ukrainians, though that is certainly not what we are. At any rate, they are determined to make Poland a racially pure country.*

I broke off reading and turned my attention to the courtyard of the former army barracks, now full to overflowing with displaced people. Most weren't as skeletal or emaciated as when we first arrived, but their hollow eyes told the stories their lips never could.

Stories of unspeakable pain, torture, and loss.

Stories of the worst of humanity.

Stories that my heart was too fragile to hear.

Just as I turned away from the window, Grośka returned with a cup of coffee for each of us. The bitter brew was rather appropriate for what I had just read.

"You look like you've lost your best friend."

I had to take several deep breaths. "In a way, I feel like I have. This letter from home says that the Polish government doesn't want Lemkos living there anymore." I sipped my coffee, burning my tongue in the process. "Did we learn nothing from the war? Was it all for naught?" My voice caught on the last word.

"I'm so sorry. Please know that not all Poles feel this way. Since knowing you, I have learned quite a bit about your people. You deserve to live peaceably on your land and not be harassed."

I tried my best to give her a smile. "Dziękuję. That means so much."

"What did he have to say about your mother and daughter?"

"I haven't gotten that far yet. I'm almost afraid to continue reading."

"Finish then." She gripped my hand as I returned my focus to the page in front of me.

Not long after the war ended, Polish soldiers came to the village and took many away. Most of those who managed to slip their net were those who could flee to the hills and forests. Your mother and daughter weren't among them. They have been taken away, and I don't know where.

I strangled the cry that rose in my throat. "Nie. Nie."

"What is it?"

"Nie. Nie. Not them. Not them." A rushing torrent of tears flowed down my face, and Grośka gathered me into a hug, one my stiff arms couldn't reciprocate. For the longest time, all I could do was weep, wetting her dress in the process.

How could they be gone? And to where? How would I ever find them? This couldn't be happening. The Nazis had stolen Risa and Jerzy from me. Now the Poles had ripped Mama and Teena away.

Was there nowhere on earth where our people were wanted? No place where we could live our lives without being bothered as we had for hundreds of years? "Mama and Teena."

"Oh, sweetie. Are they. . .?"

"I don't know. That's the worst part. I don't know. The letter comes from an old friend, Pawel, who says the Poles and Soviets came in and took them. No one knows where they went. How am I supposed to find them if I don't know where they are? How are we ever going to be together again?"

"You will find a way. I know you. You are determined enough to do it, no matter what. Soon you will be reunited."

"Where should I search? If someone could tell me where they are, I could find them. But I don't even know where to start." I stood, the letter fluttering to the floor. "I have to go home. Maybe there is some clue there. Perhaps Pawel can help me trace them. I cannot keep relying on the post. It is too slow, and letters get lost."

"Then I will come with you."

"Nie. The journey is long, and I have no idea what I will find when I return. For all I know, Dubne may be empty. I could get taken too. But the risk is nothing as long as I find them."

She handed me a handkerchief. "Are you going to be able to get travel papers?"

"None of that matters. I will do whatever I have to in order to find them. They are all I have left in the world. Without them, I am nothing." Another hollow shell left to wander the earth by this horrible, horrible war.

"Nie, that's not true. You have me. You always will."

I dried my eyes. "You have been so good to me. How can I ever repay you?"

"There is no need for such things among friends. We survived the worst humanity can dish out. I trust you will be fine in the end."

"I know you don't believe in prayer, and I am not sure how much I do anymore either, but can you say one for me?"

"Of course. It can't hurt."

"In the meantime, I am going to speak to Doris and see what help these people can provide me."

In the end, after much negotiating between me, Doris, and the Americans in charge of the camp, I managed to secure a train ticket and some money for traveling. I wanted to leave, and though they once cautioned me not to travel, now that the camp was overflowing with former prisoners of war and concentration camp survivors, the overwhelmed relief agency was happy enough for me to go. One less mouth for them to feed. One less body for them to house. Now that the war was over, they had begun pushing us to leave as soon as possible.

I still possessed both my rucksack and Jerzy's. The leather was worn, but it was soft, as soft as a summer's night in the Carpathian foothills. All I had to remind me of my marriage to one of my very best friends.

So a few days later, while a rainstorm soaked the world around us, Groska and I stood on the train platform and hugged. "Farewell, my dear, dear friend. I would never have come through these past stormy years without you." I kissed her on both cheeks, and she reciprocated.

"And I wouldn't have been able to make it without you either. Remember me. If you can, keep in touch. Here is my cousin's address." She tucked a slip of paper into my hand. "You can always write to him, and he will know where to find me. May you have great success in locating your family."

"And may you find a wonderful new life waiting for you in America. I hope it is everything you have always dreamed it would be. Perhaps you will marry an American cowboy." My laugh at my own joke was weak, but hers was hearty.

She gave me a small shove. "Go now, before you miss your train."

Shoulders steeled, I moved up the metal steps and into the coach, settling in a seat beside the window, though I couldn't bring myself to look out and see Groska standing alone. My sole focus had to be on finding Mama and Teena. If I didn't...

If I didn't, I would fall apart into little bits and pieces.

And the enemies that pressed in on all sides would claim victory.

The landscape whipped by, but I paid little attention. Not until I saw the green hills of Lemkovyna would I care. Oh, how my heart ached for that sight, more than in the previous years combined.

When we crossed into the Soviet Zone of Germany, the train halted, and Soviet officers in their black-billed hats with red stars entered the car, demanding to see everyone's papers. I dug mine out of the rucksack and handed them to a soldier with hair graying at the temples.

"Where are you going?" He glanced between my identification and me.

"Home. Poland."

"Why?"

"To find my family." My stomach tightened. Was he going to allow me to continue? I held my breath. What if he took me right here?

"Very good. Have a pleasant journey." He handed the papers back, and I released my pent-up air.

I wouldn't be able to be off guard until I walked up the path, up the little rise to my home. Even then, without Mama and Teena there, it wouldn't feel the same, but just being among my people again would be a comfort.

The train clattered down the tracks, clicking away the kilometers, bringing me ever closer to my destination. I only slept a little here and a little there and didn't eat much at all. My nerves were wound as tight as guitar strings.

At last we pulled into the station in Kraków. I couldn't swallow away the lump in my throat. The last time I was here had been when Jerzy and I fled. Not much was changed. Though German boots had trod this land for five years, they hadn't left their imprint here.

Instead, Soviet forces replaced them, the thunk of their boots every bit as grating as the Nazis'. Once again, Poland was occupied. Would any of us ever breathe freely? At least Grośka was headed to a place where she could.

Keeping my head down, staring at my battered brown oxfords, I made my way across the station to the ticket window. People bumped against me, but I didn't pay attention to them, didn't acknowledge them. I waited my turn, and when I reached the balding agent, asked for a ticket to Nowy Sącz, pushing a few złoty across the counter.

"Travel documents."

I handed over the papers Doris had given me.

"I'm sorry, ma'am, but these are only good to Kraków. You don't have permission to travel farther."

Now I did meet the agent's spectacled eyes. "What do you mean?"

"I mean that you don't have permission to go beyond Kraków. Those are the laws now."

And how were they any different than the laws under the previous occupiers? From the looks of it, Poland had traded one tyrannical regime for another.

"How am I supposed to get home? I have been a prisoner in Germany for three years. I have to get to my family. Am I now to be a prisoner here?"

"I'm sorry. For your sake, stay put. It's safer that way." He peered around me. "Next."

With that dismissal, shoulders slumped, I retreated to a corner of the station. Porters emptied luggage onto carts, and passengers made their way to and from the platforms. While the world bustled by in front of my eyes, I planned my next move.

I had not come this far to give up now. No little slip of paper, or lack thereof, was going to discourage me. Not when I was so close to Lemkovyna. Not after all these years.

Already I had wasted too much time. If I had come home as soon as I had been freed, I might have been with Mama and Teena when they were taken.

Maybe I could have even prevented it.

Out of habit, I found myself praying. Then I gave up. What use was it? God was against me at every turn.

Wait. I had contacts in the city. My former colleagues might feel the same way as the rest of the Poles, but the worst they could do was slam the door in my face. Then again, there was no telling if any of those I had taught alongside were still here. The Soviets could well have brought in their own professors to pontificate on the superiority of communist ideals.

I traversed the familiar old streets, unchanged for hundreds of years.

Soon I came to Planty Park, the branches of the trees lining either side of the path, shading it from the summer sun. And then the Collegium Novum stood in front of me, its arches welcoming me home.

Students hustled by, rucksacks slung over their shoulders. No one gave me a second glance. At least the university was operating.

I drew in a deep breath, pulled open the heavy door, then entered the vaulted hall. Memories rushed at me, familiar faces and voices playing a cinematic show in my head. As fast as possible, I hustled past Jerzy's old office. And mine.

The plaque on the next door still read JADWIGA LIPSKA. Since being turned away at the train station, this was the first bit of encouragement. I knocked, and Jadwiga called out for me to enter.

When she saw me, her mouth fell open, and she rushed from her chair to envelop me in a hug. "Oh, my dear, dear friend. We thought you and Jerzy were dead. What a relief to see you. Where have you been? Where is Jerzy?"

I held up my hand to stem the flow of questions. "It's good to see you too." I relayed some of what had happened in the past five years.

"Oh, I'm so deeply sorry. What a tragedy. We had all hoped he would show up one of these days and resume teaching here."

"That had always been our plan. But plans change. What I need now is your help. I need to get home, to Dubne, but I have no way of getting there—not the right papers, not a means of transportation. Can you help?"

Jadwiga thumped into her chair and rubbed her powdered face. "Oh, Helena, I don't think I can."

CHAPTER THIRTY-FIVE

Our mountains, holy mountains
The Besides and Carpathians,
This is where our ancestors lived,
The White Croats.

~From "Song of Lemkovyna"

Monday, October 9, 2023
Muszyna, Poland

Standing on the side of the hill, her heart pounding, McKenna clicked on the link and pulled up her DNA results. Perhaps here would be the answer to Baba's question.

She studied the little pie chart and the breakdowns in ethnicity. This was different than the first site where she'd had her test done, so it took her a bit to figure it out.

None of it was surprising. Scottish and Irish mixed with a little French on Dad's side of the family. And from Mom's side, it zeroed in on Southern Poland and Northern Slovakia, just as it should if she was descended from Lemkos.

She handed her phone to Filip. "There's nothing I wasn't expecting. Nothing, I'm afraid, that's going to lead me to Teena."

"Here is where my expertise comes in handy. These results are good. We know for sure that you are Lemko Rusyn. But there is so much more. We can look at your matches and see if that sheds any light on Teena. She might have descendants who tested, or she might have tested herself."

"Oh, I never thought of that."

"Come on. We are not that far from the top of the hill. We can rest there, and I can have a better look."

They hiked farther. By the way she was panting when they finished their climb, they hadn't been almost at the top of the hill like he'd said. But the view from this place was stunning.

It was a sight she would never forget, no matter how long or short her life. Hill after hill rose and fell in front of her, each covered with trees in a multitude of greens. Above was the bluest sky, untouched by pollution. Here God had painted a masterpiece. Perhaps His finest work ever.

For a moment, McKenna forgot to breathe.

"It is spectacular, isn't it?" Filip stood beside her, not panting at all.

"Why does it feel so right for me to be here? Even if I didn't know this is where my family is from, I would feel at home here. At peace." Something she'd had precious little of since Yasmine's death.

"It's the magic of Lemkovyna. It has this way of drawing its people home. Somewhere along the line of my research, I read a letter written by a Lemko woman in the United States to one of her relatives still in Poland. In it, she included a prayer that one day her grandchildren or great-grandchildren would return to the place that had given them birth."

At that, McKenna clutched her chest. What a beautiful wish and dream that woman had. She whispered into the soft breeze. "I've done it, Helena. I've come home."

She gulped in great breaths as the enormity of what she'd undertaken hit her. If the story was to be believed, her great-grandmother had somehow been separated from her daughter, and Baba had tasked McKenna with finding this missing child, likely now a grandmother.

She evened out her breathing and steadied herself. "Sorry about that. I'm so glad I could come here and so glad that I'm able to do this for Baba. It's just a huge task."

"I understand. Trust me, you are not the first person I have worked with who has gotten overwhelmed. Discovering your roots is a very personal matter. Your reaction is normal. Now how about we look at some of your DNA matches and see what we can glean from them."

"Sounds like a good plan."

He found a large rock with a smooth top for them to sit on, and he scrolled through the website that contained her information. All the while, she peered over his shoulder.

The first and second cousins that came up weren't a surprise to her. She knew pretty much all of her family that was close and in the United States.

Filip continued to scroll, biting the corner of his lip every now and again. An hour or so passed as he clicked on a few of her matches then moved on from them. The light was slipping behind the hills. "Ah ha." He leaned closer to her, and she had a better view of her phone. "Look at this."

He pointed to a name. Olya Yurkevich. "That sounds Eastern European. It says on her family tree that you share a common last name, Bielski, even though you aren't a DNA match. It's possible she wasn't tested."

"It's a good thing I added Helena's first husband Jerzy Bielski to her profile."

Filip again pointed to something on her phone. "Unfortunately, her tree isn't very large, and she doesn't have her grandmother or great-grandmother added, but she does have her great-grandfather. Jerzy Bielski."

McKenna's breath hitched.

"We have to do more digging to find out if this is the right Jerzy Bielski. No birth or death date is listed for him. It might take some time to figure out if she is a relative of yours. Why don't you message her via the website, and I'll go to Facebook to see if I can find Olya Yurkevich. Too bad she doesn't have a profile picture on this DNA site."

She worked to craft the perfect message to Olya while he scoured social media.

"Okay, I already spot a couple of possibilities."

She leaned over, and he pointed to two of them.

One's name was in Romanized letters, but the rest of her information was in Cyrillic except for the town name. McKenna pointed to it. "It says she lives in Novoiavorivsk. I'm sure I butchered how to say that. Do you know where that is?"

"I do. That's outside of Lviv, Ukraine."

"Ukraine? Is there bombing there?"

"Not too much in the western part of the country. Hold on just a minute." He clicked on another result. No information was listed for this Olya, but her cover photo was of the Ukrainian flag.

"I'm not understanding."

"One more second."

Before he tapped on the third result, she caught a glimpse of the information. Again, it was in Cyrillic except for the name of where she lived. "Don't tell me Sambir is also in Ukraine."

He searched for it. "Just as I thought. Also just outside of Lviv."

"Okay, so here comes the point where you're going to have to fill in some of the blanks I have. Why would it interest you so much that someone related to Jerzy Bielski is in Ukraine?"

"This is why I told you to do your history research on the Lemko people."

"So I flunked that assignment. Will you still teach me?"

"Well, I don't know." He tapped his chin as a chorus of birds broke out in song overhead. "I should make you do the required work yourself." Then a dimple appeared in his right cheek, and he burst out laughing.

"You're incorrigible."

"That is not a word I'm familiar with."

"Then you should do your own homework." This time they laughed so hard, they both ended up holding their sides.

At last the giggles cleared. It was nice to spend time with Filip. He was easy to be with. So very different from Chris, who she wouldn't ruin her day thinking about.

Filip leaned back on the rock. "So I think it's about time you learn what happened to the Lemko people after WWII."

His ominous tone twisted her stomach.

CHAPTER THIRTY-SIX

We will remember for a long time,
As long as our Motherland lives
Our loving Lemkovyna
The land given us by God.

Remember everything,
So you can take it with you.
But will that be possible for all possessions—
Attire, clothes, bread and animals?
To put them into a sack on your shoulder
And march into the world . . .

~From "Song of Lemkovyna"

Monday, March 11, 1946
Dubne, Poland

A chill wind blew through the cracks between the slats of wood that made up my small home. As I sat staring at the cold fireplace in front of me, I pulled my embroidered shawl around my shoulders.

This was the same fireplace I had worked so hard to afford a chimney for. That I had sacrificed so much time with Mama to make a reality for her.

And she was not here to enjoy its warmth.

I had no energy to feed its hungry mouth, so it provided me no heat. The outside of my body was as cold as the inside.

Months had passed since I had arrived. Months with no more clues as to where Mama and Teena were. I had no idea where to turn or what to do. Soon the small amount of money I had would run out, and I would likely have to return to Kraków to teach to keep body and soul together. And that only because I clung to the thin, delicate thread that I might locate my family.

Jadwiga had helped me and had given me a place to stay while I got the papers I needed to return here. Long days and weeks passed while I waded through the ocean-sized bureaucracy, but I persisted. I would not be denied. Finally, the authorities relented, and I was allowed to come home.

I returned to a place almost unrecognizable. So many people gone. Friends. Neighbors. Relations. A handful remained.

My home, the only true one I had ever had, sat empty and desolate, as if it mourned the loss of its occupants. Their clothing and blankets and pots and pans were gone. So was my prayer book. At least they had that part of me.

Where there had been love, there was only loneliness. Where there had been joy, there was only despair. Where there had been family, there was only me.

Just me. And I was not the same woman who had once lived here and loved here.

I rose, my back and legs stiff from sitting in one position so long. After stretching, I turned to the window as a flash of black and white passed by, and without a knock, Pawel Dudiak rushed inside, his wavy brown hair disheveled, the tail of his shirt untucked from his pants.

I spun, and he stood smack in front of me, waving a piece of paper in my face. "Look, look. I have a letter from my family in Ukraine."

For the first time in months, I straightened and took notice of something, grabbing the letter, all but tearing it from his hands. "Ukraine?"

"Well, the Soviet Union now, but that's where they are. Near Lviv."

Relatively speaking, not so far away. I studied the letter, drinking in the words it contained. Pawel's relatives were safe though scattered. Some had been taken deeper into the Soviet Union. There was news of some of the deported residents of Dubne. Then came the words that stopped my heart.

Unfortunately, Pani Kostyszak has passed to glory. Her heart, broken by the loss of her daughter, just gave out. What happened to Teena, who had been with Pani Chomiak, I don't know.

"Nie, it can't be true. Mama can't be dead." I threw the letter at him. As soon as it hit the dirt floor, I scooped it up and scanned it once more. Those black marks on the page must say something else. Something other than that Mama was dead.

Above all, not that.

But there it was, printed in almost-perfect Cyrillic letters.

A lump swelled in my throat, but I couldn't cry. Refused to allow myself to weep. My heart had turned to stone. Cold. Hard. Unfeeling.

No more alive than the rocks and boulders that littered the hill behind my house.

Pawel touched my arm. "I am so sorry. How I wish I brought better news."

"I have to go find my daughter." I scurried to the bedroom and pulled the rucksack, battered by time and wear, from underneath the bed and knelt beside the chest to pack my clothes. "She is alone in the world, without father or mother or even grandmother. My poor, poor baby. So much loss. Too much for any person old or young."

"How are you going to locate her?" Pawel followed me into the bedroom. "You have no idea where she is, and no travel papers to get there."

And no money, but I refused to mention that. None of it mattered in the end. I had to go, had to find Teena. "I will figure out something. There must be a way I can get those papers. My persistence in Kraków paid off and got me here. If I have to, I can do it again."

"Unless you plan on staying there, I wouldn't leave."

I stared at Pawel and furrowed my forehead. "Do you not understand a mother's love? This is my child, my only child. Everyone else in my family is dead. Dead." My voice rose in pitch with each word. "She is all I have, and I am all she has. Without her, I am empty. For three years, I have been without a part of my soul. I am going to find her."

Pawel held up his hands. "True, I have never been a father. But I can sympathize and imagine what Mama would have done if I had gone missing. She would have moved heaven and earth to find me."

"And that is what I must do for Teena."

"Then I will go with you."

"What? Nie. You have a life here, a farm, a way to earn a living."

"But like you, I have no one. My family has all been deported, all of them to Ukraine. There have been many times over the past several months that I wish I had never gone to hide in the hills, that I had allowed myself to be taken with them. No matter what the future held, at least we would have been together."

I softened my stance just a little. "Maybe you do understand in a way."

"There is none among us who hasn't experienced loss. Life has been brutal."

I nodded, no longer able to speak. The tears I had so desperately held back burst from behind my eyes. As I wept, he knelt beside me and gathered me close.

Mama, gone. All I had promised to do for her come to nothing. "When will it end?"

"Not until glory."

Was there such a thing? Such a place where death and fear and separation were unknown? If so, my heart longed to be there. But I still had a job to do, the most important one ever. "Will you help me?"

"Of course. Don't you know, Helena, that I have loved you for a very long time? Always, though, I believed you to be too good for me. What would you want with a man like me, who didn't have your education, who could barely read or write and worked with animals all day?"

"You what?" This was too much information being thrown my way all at once. Already today my world had been overturned. Now this?

"Love you, Helena. I have loved you ever since we were small children. It was torture for me to watch you return with an intelligent husband and a daughter. Your clothes were so stylish, and you spoke so well."

"I never knew." I had thought him cute and nice when we were children, but I was so young when I left Dubne, always with one thing and one thing only on my mind. Knowing then wouldn't have made a difference. I would have rebuffed him in favor of an education.

I had loved Jerzy. Yet my bruised, broken heart stirred when I gazed at Pawel beside me, such earnestness in his blue-gray eyes. "Pawel."

"If we were married, it might make it easier for us to obtain the papers we need. Especially if we decide to remain in Ukraine."

"This is all so sudden." I rubbed the back of my head. "Right now I don't know which way is up and which is down. And there are things about Teena, about me, that you don't know."

"Then tell me." He rose and assisted me to my feet.

"Nie, nie." I shook my head. How could I trust anyone these days? How would he feel if he learned the truth about Teena's parentage? Too many scars covered my heart for me to bare it on a whim.

He rose and stepped back. "Okay. But I will still help you, and I will still travel with you, if it is even possible for us to go anywhere."

"Anything is possible if you put your mind to it." Then again, the last time I had traveled without the proper authorization, it had not ended well. But nothing would keep me from my child.

Sunday, May 4, 1947

By rote, I sang the ancient chants along with the priests who swung incense in front of the icons with the clanging of the censer chains keeping time to the unaccompanied music.

By rote, I crossed myself at the appropriate times.

By rote, I accepted the Holy Eucharist, no thought for the significance of the sacrament.

All this time the congregation stood, as there were no pews, men on one side, women on the other. Every now and again I stole a glance at Pawel.

This was to be our last Sunday worshiping in the little wooden church on the hill. Later today the priest would marry us. Tomorrow we would set out on our journey eastward toward his family. And if there was a God in heaven, toward mine.

For over a year, we had worked to find any trace of Pani Chomiak and Teena, to no avail. We scrimped and saved every grosz we could to make the trek eastward, toward Ukraine, toward where I prayed Teena was.

Pawel caught me peeking at him once and sent me a half smile. One that he had flicked my way dozens, maybe even hundreds, of times. And never before last year had I noticed the meaning behind it. He had been patient to wait for me, to make plans with me before we married. Now that the time had come to leave, so had the time to have a wedding.

I forced my concentration to the front of the church as the service neared its conclusion. Tonight I would sleep in my bed, perhaps for the last time. Then again, I had thought that before. Somehow I always ended up in Dubne.

Throughout all my wanderings, it always called me home.

The service concluded, the odor of incense lingering in the air, the din of conversations rising. The few families remaining in the village greeted each other, men slapping each other on the back, women kissing each other on the cheek. A handful of children, all that were left in town, threaded their way around the adults and headed to the door.

The way it had been for hundreds of years. The church a touchstone. Somewhere solid that would always remain and never change.

As the congregation turned to leave, a commotion came from the back door. The noisy protest of the door opening. Scuffling on the wood floors. A woman screamed and a small child wailed.

Two soldiers blocked the exit, arms crossed over their wide chests, rifles in their hands. What was going on? This time, when I glanced in Pawel's direction, he wrinkled his forehead.

"Listen, comrades." The soldier's deep voice filled the sanctuary. "We have an edict to relocate you from this place. You have two hours to collect any belongings you wish to take with you. Then you are to meet in the churchyard, ready to go."

The broad-shouldered soldier consulted a clipboard. "These are the family names I have listed as living here. You will come forward when I call you and verify this information. Anyone on this list who does not appear at the designated time will be hunted down."

He made methodical work of ticking off the names of all those who had dwelt on this land, who had worshiped in this church, for generations.

Pawel stepped forward when his name came up. What choice did he have? He spoke with the soldiers for a moment or two before exiting the church, shoulders slumped, no little grin for me.

The familiar numbness that had brought me through the war and through these agonizing years since once again took over. About half of the people had left before the soldier said my name. I stepped forward, careful to hold my shoulders straight.

Too many times had soldiers humiliated me. Not anymore. Not if I could help it.

"I am Helena Kostyszak. Actually, Helena Bieliski."

"No matter. You have less than two hours now to pack whatever belongings you can. Report to the churchyard."

"You cannot take us from our homes, from our land. These hills give us the very breath in our lungs."

"All Ukrainians must be resettled."

"We are not Ukrainians. We're Lemkos. There is a difference."

"Ukrainians, Lemkos, it matters not to me. Your people, maybe even you, are in cahoots with the UPA, that Ukrainian insurgent army threatening Poland. That terrorist group infiltrating our country and polluting it.

"Your time is ticking away. I suggest you hurry and collect your belongings. Otherwise, you will leave here with nothing more than the clothes on your back."

"I have little more than that. The Nazis made sure of that. And now the Polish people, whom we have lived with in peace all these years, are removing us from our beloved Lemkovyna? I refuse to believe it."

"Believe it or not, it is true. The UPA has been making life very, very difficult for us. You should never have collaborated with them, should have turned them over when you had the chance."

"I have no affiliation with such a group. None of these people do or ever have."

"Our orders remain. Now go. You are taking time from the others."

The people behind me murmured.

"One more question."

The soldier blew out a breath. "What is it?"

"Where are you taking us?"

"To the reclaimed lands."

"The reclaimed lands?"

"Do you have difficulty hearing? Or comprehending?"

"But that is west."

"Precisely. You are not as stupid as I made you out to be."

"My family is east. I beg you to allow me to go to Ukraine where they have been deported."

"Then you should have not hidden when the first resettlement orders came."

"I was in a displaced persons camp."

"That is not my business." The burly man pushed me forward and called the next name.

I could run away, flee east.

But when I stepped through the door, soldiers and their trucks ringed the village. How did I never hear them come?

There would be no escape. In mere minutes, I would be forced west. Away from Teena again.

CHAPTER THIRTY-SEVEN

They cried coming out of their houses
Threshold and walls were kissed in tears
They kissed the ground which they walked upon
Which they tilled and loved very much.

~From "Song of Lemkovyna"

Monday, October 9, 2023
Muszyna, Poland

McKenna gazed over the hills in front of her, behind her, and to each side of her. Fall had yet to touch the leaves with her paintbrush. All was lush and green.

Beautiful. Peaceful. Undisturbed.

And yet violence had marred this place too. Nowhere was an Eden. That didn't exist.

But in the quiet solitude of Lemkovyna, it was almost impossible to conceive of the weeping and wailing that had once filled this valley. Families rent asunder, a culture stomped underneath soldiers' feet.

For all of human history, people had been driven from their homes and resettled elsewhere. It happened even in McKenna's day, not so far from here where war once again uprooted people and sent them from their homes. But to know that her family was forced from the land they loved, that they had possessed for many generations, was almost unthinkable.

"Oh, the poor Lemkos." What Filip had told McKenna shook her to the core. "And my great-grandmother, to suffer that same fate. Are you sure she was resettled also?"

"There's little doubt about it. The man might remember the Kostyszak name, but his family is the only Lemko left in Dubne. Everyone else is gone, nothing more than a distant memory."

"No, that's not true." McKenna shifted her gaze from the green hills to Filip's blue eyes. "As long as I live, as long as my children and grandchildren do, the Lemkos will be more than a memory. My people were part of this land for hundreds of years, and I am part of them. Today I'm here, in the spot where my family's journey began."

"I think your great-grandmother would be very happy to know that one of her descendants returned. Not many do."

"I think that's because not many know about their heritage. I certainly didn't. But that's going to change when I get home. It's time for us to know where we came from and what kind of people preceded us."

"A very noble cause. In my research, I have found a Lemko organization in the United States. I will send you the information. Maybe you will be interested."

"That would be fantastic. Thank you so much. And in the meantime?"

"In the meantime, I will try to look up records about your great-grandmother, to give us an idea of where she might have been taken. That could give us a clue as to which Olya Yurkevich is your relative."

"So you think Helena and Teena might have been resettled in Ukraine?"

"It is possible, very possible. We will have to find out. The records aren't complete, especially for such a small village as Dubne. In towns with larger populations, there is a better chance of finding the relative."

"Okay." She gazed at the lush surroundings. Even if she never learned more about her ancestors, at least she had come to the place that had birthed them.

"Don't sound discouraged. Sometimes it's a hard and frustrating process, finding the relatives you want, especially if they are Lemko. But it can be done with a bit of patience. And for you, I will do my best."

"I can't tell you how much I appreciate this."

"That is my job."

"You're doing more than your job in helping me."

A tiny bit of pink colored his cheeks. So maybe Tay was right after all. Hey, she could do worse. She almost had.

"Are you ready to go back?" He reached out for her and helped her stand.

"I'd like to never leave. That must have been so hard for Helena, to move away from this beautiful land, the place of her birth, knowing she would never return. I can't imagine the pain that caused her."

"To this day, the Lemkos sing about those times and how difficult they were. Little by little, the Polish government is beginning to recognize the unfair way they treated the people in those days. They even offered an apology."

"Sounds to me like they have a long way to go toward making things right." McKenna picked her way around rocks and a few tree roots that protruded from the ground, the coming darkness making the job more difficult.

"Allowing the people to return to their homes would help. Some have managed it by saving enough money, but many have assimilated into the Polish culture. Just like many in America, they don't know much about their past."

They completed their descent and returned to the inn.

Filip held the door open for her. "Tomorrow we will go back to Kraków so I can do some work. Maybe you will get brave enough to drive so that you can return whenever you want."

McKenna snorted. "Highly unlikely. At home I drive, but I don't enjoy it. I wouldn't say I'm the best driver in the world. Here I would be petrified. The last thing I need is to get into an accident in a foreign country."

Before heading upstairs, they discovered Taylor in the little dining room reading a book and eating a piece of cake. McKenna's mouth watered. "Is that good?"

Tay glanced at McKenna. "The story or the dessert?"

"Both."

"Yes."

"What is it?"

"The book is a cozy mystery. Kind of funny, actually, if murder can be. The cake is a plum cake, and it's delicious."

"*Ciasto z śliwkami.* That's its Polish name. One of my favorites. The season is almost over for it." Filip pulled out a chair and, after going to the sideboard and cutting himself a slice, joined Taylor at the table.

McKenna followed suit. Sitting there, just the three of them, chatting, eating, laughing, they had a really nice time. Even though they came from such different places, people were people.

They were just finishing up and about to head to their rooms when Filip's phone dinged. "Ah, I have an answer from one of the women on Facebook we contacted."

McKenna sat up straighter and leaned forward, her heart in her throat. This could be it. Perhaps she had found the thread that would lead to Baba's sister.

He scanned it then frowned. "She says that she does not have a grandmother named Teena or any Kostyszaks or Bielskis in her family that she is aware of. So she is not the woman we are searching for."

McKenna leaned back. "That's disappointing."

"Remember what I told you on the hill. This might take some time."

Tay placed her napkin on the table. "That is not one of Ken's strong suits. She hates waiting for just about everything. And that includes Christmas and her birthday."

McKenna shook her head. "Not my birthday so much anymore. That impulse lessens more with each passing year."

Soon afterward, they said their good nights and headed upstairs. McKenna flopped on her bed. "Do you think he likes me?"

"Only someone with eyes in their head could tell. And anyone can see that he's way better than old what's-his-name."

"Ugh. Don't remind me about him. I guess we'd better get some rest. Sounds like Filip wants to get an early start tomorrow, though I don't want to leave this place."

"Let's make a deal we'll come back before we have to go home."

"Sounds perfect to me."

Once they had the lights out, McKenna lay in the dark, scrolling through her phone, going over some of the pictures she'd taken in the past couple of days. There were so many. She sent a few to her parents and Baba.

Then a notification popped up. A reminder for tomorrow.

Yasmine's birthday.

She would have been three.

The realization that this precious little girl would never get to celebrate three or thirty-three or sixty-three smacked McKenna right between the eyes and stole her breath.

It's not right, Lord. It's not fair. She'll never experience her first kiss or hold her first child. Why did You have to snuff out such a bright light so soon?

A few moments later Tay left her bed and crawled in with McKenna. "What's wrong?"

"Nothing."

"You're crying."

"I am?" She touched her cheek, only to have her fingers come away wet. "I didn't even realize I was." Which made her cry all the harder.

In the dark, quiet room in the middle of nowhere in Poland, Tay held her and allowed her to mourn. "Why? Why did Yasmine have to die? And in such a horrendous way?"

"We can't know God's ways."

"That's a pat answer." The flow of tears subsided, and heat built in her chest. "I want a real answer. One that will help me make sense of a little girl's death. Of people being forced from the only homes they ever knew. Of a mother separated from her child."

"If I had the answer to that, I'd be a millionaire. But in fact, I think I do. Faith. Trust in God's goodness and His wisdom. We're mere mortals and will never comprehend the mind of the Almighty. But He calls us to trust and to follow wherever He might lead. No matter what."

That was still too trite for McKenna. On an intellectual level, as someone who had grown up in the church, it was the explanation she'd heard all her life. But now that something bad had happened to someone she'd grown to love, she couldn't make sense of it.

"Don't worry if you can't figure it out today or tomorrow or at any point in this life. In eternity God will give us the answers we don't have now."

Not wanting to offend someone as kindhearted as Tay, McKenna kept her retort to herself. The problem was that she didn't want to have to get to heaven to understand. She needed it to make sense now. "I put this reminder on my phone that tomorrow is her birthday so I wouldn't forget to buy her a gift."

"Is that what brought this on?"

"Yeah. How am I ever supposed to get through the day?"

"One minute, one second at a time."

Tay meant well, but she'd never been in a situation like this. Perhaps the drive back to Kraków would be enough to take McKenna's mind off what the day was. Hopefully she wouldn't be a soggy mess.

Before she fell asleep, her phone rang. It was Baba, so of course she had to answer. "Hello." She kept her voice as low as possible.

"McKenna? This is Baba."

"Hi, Baba."

"Well, isn't this something. I would never have dreamed that I would be able to talk to my granddaughter in Poland over the phone. For free to boot. It's always something new."

"Yes, technology is pretty great, especially when it works."

"How late is it there?"

"Not too bad." She wouldn't tell Baba it was past bedtime.

"I'm glad I didn't wake you. That would have been awful. Tell me about your trip so far."

So McKenna filled her in on what she'd learned and what she'd seen.

"Wow. Imagine being in the place where Mama worshiped and seeing the place where her house once stood. I don't understand how you figured all that out."

"Filip is helping us a great deal. He's very knowledgeable."

"Oh, is he now?"

"Don't read anything into that, Baba."

"I won't. I won't. Now to the real reason I'm calling you."

McKenna leaned up. "Oh? What's that?"

"I looked at my calendar and saw what tomorrow is. Or is it today there?"

"It's still tomorrow. I think." The way Baba had phrased it was super confusing.

"Well anyway, I noticed that it's going to be Yasmine's birthday."

"How do you know that?"

"With this forgetful mind of mine, I have to write everything down because it doesn't stay in my brain. You mentioned it last year, though you couldn't tell me her name, and I was going to give you some money to get her a present."

That lump in her throat grew again. "Oh, Baba, that's so thoughtful of you."

"You always spoke so highly of her that I came to love her just like you did."

McKenna sniffed and couldn't get any words past the swelling in her throat.

"Oh, honey, I know it's hard. Such a terrible thing to happen to one so young, especially."

"I know. I wish there was something I could have done."

"You loved her, and that's what mattered the most. You and her mama loved her. You can take comfort in that."

"I suppose."

"You know that my mother never spoke about the past. She kept it closed up and hidden inside of her, and in a way, I think it ate her up. Sure, she smiled and laughed and hugged and loved, but there was always this sadness in her eyes."

"That's too bad. But from what I learned today, it's not surprising."

"No, I suppose not. I never realized that she suffered quite so much. But there was something she always said when things went wrong."

Maybe Helena had figured out the answer to McKenna's questions about God. "What was that?"

"No matter what, God."

"No matter what, God." That would take some pondering to unpack what Helena might have meant. "Thanks, Baba. I'll try to keep that in mind."

"I hope it brings you some peace."

She'd have to wait until tomorrow to find out.

CHAPTER THIRTY-EIGHT

"Mountains, our mountains, we bid you farewell,
Because we are leaving, leaving you in sorrow."
We were leaving in sadness, to a distant unknown,
Each heart sliced to pieces by sorrow.

~FROM "SONG OF LEMKOVYNA"

Sunday, May 4, 1947
Dubne, Poland

In silence, I turned my back on the green hills that had birthed generations of my family. I couldn't bear to watch them grow smaller and disappear. Pawel too set his face away from the land that had sustained the Lemkos for hundreds of years.

We marched side by side, leading the donkey that pulled the cart that held our most essential items. Two mattresses, some pots and pans, my blanket chest, a pile of clothes. With soldiers lining the way, ensuring that every last Lemko left their land, more and more refugees joining the rising stream, we headed toward Nowy Sącz. Away from Teena.

My heart was heavier than a ten-kilo weight.

Would I ever be reunited with Teena? Not if the Poles had their way. If only I had left earlier. If only Jerzy and I had never gone to Jasło.

Life was nothing but one big *if only.*

Nie, if I was honest with myself, I was in this predicament because of my unwise choices. The trouble was that Teena was paying the price for them.

Once in Nowy Sącz, the soldiers led us to the train station. There, hundreds of other Lemkos milled about, many with carts, some with animals, some with not much at all. Sheep bleated, donkeys brayed, and children ran and shouted.

But to me, all sounds were muted. The world was gray.

Each of us carried a loss the size of Lemkovyna in our hearts.

I sat on the edge of the cart, hundreds of families from various villages surrounding me. Young and old, rich and poor, weak and strong. All joined by a common tongue, common traditions, a common religion.

And now, united in a common grief.

Pawel came and sat beside me.

I rested against his shoulder. After all this time, having someone else to be strong for me was wonderful, but it didn't make life right. "What can we do about this?" I gestured to the scene in front of me.

He shrugged. "Face the fact that we're defeated. For two years we held out, but now we have lost. There is nothing we can do. They took all of us. Every last one."

A man with a battered, tattered hat who had been wandering past stopped. "You're from Dubne, nie?"

Pawel nodded.

"At least they didn't burn your village to the ground. They torched ours, even the church."

"How awful." It didn't matter that I questioned God and His ways. The triple onion-spired shingled churches were beautiful. Lovelier than any cathedral anywhere in the world. "How could they?"

"They want a homogeneous society."

"That's Nazism all over again."

Both men murmured their ascent, but none dared speak it aloud. Not with Polish soldiers roaming the station with guns.

We had traded one form of oppression for another.

Not too much later the soldiers closed in on us, herding the crowd toward the train. Not into the coach seats but to the cattle cars.

And not just the livestock we had with us.

The people too.

Not again.

My throat constricted, and my knees went weak. I clung to Pawel's arm. "I can't."

He gazed at me, his weary face soft. "We don't have a choice."

"Nie. I would rather die first."

He pulled me close and rubbed my back as I trembled. "I promise to be right beside you."

"That doesn't matter. I can't." My voice pinched. "I can't. I can't." I would be packed inside again, boiling hot, nothing to eat, nothing to drink.

I would die.

With the way my heart throbbed, I just might. If I had to stand packed against other people, all unwashed, the incredible stench, I would scream. I opened my mouth to do that, but no sound came out.

Now I couldn't even speak. I wouldn't survive. I just wouldn't. With my free hand, I clawed at my chest.

"You can. You can. No matter what, God."

Pawel's statement cut off my racing thoughts. "What?"

"No matter what, God."

"That means nothing."

"It means everything. Think about it. No matter what happens in our lives, whether good or bad, God is there. He is in control of all situations. He has promised to never leave us nor forsake us. Whatever you experience, He will be by your side, walking with you. Holding you and sustaining you through both the darkness and the light."

By this time, we had arrived at the car, and I couldn't ask him to explain anymore.

This train was different from the one that had brought me to Germany. The Poles weren't shoving us into the cars like the Nazis had. In the carriage the soldier pointed us to, there were two families, both with only a couple of children each. There were, however, a pig and a cow traveling with us, in addition to Pawel's donkey.

The stench hit me and closed my throat again. Pawel squeezed my hand. "No matter what, God." He helped me into the car, and I took a spot on one of the benches that ran along the outer wall.

Pawel soon joined me and held me close. He took over introducing us and speaking to the others who would be our companions on the trip.

The soldiers crunched along the gravel and bolted the doors shut with a clang. The noise, ricocheting in my skull, sent me jumping to my feet. I couldn't stay in here. Not thinking, I ran to the door and pounded on it. "Let us out. We're going to die."

No one came. I paced in front of the entrance. "Open up. Let me out. I want to get off. You can't take me away. Proszę, don't take me from my baby."

Pawel came to my side but didn't touch me. Instead, he spoke to me like Nyan'o had so many years ago when I was but a child. The words fell like velvet over me, cocooning me in their peace and warmth.

After some time, I managed to take a deep breath, even though my entire body shook. My cries now came as a muffled sob. "Proshu. Proshu."

Pawel wrapped me in an embrace and held me tight. "No matter what—"

"I don't want to hear it." I tore myself away. "Don't talk to me about God right now. I can't hear it. He's not beside me. He has forsaken me and my daughter. My mother and my husband as well."

The train lurched forward. I fell to my knees, my fingernails scraping the metal door as I went down.

I lay there in silence—no tears, no screams, no feeling—until darkness snuffed out the thin shaft of sunlight coming through the grate.

Pawel knelt beside me and offered me a piece of bread and a drink of water. "For Teena, do this."

Only because he invoked my daughter's name did I choke down the dry bread and a small amount of liquid. How many loaves had I consumed over the years just for her sake?

Throughout the long night and even longer days, the train chugged north and westward. Every now and again it stopped, and the occupants, always under guard, were allowed to disembark. A couple of times Pawel went into town and purchased us a little cheese or a piece of kielbasa.

I ate to stay alive for Teena. Otherwise, I would have been happy to curl in a ball, go to sleep, and never awaken.

Though my lips remained silent, my mind did not. Morning, noon, and night, what Pawel said to me played in my head like a stuck record.

How could God be in this place? This stinking hole of a place? There were no icons here, no depictions of the Christ, the Holy Mother, or the apostles. The priests didn't come here with their incantations and act as mediators between the people and God.

Yet Pawel spoke of Him as if He were approachable without the priests and the church rituals. Like He lived outside of the walls of the wooden church on the side of the hill.

I didn't even have my prayer book. When I arrived at home after the labor camp to find Mama and Teena gone, it was among the missing items.

At least I had left something for my daughter to have. A piece of me had gone with her.

So how could I make sense of what Pawel had said? God would never leave me nor forsake me.

Those words rang in my head. Never leave me nor forsake me. They held a kernel of familiarity.

The next time Pawel came to me with food, I spoke to him. "God will never leave us nor forsake us. Where did you come up with that?"

"It's in the Bible."

"It is? Where did you get one?" My family had never owned one. Even when I went to Kraków and read so many books, the Bible wasn't among them. All I knew about faith was what was taught to me at home, passed down from generations.

"I saved up my money from working on the farm. After I bought it, I read it at night. Father Dmitrii helped me. For a while, I thought I wanted to be a priest."

"I never knew that."

"Anyway, as Jesus was going to heaven where His disciples wouldn't see Him any longer, He told them that He would always be with them. Though they faced much persecution for their faith, they had the comfort of knowing their Lord was beside them."

"You believe Him to be here, in this filthy railroad car somewhere in Poland?"

"Through His Holy Spirit that lives in every believer, He is everywhere."

"So we carry Him in our hearts?"

"Precisely."

I took the piece of bread that he offered me and chewed on both the food and his words. What he was telling me was so different from anything I had ever learned from my parents or the priests. Radical, even.

And yet it was beautiful. Looking back over the past years, even before the war, I was never alone. Not when I left home to study, not when I rescued Teena, not when I was in the prison camp.

All along, though I faced death many times, God preserved me and brought me to the place I was right now.

But oh, why wasn't that place with Teena in Ukraine? Why did He have to bring me to this train and keep me apart from the one I loved the most in this world?

And Mama wasn't even in this world anymore.

That was what I couldn't reconcile. If possible, the gaping hole in my heart widened.

I missed them so much. So very, very much. The number of kilometers that separated me and my daughter grew larger and larger with each clickety-clack of the train wheels.

Though I didn't have my prayer book, I closed my eyes and, for the first time in my life, spoke to the Lord from my heart. *Holy Father, be with my daughter. Watch over her. Don't forsake any of us or leave any of us alone. Help all of us to survive. Bring us together once again.*

I opened my eyes to see Pawel staring at me. "You look better. Calmer."

"You have given me much to think about. I didn't remember those words from the Bible, but I will trust you are telling me the truth."

"I will show you when it is light again."

"You brought it with you?"

"Of course. I never go anywhere without it. It's my greatest treasure."

"Still, even if God is with me, I'm lonely. Mama and I were very close, and I have been away from my daughter for so long, she surely doesn't know me anymore."

"Perhaps there will be a chance for you to find her. Whatever I can do, I will help you."

"Why?"

"As I told you, I have loved you for a very long time. If not for this raid, we would be man and wife now. I hate to see you as sad as you are. And you're right, no mother should be without her child. What the Nazis did in taking you away from her was wrong, and what the Poles are doing in taking us away from our homeland is also wrong."

"Ďakujem. But don't let the soldiers hear you say that."

"You're welcome. Remember what I said. I want to be of any assistance to you that I can. You need to rest and heal."

"And find my daughter."

"If there's a way to do that, I promise, we will do that."

Pawel truly was a good man.

CHAPTER THIRTY-NINE

People were beaten and tortured
They forced them to work,
Everyone was abused
And the innocent were murdered.

~From "Song of Lemkovyna"

Tuesday, October 10, 2023
Muszyna, Poland

By three thirty, McKenna was wide awake, her sleep restless and uneasy, especially once the time crossed midnight and it was Yasmine's birthday.

Just three years previous, that precious child had entered the world.

And already she had left it. Where was the fairness in that? Where was the fairness in anything? All the tragedies that befell her great-grandmother and all the Lemkos after the war, the forced resettlement to either the Soviet Union or Western Poland, wasn't fair.

She pounded her pillow, stopping the scream in her throat. And then came the tears that she struggled to keep as silent as possible.

Tears for all those who had lost so much. Helena and Baba. Yasmine and Belinda. Even a few self-pitying tears for herself.

Yes, loss was part of life, but these losses were all unnecessary.

How in the world did Helena find the strength to go on after she lost her first husband, her mother and daughter, her homeland?

No matter what, God.

McKenna woke up her phone and opened it to her Bible app. She loved the book of Isaiah, so she went there and read a few chapters. And then verse 10 of chapter 41 struck her. *Fear thou not; for I am with thee: be not dismayed; for I am thy God: I will strengthen thee; yea, I will help thee; yea, I will uphold thee with the right hand of my righteousness.*

Wow. Could this be what Baba and Helena meant? God would be with them, strengthen, help, and uphold them. That was powerful. And there were no conditions on it. In fact, it sounded like the Israelites were in fearful circumstances when God told them this. Why else would He command them not to be afraid?

No matter what, God.

Perhaps it was as simple as that. As recognizing that no matter what, God was there. And that was enough.

Many times in church they'd sung the old hymn "Leaning on the Everlasting Arms." *Lord, that's what I need to do now, isn't it? Lean on You. Please, help me to realize that no matter what, You are God. You're in control and taking care of everything. I can't see what You see or know what You know. That's where faith comes in, I guess. So give me the faith to depend on You.*

She continued praying until she fell into a deep, dreamless sleep.

The sun was streaming through the window by the time she woke up, and Taylor was already out of bed. McKenna stretched and got up. Tay wasn't even in the bathroom.

She dressed as fast as possible and made her way to the dining room where the same Polish-style breakfast awaited her. Taylor and Filip sat at the table chatting, though Tay turned around when McKenna entered.

"Good morning, sleepyhead. I can't believe you managed to get such a good night's rest."

"It wasn't good until after four this morning, but I'll tell you more about that later. Right now I'm famished."

Tay quirked an eyebrow but went back to her tea and her conversation with Filip.

As McKenna filled her plate with bread, cheese, and lunch meat, thoughts of birthdays filled her head. They should be happy days, days of celebration, not ones of sorrow.

Mom and Dad always made sure McKenna had wonderful birthdays, as far as they could help it. There wasn't much they could do the year she had bronchitis, but otherwise, they were days complete with special little touches. Brunch out with the family. Her favorite movie after her favorite dinner. A few gifts wrapped in pretty pink paper, often with sparkles.

Had Yasmine ever had such a celebration? Mom had a bunch of pictures from McKenna's first birthday, McKenna covered in pink frosting, a wide smile on her face. Did such photos exist of Yasmine?

Then an idea sprang to mind, so powerful that she dropped the fork onto the floor with a clatter that garnered Filip's and Tay's attention. "Are you okay?" Tay asked.

McKenna picked up the fork and set it to the side. "Never better." She carried her plate to the table and sat next to her friend. "I just had an idea."

Filip placed his napkin on the table covered with a plastic cloth. "Must be some idea."

"It is." She turned to face Taylor. "A foundation."

Tay crinkled her forehead.

"A foundation for underprivileged kids, at-risk kids, who might not have birthday parties. We could organize those for them and their families. Give them a special day." She spoke so fast her words almost ran over each other. "Perhaps other organizations would be willing to donate things like cakes, gifts, special dresses, decorations. Or maybe a place like a trampoline park or something like that would allow the kids in for free."

"Okay, okay." Taylor waved. "Slow down just a little so I can process everything you're saying."

"What do you think?"

Tay sipped her tea for a minute or two. "I like it. It's a great idea, but if you move forward, it's going to be a ton of work. How would you manage it with everything else you have going?"

"I'll figure it out. Obviously, we'd have to start slowly."

" 'We'?" Taylor widened her eyes.

"Sorry." McKenna grimaced. "I figured you'd want to be part of it. We could get a bunch more done if there were two of us. What do you say?"

"I'm going to have to think about this for more than thirty seconds."

"Fair enough."

"So what are you talking about?" Filip leaned forward.

"Giving birthday parties to kids who wouldn't otherwise get one. Today would have been the third birthday of a little girl I knew. She was murdered by her mother's boyfriend a couple of months ago." McKenna's eyes stung, but she blinked the burning away. "I was wondering if she ever had a party like my parents gave me, and that's when the idea struck."

"I think that is a wonderful thing to do. I wish you success."

"Thank you." While she finished her breakfast, she typed a bunch of notes into her phone. Concepts. People to talk to. Organizations she could approach. Her fingers couldn't keep up with her ideas.

An hour later the three of them were on the road to Kraków. McKenna stared out the window as the high green hills flattened little by little. But she would be back. She would return to Helena's homeland, her homeland, one of these days very soon.

Before she knew it, they were on the outskirts of Kraków, the homes and traffic not so different from any American city. Then they wound their way into the old part of town and to the hotel. They grabbed their bags before Filip blocked traffic for too long and bade him farewell.

Once in the room, Taylor opened her case and pulled out her charging cable to plug in her phone. "So how are you really doing today?"

McKenna sat cross-legged on the bed opposite her. "I won't lie. It's not easy. But Baba told me something last night that finally made sense in the wee hours of the morning. No matter what, God."

"Meaning?"

"It's really simple. No matter what happens, no matter what trials come our way, God is always there. 'Yea, though I walk through the valley of the shadow of death, thou art with me.'"

"I'm glad it's giving you a measure of peace."

"It is. The feeling of wishing I could have done something for Yasmine will probably never go away. I imagine that's how Helena felt. But if this foundation takes off, maybe, just maybe, her death won't have been in vain."

"I love the idea."

"You do?"

"Yeah. I thought about it on the way here, and it's growing on me. Kind of like those groups that give seriously ill children their wishes."

"Exactly. I hadn't even thought of it that way, but that's it."

"I have to keep my day job, but whatever help you need along the way, I'll be there."

"Thank you. That means so much to me." McKenna got up and gave her friend a big hug.

"Okay. Now let's go out and explore Kraków a little bit."

"I know. How about the Wieliczka Salt Mine? I hear that's an amazing place."

Even though the internet said it was tough to get tickets, they managed to snag a couple and, after a ten- or fifteen-minute drive from Kraków, soon found themselves there, descending three hundred wooden stairs into the heart of the earth. It was fascinating to wander through the maze of tunnels where mine workers had carved statues and various scenes out of salt.

The tour led them to a breathtaking chapel. Everything was made of salt—the floors, walls, ceilings, even the chandeliers that hung from the high ceilings and illuminated the cavernous space. Each carving along the lengthy side walls was a scene of Jesus' life, from His birth to the Last Supper and beyond.

But what drew McKenna was the altar in the front. A central, lighted figure—she had no idea who it was—was surrounded by four salt columns and two statues of what appeared to be saints. Unlike traditional Catholic churches, there weren't pews to sit in or candles burning. Despite the place being full of tourists, and despite the fact that McKenna wasn't Catholic, Yasmine's family had been, so it was right that she bow her head here and pray for them.

While losing Yasmine and Belinda had been a blow to McKenna, how much worse must it have been for Belinda's mom and dad and other relatives. She asked the Lord for peace and healing for them and the opportunity to serve them as well. Perhaps her idea for a foundation would give her that chance.

If she could make one child smile for one day, whatever she had to do to make that possible, she would do.

Before she was really ready, Taylor tapped her on the shoulder. "The group is moving on."

"Okay. Isn't this place amazing?"

"It sure is. I never dreamed of seeing anything like this when we were here. In fact, when you suggested it, I figured it would be one great big tourist trap. But it's beyond what I expected."

They completed the tour and took a rather claustrophobic old-fashioned elevator ride to the surface. At least they didn't have to climb those three hundred-plus stairs. Their driver gave them some time to browse the gift shop, and they each got some kitchen salt. "I'm going to need another suitcase just to bring back everything I've bought." McKenna replaced her credit card in her purse.

Taylor hoisted her own bag that boasted several other items including bath salts and facial scrub. "I might need two."

"I'm going to have to cut you off. Hand over your credit card."

She pulled her purse closer to her body. "No way. You only go to Poland once."

"Actually, I think I'll be back more than that."

"I can understand. There's something about this land and its people that draws me."

"That's because of me."

"Ha ha. So funny. But truly, it's good to see you laugh on a day like today. Something has changed in you."

"My view, my outlook on things. A deeper trust in God and a way to help the community that will honor Yasmine and give meaning to her far-too-short life." The salty taste in the back of her throat wasn't from licking her finger after touching the mine's walls.

"I'm glad. I knew this trip would be good for you, but I didn't realize until now just how good."

Their beefy driver, who had a leathery, been-around-the-block-a-few-times appearance, motioned to them. At that same moment, McKenna's phone rang. "Filip." She answered it. "Hello. I didn't think we would hear from you today."

"Where are you?"

"The Wieliczka Salt Mine."

"That sounds like fun."

"Yeah. We got a driver to bring us here. What's going on?"

"I wish you were sitting down. I have some news."

CHAPTER FORTY

In every village a church stands,
Because a Lemko fears God.
Often they gather there,
And sing praises to God.

They carry God in their hearts
And they ask God for mercy,
So that they would live a happy life
And after death go to heaven.

~From "Song of Lemkovyna"

Wrocław, Poland
Wednesday, February 25, 1948

I leaned over the official's desk a little more, getting close to his acne-scarred face to beg my case. "Proszę, there has to be something you can do to help. Anything at all. Surely the authorities kept a record where they sent the Lemkos taken on that date. I have been searching for my daughter since the end of the war. I've been coming here for a year to try to get some information." Was Teena dead or alive?

"There is nothing I can do." He brushed invisible dust from his suit coat as if brushing me away.

Not even a hint of an apology in his voice.

"I am desperate. This is my young daughter, and she is alone. There has to be something."

"There is not. Go home and forget about her. Forget that you are Lemko. If you assimilate, life will go better for you."

I straightened and crossed my arms over my chest. "That, I will never do." I itched to tell him that the government might have taken us from our homeland but they would never kill our culture. We would forever be Lemkos.

"Go home. And don't return. I am tired of your whining and sniveling. If you keep it up, you will regret the consequences."

I stepped back. "Is there anyone here who can help me or anyone you can direct me to for some assistance? I have money." Not much of it, though Pawel and I worked hard. Because of our ethnicity, we were denied jobs that would better suit us. But I would give every last złoty to hold and kiss my daughter.

"Even your bribery won't work. Do you want me to call someone to escort you from the building?"

"Imagine if you were separated from your family. Wouldn't you move heaven and earth to find them?"

"We are not Lemkos." As if that settled the matter.

But it didn't for me. "I will be back tomorrow and the next day and the day after that. As water wears down rock, so I will be to you until you give me the help I'm requesting."

"That would be a very unwise move. Stay away. That is not an idle or empty threat. Leave the premises before the police arrive."

I lifted my chin and turned on my heel, holding my head high while the man could still see me. But as soon as I strode out the front door, I slumped my shoulders, my focus on the steps in front of me.

Like yesterday and the day before and the day before that, I had no success in getting anyone to give me information about Teena's whereabouts. Perhaps they were glad enough to get rid of the Lemkos that they genuinely didn't have any record of us.

I could take the tram home, but the walk in the fresh air would do me good. And would save me money. Back to my miserly ways when every small coin counted. Just in case I managed to get someone to help or if I needed to travel, I would have the cash to do it.

A half hour later my cheeks stiff from the cold, I arrived at the small building where I had a tiny flat on the third level. Pawel and I remained unmarried. Almost without thinking, I entered the dingy apartment, put the kettle on, and measured out the tea leaves.

I had just sat in the second- or third-hand chair, the only one I owned, when someone knocked on the door. For a moment, I didn't move, wishing them to go away.

The knock came again. "Helena?"

Pawel. The one and only person I could bear to see right now. I opened the door, sighed, and then turned back to my chair.

"Another roadblock?"

"Now they're threatening me with arrest if I show up again. What am I supposed to do? How am I supposed to find her?"

"I'm so sorry. I would do anything to take away your pain and bring your daughter to you, but you might have to accept that doing so won't be possible, at least not in this life."

"Mama is gone. Who is going to take care of her?"

"The letter I received from Ukraine said Pani Chomiak had her. She was always very fond of Teena, so I'm sure she's watching over your daughter."

I swung a wide gesture that took in the entire room. "Look at us. They have separated us from everyone we knew. Praise the Lord that you told them we were married so that we could stay together. I don't know what I would have done without you these months.

"But we aren't close to anyone else of Lemko heritage. If they can't ship us off to parts unknown, they are going to make sure that nothing of our culture survives. And we're fellow Slavs, just as they are."

"It's not right. No one said it was. But what are we to do? We must live within the law."

"That is the same attitude that got three million Polish Jews killed." I paced the small space. "Back to the problem at hand. How am I supposed to locate my family? Do you have any suggestions?"

Pawel held his old brown hat in his lap and shook his head. "I'm afraid not. Even though we asked my family in Ukraine for help, they have come up empty-handed. They were our best shot at locating her. And I've come to tell you something else." He stared at his hands and fingered the brim of his cap.

"It doesn't sound like good news."

"We both know that we have no opportunities here, especially with how we are being persecuted. Neither of us can do what we love or bring in a comfortable income. But I have a cousin who lives in America. He says there are plenty of jobs there for anyone who will work hard."

"You're going to America?" Ice encased my heart, and the chill spread to my limbs. "Who would I have here if you left?" A few women who weren't too unkind to me at my bookstore job, that was about it.

"That is what I want to speak to you about. Come with me to America." As I paced, he rose to meet me and held me by my arms. "Marry me and travel there with me."

"That is so much to ask of me. What about Teena? I have no desire to put that much distance between us. If I come with you, I will be admitting defeat."

He shook his head, his brown hair as unruly as ever, his stormy blue eyes firm. "Just the opposite. We can earn enough to hire someone to help. We will have the means that we don't have here."

"And with the Soviets in control of both Poland and Ukraine, do you think we will be allowed to return if we leave? Or will Teena be able to move to the United States if we do locate her?"

"Those are bridges to cross when we come to them. One step at a time. We need money. That is without question."

There was no arguing with him there. Funds were so tight, there was almost nothing left after I bought food and paid my rent, even as miserly as I lived.

"If we were married and both working, by only supporting one household, we could save on expenses."

He was right again.

Yet tears threatened, and I pinched the bridge of my nose to keep them from coming. "You ask such a hard thing."

"I understand. Look at it with your head and not your heart."

I broke from his grasp, turned my back on him, and stared out the window. The town square, bounded by colorful buildings, was smaller but not so different from Kraków.

He came to me and stood beside me, not quite touching me. "You still think of me as the annoying boy from the village who pulled off your headscarf in school and who bumped you and made you fall down the church steps after service on Sunday."

I couldn't stop the upturning of my mouth at the memory. Truth was, he had been the kid that pestered me all the time. Only a firm warning from Mama kept me from going after him and punching him in the mouth. Especially when the fall on the church steps tore my one good pair of stockings.

But along the way, he changed. When I came home for visits on school holidays, he was kind and attentive to me. He held the church door open and shared his Christmas sweet. That was because he was in love with me.

Could I marry him? Be happy with him? For a few moments, I concentrated on inhaling and exhaling deep breaths, the clock in the background ticking away the seconds. The moments of my life passing by.

There wasn't one to waste if I was to find Teena. And I would find her, no matter what that took.

When I married Jerzy, it had been for Teena's sake, though I had loved him in a comfortable sort of way. Even though we were in a form of exile and even though life was tough in a Lemko village during war, we were happy. That wasn't an inflating of his virtues because he was dead.

He had truly given me a good life.

I turned around and studied Pawel. Fine lines radiated from his blue eyes, and even now the dirt of our beloved Lemkovyna stained his hands. It would forever. He was hardworking and wise and would provide me with a good life, with stability and an easy friendship.

And the ability to earn the money I desperately needed to find my daughter.

I reached up and stroked his clean-shaven cheek. Though he had logged many hours in the sun, working land that only the Lemkos could eke an existence from, his face was still smooth.

He captured my hand and held it. "I believe we can make each other happy. And I promise to help you do everything in our power to find Teena."

"There isn't even a Greek Catholic Church where we can be married."

"Nie, there isn't, and I'm sorry about that, but God knows, and He sees, and He will bless our union no matter what kind of church we're married in."

"Are you even Greek Catholic anymore?"

"I don't know. But I believe in Jesus and that salvation comes only through Him. And I believe that we can have a personal relationship with Him. But that's a discussion for another day. I have the feeling that you're stalling in answering my question."

"Just give me a day. Twenty-four hours to think about what you have proposed." This wasn't a decision I could rush into. It had to be right for both of us. Good for both of us.

"Okay, but you will think about this? Really think about it?"

"Tak, I will. And I will pray like you do for guidance to make the right decision for me, you, and Teena."

He went home a short time later, leaving me with the biggest decision of my life.

CHAPTER FORTY-ONE

Our mountains will rejoice
And the sun will shine
The forests will sing out—
Lemko returns!

~From "Song of Lemkovyna"

Tuesday, October 10, 2023
Wieliczka, Poland

While visitors to the salt mine bustled and chatted around McKenna, she stood in the weak October sun outside the gift shop and pressed the phone closer to her ear. "What's going on, Filip?"

"Are you starting the tour, or are you finished?"

"We're done. In fact, I think the driver is eager to leave." Then again, he leaned against the van, smoking a cigarette.

"When you get back, come to the office. It will be better to tell you in person."

McKenna's chest tightened. "You're going to kill me, you know that, right?"

"Don't worry." He chuckled. "I don't think you will die."

"But you're willing to take that chance."

"Yes. I will see you in a little while."

McKenna returned her phone to her crossbody sling bag. "He has news for me that he wants to tell me in person."

"Oh." Tay crinkled her face. "That's not necessarily a bad thing, you know. It could be good."

"Could be. Could not be."

"Ah, there's the McKenna I know and love. The eternal glass-half-empty girl."

"You're a laugh a minute, you know that?"

"And proud of it."

They both caught a case of the giggles, only brought to a halt when their driver crushed his cigarette butt on the ground and opened the van door.

The ride back to Kraków wasn't long, though it was nearly dinnertime before they made their way to Filip's office. He waved when they entered. "Good, you are here. I was soon to go home for the day."

"Oh, I'm sorry. But not sorry, really, because I can't wait until the morning to hear what you've found out."

"I've had my assistant working on this for a few days. It's coincidental that she would unearth these things now. Anyway, I have a few records I would like to show you."

McKenna took the papers he offered and studied the top one. "I have no idea what this says. It looks to be in German." She perused it more. "Wait. I think I found her. Her first husband's name was Bielski, right?"

"Yes."

"Then this is her. Helena Bielski. I also see Teena listed and Maria Kostyszak. My great-great-grandmother."

"You are right. And yes, it is in German. A list of people sent to work camps in Germany."

"What?" She widened her eyes. "Helena was in a work camp?"

"That's right. In 1943 she was sent to a textile factory, where she made clothes for the soldiers. It was dangerous work, long days. With little food and poor sanitation, some died. She likely had a hard time of it."

McKenna had nothing to say. Helena was an extremely intelligent woman, and then to be treated in such an inhumane way. . . It was a miracle she survived.

"This is how we believe she was separated from Teena. Helena's mother and daughter are listed as still living in Dubne, so for whatever reason, they weren't arrested. Likely because one was too old and the other too young to work."

"I—I can't get over it. It must have been awful."

"It wasn't easy, that much is certain. But she must have been very resilient. Here is another record. This one, I think you can read."

He was right. This one was in English. From a displaced persons camp in a town in Germany. Osnabrück. She was discharged in the summer of 1945, returning to Dubne. "She went home. So why do you say she was separated from her family? She went back to them."

"I'm afraid not. Poland had been liberated months before. By the time she arrived in Dubne, the first wave of deportations had already taken place. Likely Maria and Teena were gone by then."

"So why didn't Helena go and search for them? Nothing would have stopped me from finding my mother and daughter. Nothing."

Filip shook his head and pushed a dark wave from his blue eyes. "There would be things, especially in those circumstances, that would stop you, no matter how determined you were. In the first place, Helena would have come back to Dubne with next to nothing. No money to conduct the search. According to our records, she did not return to the university to teach, so our assumption is that she stayed in Dubne.

"And the Soviets and Poles weren't as good about recordkeeping as the Germans, so she possibly didn't know where her family was. The Lemkos were scattered throughout Ukraine and the Soviet Union. Some of them moved many times."

"Yeah, I guess I can see how that might have kept her from finding them. She must have been so frustrated. And then to never find them. How heartbreaking is that?"

"She went to Wrocław in the spring of 1947 as part of Akcja Wisła, Operation Vistula, the final cleansing of Lemkovyna."

"No wonder she didn't like to talk about the past. It was all too terrible for her. Too awful to process."

"That is the case for many who survived the horrors of WWII. It was a terrible time for all Europeans."

The old familiar weight fell on McKenna's chest again. Baba's advice, her prayers, and Taylor's fun-loving spirit had helped dispel the gloom from this day, but this news was heavy.

How was Helena able to throw off that mantle and live a productive life? Be a good mother and grandmother? Have a successful career? Not knowing where her family was would have eaten McKenna up. Mom and Dad and Baba were always touchstones for her. There whenever she needed them.

Perhaps having Baba helped ease the pain of losing Teena, though one child could never replace another. That was what some clients who had lost kids told her. It never got easier for them.

Helena had been strong to survive all she had. And even stronger to hold all her hurt, pain, and longing in her heart for the rest of her life.

Until that very last moment.

Filip gathered the papers, tapped them on the desk, then slipped them into a folder. "These are for you to keep. I have my own file." He handed them to her. "And now it has been a long day with not all good news, so we will go get pierogi to eat."

Taylor shook her head. "But we had—"

McKenna elbowed her in the ribs and smiled a placating grin. "Pierogi sound wonderful."

"I will show you what I think are the best in Kraków. Maybe not so good as last night, but very, very good. You will be impressed."

"Okay, then. Lead the way." As McKenna passed Taylor on the way out, she shot her a side-eyed death gaze.

"What?" Tay shrugged.

McKenna kept her voice low, though by this point, Filip was quite a bit ahead of them. "We do not turn down pierogi in Kraków. Of course I want to try everything, but we are in Poland, after all. Home of the pierogi. Baba would kill me if she found out I went for fast food or something."

"Not fast food. Maybe pizza though."

"Have what you want. I'm eating pierogi." She hurried to catch up to Filip.

They strolled a bit before they came to a spot just off the Old Town square. Charming couldn't adequately describe it. Some of the walls were brick while others were white plaster. Green vines with bright red, yellow, purple, and pink flowers were painted on the plaster arches.

On one wall hung a number of sheets of paper, each a description of a variety of pierogi. This was the menu. They were all tempting. She turned to Filip. "What do you recommend?"

"Any of them would be good. Pierogi Ruskie are the kind that are closest to what the Lemkos make."

She studied the papers a few more minutes. "Oh, Tay, these are for you.

The ones with mozzarella and dried tomatoes."

"Sold."

Filip stepped closer, his musky scent mingling with the fried onions from the kitchen. "If I get the Ruskie and you get the ones with duck and apple, we can split."

"That's perfect."

"And then we can all share the ones with cherry and mascarpone for dessert."

"You, Filip, are a man after my own heart."

Filip pinked. Oh, why had McKenna gone and blurted that out?

She turned so suddenly that she almost bumped into someone. "I'm sorry."

"No problem. We're as anxious as you for these pierogi." Other Americans. Understanding ones at that.

A little while later the three of them were seated at a table enjoying their dinner.

"I can't help but think of Helena in the work camp. Tired, not fed enough, longing for home." McKenna forked a bite into her mouth. "Did you ever find out what happened to Jerzy?"

"Helena was listed as a widow on those camp records. Somewhere along the way, he died."

"Another blow for her. How did she manage to handle all that?"

Tay wiped some tomato from the corner of her mouth. "I know your baba. If Helena was half the woman your baba is, that's how she made it through."

"Every person living in Poland during the war—Pole, Jew, gypsy, Lemko, Ukrainian, German—they all suffered. Everyone in Europe did."

"Baba told me last night that Helena always said, 'No matter what, God.' She must have clung to that as a lifeline. I can't imagine experiencing anything like that without Him."

"That is very right. My own grandmother was a small child at that time. She remembers much, but most of all, she remembers the prayers her parents and grandparents lifted. The Poles have always had their faith. Even during the communist regime when many countries forbade religion, it flourished here."

"From what you tell me, Helena had little when she was driven from Dubne."

"No one had much. During the war, the Nazis stole most of the livestock, badly needed livestock. Being a forced laborer would have left her destitute."

"I have no right to complain about anything in my life. Except for men who kill their own children."

"But evil will never win. God's good always triumphs."

McKenna sipped her water. "It's hard to see sometimes."

"It must have been hard for your great-grandmother as well. But good came from it. You came from it."

"I did, didn't I? I just hope she had a happy life when all was said and done. Baba said she always had this sadness behind her eyes. But maybe I can close that story for her. For us, her descendants."

Tay bumped her arm. "You're one of the most determined people I know. If anyone can make it happen, that's you."

"Aw, thanks."

They finished their delicious dinner, licking the last of the powdered sugar from the sweet pierogi off their fingers. Just as they were gathering their coats and getting ready to leave, Filip's phone dinged. He opened it and read the message.

"Oh, McKenna, wait until you see this."

She just about jumped across the table to grab the phone from him. "What? What is it?"

CHAPTER FORTY-TWO

It was difficult to depart,
To bid farewell to you,
For you are our loving mother,
Pain, sorrow, crying out,
To seek our fate out in the world,
Crying out bitterly often.

~From "Song of Lemkovyna"

Thursday, February 26, 1948
Wrocław, Poland

There was nothing special or unusual about the day. People conducted their business as they always did. From down the street came the plinking of a piano, and a ballet teacher called out the positions to her students. A child pressed her nose against a shop window as a woman inside, her mouth full of pins, fitted a wedding gown. A group of young men sauntered down the street, taking the cigarettes out of their mouths to whistle at a young lady in high heels.

I clutched my handful of złoty as I entered the corner pharmacy. Behind the counter, a man in a white coat handed a bag to a woman, her rounded belly peeking from underneath her warm red jacket. A couple of young girls looked over the cosmetics. Not that anyone had much money to spend on frivolities, but it was a break from the pressures of school. Risa and I had often done so. Jadwiga had come along too.

It cut me to the quick to have to part with as much money as I was about to, but when I was facing a life-changing decision, it was worth it. We would have to speak fast, but I needed advice.

No longer did I have Mama to give it to me. Jadwiga wouldn't understand. But Grośka would. She was there, in America, and knew what it was like. Was it everything they said? My uncle had done well for himself. That much was obvious because he had been able to pay for my schooling.

Should I sacrifice my chance at love for a chance to find my daughter? If I even could. Pawel gave me no guarantees. And I understood that.

The wooden floors beneath my feet squeaked as I made my way to the counter. The man tending the store rubbed his mustache as he helped me place the call. "You have five minutes."

Five minutes? That was all to get enough advice to decide my future?

"Helena!" Grośka's voice came through the crackling line when I announced who was calling. "It is so good to hear from you."

"How is America?"

"Fine. The work here is hard, but there are opportunities. Once I learn English, then it will be better. This is expensive, but I could tell you so much more in person. I miss you."

"And I miss you." I cleared my tightening throat and went on to explain what had happened to us and to tell her about Pawel's proposal.

"Not very romantic. Nothing like in the movies."

"Nie. But we are comfortable together and have known each other all our lives. He loves me."

"And does he know how you feel?"

"Tak." I drew in a deep breath. "He still wants to marry me. If we come to America, he says we won't be persecuted the way we are here. People know we're Lemkos, and they don't want to give us a good job or rent to us. There we might earn enough money to hire someone to help us search. Especially with communism, that might never happen here."

"You have such a caring heart. The way you took Lonia under your wings was beautiful to watch."

"Pawel is a wonderful man. He would be a good companion and a great father, God willing."

"In time, you may come to love him. You never know what the future holds. If you married him, would you be happy?"

That was the big question. I chewed on the corner of my lip. Happiness had been as elusive as a rainbow, just out of my grasp. Never had I been one of those giddy girls giggling over the least little thing.

Every now and then there had been sparks of joy. Joy in achieving my educational dream. Joy in a village wedding. Joy in the hours and days spent with Teena.

But contentment, that I knew. Contentment in my work. Contentment in the green hills of my home. Contentment with Jerzy.

And that was good. Happiness flies away on butterfly wings. Contentment is enduring. Lasting. "I think I would like life with Pawel very much."

"And I know you would love America. There are places here that will remind you of your homeland. Green hills."

"You have seen them?"

"I live in Chicago, but people tell me about them. In Pennsylvania. They say there are hills and small mountains there. Many Polish people go there."

"Our time is almost up, but dziękuję, my dear friend. I think I will be seeing you in America."

Grośka squealed. "I would love to have a friendly face, someone I know from home, here with me."

"We have much to work out, but I will keep in touch."

We hung up soon afterward.

I had made my decision. In a way, I was lighter. Had a little more confidence in the future. And yet once more I would head west, in the opposite direction of my daughter.

But it was right. Wise. Prudent. I would have a husband who would care for me and who truly loved God like no other man I had ever known. In a way I had never known.

All I could do, either from Poland or from America, was to pray for Teena. Pray that someone good was watching over her. That she was safe and happy. That she would know that she once had a mama who loved her.

And who was doing all she could to find her.

Maybe one day she would come to me. Then again, with the deportation, how would she be able to do that?

I couldn't allow myself to dwell too long on such matters. They only increased the weight on my already sore and tired shoulders.

By the time I returned to my tiny flat, I was fatigued. Sitting on the front stoop was Pawel. "What are you doing here?"

He stood, a smile strung across his rather handsome, dimpled face. "Waiting for you. Since it is Saturday and neither of us have to work, I thought we could go for a stroll."

"I was just at the pharmacy making a telephone call, and I'm rather tired."

That grin inverted the moment the words left my lips. I had disappointed him, and I shouldn't have done that. "Maybe a short walk would be nice."

"I won't keep you long."

We set out, wandering the streets that now bore some familiarity to me. "Did you have something you wanted to talk about?" Of course, he did.

"Have you thought any more about what I asked you?"

We went about half a block before I could settle my jumping stomach enough to answer him. "I have. In fact, that is what my phone call was about. I needed to speak to a friend in America."

"Grośka, right?"

He paid attention to what I said. Another attractive feature. "Tak."

"And what did she say?"

"That America is a wonderful place, a land full of opportunities. She said it is hard because she doesn't speak English, but I do, so maybe I could get a good job."

He pulled to a halt and grabbed my hands. "Are you saying what I think you're saying?"

All I could do was nod.

He picked me up and swung me in a circle, laughing enough for both of us. When he set me down, he kissed my hand. "I promise to be the best husband I can to you. And I know the most important thing is for you to find Teena, so I will work every day at making that a reality."

"I said yes to you because I know I can trust you. And I do. I cherish you, Pawel, and I am so thankful to have you in my life."

He kissed my hand again. Then we turned and went home, speaking of nothing but what a good life we had ahead of us, one filled with the promises and hope America offered and the dream of Pawel, me, and Teena becoming a true family.

CHAPTER FORTY-THREE

When boys will sing as they return
Home from the mountains,
They have beautiful voices
And they have plenty of songs,

And the girls will join them
When they hear the song
Then you will forget all sorrows
Even though you might have an ocean full.
Songs will make hearts happy,
Happiness will remain.
Oh! That concert is as though from heaven
The heart does not need anything else.

~From "Song of Lemkovyna"

Tuesday, October 10, 2023
Kraków, Poland

Filip allowed McKenna to take his phone. It was open to WhatsApp, the message in English. As she read the message, she stopped breathing.

Yes, my grandmother is Teena Bielski Shevchenko, and she was born
in Poland. I have talked to her, and she said that she grew up with the

*Chomiak family, but that was because her mother died during the war
and her grandmother, Maria Kostyszak, died soon after they came to
Ukraine. She doesn't remember either one of them.*

*She was amazed to learn that her mother didn't die and that she
has a sister. Your message brought her to tears.*

*We are not in Ukraine anymore. When the war broke out, I
was afraid for my family, even though we lived near Lviv. I am
here in Kraków with my grandmother while my parents remain in
Ukraine. Baba would be happy to meet you and her great-niece at your
convenience.*

By the time she got to the end of the message, McKenna was just about
jumping up and down. "I can't believe it. I can't believe you found her."

"What?" Tay leaned my way and peeked at the message. "She's here?"

"That's what it says." McKenna handed the phone back to Filip. "It's so
providential. Unbelievable. I can't wait to call Baba and tell her. . ." McKenna's
voice broke, and she couldn't form any more words.

"She's going to be excited." Tay squealed. "At least she knew she had a
sister. It must have been such a shock to Teena to discover that."

"So what do you want me to tell her?" Filip refolded his paper napkin.

"Yes! Tell her yes, we'll meet her as soon as she has free time. Maybe we
could take her and her granddaughter out to dinner."

"Okay, I will let her know. It is amazing that she is here. But with God,
all things are possible."

McKenna nodded. "Even bringing family together after being separated
for eighty years."

Filip replied to Olya. "There. We will see what they have to say."

I sat back in my chair, my heart full. "I'm going to burst before I can
talk to Baba. Too bad it's the middle of the night at home, or I would do it
right now."

"Well, there is nothing much we can do this minute." Filip stood and
pocketed his phone. "How about we take a walk and see a little of the city?"

Taylor came to her feet too. "Actually, you two go ahead. I have a headache,
so I think I'm going back to the hotel. Enjoy exploring." In a flash, she was
out the door.

"I think we've been set up." McKenna shook her head. "She didn't leave here like someone who wasn't feeling well. Sorry about that."

"No apology needed. It is fine. If you would rather go with her, I understand, but I cannot object to showing you Kraków."

He was nice enough, so there was no harm in walking around with him a little. "Sure. We've done some exploring on our own, but I'm open to what you have to show me."

"Have you seen the dragon yet?"

"A dragon?"

"Apparently not, then. Come, we will go to Wawel Castle and the dragon."

They meandered along the paths through Planty Park, passing the university she and Tay had visited, where Helena had learned and taught, then climbed a winding road up a hill to a complex of buildings. A tower rose above them all. As they went, Filip told her about the castle, including how it had been the Nazi headquarters for this part of Poland during the war.

"Of course they would take the best place for themselves."

The view from the backside—or was it the front?—offered two spire-topped domes, one covered in gold. McKenna turned around, and a multi-colored flower-lined path overlooked the Vistula River.

"That's the river Operation Vistula was named after." She leaned against the low wall. "The one that took Helena's mother and daughter to Ukraine, right?"

"Yes."

She gazed over the water. "It's too beautiful to be associated with something so ugly."

"Choose to remember the good."

"You're right. Things worked out, didn't they? It's just too bad that Helena had to suffer so much."

"Come. I will show you the dragon."

"Oh, I almost forgot about that."

They made their way down the hill to a paved walkway along the river until they came to what had probably once been a copper statue of a dragon with its mouth open that had now turned a green patina. It was a statue. Just a statue. "Is there something special about it?"

"The dragon is the, um, mascot of Kraków. But wait. Just wait."

They stood there staring at it for a minute or two before fire spit from its mouth.

"Oh." McKenna jumped backward. "You didn't tell me there was going to be a surprise."

"Ah, that is the fun of it. You should have seen your face." He opened his eyes extra wide and the same with his mouth.

"I didn't look like that."

"You did."

She feigned a pout. "You're crazy. What other surprises do you have for me?"

"No surprises, I promise. Let me show you around."

So they wandered, strolling through Cloth Hall and its many souvenir stalls, standing in the square and listening to the trumpeter in St. Mary's Basilica, and hearing two amazing accordion players perform a Bach fugue so well that it sounded like an organ.

No doubt about it. McKenna was falling in love with Kraków. "Now what, O esteemed guide?"

"I was going to suggest earlier that we get some chimney cakes. There's a place on the other side of the castle."

"Perfect. Let's go."

The walkway was too narrow, but she and Filip sauntered side by side, bumping shoulders or elbows now and then.

"Are you this solicitous of all your clients?" McKenna gave Filip a big grin. "Or am I paying for this tour?"

"This is free. I like to show off my city."

"It is amazing." And so was he. She needed to guard her heart. Only a couple of months ago, she had been planning to spend the rest of her life with Chris. No, she wasn't even going to think of him and ruin such a wonderful evening.

They came to the popular dessert spot in a short amount of time. Even had it not been busy, there was no place to eat inside. The odor of yeast and cinnamon tickled her nose as the man behind the counter wrapped long strips of dough around a wide cylinder with a long handle then baked them until they were golden brown. After he spread Nutella on the inside and sprinkled the outside with cinnamon sugar, he handed McKenna hers.

It was delicious.

"As much as I love your city, Filip, I don't think I could live here."

He took his, filled with ice cream, from the young man behind the counter. "No? Why not?"

"You have too much good food. I would double my body weight in less than six months."

He chuckled. "But you see how much we walk. That is how we stay thin."

"Even that wouldn't be enough for me." They found a bench in Planty Park and sat to finish their chimney cakes. While they ate, they chatted about life and normal things. To McKenna, normal was a breath of fresh air.

Filip's phone dinged, and he studied it for a moment. "Are you ready for some good news?"

"Always."

"How does it sound to have dinner tomorrow evening with Teena and Olya?"

"Really?"

"Yes. I'm working out the details with them."

A reunion eighty years in the making. "Wait until I tell Baba."

CHAPTER FORTY-FOUR

Friday, October 13, 2023
Kraków, Poland

Does my hair look okay?" McKenna studied her reflection in the mirror. "I wish it wasn't so straight. How about my outfit? Maybe a skirt instead of pants? Yeah, I think I'm going to change."

"That'll make it three times." Taylor peered at herself in the mirror.

"But I don't like this. I want something that looks nice but not too nice. Like somewhere in between. They're refugees, so they probably don't have a lot of money."

Tay grabbed her by the shoulders. "You look fantastic. You always do. They're going to love you for who you are, not for what you wear."

"Easy for you to say. You aren't meeting your long-lost relatives."

"Do you think you should have told your baba?"

"I will. At first I was bursting, but I want to see how it goes. Don't worry, I have something in mind if this turns out well."

"Okay. Whatever you say. You're the boss."

"And don't you forget it. Now let's hurry downstairs before we leave Filip waiting for us."

A few minutes later he pulled in front of the hotel, and she and Tay climbed into his little car, with McKenna beside Filip. He gave her a thumbs-up. "Ready for this?"

"I don't know." She pressed on her stomach.

WHAT I LEFT FOR YOU

"I talked to Olya on the phone today, and she sounds like a lovely woman, so you have nothing to worry about. And I have a surprise for you."

"What?"

Tay leaned between them from the back seat. "Remember that patience isn't her strong suit."

McKenna turned around and shot Tay a dirty look.

"You're going to have to wait and find out what that surprise is."

"Might it have something to do with where we're going for dinner?"

"It might, and it might not."

"Well, that's helpful."

"I know." There came his goofy, now-familiar grin.

They left the historic center of the city and made their way to the outlying area. McKenna had no idea which direction they were even going. After fighting a bit of end-of-the-day traffic, they came to what was more of a suburban area with restaurants, offices, shops, and a gym. Filip then turned down a residential street, neat white houses with red roofs lining the way, each with a small yard and a short driveway.

Filip pulled in front of one and stopped. "This is it."

"What is it?" McKenna furrowed her brow.

"Teena's home that she shares with her granddaughter."

"No. I don't want them to go to all that trouble for us. Do they have enough?" As soon as the words came out of her mouth, she clamped her hand over it. "I didn't mean that the way it sounded, like we're better than them. But they're refugees."

"Like you, Olya has a college degree and has managed to find a good job here. She and her grandmother have plenty."

"If you're sure. I should have brought a gift." Though she did carry something in her purse she hadn't told either Filip or Tay about.

While they waited for someone inside to answer the door, McKenna's knees trembled, and she was lightheaded. "What if they don't like me?"

"This is about your baba."

Tay's words stopped a little bit of her shaking, but it started right up again when a young woman about McKenna's age opened the door, her hair pulled into a ponytail. She wore a pair of black pants and a soft pink sweater.

Before she knew what was happening, Olya wrapped McKenna in an embrace. "It is so good to meet you."

Olya smelled of a floral perfume, and McKenna returned the hug. "Good to meet you as well."

"And these must be Filip and Taylor." Olya stepped back and ushered them inside. "Baba is fussing in the kitchen."

McKenna chuckled. "My baba does the same thing. She's never happy unless there is a fork or a ladle in her hand."

"Ah, then it is for sure that we are related."

The group made their way inside a neat living room with a gray sofa, a few chairs, and a bookcase with numerous framed pictures. Also in the spacious room was a table set with white dishes and gleaming silverware.

An older woman entered from what McKenna presumed was the kitchen and burst into tears. She also embraced McKenna, weeping and saying something in a language McKenna didn't understand.

Olya spoke to her and then stepped backward, wiping her eyes with the hem of her black, red, and green apron.

"This is my baba, Teena Shevchenko."

"It's so nice to meet you."

"Baba speaks no English, so I will have to translate."

"I can't wait to hear everything she has to say."

"Eat. Eat." Apparently Teena could say a few English words. She led them to the table. Within moments, Teena loaded the table with stuffed cabbage, pierogi, and kielbasa, all foods that McKenna was very familiar with.

At Olya's urging, Filip led them in prayer, and then Teena passed the plates around the table.

Throughout the course of dinner, they chatted about Olya's job, how they were settling into Poland, how Olya's parents remained behind in Lviv, and numerous other subjects. McKenna provided them with details about her life in America.

Just when McKenna didn't have room for another bite of the delicious meal, Olya got up from the table. "I have tea and cake."

"I couldn't possibly eat another bite. Let me help you with the dishes."

"There will be time for dishes later. Baba wants to talk now. Sit, and we can do that."

So once the table was cleared, McKenna carried one armload of plates to the dining area and brought out two cups of tea while Taylor carried the cake, and Olya and Teena set out the rest. A few minutes later they all settled back into their seats.

"Tell me about your life, Pani Shevchenko." McKenna perched on the edge of her chair.

She spoke so fast, it was amazing Olya could keep up with her. "I never knew my mother or my grandmother, but the Chomiak family raised me outside of Lviv. She always told me, though, about them. That my mother was a very smart woman who taught at the university in Kraków. My father too."

"Do you know why you were separated from your parents?"

"They were away freeing some prisoners and never returned. I was always told they had died. Soon after liberation, we were taken to Soviet Ukraine."

"Helena did what?" McKenna must have heard wrong.

"When they came from Kraków during the war, my father worked with the partisans. Some had been arrested, and he and Mama went to free them. We never heard from either of them again. Mama Chomiak never knew what became of them."

Olya sipped her tea. "We didn't find anything out until Filip contacted us. If not for him, we still wouldn't know. So thank you very much for giving Baba some answers."

"And I didn't know that my baba had a sister until she told me right before I came here."

"That's amazing."

Teena said something and motioned for Olya to translate. "She is amazed at technology and what it can do. Growing up as poor as she did, an outcast in Ukraine, a Soviet country, she would never have imagined it."

"I'm so glad. I only wish Helena could have known that her daughter was alive and well."

"Tell us about her."

So while Olya translated, McKenna relayed what Mom and Baba had told her.

The light from the lamps danced in Teena's eyes.

McKenna shook her head. "I can't imagine what it must be like to be in your eighties and finally learn about your mother."

"Some things, Mama Chomiak told her. But you have told her more."

"Mama Chomiak sounds like a remarkable person."

Teena nodded, her short, curly, gray hair bouncing with the motion.

McKenna studied her, her long face, dark eyes, tall frame. So different from Baba. "You two hardly look like sisters."

"That's because they aren't related by blood."

The way McKenna's stomach plummeted, it might as well have been dropped from the top of the US Steel Tower in Pittsburgh. "What? What do you mean they aren't related?"

"That is why I was not a DNA match to you."

"So you were tested."

"Me, my mother, and Baba. We all were. And we got quite a surprise when the test came back that Baba was one hundred percent Ashkenazi Jew."

"Jewish?" McKenna turned toward Filip, who lounged with one leg crossed over the opposite knee. "Did you know this?"

"Not until today."

"When we came to Poland at the beginning of the war, after we were settled, I decided to investigate, so I started at the university, much as you did. I found that a woman name Risa Birkha also taught there. She and her husband died during the Holocaust, but there was no mention anywhere of their daughter."

"And so you put two and two together."

Olya laughed. "I only know that expression because I studied in the States. And yes, I did. So far, I haven't discovered any living relatives of Risa or her husband. They both died in the Kraków ghetto. But from what I can find, I would say that Baba is Risa's daughter. The two women would have known each other for sure."

Filip nodded. "It makes sense to me. I visited the university today, and it is very plausible. Their offices were next to each other, and as the only women on faculty, they must have been friendly. It's just about the only explanation we have for a Jewish baby ending up with a Lemko family."

"That's absolutely amazing. What a wonderful plot twist. And Baba is going to be so surprised. Do you think your grandmother would be willing to FaceTime with mine?" On Wednesdays, Mom and Baba went to Bible study together and then out for a late lunch, so they would be with each other now.

"I don't even have to ask her." Olya set her plate with her half-eaten slice of cake on the bookcase. "She would be thrilled."

Once on Olya's Wi-Fi, McKenna placed the call to Mom.

"Hello, honey. What's up? Where are you?" She squinted into the phone.

"There is someone here who would like to meet Baba. Is she around?"

"Yes. We just stopped at my house to pick up a gift card I have before going to lunch."

"That's perfect."

A minute or two later Baba joined Mom on-screen. "Well, hi there, McKenna. That's not your hotel room, is it?"

"No. But quite a few things have happened since we've been back in Kraków. In fact, there's someone here who would really like to talk to you." McKenna handed the phone to Teena, who had tears waterfalling down her cheeks.

"Is that. . .?"

"It's your sister, Teena Shevchenko."

Now everyone on both sides of the Atlantic had tears in their eyes. And then Baba spoke in a language McKenna had never heard from her before.

"What's going on?" Taylor handed out tissues from her purse.

"I don't know, but I think Baba and Teena are speaking Lemko to each other."

They conversed for a long time, almost an hour. Not even Olya could translate. "Growing up, I didn't want to be different from my classmates. I hated that I was Lemko and not Ukrainian. At least that's what I thought I was at the time. Baba is teaching me some words, and some are similar to Ukrainian, but most goes by too fast for me to catch."

It was enough for McKenna to sit back and listen to the words flow from the women's tongues. Teena's facial expressions drifted from joyful to sorrowful to joyful once more.

At one point, McKenna excused herself to use the restroom. She leaned against the sink and took a few minutes to absorb what was happening in the other room. Two women, separated by war, an ocean, and a lifetime, were reunited. God had taken an ugly, broken situation and terrible evil and had brought good from it.

He was the ultimate healer and the perfect planner.

Though she may never see it in her lifetime, He would even be able to bring beauty from Yasmine and Belinda's deaths.

And that was enough.

Except for the two surprises she still had up her sleeve.

CHAPTER FORTY-FIVE

But there will come a time
That our fate will bring us together,
At that time no hostile force
Will separate us.

~From "Song of Lemkovyna"

Friday, November 17, 2023
Kraków, Poland

With the sun setting behind her and a decided chill to the air promising of the coming winter, McKenna stood on the stoop of the now-familiar house on the outskirts of Kraków and knocked on the door.

Because he had other clients to take care of, Filip wasn't with them tonight, though he had promised to visit her in Pittsburgh after the holidays. And from there, who knew what would happen? Compared to the frantic person she'd been when she'd arrived here over a month ago, she was happy to wait to see what God had in store.

It was too bad he wouldn't be here for this surprise she had planned for Teena and Olya.

A moment later Olya pulled the door open, her mouth rounding into an O. McKenna shushed her. "Don't spoil it."

"Come in, come in."

WHAT I LEFT FOR YOU

They entered just as Teena rounded the corner into the living room. She stopped and stared at them with the same open-mouthed expression as her granddaughter. "Nie, nie!"

"Tak, tak, *mojou sestrou*." And Baba rushed forward into Teena's arms.

For a long while, the two women who had never met but who were bound together by a mother's love embraced each other and cried, stopping every now and then to speak to each other then starting the process again.

What first the Nazis and then the Poles and Soviets had labored so hard to destroy had withstood the ravages of the decades. They might not have been bound together with common DNA, but Helena Kostyszak's commitment to them was stronger than any gene.

They touched each other's faces as if they were mirages that might disappear in the hot afternoon sun.

Olya escorted Mom and McKenna into the kitchen. "We will let them have their privacy. It is very nice to meet you, Mrs. Muir. Thank you for bringing your mother here to meet my baba. What a precious gift you have given her."

"If not for McKenna and her tenacity, they might never have had this moment. I'm so thankful that I'm able to be here for it."

"And tomorrow, since it will be the weekend, we're all going to Dubne, to bring Teena and Baba home once more. And you too, Mom. Tay is going to hate that she missed out, but work called."

Mom smiled at Olya. "I'm so grateful to be here, and I'm looking forward to getting to know you and your baba better."

After a few minutes, Olya pulled the fried pork chops from the oven and called Baba and Teena to the table. The five of them, their lives intertwined by one woman's courage and strength, enjoyed the meal. Laughter and tears flowed as freely as the tea.

The hours weren't enough for them to catch up on a lifetime apart. Before anyone was ready, Baba was yawning. "This jet lag is hard on an old woman."

"We can't leave yet. I have one more surprise." McKenna reached into her large purse on the floor and brushed the paste paper cover of the book. She inhaled and withdrew it.

"When I first came to Kraków, I met a woman who held on to the prayer book that Helena left behind when she fled the city. She was so happy to return it to one of Helena's descendants." She opened the cover where Helena had penciled her name. "Baba had the privilege of growing up knowing her mother and father. Teena, you knew neither. With Baba's permission, I'm presenting you with your mother's prayer book."

She held out the book with the angels and cherubs, the chalice, and the Ten Commandments printed on the title page. "Maybe you can even read it."

Instead of taking it, Olya scurried down the hall. A few moments later she returned with a book in her hand.

This one was battered and well-loved, and Olya held it with tender care. "When Helena left for Jasło, other than leaving Baba behind, she also left her prayer book. Baba has treasured it all these years." Olya opened the cover to reveal words penciled in Cyrillic.

She turned and translated what was going on for Teena, who replied.

Olya relayed her answer to them. "She says that her mama left beautiful gifts for her daughters. A piece of her for both of them to cherish."

Saturday, November 18, 2023
Dubne, Poland

Baba, Mom, McKenna, Teena, and Olya stood at the edge of the churchyard, arms and hearts intertwined.

McKenna swallowed hard. "We're here, Helena, we're here. All of us."

They had returned. Returned to the hills that had given them life and sustained them, some through the darkest chapters of human history. Returned to the simple, three-spired wooden cathedral that had planted the seeds of faith in each one. Returned to the ground that held such pain and beauty in a single package.

Though this was no longer home to any of them and had only been home to one of them many, many years ago, it was a place where they all belonged. Here was where they were separated and here was where they were united.

CHAPTER FORTY-SIX

Do not rejoice, cruel enemy
About our bitter plight,
God's wrath will come upon you—
We will be free.

Our mountains will rejoice,
The sun will shine,
The wind will blow through the forest,
That evil doing is ending.

~FROM "SONG OF LEMKOVYNA"

Western Pennsylvania
Saturday, June 16, 1990

The rocking chair creaks beneath my weight as I move forward and back, forward and back. My eyes, a little dimmer now with age, have not tired of the view of the green hills that rise just outside my window.

They aren't the hills of Lemkovyna. Not the slopes I climbed as a child and a young woman. Yet they remind me enough of the land of my birth that I am content.

More than that, I am at peace.

I miss Pawel. He has been gone three years now. His laughter, his gentle kisses, his prayers. When I married him, it was because I thought he would be a good husband. He was even more than I could have hoped for.

In the end, I loved him. Not the passionate love of youth, but the content, settled love of those who have seen the worst of humanity and come out the other side. The love of those who, together, love the Lord and enjoy each other's company.

There are too many married couples who claim to be so much in love with each other but who have so much less than Pawel and I shared.

For the years we had together, we were blessed.

And I have my Julia, who still lives nearby, even though she is married with a daughter of her own. What a comfort she is. And watching her daughter grow has been a joy. Like the spark that was Teena, so is she. That bright light in a life shadowed by so much darkness.

Though I no longer teach at the university, some days I still go there to lecture. Not on anthropology anymore, but in the department of Eastern European studies. There are those of Lemko descent in this area. Those who work to keep the language and culture and customs alive.

I found a home here. And it has been a good one.

I stare out the window, my prayer book in my lap. The one I purchased as soon as we arrived here and had an extra dollar or two. The one I left in my flat in Kraków probably no longer exists. And somewhere, I pray, on the other side of the world, is a woman now nearing middle age who has a similar prayer book.

Perhaps she is sitting in a chair, staring over the countryside, thinking of the mother she never knew.

My heart will forever ache for Teena. For what could have been for us. For not fulfilling my promise to Risa that awful night in the Kraków ghetto when the world was mad.

No matter what, God.

Four little words that Pawel lived by. That I now live by as well.

My peace does not come from the hills outside my window or even from the prayer book in my lap. My peace comes from the assurance that God oversees all things. No matter that our dim eyes cannot see and our weak minds cannot understand.

It is that trust, that faith, that has seen me through over four decades not knowing where my daughter is. Like a flash of lightning is all the time I had with her. Such a brief period compared to the length of my days.

But impactful.

The heavy, impenetrable iron curtain made searching for her next to impossible. We spent much money, sacrificed vacations and new shoes and a bigger house, in pursuit of her. In the end, heaven's answer to my prayers was no.

But I am content. I left that little piece of me with her. Not even intentionally, but I left it all the same, my notes scribbled in the narrow margins of the pages.

Perhaps through that, she got to know me. To know my heart and the woman I am.

A woman who loved her with the fierceness of a lioness. A woman who lived her life praying for her and searching for her. Who made mistakes that tore us apart.

I will likely never receive her forgiveness in this life, but I believe that God can take even my mistakes and create something beautiful from them. *Lord, may You have done that for Teena.*

The clock advances toward dinnertime. With Pawel gone, I don't cook much for myself. Yesterday, when Julia and her husband and daughter came, I made pierogi. It's their favorite dish. Perhaps I will take a couple of the leftovers and throw them in boiling water to reheat them.

When I stand, the prayer book falls from my lap to the floor. Though my bones now crack, I bend over and pick it up, smoothing out the pages.

The prayer jumps out at me. Perhaps it has for Teena as well.

O Creator of all things, Word of God made flesh, O Christ, the perfect Son of God, Thou who art the spotless Lamb of God: for Thy mercy's sake, never leave Thou me, but indwell me, Thy servant, by Thy Holy Ghost.

"Teena, above all, may you pray this prayer and know this indwelling love that surpasses even mine."

I gaze for another few seconds at the waves of hills before me then place the prayer book on the table and leave it there.

AUTHOR'S NOTES

What an amazing opportunity and true privilege it was to write this book. While it is a work of fiction, much of it was drawn from true-life places and events.

Historically, what really happened?

It is true that most Lemkos were very, very poor, many not even able to afford the expense to hire someone to build a chimney. They lived in "black houses," homes where the smoke had no way to escape, thus coating the walls and turning them black. Many died young because of these poor living conditions.

Most Lemkos wouldn't have been able to pay for education. There would have been little chance that any notice would have been given to how smart Helena was. That's why I invented the uncle in America who knew of her talent and who paid for her to go to the university. Even that would have been difficult, as he likely wouldn't have had much of an education himself.

Jagiellonian University does stand in the heart of Kraków's Old Town. It began admitting female students in the 1930s. Women weren't allowed to be full professors. Only a handful were lecturers in any institution of higher learning in Poland, and it was still difficult for women to be treated as peers.

The reference to Jerzy being taken to a concentration camp at the beginning of the war is based on Sonderaktion Krakau, which took place on November 6, 1939. The plaque that McKenna and Taylor read in the Collegium Novum is real and accurately describes the events of that day. Several professors lost their lives because of Sonderaktion Krakau. There was a professor who lied to the Germans about an older man at the university, telling the soldiers the man was a janitor, thus sparing him from being taken.

Józef Adamowicz and Dr. Julian Aleksandrowicz were real people. Józef did go to the ghetto gate every day carrying supplies, trying to help in some small way to ease the immense suffering of the people inside.

The Kraków Ghetto hospital stood at Jozefinska Street 14. The orphanage I describe was at Jozefinska Street 22. The one for younger children was liquidated in 1942. This one was liquidated with the rest of the ghetto, and everyone, including children and staff, was killed. It was meant for six- to fourteen-year-olds, so I did have to fudge history here a little bit.

When Helena and Jerzy went into the ghetto the second time, I had them sneak in with work details. Helena brought Teena out in a coat with large pockets. This is based on the real story of Lena Kuchler-Silberman, who did the same thing to rescue a friend's child. You can read more about her in the book *My Hundred Children*.

The reopening of the university in 1942 was real, though it was forced to operate underground because of the Nazi regulations against higher education. Among the students at the time was the man who would go on to become Pope John Paul II, who is much revered in Kraków. Again, I fudged history a little bit to have it reopen in 1943.

When I describe the weeping and wailing that could be heard throughout the valley as the Nazis took reprisals for Gładyszów in June 1943, I use the description of a firsthand account. While it might have been hyperbole, nevertheless, Helena would have viewed it much the same.

The raid on the Jasło prison also took place, and I based my description on another firsthand account using the actual code names of the men involved. There were no women, but I had to have Helena go to continue her story. Jasło prison no longer stands. Only four Lemkos were freed by the Polish Home Army. Of the many who had been taken, all the rest were executed. None of the Lemko partisans were actually involved in freeing the prisoners from Jasło.

The scene where Jerzy is shot when he runs from the train into the grain field is taken from an account of Lemkos arrested and sent to work in Germany. The people were desperately hungry, and several of them resorted to this measure at the cost of their lives. The actual event is found in the book *Lemkovyna: A History of the Lemko Region of the Carpathian Mountains in Central Europe* by Father Ioann Polianskii, translated and edited by Paul Best, Michael Decerbo, and Walter Maksimovich. It was my primary research book.

Lonia's story of how she came to be in the work camp is based on a true story, one told in the book *Wearing the Letter P: Polish Women as Forced Laborers in Nazi Germany, 1939–1945* by Sophie Hodorowicz Knab.

The factory where Helena worked in Germany is a conglomeration of stories of Polish women working in Germany. They labored in textile factories as well as other factories and on farms. If a prisoner managed to go to a good farm couple, they might be treated very well, almost like a member of the family. Or they might be treated very harshly. The conditions in the factories were deplorable. Many in the textile factories died from inhaling fabric dust floating in the air. The spinning rooms, as stated, were particularly dangerous. Surprisingly, the Nazis did require their workers to attend religious services and did give them time off on the Sabbath. Although as the war came to a close, this privilege was sometimes revoked, depending on the factory.

While Helena is encouraged to remain in the DP camp while the war continues, soon after Germany surrendered the camps surged in numbers, overwhelming the Allied relief organizations. Their stance shifted, and they urged the people to go home as soon as possible. Unfortunately, too many of them no longer had homes.

The UPA was the Ukrainian Insurgent Army, which was formed in 1942, and during the war fought against the Germans, the Soviet Union, and the Poles. They conducted a Polish ethnic cleansing in 1943, which resulted in between 50,000 and 100,000 deaths. After the war, they contested the removal of "Ukrainians" from Lemkovyna. Thus, the Poles believed that the Lemkos were part of the UPA and determined to forcibly resettle the Lemkos. Akcja Wisła took place from April 28, 1947, until July 31, 1947. The date that the Lemkos were taken from Dubne is one I picked, as there is no record of when that actually took place.

McKenna's journey to discover her family's heritage is based on my own journey of discovery about my family's Lemko-Rusyn background. It has been a long one, as records are missing, names are confusing, and Lemkos are scattered. When McKenna finds the immigration record for Anna Kostisak, who was going to her uncle's house in Johnstown, Pennsylvania, and that led to her family's hometown of Dubne, it is very similar to my discovery of my family's place of origin. I had already suspected where they were from, but this particular record got me one step closer to verifying it.

While in Poland, my daughter and I spent a couple of days with a genealogical guide who took us to Dubne. This closely mirrors McKenna's trip there, though I was unable to confirm what number house my family lived in or where that house would have stood. Unfortunately, there was no little book listing the residents. The Lemko at the farmhouse was friendly and apologetic that he couldn't tell us more, though he did recognize our family name. His father, who would have known my family, had passed away a few years before. Our guide did find the mayor, who opened the door to the gorgeous church where my ancestors worshiped.

McKenna's feelings in Dubne were the same as mine. The area was beautiful, and in some inexplicable way, I felt as if I had come home. As if I belonged. The land truly did call to me and spoke to my heart. There is something about Lemkovyna that draws its people back.

Filip says, "Somewhere along the line of my research, I read a letter written by a Lemko woman in the United States to one of her relatives still in Poland. In it, she included a prayer that one day her grandchildren or great-grandchildren would return to the place that had given them birth." There really is such a letter, and it can be found online. I was able to fulfill a wish that perhaps my great-grandmother made. Standing in Dubne, I had indeed come home.

The little inn where Filip, McKenna, and Taylor stay is based on Chata U Bożeny in Muszyna, where my daughter and I and our guide stayed. It was charming. We weren't fortunate enough to have dinner there, but the breakfast was just as I described.

On our way to Lemkovyna, our guide took us to Krynica-Zkrój, a spa town, where we tried the mineral water. It did taste just like it came from a fish tank. But overall, the town, very Alpine in its feeling, was beautiful.

I found a photograph of an old Lemko prayer book online. When McKenna and Taylor try to read the Lemko words to figure out what the book is, it's the same process and same results I came up with.

The pierogi restaurant in chapter 41 is real, as were the pierogi my daughter and I ate there. Pierogarnia Krakowiacy was out of this world. It sits just off the Old Town square and was recommended to us by a local.

As you may have been able to tell by the numerous references to food throughout the book, my daughter and I love to eat when we travel. And we did declare every day to be pączki day. In Milwaukee, prune pączki are said to be the traditional ones, but in Kraków, I didn't find any. There they are known for the ones filled with rose-flavored cream. My daughter and I enjoyed the Nutella or chocolate-filled pączki the most.

I wrote the last scene of the book in December 2023 or January 2024. In June of 2024, I took a break from writing to spend a few minutes looking for 100 percent proof that my great-grandmother was born in Dubne. While I didn't find that (yet), I did run across her oldest child's birth record in Johnstown, Pennsylvania. It listed the address where the family was living, so I went to Google Maps to see what it looks like today. I don't know if the boarded-up building was there in 1899, but I did spin around and look across the street. What was the view from their home? The green hills of Southwest Pennsylvania, much like I describe Helena's view. It took my breath away to think that they chose a place that would remind them of their home and that it so closely mirrored what I wrote.

Poland is an amazing country, filled with astounding beauty, friendly people, and a tragic past. Throughout the course of my research and my trip to Lemkovyna, I learned to be proud of my Lemko-Rusyn heritage. I descend from a long line of strong, proud, and determined people who lived difficult lives but who loved, worked, and worshiped with passion. War and hatred have erased much of the Lemkos' way of life, especially from their historical homeland, but their legacy lives on in their children, grandchildren, great-grandchildren, and all the generations to come.

Slava Isusu Kyrustu.

ACKNOWLEDGMENTS

The list of people I have to thank for making this book possible is long, as always. First of all, my deepest appreciation to Becky Germany, Shalyn Sattler, and the entire team at Barbour Publishing for bringing this story to life. You made my dreams come true in allowing me to tell the world about the Lemko people, their suffering, and their proud heritage. By doing so, you have brought to many the knowledge of this people group and the terrible way in which they were treated.

Thanks a million to Ellen Tarver, my amazing editor. You are fabulous to work with, and I appreciate your encouragement along the way. I have learned a ton from you.

Tamela Hancock Murray, my top-notch agent, I appreciate you more than you know. You are always ready with a listening ear and helpful advice. Without you, I wouldn't be where I am today. Thank you for sticking with me along this bumpy journey.

My fabulous readers, I appreciate each and every one of you. Thanks to each of you who picked up this book and read it, who left a review of it, and who shared it with others. I hope you learned something from this book, that you were entertained, and that you maybe even laughed and cried. I love to hear from all of you, so please drop me a line and let me know what you thought about the book.

To Laura, Dawn, and Jenny, my first readers. You ladies are fabulous, patiently working your way through a messy manuscript and giving me a reader's perspective on the story. With your input, this is a much better story now than when you read it. Thank you!

Thank you so much, Sarah, my wonderful niece, for your insight into social workers and their responsibility in cases like this. I would have gotten it all wrong if not for you. Thanks, also, to Lakiesha, from my local writers' group, for your help with police procedure. You helped me fix another mistake.

Dear Alyssa, my precious daughter, thank you for traipsing over Lemkovnya, Kraków, and Europe with me. I will never forget the adventures we had in the course of researching this book. I'm so glad I got to share with you the place where your great-great-grandparents came from. What a special time it was. And what fun we had in the duty-free shop in Amsterdam. I'm sure the lady there is still laughing at us. Thank you for taking such good care of me when I wasn't feeling well on the way home.

Doug, my wonderful husband, I cannot thank you enough for being willing to stay home and hold down the fort when I was in Poland and when I was under deadline. I love our life, and I love you. God couldn't have sent me a better spouse. Without your support, I wouldn't be able to live this dream.

To Mom and to Muriel, the granddaughters of those Lemko ancestors who courageously traversed the sea to make a better life for us all, I hope the information I found about our family helps you to better understand where we came from and who we are. I wish I could have taken you to Lemkovyna with me, but perhaps, through this book, I have.

Thank You, Holy Father, for the strength to travel to research this book, for the technology to take a peek into my family's past, and for the ability and opportunity to write the story of my people. *Soli Deo gloria.*

Liz Tolsma is the author of several WWII novels, romantic suspense novels, prairie romance novellas, and an Amish romance. She is a popular speaker and an editor and resides next to a Wisconsin farm field with her husband and their youngest daughter. Her son is a US Marine, and her oldest daughter is a college student. Liz enjoys reading, walking, working in her large perennial garden, kayaking, and camping. Please visit her website at www.liztolsma.com and follow her on Facebook, Twitter (@LizTolsma), Instagram, YouTube, and Pinterest. She is also the host of the *Christian Historical Fiction Talk* podcast.

OTHER BARBOUR BOOKS BY LIZ TOLSMA:

The Pink Bonnet (True Colors series)

The Green Dress (True Colors series)

The Gold Digger (True Colors series)

The Silver Shadow (True Colors series)

Picture of Hope (Heroines of WWII series)

A Promise Engraved (Doors to the Past series)

What I Would Tell You (Echoes of the Past series – book 1)

What I Promise You (Echoes of the Past series – book 2)

ECHOES OF THE PAST

Tolsma uses split-time storytelling and DNA testing to uncover a family's courageous story that was lost to the horrors of WWII.

What I Would Tell You

AWSA 2023 Golden Scroll winner for Historical Novel of the Year

BOOK 1

When college student Riley Payton takes a DNA test for fun, she never imagined it would change everything she knew about her family and send her on a journey to uncover a mystery in her ancestry lost to the horrors of WWII. Will what she discovers change what Riley believes about herself and her faith? In 1940s Greece, Sephardic Jew Mathilda Nissim is angry that her people have not stood up to their invaders, so she continues printing her newspaper in secret, calling them to action. She trusts no one to help them—not even God. But is her resistance futile with generational consequences?

Paperback / 978-1-63609-459-5

What I Promise You

Book 2

Noémie Treves, a young, pregnant Jewish woman, is arrested in 1942 and sent to the Camp de Rivesaltes transit camp in Southwest France. Drawn to helping other young women escape, she seeks refuge for herself and others at a maternity hospital. But nothing is simple in occupied France, and she finds herself doing the unimaginable to save one precious life. Eighty years later, Caitlyn Laurent takes a break from training to be a missionary nurse in Spain to visit nearby France, hoping to find her grandfather's birthplace. But what she uncovers are secrets long buried by WWII atrocities.

Paperback / 978-1-63609-777-0

JOIN US ONLINE!

Christian Fiction for Women

Christian Fiction for Women is your online home for the latest in Christian fiction.

Check us out online for:

- Giveaways
- Recipes
- Info about Upcoming Releases
- Book Trailers
- News and More!

Find Christian Fiction for Women at Your Favorite Social Media Site:

 Search "Christian Fiction for Women"

 @fictionforwomen